THE NEST

THE
NEST

CYNTHIA D'APRIX
SWEENEY

ecco

An Imprint of HarperCollinsPublishers

HarperCollins books may be purchased for educational, business,
or sales promotional use. For information please e-mail the Special
Markets Department at SPsales@harpercollins.com.

A hardcover edition of this book was published in 2016 by
Ecco, an imprint of HarperCollins Publishers.

FIRST ECCO PAPERBACK EDITION PUBLISHED 2017.

Designed by Shannon Nicole Plunkett

Library of Congress Cataloging-in-Publication Data has been applied for.

ISBN 978-0-06-241422-9

17 18 19 20 21   OV/LSC   10 9 8 7 6 5 4 3 2 1

For my family: my parents, Roger and Theresa;
my sister, Laura; and my brothers, Richard and Tony—
who all love nothing more than a good story, well told.

There was always this dichotomy: what to keep up,
what to change.

—WILLIAM TREVOR, "THE PIANO TUNER'S WIVES"

That's how I knew this story would break my heart
When you wrote it
That's how I knew this story would break my heart

—AIMEE MANN, *THE FORGOTTEN ARM*

ACKNOWLEDGMENTS

For so generously offering their support, time, and wisdom (and sometimes letting me borrow from their lives), I owe a million thanks and nearly that many cocktails to: Belinda Cape, Madeline Dulchin, Rory Evans, Kate Flannery, Robin Goldwasser, John Hodgman, Natasha Lehrer, Jenny McPhee, Liza Powel O'Brien, Rebecca Odes, Rachel Pastan, Amy Poehler, Amy Scheibe, Katherine Schulten (who enthusiastically read so many drafts of these pages that I began to fear for her sanity), Jill Soloway, Jen Strozier, Sarah Thyre, Janie Haddad Tompkins, and Paul Yoon. And to the late, great David Rakoff.

The Bennington Writing Seminars is an ideal place to invest two years of your life, and it was there that I found *my* Nest—true friends, trusted readers—Rob Faus, Erin Kasdin, Melissa Mills-Dick, Kathryn Savage, and the (sorely missed) Megan Renehan. Thanks to my workshop peers and to the faculty and staff at Bennington, especially Bret Anthony Johnston, who read the first thirty pages of what I thought was a wreck of a short story and told me it was the beginning of a novel. His enthusiasm gave me the confidence to start this book and his advice, insight, humor, patience, and friendship guided me to the finish.

My agent, Henry Dunow, and editor, Megan Lynch, not only made everything in these pages better but are an absolute joy to work with in every way. I don't know what village I saved in a previous life to deserve them, but it must have been huge. Thanks also to Daniel Halpern and everyone at Ecco for working so hard on my behalf, especially Eleanor Kriseman and Sonya Cheuse.

I am grateful to my parents, for reading to me and passing along their love of books and language. I am grateful to my children, Matthew and Luke, for letting me read to them until they started staying up past my bedtime, for growing into remarkably interesting, intelligent, and entertaining people, and for filling our house with music.

Finally, and most importantly, a world of love and thanks to my husband, Mike, whose belief in me was so absolute on such flimsy evidence, that this book is my attempt to stop him from looking like a fool. As long as we're making each other laugh, all is right in the world.

THE NEST

PROLOGUE

As the rest of the guests wandered the deck of the beach club under an early-evening midsummer sky, taking pinched, appraising sips of their cocktails to gauge if the bartenders were using the top-shelf stuff and balancing tiny crab cakes on paper napkins while saying appropriate things about how they'd really lucked out with the weather because the humidity would be back tomorrow, or murmuring inappropriate things about the bride's snug satin dress, wondering if the spilling cleavage was due to bad tailoring or poor taste (a *look* as their own daughters might say) or an unexpected weight gain, winking and making tired jokes about exchanging toasters for diapers, Leo Plumb left his cousin's wedding with one of the waitresses.

Leo had been avoiding his wife, Victoria, who was barely speaking to him and his sister Beatrice who wouldn't stop speaking to him—rambling on and on about getting together for Thanksgiving. *Thanksgiving.* In July. Leo hadn't spent a holiday with his family in twenty years, since the mid-'90s if he was remembering correctly; he wasn't in the mood to start now.

Cranked and on the hunt for the rumored empty outdoor bar, Leo first spotted Matilda Rodriguez carrying a tray of champagne glasses. She moved through the crowd with a lambent glow—partly because the setting sun was bathing the eastern end of Long Island an indecent pink, partly because of the truly excellent cocaine wreaking havoc with Leo's synapses. The bubbles rising and falling on Matilda's tray felt like an ecstatic summons, an invitation meant just for him. Her sturdy black hair was pulled away from the wide planes of her face into a serviceable knot; she was all inky eyes and full red lips. Leo watched the elegant weave of her hips as she threaded her way through the wedding guests, the now-empty tray held high above her head like a torch. He grabbed a martini from a passing waiter and followed her through the swinging stainless-steel doors into the kitchen.

IT WOULD SEEM TO MATILDA (nineteen, aspiring singer, diffident waitress) that one minute she'd been passing champagne to seventy-five members of the extended Plumb family and their closest friends and the next she was barreling toward the Long Island Sound in Leo's brand-new leased Porsche, her hand down the front of his too-tight linen trousers, the fat of her thumb inexpertly working the underside of his penis.

Matilda had resisted when Leo first pulled her into a side pantry, his fingers cuffing her wrists while he pelted her with questions: *Who are you? Where did you come from? What else do you do? Are you a model? An actress? Do you know you're beautiful?*

Matilda knew what Leo wanted; she was propositioned at these events all the time, but usually by much younger men—or ludicrously older men, *ancient*—with their arsenal of lame pickup lines and vaguely bigoted attempts at flattery. (She was constantly being called J. Lo in spite of looking nothing like her; her parents were Mexican, not Puerto Rican.) Even in this moneyed crowd, Leo was unreasonably handsome, a word she was quite certain she'd never employed for someone whose attention she was almost enjoying. She might think *hot,* she might think *cute* or maybe even *gorgeous,* but *handsome?* The boys she knew hadn't grown into handsome yet. Matilda found herself staring up at Leo's face trying to determine which variables added up to handsome. Like her, he had dark eyes, dark hair, a strong brow. But where his features were angular and sharp, hers were round and soft. On television he would play someone distinguished—a surgeon maybe, and she would be the terminally ill patient begging for a cure.

Through the pantry door she could hear the band—orchestra, really, there had to be at least sixteen pieces—playing the usual wedding fare. Leo grabbed her hands and pulled her into a little two-step. He sang close to her ear, above the beat, his voice pleasantly lively and rich. "*Someday, when I'm awfully low, when the world is cold, I will dah-dah-dum just thinking of you, and the way you look tonight.*"

Matilda shook her head and laughed a little, pulled away. His attention was unnerving, but it also made something deep within her thrum. And fending off Leo in the pantry was marginally more interesting than wrapping asparagus with prosciutto in the kitchen, which was what she was supposed to be doing. When she shyly told him she wanted to be a singer, he immediately offered that he had friends at Columbia Records, friends who were always keen to discover new talent. He moved in again and if she was alarmed when he stumbled a little and seemed to need to keep a palm on the wall to maintain balance, her worry evaporated when he asked if she had a demo, something of hers they could listen to in his car.

"Because if I like it," Leo said, taking Matilda's slender fingers in his, "I'd want to get on it right away. Help you get it to the right people."

AS LEO DEFTLY MANEUVERED MATILDA past the parking valet, she glanced back at the kitchen door. Her cousin Fernando had gotten her this job, and he would be furious if he found out she'd just up and left. But Leo had said *Columbia Records.* He'd said, *Always looking for new talent.* When did she ever get opportunities like this? She would only be gone for a little bit, just long enough to make a good impression.

"Mariah was discovered by Tommy Mottola when she was a wait-ress," she said, half joking, half trying to justify her behavior.

"Is that right?" Leo hustled her toward his car, scanning the windows of the beach club above the parking lot. It was possible that Victoria could see him from the side terrace where everyone was gathering and quite probable she'd already noticed his absence and was stalking the grounds looking for him. Furious.

Matilda stopped at the car door and slipped off her black-canvas work shoes. She took a pair of silvery stilettos from a worn plastic shopping bag.

"You really don't need to change shoes for this," Leo said, resisting the urge to put his hands around her tiny waist right then and there in plain sight of everyone.

"But we're getting a drink, right?" Matilda said.

Had Leo said something to her about a drink? A drink was not possible. Everyone in his tiny hometown knew him, his family, his mother, his wife. He finished off his martini and threw the empty glass into the bushes. "If the lady wants a drink, we'll find the lady a drink," Leo said.

Matilda stepped into the sandals and gently slid one slender metallic strap over the swell of her left heel, then her right. She straightened, now eye level with Leo. "I hate wearing flats," she said, tugging her fitted white blouse a little lower. "They make me feel flat all over." Leo practically pushed Matilda into the front seat, out of sight, safely behind the tinted glass.

SITTING IN THE FRONT SEAT OF THE CAR, Matilda was stunned to hear her tinny, nasal voice coming through the car's obscenely high-quality speakers. She sounded so different on her sister's ancient Dell. So much better.

As Leo listened, he tapped his hand against the steering wheel. His wedding ring glinted in the car's interior light. Married was most assuredly against Matilda's rules. She could see Leo struggling to summon an interest in her voice, searching for something flattering to say.

"I have better recordings. I must have downloaded the wrong version," Matilda said. She could feel her ears flush with shame. Leo was staring out the window. "I better get back," she said, reaching for the door handle.

"Don't," Leo said, placing his hand on her leg. She resisted the impulse to pull away and sat up a little straighter, her mind racing. What did she have to sustain his attention? She hated waitressing, but Fernando was going to *kill* her for disappearing during dinner service. Leo was boldly staring at her chest. She looked down at her lap and spotted a small stain on her black trousers. She scraped at the spot of balsamic vinaigrette with a fingernail; she'd mixed gallons of it. Everyone inside was probably plating the mesclun and grilled shrimp now, squeezing the dressing from bottles around the edge of each plate into a pattern that was supposed to approximate waves, the kind a child would draw to indicate a sea. "I'd like to see the ocean," she said, quietly.

And then, so slowly she wasn't sure what was happening at first, Leo took her hand in his (for a foolish moment she thought he was going to kiss it, like a character in one of her mother's telenovela shows) and placed it on his lap. And she would always remember this part, how he never stopped looking at her. He didn't close his eyes or lean his head back or lunge in for a sloppy kiss or fumble with the buttons on her blouse; he looked hard and long into her eyes. He *saw* her.

She could feel him respond beneath her hand and it was thrilling. As Leo held her gaze, she applied a little pressure with her fingers and the balance of power in the car abruptly shifted in her favor. "I thought we were going to see the ocean," she said, wanting to get out of sight of the kitchen. He grinned and put the car into reverse. She had his pants unzipped before his seat belt was fully fastened.

YOU COULDN'T BLAME LEO for the rapidity of his climax. His wife had cut him off weeks earlier, after she caught him fondling a babysitter in the back corridor of a friend's summerhouse. Driving toward the water, Leo hoped the combination of booze, cocaine, and Wellbutrin would stall his response, but when Matilda's hand tightened with resolve, he knew everything was happening too fast. He closed his eyes for a second—just a second—to collect himself, to stop the intoxicating image of her hand, her chipped blue fingernails, moving up and down. Leo never even saw the SUV barreling down Ocean Avenue, coming from the right, perpendicular to their car. Didn't realize until it was too late that the screech he heard wasn't Matilda's voice coming from the sound system, but something else entirely.

Neither of them even had time to scream.

PART ONE

SNOWTOBER

CHAPTER ONE

Because the three Plumbs had agreed on the phone the previous evening that they should not drink in front of their brother Leo, they were all—unbeknownst to one another—sitting in separate bars in and around Grand Central, savoring a furtive cocktail before lunch.

It was a strange kind of autumn afternoon. Two days earlier, a nor'easter had roared up the mid-Atlantic coast, colliding with a cold front pushing east from Ohio and an arctic mass dipping down from Canada. The resulting storm had dropped a record-breaking amount of snow in some places, blanketing towns from Pennsylvania to Maine with a freakishly early winter. In the small commuter town thirty miles north of Manhattan where Melody Plumb lived, most of the trees were still shouldering their autumn foliage, and many had been destroyed or damaged by the snow and ice. The streets were littered with fallen limbs, power was still out in some towns, the mayor was talking about canceling Halloween.

In spite of the lingering cold and spotty power outages, Melody's train ride into Manhattan was uneventful. She was settled in at the lobby bar of the Hyatt Hotel on Forty-Second Street where she knew she wouldn't run into her brother or sister; she'd suggested the hotel restaurant for lunch instead of their usual gathering spot, Grand Central's Oyster Bar, and had been mocked by Jack and Beatrice, the Hyatt not landing on their list of venues deemed acceptable by some arcane criteria she had zero interest in decoding. She refused to feel inferior to those two anymore, refused to be diminished because she didn't share their veneration for everything old Manhattan.

Sitting at a table near the soaring windows on the upper level of the hotel's massive lobby (which was, she had to admit, completely unwelcoming—too big and gray and modern, some awful kind of sculpture made of steel tubing lurked overhead, she could hear Jack's and Bea's pointed ridicule in absentia; she was relieved they weren't there), Melody ordered the least expensive glass of white wine (*twelve* dollars, more than she would spend on an entire bottle at home) and hoped the bartender had a generous pour.

The weather had remained unseasonably cold since the storm, but the sun was finally breaking through and the temperatures beginning to rise. The piles of snow at every Midtown crosswalk were rapidly melting into unnavigable puddles of slush and ice. Melody watched a particularly inelegant woman try to leap over the standing water and miss by inches, her bright red ballet flat landing squarely in the water, which had to be frigid, and filthy. Melody would have loved a delicate pair of shoes like those and she would have known better than to wear them on a day like today.

She felt a twinge of anxiety as she thought of her daughters heading uptown and having to navigate the treacherous street corners. She took a sip of her wine (so-so), removed her phone from her pocket, and opened her favorite app, the one Nora called Stalkerville. She hit the "find" button and waited for the map to load and for the dots that represented her sixteen-year-old twins to materialize on the screen.

Melody couldn't believe the miracle of a handheld device that allowed her to track Nora's and Louisa's precise whereabouts as long as they had their phones. And they were teenagers; they *always* had their phones. As the map started to appear, she felt the familiar panicky palpitations until the tiny, blue pulsating circles and the word *Found!* popped up at the top of the screen, showing the girls exactly where they were supposed to be, at the SAT tutoring center uptown.

They'd been taking the weekend classes for over a month, and usually Melody tracked their morning progress from her kitchen table, watching the blue dots slowly glide north from Grand Central according to her meticulous directions: From the train station, they should take the Madison Avenue bus to Fifty-Ninth Street where they would disembark and walk west to the tutoring center on Sixty-Third just off Columbus. They were *not* to walk along the park side, but were supposed to walk on the south side of the street, passing by the parade of uniformed doormen, who would hear them scream for help if they were in trouble. They were strictly forbidden from entering Central Park or deviating from their route. Melody put the fear of God into them every week, filling their heads with stories of girls being snatched or lost, forced into prostitution or murdered and dumped in the river.

"The Upper West Side is not exactly Calcutta," her husband, Walter, would gently argue. But she got scared. The thought of them wandering the city without her protecting their flank made her heart thud, her palms sweat. They were sweating now. When they'd all disembarked at Grand Central that morning, she hadn't wanted to let them go. On a Saturday, the terminal was full with tourists checking guidebooks and train schedules and trying to find the Whispering Gallery. She'd kissed them good-bye and had watched until she could no longer see the backs of their heads—one blond, the other brunette. They didn't look like visitors; there was nothing tentative about how they moved through the crowd. They looked like they belonged to the city, which filled Melody with dread. She wanted them to belong to *her*, to stop getting older. They didn't confide every last thought or desire or worry anymore; she didn't know their hearts and minds the way she used to. Melody knew that letting them grow and go was the proper order of life. She wanted them to be strong and independent and happy—more than anything she wanted them to be *happy*—but that she no longer had a fix on their inner workings made her light-headed. If she couldn't be sure how they were moving through the world, she could at least *watch* them move through the world, right there in the palm of her hand. She could at least have that.

"Leo's never paying you back," Walter had said as she was leaving for the train station. "You're all dreaming, wasting your time."

Though Melody feared he was right, she had to believe he wasn't. They'd borrowed a lot of money to buy their house, a tiny but historic building on one of their town's most beautiful streets, only to watch the economy collapse and property values sink. The fluctuating interest rate was about to rise on the mortgage they already couldn't afford. With little equity in the house, they couldn't refinance. College was approaching and they had next to nothing in the bank; she'd been counting on The Nest.

Out on the street, Melody watched people tug off their gloves and unwind scarves, lift their faces to the sun. She felt a tiny surge of satisfaction knowing that she could spend the entire afternoon indoors if she wanted. The main reason Melody loved the bar at the Hyatt was because she could access it through an underpopulated, nondescript hallway connecting the hotel to Grand Central. When it was time for lunch, she'd return to the terminal through her secret corridor and head downstairs to the Oyster Bar. She would spend hours in New York City and not have to step one sensibly shod foot onto pavement, could entirely avoid breathing the Manhattan air, which she always pictured as rife with gray particulate. During her and Walt's brief stint living in Upper (upper) Manhattan where the twins were born, she'd waged a ferocious, losing battle with the city's soot. No matter how many times she wiped the woodwork with a dampened cloth, the flecks of black would reappear, sometimes within hours. Minus any verifiable source, the residue was worrisome to her. It felt like a physical manifestation of the city's decay, all the teeming masses being worn down to grimy, gray window dust.

She caught sight of another woman across the room holding a wineglass, and it took a moment for her to recognize her own reflection. Her hair was blonder than usual—she'd chosen a lighter shade at the drugstore and hoped the color would soften the elongated nose and strong chin both she and her sister, Beatrice, had inherited from their father's New England ancestors. Somehow, the strong features that worked in Bea's favor (*Madam X,* Leo used to call Bea, after the Sargent portrait) just made Melody look unintentionally dour. She particularly resented her face around Halloween. One year when the girls were little and they were out shopping for costumes, Nora had pointed to an advertisement featuring a witch—not an excessively ugly one, no warts or green face or rotten teeth but still, a *witch*—standing over a boiling cauldron and had said, "Look! It's Mommy!"

Melody picked her bar bill up from the table and handed it to the waiter with a credit card. *He's never paying you back,* Walt had said. *Oh yes he is,* thought Melody. There was no way that one night of Leo's stupidity, his debauchery, was going to ruin her daughters' future, not when they'd worked so hard, not when she'd pushed them to dream big. They were *not* going to community college.

Melody looked at the map on her phone again. There was another private reason she loved the blue dots with their animated ripples so much; they reminded her of the very first ultrasound where she and Walt had seen twin heartbeats, two misshapen grayish shadows thumping arrhythmically deep inside her pelvis.

Two for the price of one, the cheerful technician had told them as Walt gripped her hand and they both stared at the screen and then at each other and grinned like the starry naifs they were. She remembered thinking in that moment: *It won't ever get better than this.* And in some ways she'd been right, had known even then she would never feel so capable, so stalwart a protector once she pushed those vulnerable, beating hearts out into the world.

The waiter was coming toward her now with a worried look on his face. She sighed and opened her wallet again. "I'm sorry, ma'am," he said, handing her the Visa she'd hoped had a little more juice on it, "but this was declined."

"It's okay," Melody said, digging out the secret card she'd activated without telling Walt; he would kill her if he knew. Just as he'd kill her if he found out that even though the SAT place in the city was cheaper than the suburban private tutor she'd wanted to hire, it was still twice as much as she'd admitted, which was why she needed the extra card. "I meant to give you this one." She watched the waiter back at his station as he swiped, both of them holding perfectly still and only exhaling when the machine started spitting out a receipt.

I like our life, Walt had said to her that morning, pulling her close. *I like you. Can't you pretend—just a little—to like me, too?* He smiled as he said it, but she knew he sometimes worried. She had relaxed then into his reassuring girth, breathed in his comforting scent— soap and freshly laundered shirt and spearmint gum. She'd closed her eyes and pictured Nora and Louisa, lovely and lithe, clothed in satiny caps and gowns on a leafy quad in a quaint New England town, the morning sun illuminating their eager faces, the future unfurling ahead of them like an undulating bolt of silk. They were so smart and beautiful and honest and kind. She wanted them to have everything— the chances she'd never had, the opportunities she'd promised. *I do like you, Walter,* she'd mumbled into his shoulder. *I like you so much. It's me I hate.*

AT THE OPPOSITE END OF GRAND CENTRAL, up a carpeted flight of stairs and through the glass doors that said CAMPBELL APART- MENT, Jack Plumb was sending his drink back because he believed the mint hadn't really been muddled. "It was just dumped in there as if it were a garnish, not an *ingredient*," he told the waitress.

Jack was sitting with his partner of two decades and legal husband of nearly seven weeks. He was confident the other Plumbs wouldn't know about this place, which was the former office of a 1920s tycoon, restored and reimagined as a high-end cocktail bar. Beatrice might, but it wasn't her kind of spot. Too staid. Too expensive. There was a dress code. At times the bar could be annoyingly full of commuters who were in mercifully short supply on this Saturday afternoon.

"Version 2.0," Walker said as the waitress placed the remade drink in front of Jack.

Jack took a sip. "It's fine," he said.

"Sorry for your trouble," Walker said to the waitress.

"Yes," Jack said as the waitress walked away, under his breath but loud enough for Walker to hear, "terribly sorry for making you do your job."

"She's just delivering the drinks. She's not making them." Walker kept his voice amiable. Jack was in a mood. "Why don't you take a nice generous sip of that and try to relax."

Jack picked a piece of mint from his glass and chewed on it for a second. "I'm curious," he said, "is telling someone to relax ever helpful? It's like saying 'breathe' to someone who is hyperventilating or 'swallow' to a person who's choking. It's a completely useless admonition."

"I wasn't admonishing, I was suggesting."

"It's like saying, 'Whatever you do, don't think about a pink elephant.'"

"I get it," Walker said. "How about *I* relax and you do what you want."

"Thank you."

"I am happy to go to this lunch with you if it helps."

"So you've said. About a thousand times." Trying to provoke Walker was mean and pointless, but Jack was trying anyway because he knew that snapping at Walker would briefly loosen the spiraling knot of fury at his core. And he *had* considered inviting Walker to lunch. His family preferred Walker's company anyway; who didn't? Walker with his rumbling laugh and kind face and bottomless bonhomie. He was like a clean-shaven, slightly trimmer, gay Santa Claus.

But Jack couldn't invite Walker because he hadn't told the other Plumbs yet about his early September wedding to Walker, the wedding to which they hadn't been invited because Jack wanted the day to be perfect and perfect for Jack meant Plumb-free. He did not want to listen to Bea's worries about Leo's accident or hear Melody's lumbering husband telling everyone who might listen that his name was Walter-not-Walker. (That Jack and Melody had chosen partners with almost the exact same name was something that still rankled both of them, decades on.)

"I'm sorry I snapped at you," Jack finally said.

Walker shrugged. "It's fine, love."

"I'm sorry I'm being an asshole." Jack rotated his neck, listening for the alarming but satisfying little pop that had recently appeared. God, he was getting old. Six years until fifty and who knew what fresh horrors that decade had in store for his slender-but-softening physique, his already-fraying memory, his alarmingly thinning hair. He gave Walker a feeble smile. "I'll be better after lunch."

"Whatever happens at lunch, we'll be fine. It will all be *fine*."

Jack slumped deeper into the leather club chair and proceeded to crack the knuckles on each hand, a sound he knew Walker loathed. Of course Walker thought everything would be *fine*. Walker didn't know anything about Jack's financial straits (another reason Jack didn't want him at lunch, in case the opportunity arose to tell Leo exactly how much the little escapade on the back roads of Long Island was costing him). Their retirement account had taken a terrible hit in 2008. They'd rented the same apartment on West Street since they'd been together. Jack's small antique shop in the West Village had never been hugely profitable, but in recent years he felt lucky to break even. Walker was an attorney, a solo practitioner, and had always been the wage earner in their partnership. Their one solid investment was a modest but cherished summer place on the North Fork that Jack had been borrowing against, secretly. He'd been counting on The Nest, not only to pay off the home equity line of credit but because it was the one thing he had to offer Walker as a contribution to their future. He didn't believe for a second that Leo was broke. And he didn't care. He just wanted what he was owed.

Jack and Leo were brothers but they weren't friends. They rarely spoke. Walker would sometimes push ("you don't give up on family"), but Jack had worked hard to distance himself from the Plumbs, especially Leo. In Leo's company, Jack felt like a lesser version of his older brother. Not as intelligent, interesting, or successful, an identity that had attached to him in high school and had never completely gone away. At the beginning of ninth grade, some of Leo's friends had christened Jack *Leo Lite* and the denigrating name stuck, even after Leo graduated. His first month at college, Jack had run into someone from his hometown who had reflexively greeted him by saying, "Hey, Lite. What's up?" Jack had nearly slugged him.

The door to the bar opened and a group of tourists barged in, bringing in a gust of air too cold for October. One woman was showing everyone her soaking wet shoe, a cheap ballet flat in a tacky shade of red. "It's completely ruined," she was saying to her companions.

"Silver linings," Jack said to Walker, nodding to indicate the shoe.

"You probably shouldn't be late." Walker lifted his wrist, presenting the watch that had been a wedding gift from Jack, a rare Cartier tank from the '40s in perfect condition. It had cost a small fortune; Walker had no idea. Just another thing to resent about Leo's fuckup, how now Jack couldn't help but mentally affix a huge neon price sticker to everything they owned, regretting briefly every single purchase of the last year, *years,* including all the not-insignificant expenses surrounding their otherwise idyllic wedding.

"I love this watch," Walker said, and the tenderness in his voice made Jack want to fling his glass against the opposite brick wall. He could almost feel the sweet relief that would flood in as the leaded crystal smashed into a million tiny pieces. Instead, he stood and placed the glass back on the table, hard.

"Don't let them rile you," Walker said, placing a reassuring hand on Jack's arm. "Just listen to what Leo has to say and then we'll talk."

"Will do." Jack buttoned his coat and headed down the stairs and out the door onto Vanderbilt Avenue. He needed a little fresh air before lunch; maybe he'd take a walk around the block. As he muscled his way through the sluggish weekend crowds, he heard someone calling his name. He turned and it took him a minute to recognize the woman in the beret, grinning madly above a pink-and-orange hand-knit scarf, waving and calling after him. He stood and watched her approach and in spite of himself, he smiled. Beatrice.

BEATRICE PLUMB WAS A REGULAR AT MURPHY'S, one of the commuter pubs that lined the short stretch of Forty-Third Street perpendicular to Grand Central Station. Bea was friendly with the owner, Garrie, an old friend of Tuck's from Ireland. Tuck approved of how Garrie pulled a pint and of how when the bar was quiet, Garrie would sing in his light and reedy tenor—not the usual touristy fare, "Danny Boy" or "Wild Rover," but from his repertoire of Irish rebel songs—"Come Out Ye Black and Tans" or "The Ballad of Ballinamore." Garrie had been one of the first to show up at Bea's door after Tuck died. He'd taken a fifth of Jameson's from his coat pocket and poured them each a glass. "To Tuck," he'd said solemnly. "May the road rise up to meet him." Sometimes, in the right light, Bea thought Garrie was handsome. Sometimes, she thought he had a little crush on her, but she didn't want to find out—he felt too close to Tuck.

"You're on the early side today," Garrie said when she arrived a little before noon.

"Family lunch. I'll take that coffee with a splash." Garrie uncorked the Jameson's and poured a generous amount into the mug before adding coffee. The sun was bright and low enough in the cloudless sky that it briefly blinded Bea as she sat in her favorite spot, next to the small front window. She stood and moved the rickety barstool into the shade and away from the door. It felt more like January than October. The room smelled like furnace and dirty mop and beer. "Aroma of the gods," Tuck would say. He loved nothing more than a dimly lit bar on a sunny afternoon. The jukebox started up and Rosemary Clooney and Bing Crosby were singing "Baby, It's Cold Outside." Bea and Garrie exchanged a smirk. People were so reassuringly unimaginative.

Bea was eager to see Leo but also nervous. He hadn't taken any of her calls at rehab. He was probably mad at all of them. She wondered how he would look. The last time she'd seen him, the night in the hospital, they'd been stitching up his lacerated chin and he'd looked wan and petrified. For months before the accident he'd looked terrible: bloated and tired and dangerously bored.

Bea worried today's lunch was going to be confrontational. Jack and Melody were becoming increasingly unhinged about the situation with The Nest and she assumed they were both coming prepared to stake out their respective plots of neediness. What Bea needed from Leo was not her primary concern. Today, she wanted to keep her ordinarily disagreeable siblings somewhat agreeable, if only for one afternoon, just long enough to get Leo to—well, she didn't know what exactly. Put some kind of plan in place that would placate Jack and Melody for a bit and give Leo enough breathing room so that he wouldn't completely shut them down—or flee.

She could feel the whiskey loosening her limbs, taking the edge off her nerves. She lifted her bag from the back of the barstool. Just feeling the heft of it gave her a little thrill. Bea was a writer. (*Used to be a writer? Was a writer who—until very recently—had stopped writing? She never knew how to think about herself.*) Sometimes, not often anymore, but occasionally at the literary magazine where she worked, someone would recognize her name. *Beatrice Plumb? The writer?* the conversation would optimistically begin. She knew the sequence by now, the happy glimmer of recognition and then the confused brow, the person trying to summon a recent memory of her work, anything other than her early long-ago stories. After a decade of practice, she knew how to head off the inevitable. She was armed with a fistful of diversionary dead-end replies about her long-awaited novel: a well-worn self-deprecating joke about writing too slowly, how if she amortized her advance over the years, it became an hourly wage best counted in half-pennies; a feigned superstition over talking about unfinished work; amused exasperation at her ongoing *perfectionism.*

From her oversized canvas bag she pulled out a deep brown leather satchel, one Leo had spotted while roaming around the Portobello

Road Market in London years ago when she was in college and had starting writing in earnest. He gave it to her for her birthday. From the early 1900s, it was the size of a large notebook and looked like a miniature briefcase with its small handle and leather straps, like something someone might have carried around Vienna at the turn of the twentieth century. She'd loved it and had thought of it as her lucky bag until it seemed all the luck she'd once enjoyed vanished. Weeks ago, she'd found the satchel on an upper shelf of a closet and took it to a local shoe repair to have one of the straps mended. They'd cleaned and polished the leather and the case looked almost new, with just the right patina of age and use, as if it had housed years of successful manuscripts. She undid the straps and opened the flap, taking out the stack of pages covered with her loopy handwriting. Bea had written more in the past few months than she had in the past few years.

And what she was writing was really good.

And she felt horrible.

YEARS AGO, when she was newly out of graduate school, Leo had persuaded her to work with him on the staff of a magazine he'd helped launch back when starting a magazine wasn't pure folly. *SpeakEasy* was smart and irreverent enough to be slightly scandalous, which made it an instant hit with the insular world of the New York media, the precise community it ruthlessly mocked. Leo wrote a column every month, media news peppered with salacious gossip that freely ridiculed the city's old guard, rife with inherited money and nepotism and ludicrously insular. The column made him a little bit famous and a whole lot disliked. The magazine folded after only a few years, but almost everyone from the original staff had gone on to bigger media ventures or bestselling novels or other highly respected literary pursuits.

For a long time, Leo had been the major success story. He'd corralled some of the younger staff to start an online version of *SpeakEasy* from his tiny apartment. He kept the snide voice and expanded the scope, targeting all his favorite objectionable people and industries, growing the business from one site to seventeen in the space of fifteen months. Only three years later, Leo and his partner sold their tiny empire to a media conglomerate for a small fortune.

Bea still missed the early *SpeakEasy* magazine days. The office was like a raucous summer camp where all the kids were smart and funny and got your jokes and could hold their booze. Back then, it had been Leo who'd pushed her to finish those early stories. It had been Leo who'd stayed up late dissecting her paragraphs, making everything better and tighter and funnier. It had been Leo who'd passed along her first story to *SpeakEasy*'s fiction editor (and her current boss, Paul Underwood) for its inaugural short story issue: "New York's Newest Voices: Who You *Should* Be Reading." It had been Leo who'd used the photo of her on the magazine's cover (with the very *SpeakEasy* caption: "The editor's sister wrote our favorite story, get over it"). That picture of Bea still popped up to accompany the occasional commemorative piece about *SpeakEasy* ("Where are they now?") or the group of young, female writers, including Bea, that some journalist had infuriatingly dubbed "The Glitterary Girls." The photo had been taken on Mott Street in Chinatown in front of a window of gleaming Peking ducks hanging from silver hooks, their still-attached heads all facing the same direction. Bea was wearing a bright yellow dress with a billowing skirt and holding a lacquered green parasol painted with tiny pink and white peonies over one shoulder. The long braids she still wore were a deep auburn then, pinned up at her neck. Chin lowered, eyes closed, profile bathed by the late-afternoon August sun— she resembled a modern-day annunciation. The photo was on the back flap of her first (only) book. For years, the green parasol had hung from the ceiling above her bed. She still had that yellow dress somewhere.

BEA MOTIONED TO GARRIE and he came over with more coffee and placed the bottle of Jameson's next to her cup. She saw him eye her notes and then quickly look away. He'd overheard enough of her whining to Tuck over the years about the novel that never appeared to know better than to ask her about work, which made her feel even more pathetic, if that was even possible.

Leo had loved—and published—her first story because it was about *him*. The character she called Archie was a thinly disguised version of a young Leo, a funny, self-absorbed, caustic Lothario. *The Paris Review* published the second Archie story. The third was in *The New Yorker*. Then she landed an agent—Leo's friend Stephanie who was also just starting out and who secured a two-book deal for so much money that Bea felt faint and had to sit in Stephanie's office and breathe into a paper bag. Her story collection (the highlight of which, the critics agreed, were the three Archie stories—"delectably wry," "hilarious and smart," "whether you find yourself rooting for or against Archie, you'll be powerless to resist his dubious charms") sold *quietly*.

"It's fine," Stephanie told her then. "This is all groundwork for the novel."

Bea wondered if Stephanie and Leo were in touch anymore, if Stephanie even knew what was going on. The last time Bea spoke to Stephanie was well over a year ago during an uncomfortable lunch downtown. "Let's meet somewhere quiet," Stephanie had e-mailed, alerting Bea to the difficult but not surprising conversation to come about her long-delayed, laboriously overworked novel.

"I can see the effort that went into this draft," Stephanie had said (generously—they both knew not a lot of effort had gone into the draft in quite some time). "And while there's much to admire here—"

"Oh, God." Bea couldn't believe she was hearing the stock phrase she'd employed so many times when she couldn't think of a single thing to admire about someone's prose. "Please don't *much-to-admire* me. Please. Just say what you have to say."

"You're right. I'm sorry." Stephanie looked frustrated and almost angry. She looked older, too, Bea was surprised to note, but then she supposed they both did. Stephanie had fiddled with a sugar packet, tearing it a little at one corner and then folding the end and placing it on her saucer. "Okay, here it is. Everything I loved about your stories, their wit and ingenuity and surprise—everything that worked in those pages—" Stephanie broke off again and now she just looked confused. "I can't find any of it in these pages."

The conversation had plummeted from there.

"Are you breaking up with me?" Bea had finally said, trying to joke and lighten the mood.

"Yes," Stephanie said, wanting to leave no doubt as to where she and Bea stood. "I'm very sorry, but yes."

"I want my novel to be *big*," Bea told Stephanie and Leo the night they celebrated her book deal, a long, boozy evening when her ebullience was so uncorrupted that she could shift a room's atmosphere when she moved through, like a weather front.

"That's my job," Stephanie had said. "You just write it."

"I'm talking about the canvas. I want it to be sweeping. *Necessary*. I want to play a little, experiment with structure." Bea waved at their waiter and ordered another bottle of champagne. Leo lit a cigar.

"Experimenting can be good," Stephanie said, tentatively.

Bea was very drunk and very happy and she'd leaned back against the banquette and put her feet up on a chair, took Leo's cigar and blew three smoke rings and watched them float to the ceiling, coughing a little.

"But no more Archie," Leo had said, abruptly. "We're retiring Archie, right?"

Bea had been surprised. She hadn't been planning more Archie stories but she hadn't thought of them as *retired* either. Looking at Leo across the table, clearing her throat and trying to focus her vision through the smoke and champagne and those tiny spoonfuls of coke in the bathroom some hours ago, she thought: *yes*. What was that Bible verse? Time to leave childish things behind?

"Yes," she'd found herself saying. "No more Archie." She'd been decisive.

"Good," he said.

"You're not that interesting, anyway." She handed him back his cigar.

"Not anymore he isn't," Stephanie said, and Bea had pretended not to notice Stephanie's fingers moving higher on Leo's leg and disappearing beneath the linen tablecloth.

How many pages written since then? How many discarded? Too many to think about. Thousands. The novel was big all right. Five hundred and seventy-four pages of big. She never wanted to look at it again.

She poured a little more Jameson's into her cup, not bothering with the coffee now, and looked again at the new pages nobody had seen or even knew existed. It wasn't an Archie story. It *wasn't*. But it had energy and motion, the same lightness of language that had come so easily to her all those years ago and then had seemed to vanish overnight, as if she'd somehow unlearned a vital skill in her sleep—how to tie her shoes or ride a bike or snap her fingers—and then couldn't figure out how to get it back.

Stephanie had left the door the tiniest bit ajar at their last meeting—if you have something new to show me, she had said, *really new,* maybe we can talk. But Bea would have to show the pages to Leo first. Probably. Maybe. Maybe not.

"When are we going to read about *your* life," he'd said, a little testily, after she published the final Archie story, the one where she'd veered a little too close to his less desirable, more predatory qualities. Well, here she was. Using her life. How dare he object? Leo owed her. Especially after the night in the hospital. What happened last July had also happened to her. It was her life, too.

NORA AND LOUISA WERE WALKING along Central Park West, hand in hand, winded from running the three blocks from the SAT classroom, breathless with anticipation. "Here we go," Nora said, squeezing Louisa's hand. "Straight to a certain death or sexual servitude or both."

Louisa laughed but she was nervous. Ditching SAT prep had started as a joke. "We could leave our phones in our lockers and just take off," Louisa had said to Nora after one excruciating session. "The only person who cares if we're here is Mom." Louisa knew by the look on Nora's face that she'd unwittingly put something inevitable into motion. They both hated the classes. The tutor who ran their group seemed barely older than they were and never took attendance or remembered anyone's name or seemed to care who did what. "This is largely self-directed," she'd say, sounding bored and uninspired while staring out a window that faced Columbus Avenue, looking as if her most fervent wish was to leap outside and stroll back into her precious weekend. "You get out of it what you put into it."

"You're a genius," Nora had said to Louisa. "Let's do it!"

"I was kidding. Mom and Dad are paying for this."

"Everything is in the book!" Nora'd pulled out the enormous SAT guide. "They paid for this book. All that tutor does is read from the chapter and make us do the exercises. We can work on the train and at home. It's not even that hard. We have *another year* before applying anywhere. We're *juniors*."

Louisa was tempted but nervous. She agreed the classes were lame, but she felt guilty. Something was up at home concerning money— there was always something up concerning money, there was never enough money—but this time seemed different and possibly more dire. Her parents spent a lot of time heatedly whispering and had even taken their discussion to the freezing and snowy yard the night before. But she knew once Nora set her mind to something that it was just a matter of time before it happened.

"Think of how beautiful the park will be today with the snow," Nora said, petitioning the second they were out from under their mother's watchful eye. "Snow in the city is evanescent. See? I just used an SAT word. Come on. Today's the perfect day."

Nobody stopped them when they bolted out of the building through a side door and ran down the street expecting to hear their names called at any second. They buried their cell phones deep in a locker in case their mother checked their location on Stalkerville (and she was their mother; she *always* checked their location).

Louisa hesitated. Melody's admonitions about Central Park and its dark pathways full of nefarious men wanting vaguely disturbing and dangerous things genuinely frightened her. But Nora wanted to find a hot dog vendor and the carousel and Belvedere Castle and other things they'd heard about but never seen. She'd downloaded and printed a map before they left home. "We'll stick to the main paths today," she said, unfolding the map and pointing to the spot marked "Strawberry Fields Memorial."

"Let's start here."

LEO PLUMB WAS LOST. He was not ordinarily an uptown guy and what he'd thought was a shortcut through Central Park had led him into an area he didn't recognize. It didn't help that the park was like a disaster area after the snowstorm. The snow and ice that had settled over the still-leafy trees had perilously weighed down the branches, destroying or damaging countless trees. Many of the park's walking paths were like obstacle courses, slippery and littered with debris. A massive cleanup was under way, and the sound of chain saws reverberated from every direction. Some areas were closed off with police tape, necessitating circuitous detours; Leo was completely turned around.

He looked up at the sky, trying to spot the distinctive peaks and gables of the Dakota on the park's west flank and take a bearing, but from where he was standing he could only see taller, unfamiliar buildings. Leo was running late for his appointment, the one he'd scheduled by phone the day he left rehab, to meet his old friend Rico at the Strawberry Fields Memorial. He had to find his way to higher ground. He used to know some trick about figuring out where he was in the park, something about numbers at the base of the cast-iron lampposts. He walked over to the nearest one. Yes! A small metal plaque affixed to the base was engraved with four numbers: 6107. Did that mean he was only at Sixty-First Street? But didn't the "07" indicate something, too? East side or west side or smack in the damn middle? Fuck Olmsted and his meandering faux-bucolic pathways. He shoved his hands in his pockets and started walking in a direction that felt like he was heading west.

"IT'S COOL, I GUESS," Louisa said, staring down at the black-and-white mosaic on the ground with the word *IMAGINE* at the center. She'd pictured something very different, with an image of John Lennon maybe. Or Strawberries. Or Fields.

Nora was bouncing on her toes, because she was excited and because it was cold. "Let's head into the park. Look at this place. It's full of people and families. The boathouse is right down that hill to the left."

Nora was right. The park didn't feel dangerous at all. It felt lively and bright. "It's downright ebullient," Louisa said, summoning another SAT word. "Lead the way."

HURRYING AS QUICKLY AS HE COULD MANAGE given the scrim of ice coating the pavement, Leo finally came to a path he recognized. He could see the Dakota now. The path was ostensibly closed, blocked off with police tape, and beyond the tape an enormous broken branch of an old elm was swaying dangerously a few feet above the ground. He ducked under the tape and started to lightly jog up the walkway. It was steeper than it looked and the soles of his expensive shoes were paper-thin. As he maneuvered around some fallen limbs, giving wide berth to the elm, he slipped on a long, nearly invisible frozen puddle that cracked under his weight and before he could catch himself, both legs went out from under him and he landed on his backside. Hard.

"Crap," he said to a flock of sparrows twittering maniacally in the surrounding bushes. Leo stayed prone for a minute. He was sweating heavily even though his extremities were freezing. Above, the vivid blue sky belied the approaching winter; it was a spring sky, he thought, a sky full of promise. He almost wanted to close his eyes and forget about his meeting. (*Meeting?* He could hear the voice of his rehab counselor in his ear, her derisive tone, her familiar snort. *Let's call things by their real name, Leo. It's a drug buy.*)

As he sat up, he heard a commotion up the path. Two teenaged girls rounded the corner, heading downhill. Their heads were bent close;

one was animated, talking quickly and gesticulating, the other was shaking her head and frowning. Leo liked something about the way the girls kept leaning into each other as they walked, almost as if they were tethered at the shoulder or elbow. The blonde looked up, noticed Leo sitting in the middle of the icy walk, and froze. Leo smiled to reassure them, gave a little wave.

"Careful," he called out. "It's treacherous down here."

The blonde looked alarmed and grabbed her friend who was staring at Leo with—was he imagining this?—recognition. The three of them faced off for a moment, and then the blonde grabbed the brunette's hand and both girls turned and hurried up the path.

"Hey," Leo yelled. "I come in peace!"

The girls moved faster, holding on to each other's arms for balance.

FOR A MINUTE, it seemed to Nora and Louisa that Melody had arranged Leo's nearly mystical appearance, had planted him there to say: *See? See what trouble lurks in the park? See how lucky you are that I'm your mother?* They were always asking about Melody's siblings, the siblings who lived in the city and seemed so interesting and exotic, especially their uncle Leo whose picture would sometimes be in the Sunday Styles section with Victoria, their glamorous aunt. (Louisa had tried calling her Aunt Victoria once at a rare family gathering and couldn't tell whether the woman wanted to laugh or spit at her.) Melody looked pained when the girls would point out the photos, her face clouding with a mix of disapproval and disappointment. Her expression made the girls feel so bad they stopped mentioning the pictures, hiding them instead in a Tupperware container in their shared closet. Sometimes they'd ask their father about Leo who would only say, "He's always been perfectly nice to me. Not much of a family man."

And here he was. Leo. Flailing about like an upended turtle. ("He wasn't *flailing*," Nora said, dismissing Louisa's attempts to describe the odd moment while they were heading home on the train later. "He was trying to get up. It was icy." But Louisa was firm, Melody-like; newly out of rehab, she insisted, Leo should not have been in the park.

He was supposed to be meeting his siblings for lunch!) At the top of the path they stopped and hid behind a tree trunk to spy on Leo.

"It's totally him," Louisa said.

"Should we say something?" Nora asked.

Louisa hesitated. She wanted to approach Leo, too, but thought they shouldn't. "He'll tell Mom," she said. Nora nodded, mouth drawn tight, disappointed. They both held still, barely breathing, and watched Leo for a few minutes. He stood and brushed off his pants. He sat on a large boulder. "What is he doing?" Nora whispered as Leo stared up at the sky. She wished they were a normal family. She wished she could run down the path, waving, and he'd smile and laugh and they could spend the day together. Instead, here they were, cowering behind a tree. They didn't have all the details of his trip to rehab, but they knew there was some kind of accident and that it was bad and involved drugs. "Who does blow anymore?" Louisa had heard her mother say to their father one night last summer.

"He might be buying drugs," Louisa said, looking at Nora, worried. "Why else would he be all the way up here right before lunch?"

LEO SIGHED AND HOISTED HIMSELF UP, brushing twigs and dirt off his pants. He sat on a nearby rock, assessing the damage to his scraped palms. Something nagged at him, something about the girls. He'd really spooked them. He assumed his fall was inelegant, but couldn't imagine that he looked dangerous. Why had they been so spooked? Kids probably weren't allowed anywhere in the park without a parent these days—not even teens, not even boys. Those girls were probably already looking for a cop.

Dammit, Leo thought. What if they *were* looking for a cop? What if they thought he was drunk or worse and gave his description to the police who were patrolling for him right now? He couldn't be caught with drugs. His lawyer had been crystal clear: *Keep your nose clean until the divorce decree comes down. No travel. No suspicious spending. No trouble.* Leo stood and headed toward the sound of traffic. At the top of the path, he turned a corner and finally knew exactly where he was. Central Park West was straight ahead. He could hail a taxi and go directly to Grand Central and not be late for lunch. If he made a right, he'd be at Strawberry Fields within two or three minutes.

He hesitated. Above him, an ear-splitting screech. He looked up to see three enormous crows, perched on one of the few trees that had already dropped its leaves. They were all squawking at once, as if they were arguing about his next move. Directly beneath, in the midst of the stark and barren branches and at the base of a forked limb, a mud-brown leafy mass. A nest. Jesus.

Leo checked the time and started walking.

CHAPTER TWO

Nobody remembered who started calling their eventual inheritance "The Nest," but the name stuck. Melody was just sixteen when Leonard Plumb Sr. decided to establish a trust for his children. "Nothing significant," he would tell them repeatedly, "a modest nest egg, conservatively invested, dispersed in time for you to enjoy but not exploit." The funds, Leonard Sr. explained, would not be available until Melody, the youngest, turned forty.

Jack was the first to argue vociferously against this distribution, wanting to know why they all couldn't have their share sooner and pointing out that Melody would get the money earlier in her life than everyone else and what was fair about that? But Leonard had given the distribution of funds, how much and when, a great deal of thought. Leonard was—and this was quite literally how he thought of himself, several times a day—a *self-made man*. It was the organizing principle of his life, that money and its concurrent rewards should flow from work, effort, commitment, and routine. At one time, the Plumbs of

Eastern Long Island had family money and a decent amount of real estate. Decades of behavioral blunders and ill-conceived marriages and businesses run amok had left next to nothing by the time Leonard was in high school. He'd wangled himself an engineering scholarship to Cornell and then a job with Dow Chemical during a time he referred to, reverently, as the Dawn of the Absorbency Revolution.

Leonard had lucked onto a team working with a new substance: synthetic polymers that could absorb three hundred times more liquid than conventional organic absorbents like paper and cotton. As his colleagues set to work identifying potential uses for the new superabsorbers—agriculture, industrial processing, architecture, military applications—Leonard seized on something else: consumer products.

According to Leonard's oft-repeated legend, the business he and his two partners started, advising larger corporations on how to use the new absorbers, was nearly solely responsible for daintier feminine hygiene products (which he never failed to mention in mixed company, mortifying his children), better disposable diapers (his proudest accomplishment, he'd spent a small fortune on a diaper service when the first three were babies), and the quilted square of revolting plastic that still sits beneath every piece of slaughtered meat or poultry in the supermarket (he was not above rooting through the garbage at a dinner party and hoisting the discarded square triumphantly, saying "Mine!"). Leonard built a thriving business based on absorbency and it was the thing he was proudest of, the fact of his life that lent a sweet gleam to all his accomplishments.

He was not a materialistic man. The exterior of his roomy Tudor house was scrupulously maintained, the interior one tick short of slovenly. He was loath to spend money on anything he thought he could fix himself, and he believed he could fix everything. The contents of the Plumb house existed in varying states of disrepair, waiting for Leonard's attention and marked with his handwritten notes: a hair dryer that could only be held with a mittened pot holder because the cracked handle overheated so quickly ("Use with Care!"), outlets that

delivered tiny electric shocks ("Use Upper, Not Lower!"), leaky cof-
feemakers ("Use Sparingly!"), bikes with no brakes ("Use with Caution!"), and countless defunct blenders, tape recorders, televisions,
stereo components ("DO NOT USE!").

(Years later, unconsciously at first and then deliberately because
it made them laugh and was a neat, private shorthand, Bea and Leo
would borrow Leonard's note vernacular for editing manuscripts—
use more, use sparingly, DO NOT USE!)

Leonard was a careful, conservative investor in blue chip stocks.
He was happy to set aside some funds to provide a modest safety net
for his children's future, but he also wanted them to be financially
independent and to value hard work. He'd grown up around trust
fund kids—knew many of them still—and he'd seen the damage an
influx of early money caused: abundance proffered too soon led to las-
situde and indolence, a wandering dissatisfaction. The trust he estab-
lished was meant to be a *soupçon,* a little something to sit atop their
own, inevitable financial achievements—they were *his* children, after
all—and pad their retirement a bit, maybe help fund a college tuition
or two. Nothing so vast as to be truly significant.

Keeping the money tied up until Melody was forty appealed to
Leonard for many reasons. He was realistic about the maturity—
emotional and otherwise—of his four children: not commendable.
He suspected if they didn't get the money all at once, it would become
a source of conflict between those who had it and those who didn't;
they wouldn't be kind to one another. And if anyone was going to
need the money earlier in life, Leonard imagined it would be Melody.
She wasn't the brightest of the four (that would be Bea), or the most
charming (Leo), or the most resourceful (Jack).

On the long list of things Leonard didn't believe in, near the top
was paying strangers to manage his money. So one summer evening
he enlisted his second cousin George Plumb, who was an attorney, to
meet for dinner and hammer out the details of his estate.

It never occurred to Leonard that evening, as he and George leisurely made their way through two Gibson martinis, a superior

Pommard, twenty-eight ounces of rib eye with creamed spinach, cigars and brandy, that in less than two years he would be felled by a massive coronary behind the wheel of his scrupulously maintained fifteen-year-old BMW sedan while driving home from work one late night. He never imagined that the bull market of the aughts, riding on mortgage-backed securities, would balloon the trust far beyond his intention, nor could he have foreseen how the staid but eerily prescient George would providentially transfer The Nest to the safer havens of bonds right before the market's decline in 2008, protecting the capital that the Plumb siblings had watched, during the decade before Melody's fortieth birthday, inflate to numbers beyond their wildest dreams. He never imagined that as the fund grew so, too, would his children's tolerance for risk, for doing the *one* thing Leonard had repeatedly warned them not to do, *ever,* in any avenue of life, from the time they were old enough to understand: count the chickens before they hatched.

The only person who could access the funds early was Francie and in spite of her casual allegiance to Leonard while he was alive (or maybe *because* of it, she married her second husband practically within minutes of shedding her widow's weeds), she abided by Leonard's wishes to the letter. Her interest in her children, anemic when she was actually responsible for them, dwindled to the occasional holiday brunch or birthday phone call. Leo was the only one who had never petitioned Francie for a loan using The Nest as collateral. Jack and Melody and Bea had all asked at one time that she consider an earlier dispersal, but she stubbornly refused.

Until Leo's accident.

CHAPTER THREE

The day Leo was released from rehab, a few days before the family lunch at the Oyster Bar, he went straight to his Tribeca apartment hoping to broker some civil temporary living arrangement with his about-to-be ex-wife, Victoria. That she had other plans became clear when his key no longer fit in the lock of the front door.

"Don't bother fighting this one," George told him over the phone. "Just find a hotel. Remember my advice. Lie low."

Leo didn't want to confess to George that Bea had taken his wallet the night of the accident. He'd arrived at rehab with nothing more than his house keys, his iPhone (which was immediately confiscated and returned to him the day he was released), and sixty dollars in his pocket (ditto). Standing at the Franklin Street subway station, paging through the contacts on his phone, he realized with deflating clarity how few people in Manhattan would be happy to lend him their sofa. How many friendships he'd let wane and diminish over the past few years while he and Victoria indulged each other's miseries and spent money as if it were somehow magically regenerating. How few people would be sorry to hear he'd had some trouble and would hope for his recovery or return. He'd lived in New York for more than twenty years and had never not had a place to go home to.

The small piece of paper with a cell-phone number on it, pressed on him by his rehab roommate "just in case," felt like a squirming minnow in his back pocket. He took the paper out, punched the numbers into his phone, and left a message before he had time to think about it, which was exactly the opposite of what he'd been incessantly lectured to do during his stay in Bridges, the recovery center where his family had dumped him for twelve endless weeks. He'd hated every minute of it. Individual therapy hadn't been half bad; he'd vented practically nonstop about Victoria and had almost exhausted his bitterness over her avarice. He almost felt like getting rid of her was worth the enormous price tag. Almost. But he should have negotiated something about the apartment for the next week or two.

The wool jacket he was wearing was not nearly warm enough. The day was unusually cold for October. He was vaguely aware of an ominous weather report. The *New York Post* headline at the subway newsstand screamed SNOWTOBER! As Leo stood waiting for a return call on his phone, he watched two panhandlers at the subway entrance compete for change. On one side, an elderly homeless guy was holding a knit cap in his hand and exuberantly addressing passersby with a hearty *Hello! Stay dry! Cold one today!* And in what Leo thought was a particularly brilliant marketing move, exhorting all the small children to *Read a book!*

"Did you read a book today, young man?" he'd say. "Don't forget to read a book!"

The kids would smile shyly and nod, chew on a finger while dropping a parent-supplied dollar bill into the paper bag at the guy's feet.

On the opposite side, a young bareheaded musical student (*smart,* Leo thought, his head of streaked blond curls was impressive) had a violin tucked under his elongated chin. He was playing popular classical riffs, lots of Vivaldi, a little Bach, and was very popular with the ladies not pushing strollers; the older ones in their fur coats, the younger ones wearing headphones or carrying reusable shopping bags.

The pelting rain that had been falling all morning was changing over to sleet. Whoever was on the other end of the phone number hadn't called him back yet. He didn't have an umbrella, didn't even have a hat, and the shoulders of his expensive jacket were soaking wet. He paged through the contacts on his phone again, looked at Stephanie's name for a few seconds, and hit "call."

"THINGS MUST BE WORSE than I've heard if you're begging to cross the bridge to Brooklyn," Stephanie said to Leo. She picked up after only the third ring.

"I'm not begging. I need to spend time with somebody normal, somebody I actually like." Stephanie didn't respond. She wasn't going to make this easy. "What *have* you heard anyway," Leo asked, "about my situation." He braced himself. This was another reason he needed to see Stephanie, to figure out how much of the story was out there, see if George had done what he promised.

"Hardly anything," Stephanie said. "I heard you checked into Bridges. That's it. Your consigliore is doing a good job. So how was it?"

"How was what?"

"The Carnival cruise," Stephanie said, trying to decide how far she could push on the phone. Probably not very far.

"You are *still* not quite as funny as you think," Leo said, trying to decide how much he'd have to cede before she invited him out. Probably not much.

"How was rehab, Leo? What else would I be asking about?"

"It was fine." Leo's fingers were starting to go numb in the cold.

"Are you all beholden to your higher power? Working through the steps?"

"It wasn't really that kind of place," Leo said.

"What kind of place was it?"

"Steph, I don't know if you've looked out the window recently, but

I'm standing outside in a monsoon of freezing sleet. I'm soaking wet. It's really cold." He stomped his feet a little to try to warm his toes. He wasn't used to being in this situation, waiting on a request.

"Come out. You know where I live."

"What subway do I take?" He cringed, hearing himself sound so eager and grateful.

"My lord," Stephanie said, laughing. "Brooklyn and not via town car? I guess the mighty really have fallen. You know there aren't tokens anymore, right? You have to buy something called a MetroCard?"

Leo didn't say anything. Of course he knew about the MetroCard, but he realized he'd probably never bought one.

"Leo?" Stephanie asked. "Do you have enough money for a MetroCard?"

"Yes."

"Come then." Her voice softened a bit at the edges. "Take the 2 or 3 to Bergen Street. I'm roasting lamb."

WHEN STEPHANIE'S PHONE RANG THAT AFTERNOON, she'd been throwing fistfuls of rock salt down her front stoop ahead of the purported storm. She knew before she answered that it was Leo. She was not a superstitious person, did not believe in second sight or premonitions or ghosts, but she'd always had an intuition around all things Leo. So she wasn't surprised when she heard his voice, realized that some part of her was waiting for him to call. She'd run into his wife some weeks prior at a bistro in Soho and found herself on the receiving end of Victoria's vituperative torrent—light on details, hard on recriminations.

"Good riddance to that narcissistic sociopath," Victoria had said, sliding her arm through her apparent date's, a television actor Stephanie recognized from one of those police procedurals. Victoria was vague when Stephanie asked why Leo was in rehab.

"Because he's a coward?" she said. "Because he'd rather sleep it off in Connecticut and hope everyone forgives and forgets? As usual."

"Forgives and forgets what?" Stephanie'd persisted. The bar was overflowing and the three of them, gently jostled by the crowd, were swaying as if standing on the deck of a boat.

Victoria stared hard at Stephanie. "You never liked me," she said, crossing her skeletal arms and giving Stephanie the self-satisfied smile of someone who'd just realized the answer to a riddle.

"I don't *dislike* you," Stephanie said, which was untrue. She very much disliked Victoria or, rather, all Victoria represented, everything about Leo that was superficial, glib, careless. Everything about him that had gone so wrong once he sold SpeakEasyMedia and left everyone behind, including her. "I don't even know you."

"Well, know this, for when Leo inevitably reappears," Victoria had said, leaning so close that Stephanie could smell garlic and shellfish and cigarettes on her breath, could see a tiny smear of dragon-red lipstick on one of her preternaturally bleached front teeth. "I'm getting everything, every last cent. Leo can rot in rehab or in hell for all I care. *Pass it on*."

So when Leo called from the subway, sounding sheepish (by Leo standards) and needing shelter, she was curious. Curious to see if rehab had rendered him even the tiniest bit transformed—sober or renewed or regretful. She knew he was probably just the same old Leo, working an angle. Still. She wanted to see for herself.

And if she was being perfectly honest—and she was because she'd fought hard to value honesty above nearly everything else—she was flattered Leo had turned to her when he needed help. Grateful she was still on his list. And because of that, she'd have to be very careful.

LEO DIDN'T HAVE ANYTHING AGAINST BROOKLYN, he just preferred Manhattan, and he believed anyone who said they didn't was lying. Still, as he walked from the Bergen Street stop into Prospect Heights and down Stephanie's block, he had to admit that the rapidly falling snow did something decidedly romantic to the streets lined with nineteenth-century brownstones. The cars on the block were already hidden under a sodden layer of white. People were shoveling their walks and front stoops; the scattered rock salt looked like white confetti against the bluestone slate sidewalks.

Hands shoved in his pockets against the cold, Leo felt like a character from an Edith Wharton novel as he lifted the latch of the black iron front gate and walked past the gas lamplight in front of Stephanie's house. The wooden shutters lining the curved bay window were open, and as he climbed the stoop, he could see into the living room where she had a fire going. He should have stopped to buy flowers or wine or something. He stood before the massive mahogany and glass front doors. Stephanie had hung life-size plastic glow-in-the-dark skeletons in the two center panes. He hesitated a minute and then rang the bell—three short ones, two long—the buzzer code they used for each other back in the day. One of the doors swung open. The skeletons clicked and swayed in the stormy breeze, and there she was. Stephanie.

He always forgot, when he hadn't seen her in a while, how attractive she was. Not standard-issue beautiful, better. She was nearly his height and he was almost six foot. Her coppery hair and tawny skin made her a peculiar brand of redhead: no freckles, quick to tan if she ever spent time in the sun, which she didn't. She was the only person he'd ever met who had one brown eye and one that was flecked with green. She was wearing admirably fitted jeans. He wished she would turn around so he could become reacquainted with her ass.

She greeted him by raising her hand, blocking him from crossing the threshold of the foyer. "Three conditions, Leo," she said. "No drugs. No borrowing money. No fucking."

"When have I ever borrowed money from you?" Leo said, feeling the welcome blast of heat from the house. "In the last decade, anyway."

"I mean it." Stephanie opened the door wider. She smiled at him then, offered her cheek for a kiss. "It's nice to see you, asshole."

CHAPTER FOUR

T hat Leo had messed up so enormously was disturbing but, his siblings reluctantly agreed, not surprising. That Leo's fuckup had activated their disengaged mother to exercise her power of attorney and nearly drain The Nest, however, was shocking. It was the one threat to The Nest none of them had imagined. It had been, simply, unthinkable.

"Obviously it wasn't unthinkable because I thought of it and your father set it up that way," Francie said, the day she finally agreed to meet them, briefly, in George's New York office, while Leo was still in rehab.

"It was our money, too," Jack said. His voice wasn't forceful as he'd intended, more whiney than outraged. "And we weren't consulted or even informed until it was too late."

"It's not your money until next March," Francie said.

"February," Melody said.

"Excuse me?" Francie looked slightly taken aback to hear Melody, as if just realizing she was there.

"My birthday's in February," Melody said. "Not March."

Bea stopped knitting and raised her hand. "I'm March."

Francie did the thing she always did when wrong, pretended not to be and corrected whoever had corrected her. "Yes, that's exactly what I said. The money doesn't become yours until February. It's also not completely gone. You will all get fifty thousand, more or less. Is that correct, George?"

"In that neighborhood, yes." George was walking around the conference table pouring everyone coffee, clearly uncomfortable.

Melody couldn't stop staring at her mother; she was starting to look old. How old was she? Seventy-one? Seventy-two? Her long, elegant fingers trembled a bit, the veins on the back of her hands were dark and prominent, the slackening skin marred with age spots, like a quail's egg. Francie had always been so vain about her hands, demonstrating the reach of her fingers by bending them forward and touching the tips to the inside of her wrists. "Pianist's hands," she used to tell Melody when Melody was little. Melody noticed now that Francie consciously placed the left (which was slightly less mottled) atop the right. Her voice had thinned, too; the slightest difference in treble had crept in, not a rasp or a scratch, but a waver that troubled Melody. Francie's decline meant they were all declining.

"You are still receiving a sum of money," Francie continued, "that would make most people incredibly grateful."

"A sum that is ten percent of what we were expecting. Is *that* correct, George?" Jack asked.

"Sounds about right," George said.

"*Ten percent!*" Jack said, practically spitting across the table at Francie.

Francie removed a slender gold watch from her wrist and placed it on the table in front of her, as if putting them all on notice that their time was nearly up. "Your father would have been horrified by that amount. You know he meant the fund to provide a modest assist, not a true inheritance."

"That's entirely beside the point," Jack said. "He set up an account. He deposited money. George managed it—*very* well. Now the deadline is approaching and it's supposed to—wait a second—" Jack turned to George. "Leo still isn't getting fifty thousand, is he? Because if he is? That is truly fucked."

"Watch your language," Francie said.

Jack looked at Bea and Melody, mouth agape, and spread his hands wide. Melody wasn't sure if he was gesturing in frustration or beckoning them to join in the conversation. She looked over at Bea who was intently counting stitches on whatever it was she was knitting.

"We're following the terms," Francie said.

"Your mother is right about that," George said. "Leo can refuse his share, but we can't refuse to give it to him."

"*Un*-believable," Jack said.

Melody wanted to speak up, but she was stuck on how to address her mother. Her older siblings had started calling Francie by her first name in their teens, but she'd never been able to do it and something about saying "Mom" in front of Jack and Bea embarrassed her. Also, she was a little scared of her mother. Her mother was a little mean. For years, the Plumbs had told one another that their mother was just a mean drunk. *If she would just stop drinking!* they'd say, *She'd be fine!* Shortly before Leonard died, she developed some out-of-the-blue alcohol intolerance and *did* stop drinking. Cold turkey. (Years later, they would realize Francie's sudden sobriety had to do with Harold, the conservative, teetotaling businessman and local politician she swiftly married after their father died.) They eagerly awaited her transformation only to discover that they already knew her true nature: She was just a little mean.

"Here's the thing," Melody said, clearing her throat and waving a little in Francie's direction to get her attention. "We've been counting on the money and have made plans and—" Melody hesitated. Francie sighed and clanged her spoon around her coffee cup as if she were stirring in sugar or cream. She let the spoon drop and rattle a little on the saucer.

"Yes?" Francie said, gesturing for Melody to wind up. "You've made plans and—"

Melody froze, unsure of what to say next.

"This is a blow," Jack said. "This is a financial blow on top of several financial hits over the past few years. Is it unreasonable to expect you—as Leo's parent and given your means—to absorb some of this financial loss?"

Melody was nodding as Jack spoke and trying to gauge her mother's reaction. There was a part of her, a tiny, contracted part of her, that thought maybe she could get her mother to help with college tuition.

"Leo's parent?" Francie said, nearly looking amused. "Leo is forty-six. And you're not the only one who has taken a financial hit over the past few years. Not that any of you bothered to inquire after us."

"Why?" Bea asked. "Are you and Harold okay?"

Francie had folded her hands in front of her and was looking down at the table. She started to speak and then stopped. Bea and Melody and Jack looked at one another nervously. "Harold and I are fine," she finally said.

"Well, then—" Jack started, but Francie put up a hand.

"We will be fine, but most of Harold's money is tied up in commercial real estate, which is a soft market right now. Obviously."

"And the money Dad left for you?"

"It's long gone. We used it to shore up Harold's business until we're on an upswing." Francie straightened her shoulders and raised her voice a little, like a teacher reassuring a room of students during a fire drill. "Everything will be absolutely fine when the market corrects the way it always does. In the meantime? We've had to cut back, too. Harold has his own children to consider. At the moment, our liquid assets are negligible, and that will be our situation for quite some time. We've all had to readjust our expectations and plans given the recent economy." Francie leaned back in her chair and crossed her arms, appraising her offspring. "Besides, Leo is your brother. It never occurred to me that you would *not* help him out of this dire situation—"

"A situation entirely of his own making," Jack said.

Francie pointed a finger at Jack. "Your father set the conditions of the account so that I could tap into it in case of an emergency for this exact reason. *This* was a family emergency."

"Which part qualifies as an emergency?" Jack said. "Leo's years of no work and all play? His marriage to a world-class spendthrift? Crashing a Porsche he couldn't afford because his dick was in a waitress's fist?"

Across the table, Francie put the tips of her unsteady fingers to her eyelids, which were creased with a violet shadow making the lids look more bruised than anything else. "I don't want to have this conversation again." She opened her eyes and looked around the table, surprised, as always, when face-to-face with her children.

Francie knew she wouldn't win any prizes for motherhood—she'd never aspired to any—but she hadn't been this horrible, had she? What had Leonard wrought with the money he thought would just be a small dividend later in their lives? How had they raised children who were so impractical and yet still so entitled? Maybe it *was* her fault. She'd wondered that often enough, what mother hadn't? She'd been twenty-five and married less than a year when Leo was born, and Jack and Bea had followed so quickly. She'd been overwhelmed to the point of being listless. And just when she felt she was coming back to her old self, gaining control of the situation—Leo was six, Jack four, Bea months away from three—everyone finally sleeping—and surprise! Melody. She was bereft when she found herself pregnant with Melody and for many years after, counting down the hours of the days until she could have a drink to dampen her anxiety. These days, she supposed, she'd be diagnosed with postnatal something and given a pill and maybe it would be different. Harold—solid, confident, reassuring Harold—had rescued her.

Maybe the fault was with her marriage to Leonard; their relationship had been fraught, disconnected (except for the sex, she still thought about having sex with Leonard, his unlikely voracious exuberance, her ability to be yielding and attentive in bed in a way she wasn't anywhere else; if only they'd been a little more careful about family planning), and probably their parenting had suffered as a result, but had they really been different from anyone of their generation? She didn't think so.

"Mom?" Francie was jolted back into the conference room by Melody's voice, away from the pleasant memory of Leonard and the unlikely places they would couple when the children were little and everywhere and wanting her constantly. The laundry room with its locked door had been a favorite, the whirring and thumping of the washer and dryer giving them a certain auditory privacy. She still had a Pavlovian type of arousal when she smelled Clorox.

And here they were—her children. Three of them, anyway. Jack, who had emerged from the womb aloof and self-contained. He was always trying to sell Francie some inferior kind of antique for her house, something from his shop that was overvalued and overpriced. She didn't know if he was dumb or if he just thought she was.

Beatrice had seemed like the easiest of the four, but then she wrote those stories. Francie was proud when the first one was published, ready to buy dozens of copies and show them to her friends—until she read the story with a character who was meant to be her, a mother described as "distant and casually cruel." She'd never mentioned the story to Bea, but she still remembered bits—a woman who "viewed the world through a prism of bottomless desire; her sole fluency, disappointment." Luckily, her friends didn't read those kinds of magazines anyway; they read *Town & Country,* they read *Ladies Home Journal.* Bea'd always had her secrets, always. Francie wondered what was going on in that bowed head now as her hands flew with needles and yarn.

And Melody. Maybe she would slip Melody some cash, enough for some Botox or a facial or something to brighten her pallor. She was the youngest and somehow the most faded, as if the Plumb DNA had thinned with each conception, strong and robust with Leo and each child after being—a little *less.* She couldn't claim to be close to Leo, but he was the least needy and, therefore, the one she thought of with the most fondness.

She'd helped Leo because Harold had insisted she take care of the situation as swiftly as possible. He didn't want any of his multiple business partners, already skittish in the current financial environment, to associate him with a publicly humiliating and possibly financially gutting lawsuit. George's connections, the family's long-standing reputation locally, and a fat check got the job done. But she'd also taken pleasure in her magnanimous gesture. She'd felt, for a change, capable and maternal. She liked being able to wipe the slate for Leo and offer him a second chance. She believed in second chances, sometimes more than first chances, which were wasted on youth and indiscretion. Her second marriage was the one she deserved even if it was a little staid, a little lacking in drama and the physical connection she had with Leonard. But Harold was good to her; she was taken care of; her "bottomless desires" satisfied.

And still she had to contend with this execution squad of her own children, complete with Madame Defarge at the head of the conference table. Who was *casually cruel* now? This was how it had always been: Nothing she did was good enough; what she did for one disappointed another. She couldn't win. When would it end? She searched their faces again, looking for some sign, some small indicator that they'd come from her and Leonard. Aside from physical traits, the easiest mark to hit, she could see nothing. Nothing. All she could think was, *I don't recognize a single one of you.*

"Mom?" Melody said again.

"This is a conversation you need to have with Leo," Francie finally said. "I'm sure he will be able to repay you as soon as he's settled with Victoria. I understand he's selling nearly everything—the apartment, the artwork. Isn't that right, George?"

George cleared his throat, made a little steeple with his fingers, and squinted as if a bright ray of sun had suddenly appeared in the windowless conference room. "He is, but I have to tell you that most of it is going to Victoria."

"What do you mean by most of it?" Melody said.

"I mean, pretty much all of it. There will be some left, enough

to tide him over for a bit, help him get settled until he finds a job."
George paused, knowing he was delivering more bad news. "As you
can imagine, Victoria could have made things quite difficult and this
was how it shook out."

"What about Leo's insurance?" Melody said. "Shouldn't he have
some kind of liability coverage?"

"Yes, well, that was another unexpected complication. It seems Leo
had lapsed payment on quite a few bills, including insurance."

Jack massaged his temples as if tending to a migraine. "So let me
recap. Essentially, all Leo's assets are going to paying off Victoria to
get rid of her, keep her quiet, whatever, and all of *our* money is going
to the *waitress* because of Leo's mess."

George shrugged. "I would phrase it in a more nuanced fashion,
but essentially? Yes."

"Matilda Rodriguez," Bea said.

Jack and Melody looked at Bea, confused. "Her name," Bea said,
impatient. "You could at least use the waitress's name."

"Are you humming?" Jack said, turning to Melody.

"What?" Melody startled. She *was* humming. It was a nervous
habit, something she did when she was worried or anxious. She was
trying not to think about the accident. "Sorry," she said to the room.

"You don't have to apologize for humming," Bea said. "For God's
sake."

"It's that song from *Cats,*" Jack said. "I want to scream."

"Before we wind up," Francie said, cutting off the all-too-familiar
bickering, "I'd like to acknowledge all George's work. I won't get into
the specifics, but suffice it to say that getting Leo to rehab, negotiating
the settlement, doing what needed to be done—at the local level—to
take care of this, keep it out of the paper, was a superb effort and we've
been remiss in not thanking him yet for his truly excellent effort,
the speed and the efficiency and so on and so forth." She nodded at
George, like a monarch recognizing a loyal subject.

"We were lucky," George said, avoiding looking at Bea, whose
hands had stilled. "Things broke our way. And your mother is right.

This could have been much, much worse. I file this one under 'best-case scenarios.'"

"I guess we have a slightly different filing system," Melody said.

"This is in *all* our best interests." Francie stood and pulled on her coat. Melody had to stop herself from reaching over to touch the rich navy fabric. "We don't want this all over the East End."

"I don't care what's on the East End," Jack said.

"Me neither," said Bea, aware that the meeting was about to wrap up and maybe she'd been just a little too quiet.

Francie was wrapping a lavender scarf around her neck. Melody stared. The scarf was so light and diaphanous it reminded her of a passage from a children's book she used to read to the girls when they were little, about a princess who had a dress that had been spun by moths from moonlight.

"Your scarf," Melody said. "It's beautiful."

"Thank you." Francie looked surprised. She fingered the cloth a little and then unwound the scarf, folded it into a neat square, and pushed it across the conference table until it was in front of Melody. "Here," she said. "Take it."

"Really?" Melody, in spite of herself, was thrilled. She had never owned anything quite so delicate. It had to be expensive. "Are you sure?"

"I'm sure," Francie said, pleased to see the appreciation on Melody's face. "It's your color. It will brighten the pallor a bit."

"Have you spoken to Leo lately?" Bea asked Francie.

Francie watched Melody wrap the scarf around her neck. It wasn't her color, but it still looked nice. She motioned for Melody to come closer and she adjusted the ends of the scarf, tucking them into place. "There," she said. She turned to Bea. "I spoke to him last week. Briefly."

"Is he okay?" Bea said.

Francie shrugged. "He's Leo. He sounded perfectly fine, considering."

"Does he understand your intentions?" Jack said. "That your incredible generosity on our behalf is not a gift but a loan?"

"I'm sure Leo doesn't need to be told to be accountable for the money; he's not dumb." Francie was pulling on her gloves now.

"But he's Leo," Jack said. "He's supposed to magically start caring about what happens to us?"

"We should give him a chance," Bea said.

"You're all delusional," Jack said. He sounded more tired than angry now.

Francie's brief sense of accomplishment over gifting Melody the scarf evaporated. She gave no one in particular a brittle flash of smile. "I'll make sure he gets in touch with you as soon as he's back in the city," Francie said. "I can do that."

"And then what?" Jack asked.

Francie shrugged. "Invite him to lunch."

CHAPTER FIVE

Meeting at the Grand Central Oyster Bar was part convenience—Melody disembarked at Grand Central, which was halfway between downtown where Jack and Leo lived and Beatrice's place uptown—and part nostalgia. On the rare occasion when the elder Plumbs had brought all four children into the city, they had always dined at the Oyster Bar, summoning plates of oysters with exotic names—Chincoteague, Emerald Cove, Pemaquid—and steaming bowls of oyster stew. The Plumb siblings loved the bustle of the dining room (where they never sat) and the ordered efficiency of the sprawling, no-reservations needed, sit-down counter (where they always sat). They loved the dramatically vaulted ceilings covered in ivory Gustavino tiles and the strings of white lights that managed to make the space feel both lushly romantic and slightly antiseptic.

Melody had arrived early to intercept her brothers and sister before they found seats at the counter. She'd made the bold move of reserving them a table in the dining room. She was sick of the counter; it was hard for a group of four to talk when sitting in a row unless they got an end spot, which rarely happened. They needed to talk today, and she'd always wanted to eat in the dining room, sitting around a table, like civilized New Yorkers would. But Leo was late and the maître d' would only seat a complete party. They'd ended up at the counter fending off the waiter with orders of shrimp cocktail and Coke.

"We could have just said we were three and then pulled up a chair when Leo comes," Jack said. "*If* he comes."

"He'll be here," Bea said.

"You've spoken to him?" Jack asked.

"No, but he'll be here."

Melody was glumly opening another pack of oyster crackers. The maître d' had snapped her head off when she'd asked if he'd save them a corner table. "Madam," he'd said, sourly, "*please* enjoy yourself at the counter seats."

"Have *you* spoken to him?" Jack asked Melody.

"Me?" Melody said, surprised. "No. Leo never calls me."

"I got an e-mail from him at work on Friday," Bea said. "But since he's not here yet, maybe we should talk about what to say when he does get here."

The three of them squirmed on their stools a bit, eyed one another warily.

"Well," Melody said. "I—"

"Go on," Bea said.

"I think we should, obviously, make sure he's okay." Melody spoke haltingly; she was unaccustomed to going first. Jack looked dubious. Bea smiled encouragingly. Melody sat up a little straighter. "I think we inquire after his health. Find out where he's staying. Offer our support."

Bea was nodding along to everything Melody said. "Agreed," Bea said.

"And then?" Jack said, pointedly.

"And then I guess we ask about The Nest," Melody said. "I don't know. How would you like to start?"

"I'd like to hand him an invoice and ask him when he's paying it," Jack said.

Bea swiveled on her stool to face Jack. "Are you guys in some kind of financial trouble? Is Walker not working or something?"

Jack let out an exasperated puff. "Walker is working. Walker is *always working.* I would like to offer Walker the opportunity to *not* work for a bit. Eventually. As in next year, which was our plan and has been our plan forever—that Walker could cut back and we'd spend more time in the country . . ." Jack trailed off. He was not comfortable talking to his sisters about any of this. He wanted to get Leo alone and make his pitch for payback priority without the other two interfering.

"I'm worried, too, you know," Melody said. "Soon we'll be paying college tuition. You can't imagine what it costs now. And the house—"

"What about the house?" Bea asked.

Melody didn't want to talk about her house, about Walter's completely insane and unacceptable idea about her house. "It's expensive!" she said.

Bea waved at the waiter and gestured for drink refills. "I get that this stinks for all of us," she said, "but I also know Leo. If we go on the offensive today—" She shrugged and looked back and forth at Melody and Jack. "You know I'm right. He'll just avoid us."

"He can't avoid us forever," Jack said.

"What are we going to do?" Bea said. "Stake him out? Garnish his nonexistent wages? Beg?"

"I think Bea's right," Melody said.

"Since when has being nice to Leo worked?" Jack said. "Since when has anything successfully forced Leo to not put Leo first?"

"People change," Bea said, opening up another pack of oyster crackers.

"More often, people stay exactly the same."

"I still don't understand why he didn't fight Victoria on the apartment and everything else," Melody said. "Why he didn't try harder to recover *something*."

"You don't?" Bea had a flash of that night in the ER, Leo's face, his sutured chin, the whispers and moans on the other side of the curtain, the sobbing parents in the hallway, the mother quietly keening and fingering a rosary. "I do," she said. "You would, too, if you'd been there."

Melody became very invested in fishing a wedge of lemon from her soft drink and not thinking about the waitress. They'd been out of town the weekend of the wedding and had missed the entire mess. Jack had missed it, too; he never attended family functions. Melody needed to keep her energy focused on where it mattered: her daughters, her husband, her home.

"Oh, please," Jack said. "That's hardly the whole story. Something else is going on." He was creating tiny origami-like folds on one corner of the paper placemat. "This is Leo we're talking about. He's got money hidden away somewhere. I know it."

"What do you mean you *know* it?" Melody said. "You have proof?"

"No, but it's the only thing that makes sense. I know it in my bones. Think about it. Since when has Leo been afraid of a fight?"

"Bea? What do you think?" Melody said.

"I don't know," Bea said, but the same thought *had* occurred to her. "How would that even work?"

"Oh, there are ways," Jack said. "It's surprisingly easy."

The waiter was circling them now, annoyed. They'd decimated countless packs of oyster crackers, and empty cellophane wrappers and crumbs littered the space in front of them. Bea started gathering the crumbs into a small pile and brushing them onto a bread and butter plate.

"He's not coming," Jack said.

Bea checked her phone. "He's just on Leo time."

Then, as if on cue, Bea saw Melody sit up a little straighter and raise her left hand and nervously fluff her too-blond bangs. A tentative smile lifted the lower half of her face. Jack straightened, too. His jaw slid forward the way it did when he was feeling defensive, but then he stood and gave a beckoning wave and before Bea could turn around, she felt a hand on her shoulder, its familiar heft and quiet preferential squeeze, and her heart did a tiny two-step, a little jig of relief, and she turned and looked up and there he was: Leo.

CHAPTER SIX

The day Leo landed on Stephanie's stoop, she immediately put him to work moving firewood from the half cord piled in her backyard to a smaller area on the deck off her kitchen and under a plastic tarp, in case the storm turned out to be as nasty as the weather report was predicting. As Leo stacked wood, his phone buzzed. It was his slip of paper calling back and, lo and behold, the voice on the other end was an old, familiar dealer, Rico. They exchanged quick pleasantries and hurriedly arranged to meet at their usual spot—in Rico's car parked off Central Park West, near Strawberry Fields, three days hence, immediately before the family lunch. Nothing major, a little weed to relax; maybe some Vicodin. Maybe he wouldn't even go. Maybe he'd try to stay clearheaded for a few more weeks, see what that was like. Leo liked options. Stephanie stuck her head out the door and asked him to bring some wood into the living room. As he moved through the parlor floor, he admired what she'd done to the house, how she'd preserved everything old but also made it feel modern, entirely her own.

Stephanie'd had the foresight to buy at the end of Giuliani's reign as mayor, only weeks after 9/11 during what would turn out to be the tiniest of real-estate dips. When she moved to the block on the wrong side of Flatbush Avenue, the non–Park Slope side, everyone—including Leo—thought she was crazy. One of the houses on the corner was occupied by a thriving drug business. Her house had ugly metal gates on the front and back windows. The door off the kitchen, leading to an unused and rotting deck, had been cemented shut with concrete blocks. But the day she looked at the building, she noticed city workers planting cherry trees along her side of the street, which she knew signaled an active neighborhood association. There was a decent garden floor rental beneath the owner's triplex. And then there was the sheer size of the place—she could fit three of her Upper West Side studios into the first floor. As she wandered the neighborhood that day, she counted three couples with strollers. Her agency was thriving, and she'd always lived frugally, saving as much as she could. She offered the asking price.

"When did you get such good taste," Leo asked her. "Where's all that crap from IKEA I had to help you put together."

"You aren't the only one who grew up and started making money, Leo. I haven't had that IKEA furniture for years." She walked into the living room from the kitchen, wiping her hands on a dishtowel, happy to admire her house along with him. She loved her house; it was her baby.

"Italianate, right?" Leo said, examining the ornate marble mantelpiece. The center medallion of the mantel was a carving of a young girl. Marble curls of hair fell around her face, her nose was long and straight, her gaze direct, her lips full. He ran his thumb over the mouth, feeling the hard edge of a tiny chip at the center of the lower lip; the imperfection made the young woman's mouth both damaged and oddly alluring.

"Isn't she perfect?" Stephanie said. "Most mantels I've seen have carved fruit or flowers. I've never seen another face. I like to imagine she meant something to the person who built this house. Maybe she was a daughter, a wife."

"She reminds me of someone."

"Me, too. I can't ever think of who."

"She has nice tits."

"Don't be gross." Stephanie knew Leo was provoking her.

"Sorry." He moved over to the fire and threw more wood onto the flames, watching it flare as he agitated the embers with an iron poker. "She has a lovely décolletage. Better?"

"Stop staring at defenseless Lillian's breasts."

"Please don't tell me you've given her a name," Leo said, shaking his head. "Please tell me someone else named her Lillian."

"*I* named her Lillian. Sometimes we chat. Don't touch her breasts."

"Truly, I'm not that hard up." He sat on one of the sofas flanking the hearth, scanning the room for signs of a male presence. "No more Cravat?"

Stephanie couldn't help smiling a little. *Cravat* was Leo's nickname for one of her post-Leo boyfriends, a guy who'd lived with her once and briefly and had made the unfortunate choice one evening of wearing a velvet jacket and a silk cravat to a book party. "He hasn't lived here in years."

"Not enough room for all his smoking jackets?"

She shook her head. "Do I really still have to defend one bad wardrobe choice from years ago?"

"I also recall a summertime straw fedora."

"You always did have great recall for anything that made you feel superior."

"What can I say? I'm not a hat and cravat guy."

"Turns out we have that in common."

Leo removed his damp shoes and put them close to the hearth to dry a little. He put his feet up on the coffee table. She sat down opposite him. "You always knew how to pick them," Leo said.

"I had some great picks."

"Like who?" Leo said, encouraged by what could have been a slightly flirtatious turn in her tone.

"Will Peck."

"The *firefighter*?"

"Yes, the *firefighter*. That guy was great. Easy."

Leo was genuinely stunned. He'd met the firefighter once, remembered him as being disturbingly good-looking and fit. An ex-marine or something equally stalwart. "Setting aside physical strength, which I will cede to the marine—"

"Don't be such a snob. Will's an intellectual, a Renaissance man."

"A *Renaissance* man?" Leo couldn't keep the mockery from his tone.

"Yes. He traveled. He read. He cooked. He *made things*."

"What? He whittled? No, no, I forgot, we're in Brooklyn. He knitted? Did he knit you that sweater?"

"Hardly," Stephanie said. "This sweater is Italian cashmere." She pointed to a custom bookcase lining the opposite wall, one Leo had admired earlier for its graceful economy. "He built that."

"Okay. I give," he said. "It's a nice bookcase."

"It's a *fantastic* bookcase."

"So why isn't *he* here if he's so great?"

"Probably because his wife hasn't kicked him out of his apartment yet."

"Right," Leo said. He deserved that one. He couldn't stop looking at the bookcase, which was, he had to admit, pretty fantastic.

"And he wanted other things." Stephanie was quiet for a minute, thinking about what good company Will was and how she hadn't been able, ultimately, to make him happy. She still ran into him sometimes with his new wife. She didn't think they had kids, yet. She looked up and thought: *Leo!*

And then, *Careful.*

The storm outside was intensifying. The streets were quiet, devoid of pedestrians and traffic. The whole city seemed to be huddling against the weather. The fire cracked and hissed and warmed the room. Leo started to relax for the first time in weeks, for the first time since the accident, really. He missed Stephanie, the ease between them, her solid and comforting presence. Sitting across from him, in the light of the fire, she blazed with health and well-being and good humor.

"I can't believe you sold your business," he said.

"I can't believe what a hypocrite you are."

"I'm not a hypocrite, I speak from experience. I never should have sold out."

"You're just saying that now. I remember those days. You were thrilled by that fat check. Also, I'm not selling out. I was acquired. My life is just going to get a lot easier. I can't wait."

"I'm telling you," Leo said. "That was the start of the end for me."

Stephanie shrugged and took a clementine from a bowl on the table, started peeling it. "You could have stayed. Nathan wanted you to stay." Nathan Chowdhury had been Leo's business partner at SpeakEasyMedia. He'd worked behind the scenes, running the money side of things, and had stayed after the acquisition; now he was CFO for the entire conglomerate. As far as Stephanie was concerned, the beginning of the end for Leo wasn't selling SpeakEasy, it was acquiring Victoria and all that came after—namely, nothing.

She still remembered the day he'd told her he was planning to sell, the day she'd visited him at work during a period when they were trying—and nearly managing—to be "just friends." Victoria had walked into his office. "Hey," she'd said to Leo, lifting her eyebrows a bit, her smile even and smug. Stephanie heard it all in that one word: *hey*. The intimate monotone of Victoria's low register. A kind of *hey* that said they'd woken up in the same bed that morning, probably could still smell each other on their hands. The *hey* wasn't inquisitive or demure or apologetic; it was territorial. Stephanie had heard that *hey* before, coming from her very own foolishly cocksure mouth. After Leo sold SpeakEasy and married Victoria, he'd practically fallen off the face of the earth. The last thing in the world she needed from him was life—or business—advice.

"You should have called me," Leo said.

"Why would I have called you, Leo? When was the last time we spoke?" Stephanie wouldn't give him the satisfaction of telling him that she *had* called. She'd left a message on his cell and someone identifying herself as Leo's *personal assistant* had called back. "Assisting what exactly," Stephanie had asked the girl, who sounded sixteen. "Does Leo have a job?"

"Leo has a number of projects in the works," the girl had said. She sounded ridiculously tentative and nervous. Stephanie suspected she was using the assistant ruse to discover the identities of all the women on Leo's incoming call list. Well, good luck to her, she thought. "Can I tell Leo what this is in reference to?" the girl had asked. Stephanie had hung up and never called back.

"I've called you," Leo said.

"Before today? Two years ago."

"That's not true."

"Two years."

"Christ," Leo said. "Sorry." He laughed a little. "If it makes you feel any better, I stopped being interesting about two years ago."

"I didn't feel particularly bad about it to begin with, but thanks."

He frowned and looked at her, still unbelieving and a little pained. "Two years? Really?"

"Really," she said.

"So come over here and tell me what else you've been up to," he said, patting the place next to him on the sofa.

HOURS LATER, after they'd eaten the lamb and replenished the firewood and she filled him in on the recent publishing news and gossip, after he'd finished clearing the table and loading the dishwasher (poorly) and rinsing some pots (even worse), he opened another bottle of wine and she dished out bowls of ice cream and they moved back into the living room.

"Are you supposed to be drinking that?" she asked him, pointing to the glass of cabernet.

"Technically, I guess not," he said. "But booze is not my issue. You know that."

"I don't know anything, Leo. You could be shooting heroin for all I know. In fact, I think I did hear something about heroin at some point."

"Completely false," he said. "Was there excess? Yes. Do I realize I should probably steer clear of speed? Yes. *This*"—he raised the glass— "is not my problem."

"So are you going to tell me what happened? Do you want to talk about it?"

"Not really," Leo said. He wasn't sure what Stephanie had heard that she might not be telling him. George assured him everything was sealed tighter than a drum. He'd paid a fortune to keep Victoria quiet, but he didn't trust anyone. Stephanie let the silence gather some momentum. Out the front window the snow accumulated, a pile six inches deep balanced precariously on the rail of a neighboring stoop. A lone car crept down the snowy street, fishtailing a little as it went. She could hear the kids in the house behind her out in their yard screeching and laughing. Their dad was yelling: "Don't eat the snow! It's dirty."

"We don't have to talk about it, Leo, but I'm a good secret keeper."

He felt the images from that night starting to surface: the sound of the car's brakes, the bite of salt air, the incongruous voice of Marvin Gaye coming from the SUV that hit them, urging him to *get it on*. He wondered if he should talk about it. He hadn't even tried at fake rehab. He wondered what Stephanie would say if he just unloaded the whole story, right then and there. At one time, they'd told each other everything or—he mentally corrected himself—she told him everything and he told her what he thought she needed to hear. That hadn't gone very well.

"Leo?"

Leo didn't even know how to start talking about it. He stared at the carved face on the marble mantel and realized why it was familiar, the swoop of hair, the slender patrician nose, the appraising gaze. "She looks like Bea," he said.

"Who does?"

"Lillian. Your stone companion. She looks like Bea."

"Bea." Stephanie groaned and covered her eyes.

"She's not bad looking. Bea."

"No, it's not that. She's called me a few times and I've been avoiding her. Something about new work."

"God. Not the novel."

"No, no, no. I told her a long time ago that I wouldn't ever read that novel again. I told her, in fact, that she needed to find a new agent. Her message said something about a new project but—I just can't." Stephanie stood and started picking up their empty bowls of ice cream, the tranquil mood broken. "This is one of many reasons I'm happy to be part of a bigger operation," she said. "I can't stand feeling responsible for the formerly talented. It's too upsetting. I can pass her off to someone else who won't have any qualms about shutting her down."

Thinking about Bea being shut down by some unnamed assistant made Leo feel unexpectedly wistful. He wasn't surprised when her first stories ended up being some anomaly of youth and fearlessness (thanks to *him),* but she had to be at the end of her rope by now. And she'd been Stephanie's first notable client, the person who'd made editors and other new writers take a very young Stephanie very seriously. He didn't like to think of Bea stuck working with Paul Underwood at some obscure literary journal, living in that apartment uptown by herself. It was hard to think about all his siblings for different reasons, so he didn't. Right now, it felt like there was nowhere for his thoughts to alight that wasn't rife with land mines of regret or anger or guilt.

"You're right," Stephanie said, standing and staring at the mantel. "She does look like Bea. Shit."

"Don't go," Leo said.

"I'm just going to the kitchen."

"Stay here," he said. He didn't like the sound of his voice, how it wavered a little. He *really* didn't like the sudden, rapid acceleration of his heartbeat, which prior to this moment he'd associated with a certain class of stimulants, not a living room in Brooklyn in front of the fire with Stephanie.

"I'll be right back," Stephanie said. Leo seemed to go slightly pale and for a moment he looked lost, almost frightened, which briefly alarmed her. "Leo?"

"I'm fine." He shook his head a little and stood. "Is that your old turntable?"

"Yes," she said. "Put something on. I'm just going to rinse these."

In the kitchen Stephanie could hear Leo flipping through her record albums. He yelled to her from the living room. "Your taste in music still totally sucks."

"Like everyone else in America, my music is on my computer. That's the old stuff. I just brought the turntable up from the basement a few months ago."

Leo was reciting from the album covers: "Cyndi Lauper, Pat Benatar, Huey Lewis, *Paula Abdul*? This is like a bad MTV segment of 'Where Are They Now?'"

"More like, guess who joined the Columbia House Record Club when she was eighteen."

Leo flinched a little hearing *Columbia Records*. He shook it off. "Ah, here we go," he said.

Stephanie heard the turntable start to spin and the familiar scratch, scratch of the needle hitting the album grooves. Then the weirdly dissonant first notes of a piano and the slurry, graveled voice of Tom Waits filled the house.

> *The piano has been drinking*
> *My necktie is asleep*

Stephanie hadn't heard that song in years. Probably not since she and Leo were together. The album was probably Leo's. He would wake her up on his hungover mornings (many mornings; most mornings) singing that song. He would pull her sleeping self into his arms, his semierection pressing into her back. She would halfheartedly try to burrow farther down into the bed, clinging to sleep and the reassuring feel of Leo's limbs holding her close.

"You stink," she would groan, feigning more irritation than she felt, not even really minding his funky breath. "You smell like my uncle Howie after a night at the bar."

He would sing into her ear, his voice pockmarked from whiskey:

> *The piano has been drinking*
> *Not me, not me, not me*

AT THE SINK, she started to rewash the roasting pan that Leo had left with a film of grease on the counter and tried to reconcile the Leo in her living room with the Leo she'd last seen almost two years ago, out one night with Victoria; they'd both seemed hammered. This Leo was slimmer and in spite of what she'd heard—and occasionally witnessed—about his recent years of late nights and marital troubles and general rabble-rousing, he somehow looked younger. He was quieter, more subdued. Still funny. Still quick. Still beautiful.

She shook her head. She was *not,* absolutely was *not,* going to get swept into Leo's orbit again. In fact, she'd better set down some hard and fast rules about how long he could stay. And she needed to run upstairs and make up the pullout sofa in her office.

Then, Leo was behind her. A hand on her shoulder. "Want to dance?" he said.

She laughed at him. "No," she said. "I most definitely do not want to dance with you. Also? You are terrible at washing dishes. Look at this."

"I'm serious," he said. He lifted her hands out of the soapy water in the sink.

"Leo"—she held herself rigid—"I was clear." Her posture was combative, but he could hear something new in her voice, a fleeting hesitancy.

He inched closer. "You said no fucking. I respect the no-fucking rule." Leo was entirely focused on her. His desire was physical, yes (it had been twelve weeks, not counting a couple of breezy flings with the rehab physician's assistant in the weight room), but he also remembered how much he'd loved this part, getting past her prickly exterior, cracking her wide open like unhinging an oyster. He hadn't thought about it in a long time, how satisfying it was to watch her steely carriage collapse a little, hear her breath catch. How good it felt to win. Fuck the firefighter.

She sighed and looked past him, out the rear windows, into the Brooklyn night and the snowflakes ecstatically spinning in the beam of the floodlight on her back deck. Her hands were wet and cold and the warmth of Leo's fingers around her wrists was disorienting.

Leo couldn't read her expression. Resigned? Hopeful? Defeated? He didn't see desire yet, but he remembered how to summon it. "Steph?" he said. She smiled a little, but the smile was sad.

"I swear, Leo," she said quietly, nearly pleading. "I'm happy."

He was close enough now to lower his face to her neck and breathe in her skin, which smelled as it always had, faintly of chlorine, making him feel as if he could swim into her, assured and buoyant. They stood like that for a minute. He could feel his racing pulse gradually slow and align with the reliable rhythm of her constant heart. He pulled back a little to look at her. He ran his thumb along her lower lip, the same way he had with the marble carving earlier, only this time the lip yielded.

And then, from the backyard, an enormous crash splitting the outdoor quiet like a clap of thunder. Then flickering lights. Then darkness.

CHAPTER SEVEN

When Leo arrived at the Oyster Bar, he worked some magic with the surly maître d'. Within minutes the Plumbs were seated and had unconsciously arranged themselves around the red-checkered tablecloth according to birth order: Leo, Jack, Bea, Melody. They shed coats and hats and made a little too much of ordering "just water and coffee." Leo apologized for running late and explained how he was staying with a friend in Brooklyn (*Stephanie!* Bea realized), and he'd taken the wrong train and had to retrace his steps. Obligatory chatter about how Brooklyn had become so crowded and expensive and why was the subway so unreliable on the weekends anyway and, well, the weather certainly didn't help, snow in October! Then they all fell uncomfortably silent— except Leo, who seemed utterly calm while appraising his brother and sisters, who all looked back at him, ill at ease.

The three of them wondered how he did it, how he always managed to be unruffled while putting everyone else on edge, how even in this moment, at this lunch, where Leo should be abashed, laid bare, and the balance of power could have, *should* have, shifted against him, he still commanded their focus and exuded strength. Even now, they were deferentially waiting, *hoping,* he would speak first.

But he just sat, watching them, curiously attentive.

"It's good to see you," Bea finally said. "You look well. Healthy." Her light affection made Jack's shoulders relax, Melody's face unclench.

Leo smiled. "I'm happy to see you all. I am."

Melody felt herself blush. Embarrassed, she put her hands to her cheeks.

"I guess we should get right to it," Leo said. In the taxi down from Central Park, he'd decided to address the unpleasantness head-on. He realized, somewhat surprisingly, that he'd given precious little thought to this moment during his long weeks at Bridges. He'd been so focused on Victoria and the dissolution of their marriage that he'd failed to consider the repercussions of Francie's actions. To be fair, he hadn't entirely understood Francie's actions until a couple of weeks ago. When George first told him that his mother was funding the Rodriguez payout, Leo'd had a brief moment of hope that she was using her own—or Harold's—considerable resources. Alas.

"I know you want to talk about The Nest," he continued, satisfied to see their surprise at his direct approach. "So first, I want to say, *thank you.* I know you didn't have to agree with Francie's plan and I'm grateful."

Bea looked at Melody and Jack, who both shifted a little in their seats; they all looked confused and troubled.

"What?" Leo said, processing what was happening a minute too late.

"We hardly had any choice in the matter," Jack said.

"We didn't know until it was done," Melody said.

"Really?" Leo turned to Bea. She nodded.

Ah. Leo leaned back and looked around the table. Of course. He mentally berated himself for that bit of miscalculation while, briefly, experiencing a wave of elation because Francie had acted so decisively and singularly on his behalf. But Leo quickly realized he was wrong about that, too. Francie hadn't come to *his* rescue; no doubt she'd rescued herself—and Harold. Leo could hear Harold now, his adenoidal voice going on and on about what was *all over the East End*.

Bea warily watched Leo absorb this new bit of information. "I tried calling you, Leo," she said. "Many times."

"Right," he said. "Okay." This complicated things.

When Leo and Victoria were first engaged, shortly after he sold SpeakEasy and "went on sabbatical" (as he thought of it) and after she refused to consider a prenup, he'd opened an offshore account during one of their diving trips to Grand Cayman. He'd acted on a whim while she was off shopping. The account was perfectly legal, and although he'd planned on telling Victoria about it, he found himself not telling her. He thought of it as a little insurance, a private pension of sorts, maybe a way to keep some of his money protected in case of a stormy day. As his marriage began to deteriorate, he started bolstering the balance. One upside to the prodigious way he and Victoria spent money was that she stopped noticing where the money went. A few thousand here, a few thousand there; over the years it added up. He thought about the money all the time and the day he would just pick up and leave. What had kept him from doing it years ago was the hope that Victoria would tire of him first, fall in love with someone else and leave him so he could avoid a financially decimating divorce. When it became clear she never would (why couldn't he have married someone just as beautiful but not so strategic?), he surrendered fully to the more libertine aspects of his life. He wasn't sorry to see the diminishing balances on their joint accounts. So even though the accident had been a humiliating and unfortunate event, it had also—in a strange way—loosened him from the life he was already desperate to escape. For months he'd expected Victoria's lawyers to find and triumphantly expose the funds, but nobody had. He had nearly two million dollars hidden away, almost exactly what he owed The Nest. He'd never touched a penny of the low-interest savings account; it was safe and sound. Liquid. If he replenished the fund to pay his siblings, his two million would be divided by four. The math hardly worked in his favor.

"I wish I had the money sitting somewhere and could write you all a check," Leo said. He placed his palms flat on the table and leaned forward, looking each one of them straight in the eye. He hadn't run a company for all those years without learning the art of a quick recalculation, without learning how to work a table. He still mostly needed to bide time. "But I don't. I'm going to need some time," Leo continued.

"How much time?" Melody said, a little too quickly.

"I wish I had the answer to that," Leo said, as if having that answer was his most fervent desire on earth. "But I promise you this: I am going to start working immediately—and hard—to rebuild. I already have some ideas. I've already started making some calls."

"What's the plan?" Jack said. He wanted specifics. "Is there a way for you to borrow the money you owe us? Pay us off and owe somebody else?"

"Very possibly," Leo said, knowing that his chances of getting anyone to lend him money at the moment were nil. "A lot of things are possible."

"Like what else?" Jack said.

Leo shook his head. "I don't want to throw out a lot of *what-if*s and *maybes*."

"Do you think you might have the money—or at least some of it—when we were expecting to get it?" Melody asked.

"In March?" Leo said.

"February. My birthday's in February," Melody said, too panicky over how the conversation was going to be indignant.

"I'm March," said Bea.

"Right." Leo beat out a little rhythm on the table with his thumb and pinkie. He looked like he was doing a complex equation in his head. They all waited. "How about this?" he finally said. "Give me three months."

"To pay us?" Jack said.

"No, but to have a plan. A solid plan. I don't think I'm going to need three months, but you know how tough financing is these days." He directed his last comment at Jack. "You're a business owner." Jack nodded in solemn agreement. Bea suppressed the urge to roll her eyes. Leo. He really was full of shit. "And figure in the holidays, when it's tough to pin people down. I think I need three months to come up with options," he said. "Ideally, more than one option that will have you seeing full payment as soon as possible. I'm not promising February, but I am promising that I'll work as hard as I've ever worked on anything to try and make good." He looked around the table again. "I'm asking you to trust me."

PART TWO

THE KISS

CHAPTER EIGHT

Paul Underwood ran his literary magazine, *Paper Fibres,* from a small warren of offices up a worn flight of stairs in a slightly sagging building that stood in the shadow of the Manhattan Bridge. He'd bought the four-story brick front before the Dumbo section of Brooklyn became DUMBO, when the masses of migrating Manhattanites had been priced out of Brooklyn Heights and Cobble Hill but still had their hearts set on the aesthetically pristine, historically important, and relatively affordable brownstones of Park Slope or Fort Greene. He'd stumbled into the small wedge of a neighborhood one bright summer Saturday after walking across the Brooklyn Bridge. Leisurely heading north, he'd found himself wandering through the industrial blocks and admiring the streets of blue-gray Belgian bricks laid out in appealing patterns, threaded through with defunct trolley tracks. He'd noted with approval the absence of expensive clothing boutiques, high-priced coffee shops, restaurants with exposed brick and wood-burning ovens. Every fourth building seemed to be an auto body shop or some kind of appliance repair. He liked the vibe of the place; it reminded him of Soho back when Soho had energy and grit, a little theatrical menace. Down by the waterfront a sign indicated that the scrubby park populated with crack dealers and their customers was slated for expansion and renovation, and he noticed that the same developer had signs all over the neighborhood heralding the arrival of warehouse-to-condo conversions.

Standing on a corner of Plymouth Street that afternoon, in the waning days of the twentieth century, listening to the clank and rattle of truck beds as they rumbled over the approach to the Manhattan Bridge to his north, watching the sun illuminate the massive arches of the Brooklyn Bridge to the south, Paul Underwood saw his future: a For Sale placard on a seemingly abandoned corner building. At the top of the building's reddish-brown façade he could make out the faded, white letters of a sign from the long-defunct business the dwelling once housed: PLYMOUTH PAPER FIBRES, INC. He took the sign as an omen. He bought the building the following week and started his literary journal, *Paper Fibres,* the following year.

Paul lived on the top floor of the building (two bedrooms, nicely renovated, meticulously furnished, spectacular views) directly above the *Paper Fibres* offices, which were crammed into the front half of the third floor. The back half of the third floor and the entire second floor housed two modest but increasingly lucrative rental apartments. At street level there was a lingerie store. La Rosa didn't sell fancy lingerie, nothing lacy or push-up or see-through, but what Paul thought of as old-lady lingerie, matron underwear. Even the plastic torso mannequins in the windows looked uncomfortable, bound tightly with brassieres and girdles that resembled straitjackets with their rows of steel hooks, dangling elastic belts, and reinforced shoulder straps. Paul had no idea how they stayed in business, had never seen more than one customer in there at a time. He had his suspicions, but the rent check was on time every month so as far as he was concerned La Rosa could launder hosiery or money, or sell whatever they liked to the odd selection of male customers who usually left empty-handed.

Paul went to great pains to keep his home and work life separate. He never brought work "upstairs," he never appeared in the *Paper Fibres* offices in what he thought of as civilian clothes, always dressing for the commute one quick flight down. Every morning he put on one of his exquisitely tailored suits and chose a bow tie from his vast collection. He believed the butterfly shape beneath his chin provided a necessary counterweight to his overly long face and inelegant hair, which was baby fine, mousy brown, and tended to stick out around his ears or at the crown.

"You can get away with colorful ties," his ex-wife had told him, diplomatically referring to his rather unremarkable features—gray eyes that were more watery than striking, thin lips, a soft, almost putty-like nose. Paul never minded his ordinary looks. They lent a valuable invisibility in certain situations; he overheard things he wasn't supposed to hear, people confided in him, errantly judging him harmless. (His looks didn't *always* work in his favor. There was the recent lunch, for example, which he'd scheduled with a young poet after their e-mail exchanges had turned flirtatious. That she'd been disappointed in his appearance versus the muscular wit of his correspondence had been abundantly clear by the look on her face. Well, he'd been surprised, too. Surprised to discover that she didn't remotely resemble her author photo with its glossy hair, hooded eyes, and come-hither glistening lips.)

Paul valued routine and habit. He ate the same breakfast every day (a bowl of oatmeal and an apple) and then went for a morning walk along Fulton Ferry Landing. On weekdays he never deviated from his route, becoming an expert chronicler of the waterfront in all its seasonal mutations. Today the wind was fierce, battering the hearty souls brave enough to be outside; he leaned into it, pitching himself forward and wrapping his scarf more tightly around his neck. He loved the river, even during the grim New York winter, loved its steely gray shimmer and menacing whitecaps. He never tired of the view of the harbor; he always felt lucky to be exactly where he was, the place he'd chosen to belong.

As he headed toward the far edge of Fulton Ferry Landing, Paul saw Leo Plumb's familiar figure sitting on one of the benches closest to the water. Leo and Paul had taken to walking together every so often. Leo looked up and waved. Paul picked up his pace. He'd actually begun to look forward to the days when Leo would join him at the bench. Stranger things had happened, he supposed.

PAUL HAD BEEN LIVID when *SpeakEasy* magazine folded and Leo hadn't invited him to help start the website that would eventually grow into SpeakEasyMedia. Leo hadn't taken everyone from the print magazine, but he'd taken those generally considered the sharpest, the most desirable, and Paul had always believed himself to fit squarely in that category. Maybe he wasn't the most talented writer, the most fearless reporter, but he was reliable and capable and ambitious and shouldn't all those things count for something? He met deadlines, his copy was pristine, and he pitched in where needed even when it wasn't his responsibility. He did everything you were supposed to do to earn the things you wanted. He was *nice*.

That no one else was surprised Paul wasn't going with Leo was also a blow. He kept waiting for the shocked looks, the crooked finger beckoning him behind a closed door, "Leo isn't taking *you*?" When it didn't happen, he realized nobody else considered him prime pickings either.

He'd mustered the nerve to ask Leo about it once. "Underwood, this is not going to be your scene," Leo'd said, putting a heavy palm on Paul's shoulder and holding his gaze in that way Leo had, the way that made you simultaneously flattered to command his full attention and slightly brain addled, unable to capture a train of thought. "You would hate it. You're an in-depth feature guy. I wouldn't do it to you. And I'm paying peanuts."

Paul comforted himself with Leo's explanation for a while. He probably *would* hate gossip; it was true that Paul specialized in the longer cultural pieces. And he wasn't willing to work for nothing. But then Paul discovered that Leo had hired Gordon FitzGerald as content editor at the new SpeakEasy. Gordon wasn't any more interested in short form or gossip than Paul, and he was sure Gordon wasn't working for peanuts. Paul had supervised Gordon—he'd recruited him!—and he knew that Gordon was nothing but trouble, a drunk and a world-class dick. For months after Leo left, Paul freely offered his opinion of the new venture: "Dead in the water in six months." He had, of course, been preposterously wrong.

Paul didn't know what had happened to land Leo in rehab because the public details were sketchy and Bea was closemouthed. He'd heard rumors about a car accident out in the Hamptons. Leo's wife, Victoria, had been seen around town with a number of high-profile dates. Leo seemed to be shacking up (*again*) with Stephanie Palmer in Brooklyn. His Porsche was gone.

When Leo appeared in his offices one morning in November ostensibly looking for Bea, Paul didn't think anything of it. But Leo was there for hours, nosing around Paul's office, asking questions about issue scheduling, advertising deadlines, print sales, subscriptions, finances. He wanted to know about the magazine's online presence (slim), writer relationships (robust), and how Paul would expand if he could—"If you had all the funding you wanted?"

And then Paul thought he understood. "Nathan sent you here," Paul said. "You two are working together again." It made sense; they used to be partners and Paul thought his recent meeting with Nathan had been promising. Leo held Paul's gaze in a way that seemed significant and said, "Officially? No. *Officially?* This is just a friendly visit."

"I see," Paul said. He didn't see but hoped to God that Leo was there on unofficial-official Nathan business. At one of the countless holiday parties he'd attended in December—he couldn't even remember which one, they all blurred, all the cheap Prosecco and waxy cubes of cheese and gluten-free cupcakes—one of his old *SpeakEasy* colleagues mentioned that he'd heard Nathan was thinking about starting a literary magazine—or investing in one.

"As a write-off?" Paul asked, unable to imagine any other reason.

"I think it's more of an ego thing," his friend had said. "Something respectable and highbrow to balance the other stuff." The *other stuff,*

Paul knew, referred not just to the gossipy lowbrow nature of Speak-EasyMedia's online presence, but to the soft-core porn site that generated most of the company's revenue.

"Any idea who he's considering?"

"None. You should call him. The money he's willing to throw at someone is chump change for him but probably massive by your standards."

Paul had been on the phone scheduling a meeting the next day. Keeping *Paper Fibres* afloat sometimes felt like trying to cross the Atlantic Ocean in a leaky skiff. He was constantly plugging one hole, just to have another appear and then another and he felt like the whole venture was going to sink more times than he cared to think about.

The rental income from his building, in addition to allowing him to work and live rent-free, provided some income—enough to pay himself, Bea, and his one other full-time employee (a managing editor who spent most of her time filling out grant applications and chatting up prospective donors and trying to keep existing contributors from turning fickle) a modest income. *Paper Fibres* had a solid subscription base—as far as those things went—and even managed a decent amount of advertising revenue, but not enough to cover all his costs and pay writers and keep his related projects thriving.

The majority of outside funding came from Paul's two elderly aunts, his deceased father's sisters who'd never married and treated Paul like a son. They were a certain type of elderly New Yorker, sharing the same rent-controlled apartment within walking distance of Lincoln Center for decades and decades. Voracious readers, eager travelers, regulars at all kinds of readings and the Broadway Wednesday matinee. They had annual subscriptions to the ballet, Carnegie Hall, and the Ninety-Second Street Y and box seats at Shea Stadium. Every January since he'd started his publication, they sent an extremely generous check. The Sisters' Fund, as he thought of it (and how he listed it on the contributors' page, which thrilled them), was how he could pay writers and manage, once or twice a year, to publish a book under his very modest imprint. Usually a poetry collection, the occasional novella, or a book of essays.

Two years ago, the January check had been a little less. The following year, less still, and last month, nearly half what it used to be. Paul would never question them, but he worried that maybe something was wrong and they weren't telling him. He invited them out, as he did every January, to thank them for their contribution—drinks at the Algonquin and dinner at Keens Steakhouse. Before Paul got a chance to ask if everything was all right, they brought up the diminishing checks, speaking in their typical fashion, almost as one person. He was used to their eccentricity by now, but on the few occasions they stopped by his office—"just to have a look around"—he realized how they appeared to others. "Like those Grey Gardens ladies," one of the interns had said once, admiringly, "minus the dementia and cats."

"We're so sorry," they told him over lunch. "It seems we're going through our retirement fund a little more quickly than is ideal."

"Our accountant has put his foot down, dear. He's trying to get us to cut all expenses by half."

"Especially ones he deems 'unnecessary,' anything charitable."

"You can imagine our distress. Of course we initially refused, but then—"

"He summoned us to his office! Like a principal bringing truants called to account. It was mortifying—"

"*Mortifying*. He had charts."

"Not charts, graphs. They were very colorful."

"*Very*." Mutual and grave nodding commenced; Paul waited.

"You see, the amount of red on the future projected income—"

"Red isn't good."

"I realize that nobody wants red on the charts," Paul said.

"Graphs." They looked so troubled, avoiding eye contact, drinking their wine too fast, that he quickly reassured them he understood.

"You've done so much already," Paul said. "You've done more than enough."

"Our check will be a little less every year but you can count on us for *something*."

"I'm afraid we've lived too long. Who would have thought?"

"Especially after all those years of smoking? All the red meat? We'll be lucky if there's anything left for our funeral when that day comes."

Paul decided to ignore the odd sentence construction, the assumption that two people would have *one* funeral—on the same day—although it was impossible to imagine one sister without the other.

Although he thought he'd have more time, Paul knew this day would come eventually; his aunts wouldn't live forever. Countless times he'd tried to get a better handle on the business side of things, his tenuous finances, but he *hated* the business side of things. He was trying to figure out how to redouble his funding efforts when he serendipitously heard the chatter about Nathan and arranged a meeting. Nathan hadn't committed to anything but he'd been engaged, curious. He'd asked lots of questions and Paul offered intelligent, thought-out answers. Why wouldn't he? He thought all the time about what he would do if he had more money. The website was pathetic, nothing more than a place to subscribe and submit, and many of his writers were frustrated their content wasn't available online. He wanted to publish more books, many more books. He wanted to expand the modest-but-respected reading series he ran, start a summer conference, and maybe open a writing center for at-risk youth. But it would all take more money than he'd ever had.

"Let's both think on it a little more," Nathan had said. "I'll be in touch in a few weeks."

And then there was Leo, standing in his office and looking around and asking questions.

"*Unofficially,*" Paul said to Leo, "is there anything specific you'd like to know about how things work here?"

Since then he and Leo had met a handful of times, usually starting at the bench in the morning. They'd stroll, get coffee, and talk—mostly about work and the challenges of running a literary magazine. But about other things, too: real estate, the rapidly expanding Brooklyn waterfront, city politics. Paul still wasn't sure what Leo was after. He assumed more than one person would be in the running for Nathan's dollars, so he was trying his hardest to impress Leo, walking him through every stage of putting the summer issue together, occasionally pretending to solicit Leo's advice and then feeling pleasantly surprised at his excellent input. Paul had forgotten—it had been easy to forget given Leo's gradual morph from new-media celebrity into his glaring life of unrepentant indulgence—how cunning Leo could be about the printed word. Leo's instincts were infuriatingly effortless and accurate, and Paul couldn't help enjoying him and their lively exchanges. It was, in fact, Leo's presence that made Paul Underwood rekindle the tiny ember he'd consigned to a much smaller place that was the thought of kissing Beatrice Plumb.

Over the years, Paul had had a few carefully selected lovers. They came and went, some more than once. He'd been married briefly, didn't seem to have the knack for it, but he had loved Beatrice Plumb for nearly always. His love for her was quiet and constant, familiar and soothing; it was almost its own thing entirely, like a worn rock or a set of worry beads, something he'd pick up and weigh in his palm occasionally, more comforting than dispiriting. Paul suspected Bea would never love him, but he thought maybe, one day, she might let him kiss her. He was a very good kisser; he'd been told so often enough to have confidence in that skill and to know that a good kiss, perfectly timed, well executed, could establish inroads to far more interesting destinations.

He'd thought about kissing Beatrice for so many years that he knew he should probably never try, that the reality would almost have to pale in comparison to his many, many years of imagining the kiss and how it would unfold (in the back of a taxi on a sultry rainy night, on a stalled subway train as the lights flickered off, under the elegantly tiled archways of Bethesda Terrace as the sun was low in the sky, and his favorite: in the sculpture garden at MoMA, both so overcome by the lush, rotund Henry Moores that they turned to each other simultaneously, needing the same exact press of flesh at the same exact moment).

Paul had spent the past decade watching Bea's light dim and it was troubling. Not only because he cared, deeply, about Bea as a writer and a person, but also because he suspected her slow fade played a part in his waning libidinous thoughts about her. He wasn't attracted to failure; he preferred his women dedicated and ambitious. Bea had stopped talking about her book years ago. He never saw her sneaking time to write or even scribble on index cards or in a notebook. Some days he wanted to fire her, make her leave the office and do something else, *anything* else. But he couldn't. He wouldn't.

Bea seemed revived lately, there was something newly engaging and ardent about her. He'd overheard her make reference to a new writing project. He knew better than to ask; he'd wait for her to bring it up. He wondered if she'd shown Leo the new stuff yet. He hoped so because he would trust Leo's opinion. If Leo thought whatever she was doing had potential, well, who knew? What could be more perfect for a newly expanded fiction imprint than the long-awaited debut novel by Beatrice Plumb. Anything she wrote would attract attention, along with the entity that published the work. Maybe he would pull Leo aside and ask if he'd heard or seen anything.

He could picture it perfectly: the publishing party at a local independent bookstore, Bea surrounded by an eager, appreciative crowd, her bright eyes and fluttering fingers, her long braids coiled and pinned up at the nape of her neck just how he loved. She would turn to him tender and eager with gratitude, flush with accomplishment, and he would touch her elbow, kiss her cheek as he'd done a thousand times before, but this time he would linger just a little longer, long enough for her to notice, a shadowy declaration. A first kiss in the book stacks. Now that was romantic.

CHAPTER NINE

The sole reason Bea Plumb agreed to accompany Paul Underwood to the dinner party at Celia Baxter's on the Upper West Side, sure to be jammed with the exact type of people—writers, editors, agents—she couldn't avoid at work but desperately tried to avoid at all other times, was because Celia was one of Stephanie's closest friends from college. Celia was not *of* the publishing world, she was *of* the art world, but those worlds often collided, especially over cocktails. Bea hoped to see Stephanie at the smallish gathering in Celia's intentionally stark and underdecorated apartment, which was only a few blocks—but worlds away—from Bea's place; it would be easy for her to duck out if the event was unbearable.

Just past the new year, heading into the dreariest weeks of the calendar, almost three months since the Oyster Bar lunch, and Bea was still dithering about showing her new work to any of the three people (Leo, Paul, Stephanie) who could or should see it. After her phone call with Jack earlier in the week, she felt a new urgency. Jack said he was heading out to Brooklyn to see Leo. He was vague about why.

"Do I need a reason to visit my brother?" he'd said. "I want to see how he's doing."

"And?" Bea had asked.

"And, okay, I want to see what's going on. Has he said anything to you?"

"No," Bea'd said, trying to think of something to tell Jack that might assuage him but also be the truth. "He looks good."

"What a relief," Jack said, his tone sour.

"I mean he looks healthy. Alert and focused. He seems optimistic. He's been hanging out with Paul. I think they're working on something."

"You're joking."

"Why would that be a joke?"

"*This* is his big plan? Working for that putz Paul Underwood?"

"*I* work for Paul Underwood," Bea said.

"I realize that—and I mean this as a compliment—there are lots of things you would be willing to do that Leo wouldn't."

"I know." Bea did know. Leo's interest in Paul was bewildering. Paul seemed to believe Leo was working with Nathan Chowdhury again, but Bea found that unlikely. And Leo had never liked Paul. Ever. He'd called him *Paul Underdog* behind his back for years and had only shown a grudging kind of interest in *Paper Fibres* or what Bea did every day. He'd been visibly shocked to discover that *Paper Fibres* was a thriving publication. Not that she ever volunteered to talk about work; nobody was more dismayed than she was to find herself still going to the same office every day. Over the years, she'd managed to assume mostly managerial duties. She eagerly took on any job that removed her from working with writers and let Paul be the editing face of the magazine, which he loved. He still sought her input and shrewd pen, but those exchanges happened between the two of them, in private.

"Apparently Leo's meeting with Nathan," Bea told Jack.

"Nathan? *Nathan* Nathan?"

"Yes." She knew Jack would be happy to hear Nathan's name. Everyone would.

"Well, that's very interesting. Sounds like the perfect time for an in-person progress report."

She didn't tell Jack what else she thought about Leo, that for all the moments he seemed terrifically healthy and eager and nearly like his old self—his *old,* old self, the Leo she loved so much and missed even more—there were nearly an equal number of times he seemed remote and anxious. Bea knew Leo better than anyone. On the surface he was fine, stellar even. But she'd also seen him staring out the office windows, jiggling his leg, eyeing the harbor and the ocean beyond like a death row prisoner from Alcatraz who was wondering exactly what distance the body could survive the open water in February. That was partly why she'd chickened out every time she thought to talk to him about what she was writing. If Jack was going to start putting pressure on Leo—and Bea realized it was a bit of a miracle he'd held off for this long—she needed to do something. Once his divorce was final, Leo would be free to roam. She didn't understand what was going on with him and Stephanie, but those two made Elizabeth Taylor and Richard Burton look like slouches in the on again/off again department. But this she knew: She needed to figure out what to do. She needed to commit to what she was writing or move on to something else *while* she was writing, before her confidence and inspiration fled. Again.

She'd been hiding in a corner of Celia's enormous living room, pretending to examine the bookshelves, which were full of what she thought of as "fake" books—the books were real enough but if Celia Baxter had read Thomas Pynchon or Samuel Beckett or even all— *any!*—of the Philip Roths and Saul Bellows lined in a row, she'd eat her mittens. In a far upper corner of the bookcase, she noticed a lurid purple book spine, a celebrity weight-loss book. Ha. That was more like it. She stood on tiptoe, slid the book out, and examined the well-thumbed, stained pages. She returned it to the shelf front and center, between *Mythologies* and *Cloud Atlas*. Satisfied, she waded into the crowd to find Paul; maybe he wouldn't mind if she left. If Stephanie wasn't here by now, she wasn't coming.

Bea heard Lena Novak before she saw her, that old familiar hyena laugh. She froze, thinking she had to be wrong, only to see her old— her old what? They hadn't been friends but they hadn't exactly been enemies either—heading in her direction. Bea could *not* handle Lena Novak right now, absolutely could *not*. She turned on her heel and fled into a nearby powder room, nearly slamming the door behind her. Seeing herself in the mirror she was only mildly surprised by how terrified she looked.

Lena Novak was another one of the Glitterary Girls who, unlike Bea, had gone on to publish a well-regarded book every few years. Bea had recently stumbled across a feature in a glossy magazine on Lena and her handsome architect husband and adorable daughter and their "ingeniously" renovated Brooklyn town house and the horse-barn-turned-weekend-home in Litchfield, Connecticut. She'd been increasingly nauseated by every paragraph and had finally tossed the magazine into the recycling bin at work. "Hey, I wanted to read that!" one of the interns had said, fishing it out of the bright blue receptacle. "I *love* Lena Novak!"

In the powder room, Bea washed her hands and found an old lipstick in the corner of her purse. She carefully applied the color, checking to make sure none of it was on her teeth. She used her dampened fingers to calm the hair around her face that had frizzed under her winter hat. She moved as slowly as possible, trying to remember where her coat had been ferried off to and the most direct route to the front door. She eyed a glass shelf housing an impressive collection of tiny antique perfume bottles. *Really?* she thought. *Where do people get the time?* (And then: *Who am I kidding? I have the time.*) Someone rapped gently on the door.

"Hold on," she said. She squared her shoulders, happy that she'd worn her favorite zebra-print wrap dress from her favorite second-hand clothing store. She took a deep breath and opened the door. Maybe Lena wouldn't even recognize her, she thought, as she walked

into the front hall. But the moment she emerged from the tiny powder room, Lena pounced, squealing and pulling Bea into an alarmingly fierce hug. "I heard you were here, but I didn't believe it!" she
said, rocking Bea a little as if they'd just been reunited after a lengthy,
involuntary separation.

The Glitterary Girls were just an invention of some journalist for
an urban magazine. Bea had been horrified when the article came
out, which made them sound like silly socialites. ("Perched on a Soho
rooftop on a languid summer night, the most buzzed about writers
in Manhattan glitter like beads on a particularly smart necklace.")
The breathless writing was awful, the designation didn't even make
sense, a meaningless phrase assigned to a group of female writers
who happened to live in New York City at the same time, happened to
be around the same age, and, for the most part, disliked one another.
At best, they were grudging acquaintances bound by a name they
all wished they could shake—except for Lena, who had adored the
catchphrase and taken it literally. (*Gliterally,* Bea had joked to the
one woman in the group she actually liked, a poet from Hoboken who
had also seemed to drop off the face of the earth in the ensuing years.)
Back then, Lena was always trying to gather "the girls," for drinks
or dinners or suggesting they go to events together, as if they were a
lounge act in Vegas.

"You look exactly the same!" Lena held Bea at arm's length and
gushed. "Come sit and talk to me." She clapped her hands, and her
bared cleavage bounced a little. Had she bought herself new breasts,
too? Bea didn't remember Lena ever being voluptuous. They sat in a
quiet corner of the dining room next to an enormous table covered
with trays of meticulously made canapés. Bea positioned herself
with her back to the room and steeled herself for Lena's interroga-
tion only to realize, within minutes, that of course Lena wanted to
talk about Lena.

"Here she is," she said, handing Bea her phone and swiping through
what seemed like hundreds and hundreds of photos of her daughter.
"She's three. I finished the edits on my last book on a Wednesday

morning, e-mailed the pages to my editor, stood up from my desk, and my water broke."

"You were always really efficient," Bea said.

"I know!"

"What's her name?" Bea asked, looking at the photo of a little girl with a party hat sitting in front of a birthday cupcake.

"Mary Patience."

"Patience?" Bea wasn't sure she'd heard properly.

"Oh, you know," Lena said, as if it were obvious, "one of those old family *Mayflower* names."

"Have you been adopted by a new family?" Bea knew Lena had grown up in a trailer park somewhere in central Ohio with a single mother who managed to raise four kids working a variety of minimum-wage jobs. You had to listen closely these days to hear any echo of the broad and nasal midwestern vowels in Lena's speech, and her unruly black hair had been straightened, and somewhere along the line *Nowaski* had become *Novak*—and there were those new impressive breasts—but there was no way Lena's round and freckled face with the slightly bulbous nose that looked like it had been raised on kielbasa had anything to do with the *Mayflower*.

"My ridiculous husband," Lena said, her voice full of admiration. "He's in the blue book."

Bea looked down at the picture of Lena's daughter again and was secretly pleased to see that the girl's nose had been inherited from the kielbasa not the *Mayflower* side of the family. She looked kind of sweet.

"So tell me about her?" Bea said, sending a fat one across the plate to Lena. "Tell me everything about being a mom."

Forty-five minutes later, she'd neatly extracted herself from the predictably dull conversation. ("They say being a mother is the hardest job in the world and it's true," Lena had said, solemnly, "many, *many* times harder than writing an international bestseller, harder than figuring out that NEA grant application!") She stood and hugged Lena good-bye. "Don't fall off the face of the earth again, *okay*," Lena had said, giving Bea a little shake, pressing her thumbs just a little too hard into Bea's upper arms. "Get in touch. Find me on Twitter."

Bea went to collect her things and to tell Paul she had a headache. Her coat was in a small maid's room adjacent to the kitchen, underneath an inexplicably huge pile of fur coats (didn't anyone in New York have any *shame* anymore?) and rooted around the left sleeve for the mittens she'd tucked there for safekeeping. She could hear Lena in the kitchen now, animatedly talking to Celia.

"—Absolutely *no idea*," Lena was saying, sounding more thrilled than confused. "I haven't spoken to her in years. I know she still works at *Paper Fibres*." Bea froze.

"God," Celia said, a touch of satisfaction in her voice, too. "Still? How depressing. Is she *married*?"

"She had that boyfriend for a long time, that older guy? The poet? Did he die? I think he was married."

"So she's not writing at all?"

"From what I gather, no." Bea could hear Lena chewing something crunchy, a carrot or a celery stick or a lesser mortal's finger bone. "Do you hear anything from Stephanie?" Lena asked Celia. "They're not working together anymore, right?"

"No, they're not. I can't ever get any good gossip from Stephanie. All she would tell me is they went their separate ways and it was mutual, which I'm sure isn't true." Celia's voice lowered a bit. Bea inched closer to the open doorway, flattening herself against the wall. "I *did* hear something interesting from another source."

"Yessss?" Lena said.

"She had to pay back part of her publishing advance a few years ago. It was a lot of money."

Bea winced, frozen in place, afraid to move.

"That's rough," Lena said, and this time the concern in her voice was genuine. Bea felt a wave of nausea move through her and she had a terrible and sudden urge to defecate. Being scrutinized or mocked by Lena was leagues better than being on the receiving end of her pity.

"Terrible," Celia said, momentarily chastened by Lena's sincerity. "Really terrible."

Both women were quiet, as if they'd just read Bea's obituary or were standing over her gravestone.

"But you know what?" Celia said, resummoning her nerve. "I'm just going to say it since Stephanie's not here. I never loved her stories. I never got what all the fuss was about. I mean, they were cute—the Archie stuff—it was *clever,* but *The New Yorker*? Please."

"They were of a place and time," Lena said, her register lowering into the interview or public reading voice Bea recognized and remembered loathing. "They worked in that late '90s kind of navel-gazing, where-did-we-come-from thing. We were all doing it. We were so young. Not everyone was able to figure out how to transition to more mature material." Bea couldn't believe how regal Lena sounded, as if someone had appointed her the fucking Emperor of Fiction.

"Well, her clothes are of another place and time, too," Celia said. "God. What is she wearing? Who still shops at thrift stores? Hasn't she heard about bedbugs?"

"Stop," Lena said, sounding guilty but still laughing.

"And those braids. Honestly," Celia said. "How old are we?"

"I feel bad for her, though," Lena said. "Stuck at *Paper Fibres.* People in that world know who she is, still recognize her name. It must be hard, being Beatrice Plumb."

Bea was grateful that she was still leaning against a wall, had flattened both hands on the cool plaster and felt sturdy, supported, and able to withstand the wave of rage and humiliation roaring over her. She closed her eyes. The room smelled like cat even though there wasn't a cat in sight and no other signs of an animal in the house. She wondered if Celia made a housekeeper or a neighbor hide the cat when she had guests so her pristine apartment wouldn't be sullied by a bowl of pet food or a scratching post; she seemed like that kind of traitor.

Bea stepped away from the wall and hurried to button her coat and pull on her hat. Celia and Lena were gossiping about someone else and moving into the living room. Bea entered the now-empty kitchen, heading for the front door; she stopped in front of an impressive array of expensive cookies destined for the dessert table. She opened her canvas tote and carefully slid all the cookies inside. Celia walked back into the room just as Bea was covering the stash with paper napkins. "Bea!" she said, stopping short, looking slightly abashed but also annoyed. "Where did you come from?"

"Nowhere," Bea said. Celia eyed the empty plate and Bea's bulging tote. "I can't stay for dessert," Bea said, "but thank you for a lovely evening." They stared at each other for a few laden seconds, each daring the other to speak, and then Bea turned and walked straight out the front door.

CHAPTER TEN

Jack was winded when he ascended the stairs after arriving at the Bergen Street stop in Brooklyn. How could he be so out of shape? He'd been to Stephanie's once before, years ago, right after she moved in and she and Leo were doing whatever it was she and Leo did on and off for all those years: fucking, teasing, staging their hetero melodramas. He and Walker had casually considered buying a brownstone once, but Jack didn't want to live so far from his shop, and reopening in Brooklyn was unthinkable; he believed he'd lose too many customers, which was probably no longer the case now that Brooklyn was unaffordable and unrecognizable. Jack remembered Stephanie's street as being fairly derelict. Today it seemed as if every third house had a construction Dumpster out front. He stopped in front of one brownstone under renovation. The doors were open and the curving mahogany staircase with freshly painted white risers was visible. He could see straight through into the rear open kitchen where two workers were laboring to fit a massive stainless-steel refrigerator into a cutout in the back wall.

Another lost opportunity, Jack thought. Well, that was the story these days if you were a longtime New Yorker and hadn't jumped on the real estate carousel at the right time. No matter where he looked lately, the city was mocking him and his financial woes. He picked up his pace and soon he was standing in front of Stephanie's building. A light in the upstairs hallway went off. Good. Someone was home. He hoped it was Leo, but if it wasn't, he'd sit there until Leo returned. He had all day. It was a Monday and his store was closed.

"Three months," Leo had said that afternoon in the Oyster Bar. "Give me three months to present you with some kind of plan."

And so he had. Three months and seventy-two hours to be exact and Leo wasn't answering phone calls or e-mails and he'd better have a fucking plan. Jack was in a near panic. He'd barely slept since the meeting with his old friend Arthur, the one who had helped him obtain the homeowner's line of credit.

Jack was concealing an enormous debt from Walker, a tangled thicket of money and deception. Walker knew that most years Jack's revenue barely covered his expenses, but he never objected because Jack loved what he did. But Walker was completely unaware of how Jack's rent had risen (dramatically, precipitously) during the last five years and that Jack was keeping the store above water with a home equity line of credit taken against the small weekend property they owned on the North Fork of Long Island. At the time, it had seemed a logical solution to what he hoped were temporary financial woes, a welcome bit of magic, when his old friend Arthur had proposed the opportunity over drinks one night when Jack complained about his balance sheet. He and Arthur had gone to Vassar together and shared an apartment the first year they lived in Manhattan.

"As easy as opening a credit card!" Arthur worked for an Internet mortgage lender and claimed he helped friends "put their equity to use" all the time. "Won't cost you a cent!"

Jack knew he wasn't alone in the mid-2000s, falling prey to this gilded logic, but he realized with a sickening heart that he'd been among the last before the financial system nearly buckled under the weight of its own greed and folly. Worse, he knew better. He'd listened to Walker rail against the loans for years, had heard him discourage their friends and acquaintances and neighbors and his clients from participating in the feverish, implausible extending of credit. "It's not just foolish," Walker had said over and over about the swollen mortgage industry, "it's bordering on illegal. It's fraud and it's completely unethical."

Unethical. The word rang in Jack's brain—*unethical* would also describe how he'd taken advantage of the signatory authority he and Walker had given each other years ago for all matters relating to the weekend cottage so they both didn't have to drive out to Long Island whenever papers needed to be signed for anything regarding the house or property.

The cottage they'd owned for twenty years was nothing lavish or fancy, but it was on a lovely piece of property with a stream running through a wooded area and a short walk to the beach. It was going to be their retirement home, a place to go when Walker could scale back his practice, relax, take more time to do the things he loved: cook, read, garden. *After The Nest* became Jack's favorite expression. After The Nest, they'd winterize the cottage, renovate and expand the kitchen, buy a car, maybe add a guest room; the list went on and on. Walker used to gently mock Jack. *After The Nest, world peace!* he'd say. *After The Nest, the lame will walk and the blind will see!* Walker was dismissive of The Nest. He'd spent too many hours with clients who showed up at his door outraged because something they thought they'd inherit didn't materialize. Walker didn't believe in inheritances, which he thought were nothing more than a gamble, and a shortcut; Walker didn't believe in shortcuts or gambling.

The entire time (all of ten days) that Arthur was processing the loan, Jack expected somebody to stop him. But no. It had proved frighteningly easy to tap into the property's equity. Whenever he voiced a hesitation, everyone—from Arthur to the bank manager who handed him a credit line of $250,000—told him how smart he was being, how wise it was to consolidate his debts and take advantage of the low-interest payments. Jack told himself he'd only spend a little, just what he needed. But every year he needed more, and some years he used the funds to upgrade the retail space and attempt to lure in more customers. Better lighting. Fresh paint. A new computer invoicing and inventory system. He told himself they were capital investments. Who wanted to shop at a pricey store that didn't have fresh flowers on display? An espresso machine up front? His initial fear about using the card waned because he'd be able to pay it off *after The Nest*. He'd have to confess his scheme then, but Walker always told Jack the money from The Nest was *his*, a gift from his father to do with as he liked. So when he did confess, the loan would be paid, there'd still be ample money left, and the weekend cottage would be safe. If it wasn't? Walker would never forgive him.

"Extension?" Arthur had said a few days ago, frowning. He gave a long, low whistle and shook his head a little. Jack's fingers went numb; his heart pounded so hard he was sure if he looked down he could see it through his shirt. "That, my friend, is an impossibility." He hit every syllable of impossibility to stress his refusal. "We set up the loan in 2007," Arthur said, squinting at the paperwork in front of him. "Another place, another time. Prerecession. I couldn't get you this kind of loan now, never mind an extension. I see a few late payments and—" He shrugged. "Is this really a problem? Are you in some real trouble here?"

"No trouble. Just exploring options." Jack wasn't going to confide in Arthur who had a big mouth. He'd spent the last few nights tossing and turning and silently rehearsing his plea to Leo for immediate help. He climbed Stephanie's stoop and rang the bell a few times. Timidly at first and then with more duration and persistence. He knocked. Nothing. He pulled his phone out of his pocket and called Leo's cell. No answer. He wanted to call the house phone but realized he didn't have Stephanie's number. He descended the stoop and backed up onto the sidewalk, trying to get another look at the upper floor where he was sure he'd seen a light. He imagined Leo inside, watching him, smug and safe behind the still curtain. At the garden level, Jack spotted someone tall and male moving about inside. Leo! Jack let himself through the gate at the sidewalk. He walked up to the street-level window and rapped, hard and insistent. He peered through, hands cupped around eyes, nose pressed to the glass that slightly fogged from his breath.

The face that appeared on the other side of the window was twisted with indignation and sitting above a policeman's navy uniform shirt. Outside, Jack raised his hands in surrender, took a step back. "I'm sorry! I'm so sorry. I'm looking for my brother." The face disappeared from the window and within seconds the door beneath the front stoop flew open and the furious man was walking toward him, fists clenched. A medium-size dog rushed at Jack, stopping short of his ankles and crouching down with a low, menacing growl.

"Please." Jack stepped backward and almost tripped over an elevated brick border that enclosed the small front garden of ragged English ivy and a struggling dogwood. "Don't shoot." He was simultaneously frightened and furious. He hated having to lift his hands to this beefy, red-faced cop. "It was an honest mistake, Officer. I'd forgotten Stephanie rented the ground floor."

"I'm not a cop. I'm a security guard and you better have a good reason for looking in my windows and I better hear it fast."

"I'm looking for Leo Plumb," Jack said in a rush. "I'm his brother. Leo's brother! He's staying upstairs."

"I know who Leo is."

"Again," Jack said, relieved to see that the cop—security guard— whatever, wasn't wearing a gun. "Please accept my sincere apologies." Jack looked down at the dog who was coming closer to his ankles and barking.

"Get back here, Sinatra." The man snapped his fingers at the dog who returned to his owner's side, whined, settled onto his haunches, and then resumed barking at Jack.

TOMMY O'TOOLE STARED at Jack for a few minutes. He was definitely related to Leo, the same WASPish features, thin lips, slightly beakish nose beneath dark hair. On Leo it all added up to something a little more impressive. Tommy enjoyed rattling the intruder. His clean-shaven face had gone green and there were beads of sweat on his upper lip and along the top of his generous forehead. His tweed coat looked like something Sherlock Holmes would wear. Jesus. Where did he think he was?

"You look through a window on some of the streets around here and people will shoot first and ask questions later," Tommy said, knowing Jack wouldn't recognize the exaggeration.

"You're absolutely right. I will be more careful." Jack lowered his hands and took a tentative step out of the garden patch. The dog lunged and Jack scrambled back inside the brick enclosure.

"Sinatra!" Tommy bent down and stroked the dog's back. "Francis Albert. Be quiet." The dog licked Tommy's hand and whimpered a bit. "Sorry," he said to Jack. "He's very high-strung. I should have named him Jerry Lewis."

"That's very funny," Jack said, without smiling. He stared at the dog who appeared to be some kind of pug mix with a short brown coat, black pushed-in snout, and slightly bulging blue eyes that were eerily Sinatra-like. Jack stepped out of the ivy one more time and looked down at his suede shoes, which were dampened with what he optimistically hoped was lingering morning dew but assumed was dog urine.

"What did you say your name was?" Tommy said.

"Jack. Plumb." He extended a hand, and Tommy reluctantly stepped forward to shake it. Tommy didn't trust this guy; there was something furtive, something not quite open about him. The kind of guy he'd keep his eye on if he were loitering around a lobby or a store.

"We've had a Peeping Tom in this neighborhood," Tommy said. "Some creep who walks up to windows looking for women inside and whips it out in broad daylight. Sick bastard."

"I assure you"—Jack placed one gloved hand over his heart—"I am not your Peeping Tom."

"Yeah, I imagine not."

"Do you know if they're home?" Jack asked. "Leo or Stephanie? I thought I saw a light go on upstairs a few minutes ago."

"I guess they're gone for the day," Tommy said. He suspected he wasn't telling the truth. He thought he'd heard Stephanie walking around a few minutes ago.

"Listen," Jack said, taking his phone from his pocket. "I'd like to call just in case someone is there and can't hear the bell for whatever reason. Do you have Stephanie's number? I've come all the way from Manhattan."

"From Manhattan?"

"Yes," Jack said. "The West Village."

"That's quite a trip. I guess you've been on the road what? Two, three days?"

Jack forced what he hoped was a self-deprecating laugh. God, he hated everyone. "I just meant I'd hate to get back across the bridge and discover they'd been in the shower or something."

Tommy eyed Jack. If Stephanie were lying low, she wouldn't answer the phone either. Also, he should probably offer Sherlock a paper towel or rag; he definitely had dog piss on his shoes.

"I'll be quick," Jack said. "I'd be incredibly grateful."

"I've got her number inside." Tommy gestured to the open door behind him. Jack followed Tommy and the dog into the front foyer, which was dark and nearly empty except for a few woolen jackets hanging on an overloaded hook by the door, a small card table with a landline receiver, and a poster on the wall from a Matisse retrospective at MoMA, which Jack assumed was left over from a previous tenant. The hallway smelled, incongruously, of potpourri. Something cinnamon heavy. Tommy stood in the doorway, watching Jack. The dog, calmer now, sniffed at Jack's ankles.

"Stay here," Tommy said. "I'll get her number. It's in the back." He moved down the hallway to the back of the apartment where Jack could see a kitchen. The dog followed him, snorting. Jack looked through the open pocket doors into the living room. The furniture looked like castoffs, what Jack thought of as the divorced-man's-special. Two overstuffed flowery and worn sofas probably bestowed by a concerned female relative or friend. A sagging wicker bookcase, which housed a bunch of true crime paperbacks, out-of-date phone books, and an abandoned glass fish tank one-quarter full of loose change. The coffee table was covered with a pile of *New York Post*s turned to completed Sudoku puzzles.

A fairly decent pedestal table, something that must have sat in a much nicer room at one time, was covered with an assortment of framed family photos. Jack stepped into the living room to look at the table. Nice but not old. He surveyed the photos, lots of pictures of someone he assumed was the ex-wife and various family tableaux: weddings, babies, kids in Little League uniforms with gap-toothed grins holding bats half their size.

He could see through to the dining room, which was empty except for a plastic collapsible table surrounded by a few folding chairs and, oddly, in a dark corner of the room a sculpture sitting on top of a small wooden dolly on wheels. Jack thought he recognized the familiar shape of Rodin's *The Kiss*. Figures, he thought, as tacky as everything else in the place, probably ordered from some late-night shopping network meant to woo the guy's divorcée dates.

Jack could hear Tommy in the back, opening and shutting drawers, rifling through papers. Jack quietly approached the statue. There was something off about the Rodin reproduction, which was polished to a sheen. As he got closer, he could see it was badly damaged. The original cast had probably been nearly two feet high, but it had lost at least six inches off its base. The right side of the man's upper body was missing, his disembodied hand still partly visible on the woman's left thigh. The woman sitting partially on his lap was mostly intact, except for her right leg, which seemed to have melted below the knee. *Melted?* Jack thought. *Was it plastic?*

He gave the thing a little shove; the sculpture didn't move, but the wheels of the dolly did. So that's why it was on wheels, it was heavy. There were deep gouges in the surface of the metal. Jack realized he was looking at a badly damaged bronze cast of Rodin's *The Kiss*. This in itself wasn't all that rare—there were quite a few on the market, some valuable, some not, depending on where and when they'd been forged. One of Jack's best customers collected Rodin and Jack had sourced some bronze castings for him over the years. The most valuable were the so-called originals produced by the Barbedienne foundry just outside of Paris. Authenticating them was a nightmare. If there was a foundry mark, he knew where it would be, but there was no way he could turn the thing over himself.

"What are you doing in here?" Tommy said. Jack looked up to see Tommy standing in the doorway, a stained and wrinkled Post-it in his hand. He looked pissed.

"I was admiring your piece," Jack said. "It's a good casting. Where did you get it?"

"It was a gift." He handed Jack the paper. "Here's Stephanie's number, the phone's in the front hall."

"What happened to it?"

"It sustained some damage during an unfortunate incident." Tommy pointed to the front hall, but Jack could see his hand tremble a bit. "Phone's in there."

"What kind of accident?"

"Fire."

"The scratches didn't come from a fire, though," Jack said, walking around the sculpture. "And for bronze to actually melt, the fire would have to be incredibly hot, incredibly strong."

"Yeah, well I'm an ex-firefighter," Tommy said. "I've seen fire do some pretty unbelievable things."

"So you recovered this from a fire?"

"That's not what I said," Tommy said.

Jack squatted and knelt before the statue "Did you say this was a gift?"

Tommy walked to the front hall, praying Jack would follow him. Now he was the one with telltale sweat on his upper lip and brow. What had he been thinking, letting this guy into his house? "I'm calling Stephanie for you right now," Tommy said.

The damage to the statue was tugging at Jack; something about it felt significant. He started to feel a familiar tingling in his fingers and at the back of his neck, a feeling he'd learned to trust when trolling through flea markets and estate sales and antique shows, a little *tick tick tick* that alerted him he might have found something of value among the piles of crap. In the front hall, Tommy was standing with the receiver to his ear. Jack stepped out of Tommy's line of sight and quickly took a few surreptitious pictures of the cast with his phone.

"No answer," Tommy said. "I'll tell them you stopped by. If there's nothing else I can do for you—"

"Nothing else," Jack said, walking into the front hall, eager now to get home and make a few calls. "You've been very helpful."

Tommy opened the door. Jack gave a quick wave to the dog who was standing like a sentry next to Tommy and who followed him as he walked down the short path and unhooked the gate. As the gate clicked behind him, he turned and bent a little at the waist, referencing the only Frank Sinatra tune he could summon. "I'll be seeing *you,* Frank," he said, causing the dog to growl and leap up and bark madly at Jack's back until he was completely gone from sight.

CHAPTER ELEVEN

The first few weeks Tommy had *The Kiss,* he'd been elated. He couldn't believe how easy it was to procure (that's how he thought of it when he was forced to assign a verb to his actions: *procure).* The sculpture had appeared on his very last day of working the pile at the World Trade Center site, early April 2002. By that time, Tommy had been working the pile for seven straight months, since the early hours of September twelfth. As a retired fire-fighter (his lower back had betrayed him once and for all years ear-lier), he was one of the first to be cleared to work rescue and recovery. The cough he'd developed somewhere around week six was only get-ting worse and his daughter Maggie was apoplectic about him going there every day.

"Ma would have hated this. She would've wanted you to take care of yourself, to be here for me and my sisters, for your grandchildren," she'd say, pushing more and more food in front of him. She'd taken to feeding others (everyone except herself) with an alarming zeal over the past seven months. She'd cook all day, layering the freezer with pans of lasagna and enchiladas, containers of chili and homemade soup, more than the family could possibly eat. Her hands were in constant motion. If she wasn't cooking, she was scrubbing a pot or polishing flatware or zealously wiping down counters as if she were eliminating scurvy from a dangerously filthy ship. The furrow between her eyes never disappeared now. She'd delivered his first grandchild three months earlier and had already dropped the pregnancy weight and then some; there was a new slackness to her jawline. Her pretty brown eyes, always so engaged and eager, were often watery and bloodshot and unfocused.

"You're working yourself into your grave," Maggie told her father.

"Poor choice of words," Tommy said, trying to keep his voice light instead of bitter.

"You know what I mean, Dad."

Tommy knew. He showed up at the pile every day because it *was* his wife's grave, as much of a grave as she'd ever have anyway. Ronnie had been an office manager for a financial services company on the ninety-fifth floor of the north tower of the World Trade Center. Before the planes hit that morning, Tommy and Ronnie had passed each other in the outdoor concourse between buildings, as they did many days when Tommy was heading home from the occasional late-night security guard shift and Ronnie was arriving. She was supposed to be off that Tuesday but had decided to go in and help her boss clear out a backlog of files.

"I'll take an extra day next week," she'd told Tommy. "I'll enjoy it more if I get this work out of the way." They'd kissed in the lobby, talked about what to do for dinner. "Load the dishwasher," she'd said, giving him a little squeeze on his upper arm.

"Roger," he'd said. She'd smiled and rolled her eyes a little; they both knew he'd forget. He was tired after working all night but not too tired to notice her short skirt, how fine and high her ass looked beneath the center seam of the gray wool, how shapely and firm her legs were after three daughters and, soon, a grandson.

Through the excruciating hours and days and weeks following that morning, he'd thought repeatedly about that moment: Ronnie's long, strong stride in the bright morning sun, how those legs should have carried her down to safety, how he should have been there to catch her. He remembered the shoes she wore that day, red patent leather with a little cutout for the toes. She always wore sneakers to commute from their house in the Rockaways, but would stop in the concourse lobby to slip on her heels. She cared about things like that.

"Appearances count," she would tell their kids. "If you want people to judge you based on the inside, don't distract them from the outside."

His eyes had followed her that morning as she'd walked to the elevators. He would always be grateful for that, at least, how he'd stopped and admired the little sway of her derriere, watched her swipe her employee ID, press the up button for the elevator, gently tug at the hem of her skirt. How his heart had softened thinking what a fierce specimen of a woman she was, how lucky that she belonged to him.

"Mom would have hated you going there every day," Maggie told him repeatedly in the following months. "She would have hated you putting yourself at risk."

Tommy didn't care what Ronnie might have thought of his days spent digging through the pile, but the concern on his daughter's face wore on him. Her husband had pulled him aside recently to delineate how poorly she was still sleeping, the frequency of her nightmares and crying jags. How her grief had transmuted from her mother's absence to fear for her father's health, a sticky certainty that he was using the pile to slowly kill himself and that he wouldn't even live to see his first grandson's first birthday. Maggie repeatedly asked Tommy if he'd help with the baby so she could go back to work part time. He knew the request was just her way of trying to get him away from the site. With the cleanup only weeks away from being finished, he decided to give notice and help with his grandson to give Maggie and her two sisters some peace of mind. They deserved it.

TOMMY SPENT HIS LAST MORNING at work walking around and shaking the hands of the men and women he'd worked with side by side for twelve-hour shifts, six days a week, for months. Soon they'd all be gone, this unlikely, contentious family of firefighters, ironworkers, electricians, construction workers, police, medics. They'd spent months dismantling the ruins of the buildings and it was time for all of them to return to their lives, including him, whatever that meant, whatever life was going to be on the unimaginable other side of the pile. He took his rake and went to his usual position, still believing that today, his last day, might be the day—the day he found something belonging to Ronnie.

It was a silly, unlikely desire and one he couldn't shake. Every morning as he crossed the Gil Hodges bridge and followed the Belt Parkway to downtown Manhattan, he imagined coming across something of hers while sifting through the debris—anything—her reading glasses in the fuchsia leather case, her house keys on the Cape Cod key chain she'd used for years, one of those red shoes.

On his worst days, he was angry with Ronnie, angry that she hadn't sent him a sign, some small reassuring object. He knew this was just one of the many irrational thoughts he'd had over the past months. For weeks he was sure he'd find *her,* still alive and huddled under a pile, dirty and tired and coated with that omnipresent gray dust; she'd look up at him, extend a hand, and say, *Take your sweet time why don't you, O'Toole?*

He knew from the first wrenching moments he saw the wreckage on television, before the towers even fell, that she didn't have a chance. Still, he'd spent the first few weeks digging frantically where he imagined she might have fallen. And then, for a disconcerting number of weeks, he'd had an overwhelming desire to taste the ash, to take it into his mouth. The only thing that stopped him was the fear that someone would see and send him to the tent for grief counseling and not allow him back. Finally, he'd gotten himself assigned to the raking fields nearest the north tower, a silly distinction because there was little rhyme or reason as to how the piles of debris arrived at his feet; still, it reassured him. He spent his days with a garden rake in his hands, hoeing for artifacts. His desire made him a fastidious spotter. He'd found countless objects. More wallets and eyeglasses than he could count, faded stuffed animals, keys, backpacks, shoes; he made sure each and every one was tagged and bagged, hoping it would give some other family relief, however anemic.

Still, this one idea persisted: that he would find something of *hers,* and as long as he was there digging through the carnage it was possible—it had happened, just not to him. Salvatore Martin, retired EMS, who worked the 5:30 A.M. shift seven days a week had drawn his rake through a tangled pile of cable and dirt one bitter, frozen winter day and staring up at him was a photo of his son Sal Jr. on a laminated corporate ID, slightly burned around the edges, picture intact. Sal had quit the following week and everyone thought seeing the plastic badge had been too much, had sent him over the edge. Tommy knew the truth. Sal had found what he'd been looking for—proof, a talisman— and so he was free to leave.

Tommy's last afternoon on the pile. He decided to find his own souvenir to take that was of this place where Ronnie had last lived and breathed—something easily pocketed to sit on his desk or the windowsill above the kitchen sink, something he could bear to look at every day. As he raked through the rubble, considering his options (a piece of stone, a pebble—it couldn't be anyone else's personal effect, he wouldn't do that), one of his coworkers hollered for him.

"Tommy!" It was his friend Will Peck. Most of Will's engine company in Brooklyn had been lost when the towers went down; Will had stayed home that morning with the stomach flu. They'd both been there since day one, embracing and exorcising their particular demons. Will waved him over to where an excavator had just dumped a heaping pile of dirt and dust and mangled metal.

"We got something here, O'Toole. Might want to come over and take a look."

WHEN TOMMY HAD BRUSHED THE DEBRIS AWAY from the sculpture and understood what he was looking at, he could barely contain his glee. Oh, she was feisty that one, waiting until practically the very last hour of his very last day, but she did it! The minute he saw the hulk of metal emerge from the dirt and dust, he knew it was from Ronnie. In spite of its damage, he could see the tenderness of the couple's embrace. The woman in the sculpture had one of her legs draped over the man's leg, exactly the way Ronnie used to sit when they were alone, when she'd move in close and swing her leg over his and put one of her arms around his shoulder and draw him close with her other arm.

Am I too heavy? she'd ask.

Never. Even when she was nine months pregnant, she was never too heavy in his lap. He loved the feel of her fleshy thigh on top of his, how she'd press against his chest. The posture was so intrinsically hers, so intimate and familiar that when Tommy saw the statue, even covered with grime and grit, it took all his restraint not to whoop and holler, to tell everyone what its appearance meant, whom it was from. But he couldn't be that cruel, couldn't flaunt his luck in front of the others. He closed his eyes for a minute, silently thanked his wife.

The Kiss sat there until Tommy's shift was over and it was night. The statue was secured to a flatbed cart and he volunteered to wheel it over to the Port Authority's temporary holding trailer, where the piece would be documented and photographed before being handed over to the authorities in charge of artifacts. In an exquisite piece of luck, the Port Authority worker doing documentation that day had gone home early. Standing at the trailer's door, Tommy knew what he had to do. It had proved absurdly easy for him to wheel the sculpture up a plank and into the back of his pickup and drive it home. He knew it would be weeks or months, possibly never, before anyone noticed it was missing. Among the piles of scorched debris—all the personal possessions and pieces of buildings and tires and cars and fire trucks and airplanes, who would even remember this thing? Who would think to ask where it had gone?

CHAPTER TWELVE

Melody had been sitting in her car outside the small consignment store on Main Street for almost an hour. Her coffee in the cup holder was cold. She was wasting gas because it was too chilly to turn the car off and sit for more than a few minutes without running the heat, but she still hadn't worked up the nerve to go inside and talk to Jen Malcolm who owned the store and whom Melody knew a little bit because Jen also had children at the high school, two sons, and because Melody had occasionally sold a piece of furniture to Jen in the past. Items she'd bought and refinished but didn't quite work in her house and were too nice, she thought, to sell on Craigslist and too bulky for eBay. Jen always liked the pieces Melody brought. Most of them sold, and Melody would earn a little extra money doing something she genuinely loved to do. Today's errand felt different.

Melody turned the key in the ignition, cutting the exhaust but leaving it in the position where the radio would still play. When she got too cold, she told herself, she'd go inside and show Jen the photos of all the furniture in her house, the many pieces she'd spent years hunting down at flea markets and estate sales, her favorite finds, the valuable items acquired for a song from sellers who didn't know any better: a neglected Stickley table that someone had criminally sponge painted, now stripped and restored; a black leather Barcelona chair pocked with cigarette burns and other unsavory stains she'd reupholstered in a bright turquoise tweed; and her favorite, a beautiful oak drafting table that tilted. Nora and Louisa had used it for years to draw or do homework or just sit, side by side, reading a book. She would sell all of it to appease Walt and slow him down. She would sell anything. Almost.

MELODY KNEW NORA AND LOUISA called her *the General* behind her back, but she didn't care. She didn't care because she also knew what it was like to grow up in a state of anarchy, in a house with parents so hands-off they were nearly invisible. Melody knew what it was like to have teachers ask, hesitant and concerned, if her parents were going to come to a parent-teacher conference. She knew what it was like to search in vain for their faces in the school auditorium during a play or a concert. She'd vowed to be an entirely different type of mother, and having twins never set her off course. Some days she drove herself crazy, running from one daughter's after-school activity to the other's. She charted the time spent with each child, making sure to even it out as far as was humanly possible. She never missed a single concert, play, soccer game, track meet, Brownie meeting, choral performance. She packed a healthy lunch every day, including one indulgent sweet on Fridays. She wrote them encouraging notes and arrived fifteen minutes early for pickup, so they would never stand in a parking lot alone, wondering if anyone was going to show up to bring them home, wondering if anyone even realized they were gone.

She remembered their first exploratory trips upstate as if they'd happened yesterday. Driving north, watching the scraggly city trees gradually replaced with the stately elms and elderly pines of the Taconic. Nora and Louisa asleep in their respective car seats in the back, both sucking away on identical pacifiers. Melody had instantly loved their small village with its quaint dress shops and bakeries, all the women pushing strollers while wearing jogging suits the color of sorbet. It was nothing like the grime and cacophony of their street that was technically in Spanish Harlem.

They rented a condo on the less desirable side of town. For two straight years Melody would put the twins in a stroller and walk the streets on the other side of the tracks, literally. The commuter train divided the town into its desirable (nearer the water) and less desirable (nearer the mall) side. She didn't know what she was looking for until the day she saw it. A small house that had managed to survive the kind of gut renovation and expansion happening on most of the surrounding streets. It was an Arts and Crafts bungalow that had clearly fallen into disrepair. The morning she passed by, a man about her age was loading a car with boxes.

"Moving out?" Melody said, trying to sound friendly but not overly curious.

"Moving my mom out," the guy said; he was staring at the girls as people tended to do. "Twins?"

"Yes," Melody said. "They're almost three."

"I have twins, too." He leaned down in front of the stroller and played with the girls for a minute, pretending to snatch a nose and then hand it back, one of their favorite games.

"So what's going to happen to the house?" Melody asked.

The man stood and sighed. He squinted at the house. "I don't know, man," he said, sounding beaten. "There's so much to do to get it in good shape to sell. The Realtor says it's not even worth the work, someone will probably tear it down and rebuild into something like that." He pointed disgustedly to the house next door, a renovation Melody had watched—and secretly admired—over the past months.

"Yeah, that place is pretty awful," she said. And then without thinking: "My husband and I have been looking for a house, but everything is so much bigger than we need—and can afford. I'd love to find something to fix up, not to change but to restore." Once the words were out of her mouth, she knew they were true.

Walt had been against the house. He thought it was overpriced for what it was and feared a real-estate downturn. The seller liked Melody, but even with all the work the house needed—and it needed everything—he held firm on the price, which was more than they should borrow given that she didn't work. (Her working had never been worth the price of child care and now who would hire her?) Walt's salary as a computer technician in Pearl River was okay but not great.

The house's interior was dated, but Melody could see past the ugly carpet and '70s wallpaper to its excellent bones and understand what it could be: a home, a place her girls would feel safe and cared for. She loved the tiny leaded glass windows, the breakfast nook, the window seat at the landing of the front stair, the enormous oak in the front yard and the sugar maples in the back turning brilliant shades of orange. She and Walt would take the front bedroom, the one under the eaves. There were two small bedrooms in the back, perfect for Nora and Louisa. She could see birthday parties in the yard under the maples, early morning breakfasts in the paneled dining room; she knew exactly where she'd put the Christmas tree. The Realtor had pulled up a corner of the living room carpet to show Melody the original heart pine floor. She fought for that house in a way she'd never fought for anything before.

"All the mechanicals are going to need an upgrade," Walt had said, frowning. "Any money we have is going to go behind the walls, in the basement, under the floors—we'll drain our savings for things you can't see."

"That's okay," Melody said. And it was. She knew how to do the other stuff, how to strip paint and steam off wallpaper and refinish. What she didn't know she'd learn. The house would be her project, her job. Alan Greenspan was on her side! And Walt couldn't argue with the concrete fact of The Nest.

But he did. For weeks. And when she thought they'd waited too long and the property would go to someone else, she'd broken out into head-to-toe hives. She'd been soaking in a tub of colloidal oatmeal, bereft, when he'd come to her to tell her the property—and hefty mortgage—was theirs. She knew his capitulation had finally come down to this: He loved her, he wanted her to be happy.

"Why can't we move to a town where everyone isn't a gazillionaire?" Walt would say to her every so often, usually when Melody was in a tizzy about something the girls needed—clothes, after-school activities, summer camp. But she didn't want to move. They lived in one of the best school districts in the Northeast. Melody had learned where to shop, how to poke around for what the girls needed. She knew how to wait for sales and who would take money off when she said she was buying for twins. She always came up with funds when necessary—for special school trips or instruments so they could take music lessons. When they joined the ski club, she'd paged through old school directories and called parents of twins who'd gone off to college asking if they had any equipment they would be willing to sell and she hit the jackpot, a bored-sounding father who told her if she'd come clean his garage of ski equipment—along with the ice skates and tennis rackets and bikes that his daughters never, ever touched—she could have it all for free.

Through all the years, the coupon cutting, working on the house every weekend until her knees ached and her hands were cracked and bleeding, rarely buying anything new for herself—or Walt—off in the distance her fortieth birthday glowed like a distant lighthouse, flashing its beam of rescue. She would turn forty and the money would drop into their account. Most of it would go toward college and some of it would pay down the house loan and all would be, if not completely right with the world, better than it ever had been. She didn't like to think about the year the girls would go away to college, how she would feel without them, but she did allow herself to think about how things might get a little easier for all of them after The Nest. Finally, the girls could have something that wasn't about price. They could line up the college acceptance letters and Melody could say, *Which-ever one you want. Choose.* Finally, she could start to relax. Finally, she was going to get a goddamn break.

She turned up the volume on the classical radio station, which she only listened to when her mind was too occupied for lyrics or talk. *Occupied* was a polite term for the current state of her amped-up brain. If she hadn't been parked in plain sight on the main commercial strip of their tiny gossipy town, she would have lain down on the front seat and gone to sleep. She was so tired lately. She couldn't manage more than a few hours at night when she'd involuntarily shift into some kind of exalted state of anxiety. She would be awake for hours, telling herself to get out of bed and brew some tea or run a warm bath or read, but she couldn't manage to do any of those things either; she would just lie next to Walt, listening to his gentle snore (even when sleeping, he was unfailingly polite), rigid and paralyzed with worry about Nora and Louisa and money and the mortgage and college tuition and global warming and pesticides in food and lack of privacy on the Internet and *cancer*—God, how often had she micro-waved food in plastic containers when the girls were little?—and whether she'd permanently compromised their intelligence by not breast-feeding and what were the repercussions of that one month she'd let them joyfully tear around the living room in hand-me-down walkers from a kind older neighbor until an unkind younger neigh-bor told her that *everyone* knew walkers delayed motor and mental development. She'd fixate on what would happen to the girls when they left home and strayed from her watchful eye (What was the range of Stalkerville? How many miles? She'd have to check) and wonder who could ever love and care for them the way she and Walt did, except that lately she felt like a big fat failure in the love and care department. Oh! And she was fat! She'd gained at least ten pounds since the lunch with Leo, maybe more, she was afraid to weigh herself. Everything felt tight and uncomfortable. She'd taken to covering her unbuttoned jeans with long shirts borrowed from Walt; she could hardly afford to buy new clothes. Nora's coat was looking particularly ratty, but if she bought Nora a new coat, she would have to buy Louisa one, too (it was her rule: parity in all things!), and she definitely couldn't afford two.

Melody remembered a day long ago when both girls had raging ear infections. Two fevers, two toddlers crying all night who both hated medicine of any kind. As she watched the doctor writing prescriptions, she wondered how on earth she was going to manage to get eardrops and amoxicillin into two cranky, sick babies (*four* ears, *two* mouths) three to four times a day for ten days.

"It gets easier, right?" she'd asked her pediatrician then, holding one squirming, sweaty child in each arm, neither one would be put down, not even for a minute.

"That depends on what you mean by easier," the doctor said, laughing sympathetically. "I have two teenagers and you know what they say."

"No," Melody said, dizzy from lack of sleep and too much coffee. "I don't know what they say."

"Little kids, little problems; big kids, big problems."

Melody had wanted to slap the doctor. Having twins seemed so hard when they were little, especially when they were living in the city. Now she found herself wishing for the days when the hardest thing she had to do was dress and load two babies into the unwieldy double stroller and make her way to the playground where she'd sit with the other mothers. They'd all show up with steaming lattes in the winter, iced cappuccinos in the summer, and grease-stained paper bags with various pastries purchased to share. They'd talk and pass bits of lemon cake or blueberry muffins or some gooey cinnamon confection called monkey bread (Melody's favorite), and the conversation would often turn to life *before* kids, what it had been like to sleep late, fit into skinnier jeans, finish reading a book before so much time passed between chapters that you had to start from the beginning again, go to an office every day and order out lunch. "Sure I had to kiss a few asses," one of the women said, "but I didn't have to wipe any."

"I was an important person!" Melody remembered another mother saying. "I managed people and budgets and *got paid*. Now look at me." She'd gestured to the baby fastened to her breast. "I'm sitting here in the park, half naked, and I don't even care who sees. And what's worse is that nobody is even trying to look." The woman detached her sleeping baby from her nipple and ran a soft finger over his pudgy cheek. "These breasts used to make things happen, you know? These breasts didn't put *anybody* to sleep."

Melody couldn't help but stare a little at the prominent veins running beneath the woman's fair skin, the darkened, engorged nipple. She'd tried to breast-feed the twins, had wanted to so badly, but had given up after six weeks, unable to get them on any kind of schedule and nearly out of her mind with lack of sleep. She watched the other mom hook her nursing bra closed and hoist the infant up on her shoulder, rhythmically thumping his back to elicit a burp. "I used to read three newspapers every morning. *Three*." Her voice was softer now so as not to disturb the baby. "You know where I get all my news now? Fucking Oprah." Her expression was rueful, but also resigned, her fingers making small circles on the baby's back. "What can you do? This is temporary, right?"

Melody never knew how to join those conversations, so she didn't. She'd sit and smile and try to nod knowingly, but what she would have said if she could have mustered the nerve was that before her daughters were born she was *nothing*. She was a secretary. A typist. Someone who blew off college because her father died the fall of her senior year of high school and her mother was checked out and Melody herself was paralyzed with confusion and grief. Not to mention her kind of shitty grades.

But then one day Walter sat next to her in their company cafeteria. He introduced himself and handed her a piece of chocolate cake, saying it was the last one and he'd grabbed it for her because he'd noticed she usually allowed herself a slice on Fridays. When Walt asked her out for pizza and a movie and only months later asked her to be his wife and only a year after that she became a mother to not one but *two* brilliantly beautiful baby girls? Well, that was *something;* then she became *someone.*

She leaned back and closed her eyes. Maybe she could just doze for a minute or two. She thought about Nora's coat and wondered if a new set of buttons would help. Something decorative—wooden or pewter or maybe a colorful glass button, emerald green maybe. She could do that, she could afford two sets of new buttons. Sometimes a small change could make all the difference.

CHAPTER THIRTEEN

After they saw Leo in the park, it took another three weeks for Nora to coerce Louisa out again and that was the day Simone spotted them leaving and asked if she could join. "I thought I saw you two skipping out of this particular ring of hell a few weeks ago," she said, stopping on the front steps of the building to light a cigarette. "I live around here. Want to go to my apartment?"

In the weeks since then whenever they skipped class, Simone joined them and she'd completely taken over their weekly excursions. It was winter, and the only thing Louisa and Nora ever did now was go to the American Museum of Natural History because Simone had a family membership card and it was free or hang out at Simone's apartment, which was always empty because both of her parents were attorneys who almost always went into the office on Saturdays. Louisa was sick of it. She wasn't only sick of the deceit—she was certain it was just a matter of time before they were caught and then what?—she was sick of Simone's apartment and even sick of the museum, a place she used to love because it was one of their family's special destinations, one of the few Melody-approved field trips into New York, and what had seemed gleaming and exotic all through their childhoods—rooms with sharks and dinosaurs and cases of gemstones; live butterflies!—had been dulled over the past few months, tainted with familiarity and guilt and boredom.

And then there was Simone—the beautiful African American girl who always sat in the front row and finished her work before everybody else and wandered the room offering help to those who wanted it. She was a junior in high school, too, and Louisa had overheard the instructor say that Simone could probably get a perfect SAT score without too much effort. "Probably," Simone had said, shrugging. Something about her made Louisa nervous. She seemed so much older than they were. She supposed it was just that Simone had grown up in Manhattan and was braver, more sophisticated. And she was free with her opinions of Nora and Louisa in a way that was discomfiting.

Every Saturday, at the start of their outing, she'd appraise Nora and Louisa, looking them up and down and pronouncing judgment on each piece of clothing and accessory: *no, yes, God no, no, no,* that *is actually nice, please don't wear* that *again.* When she laughed, she threw back her head and hooted a little and was so loud people turned to stare. She smoked. She applied bright orange lipstick without even looking in a mirror, flicking a pinkie into the cleft of her upper lip and the corners to be sure it was perfect.

"This is my signature color," she'd told them, snapping the tube of lipstick shut and tucking it into her back pocket. "Black women can wear these shades. Don't you two even think about it." That day she'd had her long braids piled on top of her head in a coiled bun, adding inches to her already imposing height, elongating her face, which could be aloof or curious depending on her mood. She wore fitted tees made out of some kind of diaphanous cotton that left nothing above the waist to be curious about. Her bras, the kind with the molded cup designed to enhance cleavage, were brightly colored and lacy and clearly visible under everything she wore. Melody still shopped for most of Nora's and Louisa's clothing, buying them serviceable lingerie on sale that sometimes verged on cute—prints of puppies or handbags or seashells—but never veered toward sexy.

Occasionally Simone would point to something one of them was wearing and say, "That is adorable," not meaning it as a compliment. As far as Louisa could decipher, *adorable* in Simone's lexicon was a combination of stupid and tacky. Simone was also fiercely critical of everything that was—to use her favorite insult—*popular,* her bright orange mouth twisting the word into an insult. If Simone liked something, it was *tight,* which made no sense to Louisa. "Shouldn't *tight* be negative?" she asked Nora. "As in uncomfortable, constrained, restricting. As in these old pants are *tight*?"

"Not everything's an SAT word," Nora said, in a drawl Louisa had never heard her employ before and which made her sound exactly like Simone. According to Simone, lots of the twins' favorite songs or television shows or movies were *popular.* And just like that, things Nora and Louisa had enjoyed became tainted—at least for one of them.

LOUISA HAD BEEN SITTING on the linoleum floor in the museum with her sketch pad for almost an hour, and the leg bent beneath her had started to go numb. She stood awkwardly and tried to stomp the feeling back into her thigh and butt, which were tingling uncomfortably. She limped back and forth under the sign for the entrance to the small corridor where she'd been drawing: The Leonard C. Sanford Hall of North American Birds. She liked that part of the museum for a bunch of reasons. First, it was named after a Leonard and so was she, after the grandfather she'd never met (Nora was named after their father's father, Norman). She liked that the hall wasn't nearly as crowded as the more popular exhibits, the dinosaurs or the blue whale—on a weekend those rooms were nearly impossible to navigate, never mind finding a spot to sit in peace with her sketch pad. North American Birds was a dated, musty exhibit of field specimens tacked onto walls behind glass. It was more a corridor to pass through than a destination.

And she loved the bird specimens, even if they were old-fashioned and a little creepy. Her favorite case was the one displaying "Swallows, Flycatchers, and Larks" because the birds were in flight and almost looked alive. Her least favorite: "Herons, Ibises, and Swans," because the large birds looked awkward and uncomfortable. Purely for vernacular, she loved the case she was sitting in front of now: "Wrens, Nuthatches, Creepers, Titmice, Mimic Thrushes, Jays, and Crows." She wished she knew what a mimic thrush mimicked and whether titmice ate mice. She supposed she could Google, but she preferred to wonder.

But even in the relatively sparsely populated corridor, she was rarely left alone. People still constantly looked over her shoulder and asked questions about what she was drawing or why or, even worse, just stood watching in awkward silence. And the kids! Pestering her nonstop and asking if they could draw, too. Their parents were just as bad.

"Maybe if you ask nicely," one mother had said to her son while Louisa was trying to sketch the larks in flight, right before her leg went numb, "this nice lady will share her paper and show you how to draw."

"These aren't for kids," Louisa said, sharply, picking up her charcoal pencils and pastels from the floor.

"How come she won't share?" the little boy whined.

"I don't know, honey," his mother said. "Not everyone is a good sharer like you."

"Jesus," Louisa said, slamming her pad shut. The mother threw her a dirty look and walked away. Louisa started to gather the sheets of paper on the floor around her. One wasn't terrible. It was of a little boy who'd thrown a tantrum after his father wouldn't buy him a stuffed seal in the gift shop. He'd flung himself to the ground and buried his head in his arms, shoulders heaving. Louisa had sketched him quickly and she'd managed to capture the bereft set of his shoulders, his legs swinging in frustration, how one of his hands reached out, fingers splayed, toward the door of the toy shop where his object of desire was cruelly out of reach.

"Seal-y! Seal-y!" the boy had wailed, his father finally having to carry him kicking and screaming into a nearby restroom.

The other drawings of people, quickly sketched as she watched visitors moving through the long halls, weren't exactly embarrassing, but they weren't great. She never got the proportion of features-to-face exactly right. The reason the little boy came out better, she knew, was because his face was concealed. She didn't want to think about what it meant that she couldn't draw eyes, the windows to the soul, the most important thing an artist had to master. It was not lost on her that all the birds in the Leonard C. Sanford Hall were eyeless, tiny bits of cotton inserted in their eye sockets.

"So are you going to art school?" Simone had asked once after Louisa let her look at some of her sketches.

"No," Louisa said. She'd mentioned art school once and her mother had blanched. Art school, to Melody, was not really school.

"Why not?" Simone said.

"Because I want to get a good general education," Louisa said, mimicking Melody's words. "Art school is more like trade school."

"What's wrong with trade school?"

Louisa laughed nervously. She wasn't sure if Simone was being serious or sarcastic.

"I mean it," Simone said, still paging through Louisa's drawings. "Medical school is trade school, so is law school."

"But that's graduate school, it's different," Nora said. Sometimes she thought Simone picked on Louisa a little.

"True," Simone said, agreeably. "But if you love art and you want to draw or paint, why wouldn't you go to a place where you can get better doing the thing you love?"

"Some of the schools we've looked at have excellent art programs," Louisa said.

"How many have you looked at?"

"Fourteen," Nora said.

Simone burst out laughing. "You've looked at *fourteen* colleges already?"

"It's fun. We like it," Louisa said. She knew she sounded defensive, and in truth she'd be happy to never look at another college again. "It's good to be able to compare, so we know which ones are the right fit."

Simone shook her head and snorted a little. "Wow. You all are *seriously* drinking the admissions Kool-Aid." She plucked one of the drawings from the pile and handed it to Louisa; it was one of her favorites, a soft pastel of the front of the museum at dusk. She'd done it quickly and kept the rendering loose; the museum looked more like a mountain than a building, and the street beneath with its streaming cars resembled a rushing river of movement and color. "This is really beautiful," Simone said, sounding more sincere than Louisa had ever heard her. "I know exactly what it is, it's realistic in that way, but it's also kind of abstract." She turned the page vertically. "Look, it even works from this angle—the perspective, I mean." Louisa was surprised and pleased to see she was right. Simone handed the drawing back to Louisa. "This is tight. Frame it. You should do more like that one. And you should really look at Pratt and Parsons. RISD, too. I'll think of some more places for your list."

LOUISA CHECKED HER WATCH. It was late and she had to find Simone and Nora who always seemed to lose track of time. They'd agreed to meet in the Hall of Pacific Peoples, which appeared to be empty except for a French family gathered around the fiberglass replica of an Easter Island head that loomed over one end of the room. As Louisa approached, they asked her to take their picture with one of their phones and thanked her profusely when she showed them a shot where everyone was smiling, eyes open. She decided to take a quick look at the Margaret Mead display, which she loved. As she headed toward the glass cases, she passed by a small dark corridor and then backed up, embarrassed, because she'd interrupted a couple in an intimate embrace, only to register before she turned around that one of the couple was wearing red Swedish perforated clogs just like hers. And Nora's.

Louisa felt her neck and face become feverish. She wanted to run, but she couldn't move. Nora was leaning against the wall and her shirt was unbuttoned to the waist. Simone's hands were moving under the shirt. Nora's eyes were closed, her arms limp at her sides. Louisa could see Simone's hand moving up toward Nora's white utilitarian bra. "Please," Louisa heard Nora say and then watched as Simone's thumb stroked Nora's nipple through the worn cotton. Both women groaned. Louisa turned and ran.

CHAPTER FOURTEEN

Corporal Vinnie Massaro knew that the kids who came into his father's pizza place called him Robocop. Whatever. One of these days he was going to reach out and grab one of them with the claw at the end of his terrifyingly complicated prosthetic arm, probably the chubby redhead; he'd wipe the smirk off that kid's face. Maybe he'd grab him with his good arm, his flesh-and-blood arm, and let the kid dangle a few inches off the ground while he stroked his fat, freckled cheek with one steel finger, making him cry and beg for mercy, apologizing through heaving sobs. Vinnie could see the bubbles of snot now.

Stop.

Rewind.

This was not the type of imaginary scenario Vinnie was supposed to indulge, it was not *positive* or *affirming,* it was not how he'd been instructed to *manage his anger.* Stop and rewind was one of the *techniques* he was supposed to *employ,* according to his anger therapist,

who shouldn't be confused with his physical therapist or his prosthetic therapist or the occupational therapist who had been the one to
suggest anger management when Vinnie used the metal pincers of his
brand-new government-financed limb to eviscerate a toy duck into a
million bits of foam the day he couldn't manage to lift and lower the
yellow duckie even once.

Vinnie took a deep breath. Closed his eyes. *Rewind. Rewind.
Rewind.* He pictured himself walking over to the table of kids and
laughing along with them, showing them his arm, genially explaining
how sophisticated the technology was, how certain of his nerve end-
ings had been surgically regenerated so that he could actually control
the artificial limb with his brain. *I guess I am Robocop,* he'd say, *part
man, part robot.*

Wow, the kids would say. *Can we touch it? Sure,* Vinnie would
reply, then laugh and cuff one of them lightly on the shoulder (with
the real arm). *Go ahead,* he'd say, *touch it. It's as good as my old
arm. It doesn't get hot or cold or cut or bruised. It's better than the
old arm!*

Better, that is, unless you were Amy, Vinnie's ex-fiancée, in which
case the new arm was definitely not better than the old arm. If you
were Amy, you'd pretend to be fine with the new arm, plaster a grim
smile on your face, spout platitudes like "It's what's on the inside that
counts" until the day when Vinnie, finally starting to feel at ease, casually put his arm around her waist and she flinched. Vinnie didn't feel
the flinch, of course (*Hey, kids! The new arm doesn't feel betrayal!*),
but he saw it; he wasn't blind. Worse, because he'd unthinkingly
touched her with the robot arm, he didn't even get the pleasure of
feeling his fingers sink a little into the soft ribbon of flesh above her
hips that he loved so much, didn't get to feel anything before he saw
her recoil and then look at him, petrified and—

Stop. Rewind.

In his mind he went back to talking to the kids at the table and
imagined how even the redhead would stop snickering. How they'd all
be impressed when he picked up the tiny, plastic, greasy saltshaker.

Not the bigger cardboard container of garlic salt, whose mere presence he found offensive. Don't get him started on how the Mexicans in the neighborhood covered their perfectly seasoned pizza with the garlic salt and sometimes even hot sauce that they'd take out of their pockets in little travel bottles, as if his grandfather, whose recipe Vinnie and his father, Vito, still followed, hadn't learned to make tomato sauce in Naples where they fucking invented tomato sauce.

Stop.

He'd pick up the real saltshaker and daintily shake a few grains into his fleshy palm, throwing them over his left shoulder to thwart the devil like his nonna taught him. The kids would applaud.

Yeah, Vinnie would say, winding up his demonstration with something *positive* and *forward looking,* trying to avoid *bitter* and *self-loathing. I'm one of the lucky ones,* he'd say, winking at them like he was a goddamn movie star.

HERE WAS THE THING: Vinnie *was* one of the lucky ones and he knew it. He could have lost more than one limb. He could be dead. When the IED exploded, he could have been walking on the left side of the path instead of the right like his buddy Justin who was alive but not. Traumatic brain injury they called it, instead of what it was, fucking retarded. Justin, back home in Virginia sitting and drooling in front of a television set all day, every day, bathed by his mother, spoon-fed by his father, wheeled out onto the porch for a little sun and fresh air so the neighbors could peer out their windows and feel blessed, shake their heads and say, *There but for the grace of God.* Justin, carried to bed by his brother every night, only to wake up the next day and start the whole depressing regimen all over again until he finally did kick it and was out of his misery for good. Justin, who had been five measly days away from completing his tour and going home—whole.

So yes. Vinnie was lucky. Fortunate. He was still strong, mostly healthy. He could take over the family businesses whenever he wanted, not only the pizza place but also a nice Italian grocery across the street, mostly imports, that his grandfather had opened on Arthur Avenue back when the neighborhood was all Italian, only Italian, before the ever-increasing influx of Mexican families over the decades. He had family around who were helpful and supportive. Fuck Amy. Maybe he got too angry sometimes, but he was working on it. He was trying.

Now that the kids had left the pizza joint (snickering at him, he knew it), he was a little calmer. Calmer that is until he saw Matilda Rodriguez coming down the street and his fury smoldered anew because there she was, walking down the street, again on the crutches, swinging herself around like she was the fucking Queen of fucking Sheba and Arthur Avenue in the Bronx was her kingdom. Waiting for people to move out of her way, hold doors open for her, offer to carry her bags. What was next? A rickshaw? A fucking velvet cape over an icy puddle?

It wasn't right. She should be walking.

He put his head down, took a deep breath. *Rewind, rewind, rewind.* He tried to *employ* an *imaging technique* using a *positive historical frame of reference.*

He thought about when he met Matilda, during her first weeks at the rehab center when he was there doing the tedious work of managing his new arm. He thought about how upbeat and determined and flirtatious she'd been then, not just with him—he wasn't an idiot—with everyone, but still, it had been nice. How she sang a lot and called everyone Mami or Papi, no matter his or her age in relation to hers. He remembered her swinging dark hair and bright smile, which reminded him about a particular pink sweater she wore during those first weeks. He thought about how that pink sweater would pull across her breasts when she was positioned on the crutches, making it apparent that she hadn't bothered with a bra, riding up to reveal her tiny waist. He thought about how he might like to touch that pink sweater, which made him think of his mechanical arm and how if he did touch the sweater, the material might snag and maybe even rip and start to unravel. Matilda would look down at her damaged sweater and her face would fill with regret and maybe even a little disgust. And then she would look back at him with her lovely almond-shaped eyes and—he could see it perfectly—they'd fill with pity.

"CORPORAL!" MATILDA, in the doorway of the pizza place now. She was with her cousin Fernando, the one who'd visited her repeatedly in rehab when he was on break from law school. He was carrying her purse and all her grocery bags. Her eyes were watery with cold, and her smile was tentative; she knew how Vinnie felt about the crutches, about her not using the prosthesis.

"I'm so hungry. I swear I could eat five slices right now," she said, moving into the restaurant, toward one of the booths. He watched Fernando help her sit and get comfortable, slide her crutches beneath the table. Vinnie concentrated on a *nonjudgmental* greeting. He counted to ten before he approached, tucking the damp dishtowel he carried into the waistband of his jeans. Matilda sat and looked up nervously as he came closer, wiping her slightly runny nose with a Vito's Pizzeria napkin. He leaned a little on the table with his good hand, moved his face closer to hers.

"Where the *fuck* is your *foot*," he said.

CHAPTER FIFTEEN

The night of the accident the previous summer, Leo had sat in the Emergency Room bracingly, horrifyingly alert. Hungover. Petrified. He kept replaying the moment of the crash, Matilda's screams, and the far more frightening moment when she'd stopped screaming and he was afraid she was dead.

They were in adjacent rooms in the ER, he and Matilda. He could hear her occasional moans and the doctors talking about the possibility of reattachment. Her right foot had been nearly severed at the ankle. A hospital translator was talking to her parents.

An old family friend from the sheriff's department had made a call to George Plumb from the accident site around the same time that Leo had called Bea. George and Bea left the wedding and arrived at the hospital together.

George immediately discussed containment with Leo. "I don't care what you remember," he said to him softly. "At this moment, you don't remember anything. You've had a head trauma." He nodded toward Leo's bleeding chin. "Got it?"

Leo was watching Bea listen through the curtain, not knowing whether to hope that her Spanish was still strong or had, along with many of her talents, diminished to ineffectual. She was listening hard; her head was bent, and Leo noticed that the tops of her shoulders were slightly sunburned. Her dress, like almost everything she owned, was vintage—short, black, and sleeveless—and she was clutching herself, as if trying to stay warm in the chill of the air-conditioned hospital.

Bea wasn't cold; she was concentrating on understanding as much of the conversation as possible, which was pretty much everything. She was losing some medical terms, but she understood when the translator explained to Matilda's parents the slim possibility of a successful reattachment. He detailed the complications, the chances of rejection, the powerful pharmaceuticals and lengthy hospitalization and rehabilitation Matilda would need in the coming weeks and months. The very, very long road ahead with a reattachment that could still result in an eventual amputation. Matilda's father told the translator they had no insurance, that they were, in fact, in the country illegally.

"That doesn't matter right now," she heard the translator say, his tone urgent but kind. "You are entitled to the proper treatment."

One of the nurses gently interrupted. "We don't have much time to decide if you want to reattach. We'd need to prepare the foot."

Bea could hear Matilda's mother address the doctor and her husband in heavily accented English. "What is a life without a foot?" she said. The anguish in her voice was harrowing. "What kind of future will she have? How will she walk? How will she work?"

"No, Mami, no." Matilda spoke from the bed, her voice slurred and dreamy, from shock and morphine. "The man from the car is going to help me. He knows people. Music people. It was just an accident. A bad accident. He is going to help me. No more waitressing."

"Your music?" the mother said, incredulous. She reverted to Spanish, her tone bitter and scared. "You lose your foot and this man is going to make you a star?"

"I need to get out of here," Matilda pleaded.

The translator was speaking to the doctor, but Bea couldn't make out what they were saying. Bea walked over to Leo, who was still clutching a bloody piece of Matilda's white blouse in his hands. The nurse had cleaned the wound and left to get sutures so she could stitch Leo's chin. George pointed to the curtain. "Pick up anything interesting?"

Bea hesitated. What she'd just heard wasn't her business; the information was not hers to pass along. She knew George.

"Bea?"

"Kind of," Bea said. "They're deciding whether to amputate."

George sighed. "Not great news."

Bea turned to Leo. In the fluorescent light of the ER, chin split, eyes bloodshot and watery, gaze unfocused, he looked beaten and scared. He tried to smile. He looked, for a minute, like a little boy, and she took his hand.

"I don't know what happened," he said to her. "One minute we were going—"

"Shhh." George stopped Leo by raising a palm. "Time for all that later."

Leo held Bea's hand so tightly her fingers were numb. "Careful, Superman," she said, wriggling her fingers and loosening his grip a little.

"Superman. Right." Leo lightly touched his chin and winced. "I could use Superman right now. Have him fly and reverse the earth's rotation to go back in time."

"Before the really dry crab cakes were passed?" Bea said, trying to distract Leo from the crying she could hear on the other side of the curtain.

"More like to early 2002," he said.

That sounded good to Bea—2002, the year before he sold Speak-EasyMedia and met Victoria; Tuck still alive; her book newly published. The year that was the dividing line, in Bea's mind, of the Leo she loved, the Leo who was one of her closest friends, gradually disappearing and morphing into someone unrecognizable.

Leo looked like he might cry. She was scared for him. "How did I get here?" he said. She was trying not to stare at the split in his chin. He was going to have a scar. "How did I fuck up this badly?"

In spite of the circumstances, Bea's heart billowed to hear something approaching self-reflection and regret, something hinting at an apology coming from Leo. It had been a long time.

"It's going to be okay," she said, feeling helpless.

"I don't know about that," Leo said. There was a slight commotion on the other side of the curtain. The parents seemed to be arguing in Spanish, and the translator was trying to intervene. "I think it might be the furthest thing from okay," he said.

Bea put her hand on Leo's back, and he leaned into her a little. She motioned George closer and spoke softly and quickly, before she could change her mind. "I heard something else."

"What?" George said.

"The parents are undocumented."

George smiled for the first time since arriving at the ER. "*That* is much better news. Good work." He pointed a finger at Leo. "This is still going to cost you a fucking fortune, but I can use this."

From the other side of the curtain, Matilda's voice rose above the ongoing bickering, louder and more insistent. "Tómelo, Mami, tómelo!"

Tómelo. Take it. Take the foot. Then the translator speaking to the surgeon: "They want you to amputate."

"I think that's the right decision," the surgeon said. "We'll get a clean cut. Leave as much bone as possible."

"Not a fiction class, something else. Poetry. Nonfiction. Just to get the wheels greased. It might be fun."

"Like go to the New School and sign up for Introduction to Poetry?" Bea was pissed. She had an MFA.

"No, of course not. Something at your level. Like how about Tucker McMillan's class at Columbia. He's amazing. You could audit."

Bea ignored Stephanie's suggestion only to find herself a few days later at a party standing before Tucker. She was mesmerized. He was appealingly craggy in the way of some older men who seemed to finally grow into their generous features in middle age. She'd seen pictures of him when he was younger and thinner and seemed burdened by his own physicality, nose too large, mouth too generous, ears too wide—but when she met him, some alchemy of time and girth and weathering of his face made him beautiful. And his voice. It was one of the biggest regrets of her life (and *that* was saying something) that she didn't have his voice on tape anywhere.

"Ah, Beatrice Plumb," he'd said, taking one of her hands in both of his and giving her his full attention. "As pretty as your picture." Bea hadn't known then if he was making fun of her. It was shortly after the "Glitterary" piece came out and although the photographer had taken what felt like hundreds of pictures of her for that article—at a desk, leaning against a window, curled in a chair—he'd chosen to use one of maybe three shots he'd snapped at the very end of the day when she was exhausted and had collapsed on her bed for a minute while he was changing lenses. "Hold it right there," he'd said and had stood on a chair at the end of the bed and shot her from above, reclining, arms stretched to her side, looking sleepy and patently alluring (she *had* been flirting with the photographer a little, but not with *the world*). The picture had been ridiculed on various media sites, written about more than anything she said in the article. She was still angry about the stupid photo, which, in any context other than work, she would have quite liked.

"Not the one I would have chosen," she'd said, trying to sound dismissive but not defensive.

"Why on earth not." Tuck stared at her so intently she backed up a few steps. "The yellow dress, the parasol, those hanging ducks. I thought it was brilliant. Strong."

"Oh," she said, relieved. "I like that photo, too."

"I didn't know there were others," he said. "I'll have to find them."

"That's the best one," she said. She could feel her face and neck flush and tried to back away. His stare was so direct. It was exhilarating.

"Stay for a bit." He put his hand on her arm and her entire being lit up. "Everyone here is dull. Stay and tell me an interesting story."

She showed up in his class the following week and every week after that for the rest of the year. She was a good student, serious and hardworking, quiet and unassuming. She wasn't a great poet, but Stephanie had been right; it was fun to do something new, something without a particular result or pressure to perform attached.

Bea waited until she was no longer Tucker's student to sleep with him. He assumed her reluctance was because he was almost twenty years older, married with grown children, but it wasn't any of those things. Bea simply didn't want to have sex with the teacher, didn't want that to be the beginning of their story and by then—when it wasn't a question of *if* but *when* they would be together—it was clear to both of them that they would, in fact, have a story.

Or at least that was the narrative she wove for Tucker, and it was partly true, but something else was true, too—she loved the power his desire afforded her. Her inability to produce anything significant of the novel made her feel like such an imposter, frightened even, and his desire was a balm. She loved the secret of what they were surely going to do. She flirted with him mercilessly at the beginning. Requesting private conferences that she dressed for as if she was going to be undressed, even though she knew she wasn't. She carried his lust around like a magic coin in her pocket that she could spend when she decided she was ready.

He acquired the apartment on the Upper West Side shortly after they began their affair, wanting a place where he could spend time with her that was not the cockroach-infested studio she rented on the Lower East Side with the occasional junkie passed out in the lobby. He would have left his wife—his kids were grown and his wife taught in Dublin most of the year—but Bea liked their arrangement. She needed solitude.

When she grouped the passing years into logical increments, it didn't feel so confounding. The story collection published and then a year in Seville, trying (failing) to write what she was calling her bildungsroman. The year after Seville when she returned to New York and accepted every invite—readings, conferences, interviews, panels—and met Tuck. The following year when Tuck made her decline every invite because she was writing (finally!) and the two subsequent years (still writing) when the invites stopped. The year she set aside what she'd started to call a *spiritual coming-of-age* and went to work with Paul Underwood because her advance was long spent. The year she threw that away and went back to the bil-dungsroman. Tucker's stroke and aftermath—two years when she tended to him and loved him and didn't write. His death and the year she spent broken by grief and trying, once and for all, to salvage the novel (now a combination of the first and second, a not-very-spiritual unwieldy coming-of-age disaster). Last year when she gave it up for good. Eleven years of life and heartbreak and work and failed paragraphs—when she broke it down like that, it didn't seem so inexplicable, but what had she done every day? How had so many years of days gone by with nearly nothing to show outside of her work at *Paper Fibres*? No impressive salary. No children. No partner. She didn't even have a lousy pet.

When Tucker died, she'd prepared to vacate the premises. It was the one time in her life she'd asked Francie for an advance on The Nest, the only time in her life she even thought about The Nest. She'd been stunned to receive the call from Tucker's attorney saying that the apartment was hers. She owned it outright, no mortgage. Tucker had worried about her; he was dismissive and dubious about the neb-ulous legal and financial structure of The Nest.

"If you're really receiving a trust, there should be financial state-ments, an executor other than that loon of a mother, someone protect-ing your interests."

She'd laughed at him. "You do not understand the people you're talking about. This is just how my family works."

Well, he'd been righter than she could have imagined. But thanks to him, she was okay with how and when and if Leo paid her back. The apartment was her nest, literally and metaphorically. She could stay there forever and manage on a modest income. She could sell and move someplace cheaper and live contentedly for a long time. Her family didn't know she owned; it wasn't anybody's business.

Bea didn't dwell on the sum of cash Tucker also left her that was almost the exact amount of the portion of her advance she ended up having to pay back to her publisher. She preferred to think of it as an unsettling but lucky coincidence and not what deep down she knew: something Tucker recognized about her that she couldn't admit to herself.

In last night's dream, Tucker was trying to tell her something important. He was jabbing furiously at a piece of paper with his good hand, and she was unable to make out the words, keep her eyes open and focus. She wondered, not for the first time, what he would think of her new work. She imagined he would approve.

She stood and started straightening the mess on the table: piles of notebooks; a handful of fountain pens and two bottles of ink; spools of merino wool and a hand spindle. Bea wanted to knit mittens for Melody's twins, had a few ideas about how to work the yarn. She picked up a small plastic bag of weed and her rolling papers. For a fleeting moment, she considered pretending it was still Sunday, get-ting high and knitting all day. She could call in sick; Paul wouldn't care. But she shouldn't. She couldn't.

The radiator finally came on. She picked up the *Collected Poems: Edna St. Vincent Millay,* which she'd been reading since she awoke, thinking about Tuck and the poems he loved. Her fingers were so stiff, she dropped all 758 pages and the book landed on the uneven, hardwood floor with a boom and a healthy reverb. Before she even had a chance to brace herself, her downstairs neighbor started banging on his ceiling with a broomstick. *He must carry that broom around the apartment with him,* Bea thought. *He must sleep with the damn broom.* Did he even sleep? Or did he just sit, alert, clutching his broomstick, waiting for her auditory trespasses.

"Sorry, Harry," she yelled down through the radiator.

She wasn't sorry. She disliked Harry, the seventysomething widower who had always lived beneath her. Over the years, she'd realized that he was easily placated by a regular string of verbal apologies. The more she ignored his banging, the more hair-trigger the banging became. He'd pound when she dropped an apple, walked two steps in her stack-heeled boots. Harry was unpleasant but she understood he was lonely and that their ritual comforted him, connected the noises of her life with the silence of his and that even if the connection was relentless complaint and apology, their call-and-response interaction settled him.

Still, when was he going to get a little deaf? Too feeble to live on his own? Sometimes she fantasized about Harry dying and his family offering his apartment to her at a good price, well-below-market-value. His son liked her; he called her sometimes to make sure Harry was doing okay. He lived in Chicago and didn't get back as often as he should. If she owned Harry's apartment, she would break through the floor, put in a simple spiral staircase like the people on the D line down the hall had done. She'd have two floors and never have to move again. She could have a real office with an actual library. A guest room.

Of course, even given some kind of ridiculously discounted insider price, she was in no position to buy anything—not without The Nest. Thinking about The Nest made her think about her new pages (they were good!) and then about Leo, which led back to Dream Tucker, and then she lit a joint. She wondered if Leo would stop by the office today. Maybe she'd ask him to lunch and take the plunge. She imagined handing him her new work and him reading and reacting with enthusiasm and excitement, saying *I knew you had this in you!*

He'd been her biggest fan once. He'd watched out for her. She remembered when she was a freshman in high school, Leo a senior, and she'd let Conor Bellingham do things to her in the backseat of his car in the school parking lot after a meeting for the literary magazine; Leo was the editor, she was on staff. As she and Conor made out, she was simultaneously ecstatic and disappointed. Ecstatic because she'd had her eye on Conor for weeks. In addition to being handsome and popular and the class president, he'd submitted a shockingly good story to the magazine and she hadn't been able to stop thinking about it, or him, or the last line of the story: "Angry, and half in love with her, and tremendously sorry, I turned away." Disappointed because he refused to talk about writing. She didn't get it. Or how someone who, frankly, seemed a little doltish could write something so moving.

"Have some more," he'd said, passing a small flask. The flask was gleaming silver and heavy in her hand. "Irish whiskey. My father's. The good stuff."

"Some of my favorite writers are Irish," she'd said.

"Yeah? Well, I guarantee they drink this stuff."

"Who are your favorite writers?" She smiled brightly, trying to get him to look at her and not out the window.

Conor shook his head and laughed a little. "You have a one-track mind, you know that?"

She shrugged and bent her nose to the flask and breathed deeply, imagining she was smelling Ireland—the surprisingly sweet fermentation and then the quick sting and heat, the heady aroma of peat and smoke.

"To the old sod," she'd said, tipping the flask and taking a long sip. She liked it. Conor liked it. Conor liked her! She drank some more and they laughed, about what exactly she wasn't sure, and then they were kissing again and his hands started moving lower and she stiffened. "Relax," he said. She took a long sip from the flask and then another. She could feel something on the cold, steely surface. She held it up toward the window and in the light of a streetlamp read the engraving.

"What does 'Trapper' mean?" she asked him.

"Nothing. A silly nickname."

"I think I should probably go." She realized she was getting very drunk.

"Don't go," he said.

"Look outside." Her voice sounded thick. "It's starting to snow. I should get home." Out the window, it was dark and she was having trouble focusing. Conor moved closer, his hand successfully creeping beneath her skirt this time.

"'The newspapers were right,'" he said, whispering into her ear, "'snow was general all over Ireland.'"

"Joyce," she whispered, turning back to him.

"Yes," he said. "Joyce. I like James Joyce. So there's a writer I like." And that was it. Her resolve melted and her clenched knees unfurled like the petals of a ripening peony. She didn't think anything when he didn't call over the weekend. And told herself he must not have seen her when she walked by his locker early Monday morning. At lunch, she strolled over to the table where he was sitting and stood for a minute, waiting for him to see her and to smile and invite her to sit. After far too many beats, after his friends were staring at her, half of them confused, half of them smirking, he looked up and raised an eyebrow.

"Hi," she said, trying to hold on to confusion because what came after that, she knew, was going to be worse.

"Can I help you with something, Beatrice?"

She knew her face was flooding with color, knew she was probably flushing from head to toe; she could feel her *knees* sweat. Somehow she mustered enough breath and energy to turn and walk away. She heard him mumble something to the rest of the table, and they all burst out laughing, a few pounding the table in uproarious amusement.

(Years later, in a feminist literature class during a discussion on pornography, she would hear the term "beaver" for the first time and would remember with shattering clarity the feel of that flask in her mouth, the sulfur taste of silver, the smell of whiskey and peat. She would burn with shame for days, weeks, realizing what "Trapper" indicated and what it had meant when Conor slid his hand beneath the elastic of her underwear that night and whispered, very much to himself, *Seventeen.*)

"I'm so dumb," she'd said over and over to Leo, crying and wiping her nose. "I just can't believe I was so dumb."

"Conor Bellingham?" Leo didn't get it. That guy was a loser.

"He wrote the best story," she said. "Did you read it? Did you read the last line?"

"The one he lifted from *The Great Gatsby*? Yeah, I read it. He's lucky I didn't turn him in for plagiarizing."

Bea didn't think it was possible to feel worse, but she bent at the waist and groaned. "I'm so, so dumb."

Leo wrote the limerick the next day using the byline "Anonymous." He typed it up and made copies and before lunch nearly the whole school had enjoyed his handiwork, featuring an unnamed student, his string of romantic conquests, and the moment in the backseat of his car when the boy would get the girl alone and inevitably, lamentably, prematurely ejaculate. The identity of the boy was obvious to the students but so cleverly done, so easily denied, that it didn't cause trouble for Leo. And then there was this: For Conor himself to object would mean casting himself as a premature ejaculator, which Leo knew he'd never do. At first, everyone thought Bea was "Anonymous," and even though she never denied it, any number of women Conor had mistreated claimed credit for the piece and then started writing their *own* punishing rhymes (with Leo's subtle encouragement and often with his assistance) about Conor and soon other school miscreants. Finally the administration stepped in and put a stop to anything by the increasingly notorious and multiheaded Anonymous that became the highlight of that school year. Later, Bea would think how the silly limerick was really the start of what Leo would create with *SpeakEasy*—at the beginning anyway, before it turned kind of desperate and dirty.

She opened her Millay to one of the poems Tuck had loved and sometimes read to her: *I pray if you love me, bear my joy.* She was too antsy to read the whole thing. She refilled her cup of tea. Jesus, she was horny. How long had it been? She went into her room and rummaged through her bedside drawer for her miniature vibrator. She pulled it out and switched it on. Nothing. The batteries were dead.

She looked up and saw herself standing in front of the mirror, braids sloppy and uneven from sleep, some of the hairs around her face turned gray and wiry. She was winter pale and her eyes were bloodshot and unfocused from the weed. Was this who she was now? A middle-aged woman with a spent vibrator and a pile of typed pages that she was hoarding like they were dead cats? She was extremely high. She could hear Lena Novak's voice as if Lena were standing in her bedroom. "It must be hard—being Beatrice Plumb."

"Must be hard to be me," she said to her reflection. "Hard to be Bea." She threw the vibrator back in the drawer and went to get her coat. *Bear my joy,* that's what she would say to Leo. Read these pages and tell me they're good and let me have them and *bear my fucking joy.*

CHAPTER SEVENTEEN

W eeks after (barely) graduating from college, Jack moved to Greenwich Village with a very particular goal in mind: to have sex, lots and lots of sex. Vassar had been somewhat disappointing in that regard. At first, Jack attributed the lack of free and easy fucking that he had assumed would come with his student ID and highly coveted dorm single to statistics: A former women's college, there were fewer gay men than women on campus. Then he assumed the problem was AIDS, which was cutting a terrifying swath through the gay community. But the gay population at Vassar seemed more angry than scared. Ninety miles south in New York City, Larry Kramer was sending up his clarion cry of outrage and the mostly well-to-do, mostly white sons and daughters of Vassar were complying—in spades. They organized, marched, protested, heckled, debated, and demanded. Outrage, Jack learned, was not an aphrodisiac; it was exhausting.

Jack wasn't against activism precisely, but campus politics seemed trivial to him, almost laughable. It was activism of the easiest sort, run by idealistic youth barely out of their teens who never left the peachy enclave of their campus in Poughkeepsie. Enlightenment fueled by a heightened sense of mortality was certainly logical, but it also seemed blatantly self-serving in a way that infuriated Jack. Years later, he would experience the same intolerance about the surge of patriotism that swept through New York after 9/11—the run on American flags by people who would also confess in lowered tones how they'd recently put their place on the market while looking at houses in New Jersey or Connecticut or in their hometowns somewhere in the Midwest, "nobody's flying a plane into the Gateway Arch." True patriotism, Jack believed, would have been for his fellow Americans to look inward after 9/11 and accept a little blame, admit the attacks had happened, in part, *because* of who they were in the world, not in spite of it. But no. Suddenly at every public function his previously godless neighbors would stand with hands on heart to earnestly intone the Pledge of Allegiance and sing "God Bless America."

"I wish Kate Smith had never been born," Jack said at a dinner party one night, inciting a nasty argument about patriotism and its relative merits. The woman sitting across the table went on and on about the duties of civilians during wartime and in the face of terrorism until he broke off a piece of his baguette and threw it at her. He'd meant to startle her, shut her up, not hit her square on the chin. He and Walker had missed dessert.

The mini ACT UP protests at Vassar felt self-indulgent to Jack. How daring was it to stage a "Kiss In" in front of one of the most sexually diverse and accepting populations for miles and miles? It had all felt frivolous and half-assed and bloated with self-regard.

Still, when Jack's best friend at college, Arthur, took a job with the Gay Men's Health Crisis and invited Jack to share an apartment on Barrow Street, Jack jumped at the chance. He would have preferred Chelsea, where the gay scene was a little younger, a little more hip, but Barrow Street was great. Barrow Street was classy in a way Chelsea wasn't, historical, only blocks away from the Stonewall Inn. Sure, he told Arthur, he'd be *thrilled* to volunteer at GMHC, was *desperate* to get to the front lines, do something that mattered.

But what Jack really wanted was to have sex. Not earnest, leftist, collegiate sex—sex that required far too much conversation and not nearly enough lube—but Greenwich Village, Christopher Street, drop your pants but leave on those leather chaps, mindless, mind-blowing, anonymous sex.

So it was with a certain karmic comeuppance, Jack would realize later, that mere months after arriving in the West Village, he would meet the love of his life, Walker Bennett.

WALKER LIKED TO SAY that he'd been born gay and middle-aged. He'd grown up in Greenwich Village; his parents were roving adjunct professors, self-anointed socialists who intermittently practiced open marriage and dabbled in bisexuality and refused the tenure track because it was nothing more than a union to protect the interests of the already-coddled upper class. When Walker came out to them in high school, it had all the Sturm und Drang of him announcing that he was switching from violin to cello.

Early on, Walker knew he wanted a different kind of life from his parents who lived paycheck to paycheck, collected furniture on the street the night before the bulk garbage pickups, counted coins in the sofa cushion to pay for take-out fried rice. After graduating from law school in the mid-1980s, he returned to the West Village, planning to work at the same corporate firm where he'd done his summer internship, only to find himself deluged by neighbors and old family friends, mostly gay men, who were suddenly getting sick and dying in alarming numbers and under mysterious circumstances. They wanted Walker to help them write a will or fight an eviction or understand their disability insurance. Within months, Walker had more work than he could handle, some funneled to him from GMHC, some from the prominent, often still-closeted gay business community. They trusted Walker. The premium he charged his wealthier clients allowed him to take on a lot of work pro bono, which he loved. After only one year, he was able to hire help, rent office space. Soon he was a neighborhood fixture: Walker, the genial, slightly overweight neighborhood attorney who would handle pretty much anything—even if you were broke, especially if you were queer.

The night Walker met Jack, he'd wandered into the raucous bar down near the Christopher Street pier on a whim. He usually preferred the quieter gay watering holes, but he'd had a long day. He was still in his work clothes, and as he made his way through the lively Friday night crowd, he spotted Jack, who was difficult not to notice, bare chested and wearing extremely short shorts, dancing by himself, ecstatically, to "I Will Survive." Walker hated that stupid fucking song. Everyone around them was most assuredly *not* surviving. Two of his clients, both sick and quarantined at St. Vincent's, had died that week, making six in just the last month. He needed a drink. He needed to get really, really drunk. As he approached the bar, Jack started waving at him, calling him over. Walker wondered if they'd met before. Was he a client? A friend of a client?

"Have we met?" he yelled at Jack, trying to be heard above the deafening, thumping disco beat. Jack shook his head no and looked Walker up and down. Then he leaned close to Walker's ear; his cheek was damp and smelled of perspiration and some kind of too-sweet cologne. "That suit looks really uncomfortable," Jack said, his voice hoarse from singing. He handed Walker a shot of tequila.

And in a move so out of character, so weirdly un-Walker-like and spontaneous and defiant and hopeful, Walker tipped back the shot, swallowed, put the empty glass on the bar, grabbed the back of Jack's sweaty head, and kissed him full on the lips.

Jack kissed Walker back, then pulled away and grinned, and said, "How about we start the weekend by undoing that belt?" They'd been together ever since.

STANDING AT HIS AND WALKER'S BEDROOM WINDOW in Greenwich Village (technically the far, *far* west village; their building was as far west as you could go without living on a houseboat in the

Hudson), Jack watched a Carnival cruise ship glide up the center of the river, heading to collect its passengers at Pier 88. He'd probably see the boat later that evening, being tugged in reverse until it reached the open harbor and could swing south. A cruise sounded good to Jack right now, anything to get him out of New York and to take his mind off Leo and his massive Leo-related migraine.

The afternoon was so cold that the bike paths along the river were deserted. The Christopher Street pier, across the way, was no longer the decrepit, free-for-all cruising spot it had been when he and Walker moved in, more than twenty years ago, a place you could go for an easy afternoon frolic or to sunbathe nude when the weather was fine. Giuliani had cleaned up the piers and transformed the entire waterfront into sanitized paths and miniparks for walkers and bikers and strollers. (*"Fooliani,"* Walker would say; he'd hated Giuliani's particular brand of dictatorship almost as much as he'd hated Koch's insistence on remaining closeted.)

Even scrubbed, the pier remained a gathering place for gay youth. No matter how biting the cold, there were always a few hardy souls out, huddled, trying to shield their cigarette lighters from the wind. Jack wondered why they weren't at school, if they were there because they didn't have anywhere else to go. He envied the teens on the waterfront, hopping up and down to stay warm, drinking beer from a paper bag—no cares, no worries. What did you have to worry about at seventeen when you were young and untethered and in New York City? How bad could it be, really? Did kids even worry about being gay, worry about having to tell their families? He wished that was all he had to agonize about. He'd give anything for that to be the thing he needed to confess.

Jack took out his phone and opened Stalkerville. Melody had shown him the day they had lunch and although he'd made fun of it, he also hadn't objected when she downloaded it to his phone and "connected" him to Walker.

"It's addictive," she said, "you'll see."

The whole thing perplexed Walker. "I always tell you where I am.

I'm always at work or with you, anyway. Why do you need to check on your phone?"

"I don't," Jack said. "It's just interesting to know I can. Creepy but interesting."

And it was creepy, but Jack had to admit that Melody was right, it was also addictive—opening the screen and seeing the icon of Walker's face appear and then the roaming blue dot—at the drugstore, at the grocery, at his office. Right now, he was at the gym, probably sitting in the sauna instead of exercising, thinking about what to make for dinner. Something about being able to see Walker move around during the day, seeing how connected their lives were, how small Walker's world was, how much of it revolved around him—*them*—made the financial mess he was in feel even worse.

Jack didn't think about this too often anymore, but he knew he was probably alive because of Walker. When he met Walker, all those years ago, in the midst of his freewheeling days in Chelsea, on Fire Island, in the bathhouses and the clubs, Walker had been the one to insist on condoms, to demand fidelity. Jack had taken umbrage at first; hardly any of the couples they knew were exclusive. They were young and out and living in the greatest city in the world! But Walker recognized what Jack refused to face then: men getting sick, being denied treatment, dying. Walker worked with the doctors at St. Vincent's; he believed what they told him about prevention, and he scared the shit out of Jack.

"If you want to spend every morning checking your exquisitely beautiful body for sores that won't heal or worry about every little cough, that's your choice," Walker had said in the early weeks, "but it's not mine."

Walker was scrupulous—condoms and fidelity were nonnegotiable. "If you want to mess around, that's fine," Walker said, "just not while I'm in the picture." Jack tried to resist Walker at first but found himself drawn to the man in ways he didn't understand and couldn't explain. Something about Walker—his goodness, his compassion (and, okay, the size of his dick, Walker was *huge*)—was more compelling than sleeping around. It was one of the nicest things Jack could say about himself: that he had recognized the value of Walker. Before they moved in together, they'd both gotten tested and Jack didn't think he'd ever been as scared as the day they went to get their results. They had collapsed into each other's arms, weeping and laughing with relief, when they were negative.

Walker had saved his life. He was sure of that. And if that certainty created a certain inequity in their relationship, a certain kind of paternalistic vibe that, Jack could admit, was sometimes not particularly sexy, not very hot, if sometimes Jack resented Walker's saintliness, his goodness and light and responsibility and needed to act out a little, spend money he didn't have, very occasionally and *very* discreetly have a late night with someone who didn't need to floss and brush and shave and apply moisturizer before dropping his pants, well, what of it? There was still a part of Jack that wondered what it would have been like if he hadn't heeded Walker's advice, had thrown caution to the wind and spent a little more time sleeping around before he settled down. Maybe he would be dead, but maybe he wouldn't. Maybe he'd be just fine—alive and better for the breadth of his experience. If Walker hadn't kissed him that very first night, maybe he wouldn't even be in this mess.

AT HIS SHOP, Jack opened the rolling gate and unlocked the door. He'd spent all week going through his inventory, trying to see if he had anything tucked away he'd forgotten about that he could sell to raise some cash, knowing the whole time he didn't. He knew his inventory down to every cast-off crystal doorknob. Whenever he found something of worth—which he did frequently, he had an eye—he knew exactly whom to call to place it. It was rare for something of true worth to linger at Jack's shop. His lucrative dealings were all private transactions with his longtime customers—designers, architects, and the esteemed ladies of the Upper East Side. The economic downturn had brought most of that business to a halt, too. Things were starting to pick up, but there wasn't time for him to accumulate anywhere near the money he needed.

If Jack didn't have a photo of the damaged Rodin sculpture on his phone, he would have thought he'd imagined the whole thing. Back at home after the aborted visit to Leo, it had only taken a few minutes on the computer to realize why it looked familiar, that it was one of the recovered pieces of art from the World Trade Center site that he'd read about years and years ago. The story was a tiny blip in the midst of all the coverage about the cleanup—how a damaged cast of Rodin's *The Kiss* had been recovered and then mysteriously disappeared. Jack had paid attention at the time because of his very good customer who collected Rodin.

Jack didn't know what to do with the information he had. He could do nothing, of course. He didn't care about the security guard in Stephanie's house or the statue, really. He could call someone at the 9/11 Memorial Museum that was under way and tip them off, anonymously or as himself; maybe there was a reward, maybe he'd get some press and it would be good for his business. Or, and this option was the one he was trying—and failing—to resist, he could approach Tommy O'Toole and offer to broker a sale for a sum of money, Jack was certain, so significant that Tommy wouldn't be able to refuse. And Jack's sizable commission would solve his immediate financial problems, release him from whatever Leo might or might not do.

He went to his little back office and printed out the photos of the sculpture from his phone. Jack had asked around and his friend Robert knew someone, some guy named Bruce who worked in the shadier places of art and antique sales. "I used him once," Robert said. "He'll know what to do. Tell him you're my friend." It didn't hurt to ask, Jack thought. It never hurt to gather information and know all the possibilities. Before putting on his coat, he took out his phone and the card stowed away in his pocket and dialed the number. "Hey," he said to some guy named Bruce. "I'm Robert's friend. I'm on my way."

CHAPTER EIGHTEEN

L eo was home alone, sitting in Stephanie's tiny second-floor
back room, the space he'd appropriated as his office, trying to
work out his pitch for Nathan whom he was finally scheduled
to meet with later in the week.

Out the window, the bare January trees and leafless shrubbery
allowed him full purview of all the neighboring yards to the side and
the rear. He could see straight down into the kitchen of the brownstone
directly behind Stephanie's, the layout just like hers but reversed—the
rooms a little more colorful, maybe a little shabbier. A spindly blonde
in black jeans and a baggy red sweater was arranging an array of
sliced fruit on a plate for two little boys bouncing and swiveling on
breakfast stools at the island counter. The boys were the same size
and coloring, twins probably. Leo wondered when twins had become
as common as the common cold. He thought of Melody's daughters
who, he dimly remembered, were a happy accident. She probably
hated that people assumed she'd had some kind of fertility treatment,

that she and Walter didn't get credit for two of his determined sperm successfully penetrating two of her enterprising ova. That type of thing would drive her crazy. He watched as one of the kids across the way shoved his brother off the seat and out of sight, presumably down to the floor because the mother raced over and bent down and when she stood the boy was in her arms, his legs wrapped around her waist, his face buried in her shoulder. He could see the boy's shoulders heaving, the mother stroking his back and mouthing *shhh, shhh,* gently rocking him back and forth. In the house next to hers, a middle-aged man walked through his kitchen with someone who looked like a contractor. The contractor was pointing at the ceiling molding with an extension of measuring tape while the homeowner nodded. Back to the right, red-sweater mom opened her back door and dumped a plate of fruit peels into what he guessed was a compost bin. He found the tableau behind Stephanie's house endlessly entertaining. He could sit and watch all the quiet lives of aspiration play out for hours. It was strangely soothing. Brooklyn was growing on him.

Though Stephanie hadn't been kidding about the drugs or borrowing money (not that he was using any drugs at the moment; not that he needed to ask for money), she'd been a pushover about the sex. They'd spent most of the power outage in bed, undressed, making their bodies sing the old familiar tune. "You can stay until you find a place," she'd said a few days later.

Victoria finally shipped Leo his belongings, no more than a dozen boxes; he didn't want much. It took leaving his life with Victoria to understand how much of it had been constructed by her (using his money) in a way he didn't miss and certainly wasn't eager to re-create. The relentlessly neutral palette with splashes of dark brown or black ("It's like living in a gigantic portobello mushroom," he'd complained to her once), the spare modern furniture, the sterile metallic Italian light fixtures, her quirky (and as it turned out nearly worthless) taste in a handful of upcoming-but-still-wildly-pricey artists—he was ecstatic to leave it all behind. Aside from recovering the years of his life he'd spent wooing, winning, and then regretting her, all he wanted from Victoria were a smattering of personal belongings and a few boxes of old SpeakEasy files. He unpacked the clothes he needed and stored the rest in Stephanie's basement. They were calling it temporary.

When Stephanie first told him about Nathan Chowdhury's alleged new project, he'd managed to keep a neutral face.

"I'm not sure exactly what it is," she'd said. "We were at a party and it was very loud and incredibly hot and, you know, he was classic Nathan, going a million miles a minute in seventeen different directions. *Genuine writers. Irreverent but vigorous. Smart but sexy. Bloody brilliant.*" She did a decent impression of him and his vaguely British accent, left over from his early years in Kilburn. "Maybe you should call him," she'd said, a little too casually. "Maybe he needs a content guy."

"Maybe."

What Stephanie had described was not a new idea of Nathan's; it was an old idea of Leo's. Back when SpeakEasyMedia was generating new sites faster than they could have imagined, Leo had wanted to create a writing hub. Something that would have a separate identity and attract serious writers, fiction and nonfiction, reportage, high-level think pieces. They had to focus on gossip at first because it was cheap and easy and fun and people would read it—but once they had a little traction, a little more money, Leo wanted to balance the gossip and blind items with something respectable. First, they needed money, and gossip was where they'd find it.

Interesting that Nathan who hadn't been taken with Leo's idea back then ("You're describing a gaping sinkhole that will suck up money and not return a proper cent") was ready to revive the concept. On his own.

"Any specifics?" Leo asked Stephanie.

"No, it sounded very early stage. He did say he was considering acquiring an existing publication to build around." (Another idea of Leo's from back in the day.) "He asked for suggestions. I told him to look at *Paper Fibres*."

"He can do better than that."

"Paul's respected, Leo. *I* respect him. He could use an influx of cash. And Paul does stuff with the public schools and literacy, and Nathan was also interested in the philanthropic angle."

"Since when is Nathan interested in philanthropy?"

"Since he got married and had a couple of kids and is probably looking to impress the private school admissions committees. He went to Darfur a few months ago."

Leo snorted a little. *Literacy? Darfur?* All he could think about in that moment was a particularly depraved evening at some bar on the Lower East Side one late, late night (early morning? probably) when a bleary-eyed Nathan outlined the SpeakEasyMedia financial model on a series of napkins: how they'd make their first million, how quickly he'd leverage it into more, how many people along the way would bend to his vision—"collateral damage, can't be helped"—how soon they'd be retired. Leo had sat next to him on the barstool, half listening, while an extravagantly pierced but fetching young musician flirted with him and then leaned against Nathan and then back into Leo, making her interest in both apparent. "Do you guys want to come home with me?" she'd finally said, as the bartender was ushering them out the door. "Both of you?" He'd been relieved when Nathan passed out the second he landed on her sofa. If he was going to engage in a threesome, it wasn't going to be with Nathan. *Pierced,* as he sometimes still fondly thought of the musician, kept Leo up until sunrise; she taught him some things.

"I feel like Rip Van Winkle right now," Leo said to Stephanie. "Like I woke up and everyone became their exact opposite. Paul Underwood's a literary force. Nathan's a philanthropist."

"Yeah, well. Things changed while you were otherwise occupied."

At first, Leo just pretended to be interested in Nathan's new venture, a way to kill time while waiting for his divorce to be final, an amusing lark that would keep everyone off his back and halt all the lame suggestions about work. But the more he talked to Paul Underwood, the more he realized the potential sitting there, untapped.

Paul's content was stellar—Leo was impressed with who and what he was publishing—so was the layout, design, art. But everything else was dismal. The office was chaotic and inefficient, like almost anything in the publishing world. Without even trying, Leo could think of a dozen things they could do immediately to raise the profile and productivity of the magazine and expand in a multitude of interesting ways, starting with a more robust online presence. Social media. A blog. An app! *Paper Fibres* could—should—publish a handful of books every year. They needed a bigger staff.

Once Leo decided to put a proposal together, take himself and Paul seriously, and approach Nathan with a multifaceted well-thought-out plan for bolstering and expanding, he started having fun. His mood lifted. He was sleeping better than he had in years, waking up before Stephanie and going for a run in Prospect Park, no matter how cold. He spent his days reading, researching, thinking, and working so hard at times he lost track of time. He'd forgotten how good it felt to be interested, absorbed, stimulated. He made dinner some nights: huevos rancheros, beef stew, French onion soup. "You're making me fat!" Stephanie complained one night. "Don't let me have seconds."

If he could get something going, Leo started to think that maybe he *could* borrow money to pay his family back and leave his investments intact, maybe even borrow from Nathan. Rebuilding wasn't unthinkable. He'd done it all before. And if his efforts stopped being interesting? If he stopped having fun? He still had money in the bank. He still had options. Doing some research, putting together his ideas, meeting with Nathan—it would all be, to use one of Nathan's favorite expressions, "win fucking win."

Downstairs, the doorbell rang. Leo walked to the front bedroom and looked out the window. Bea was standing on the front stoop, shivering and clutching something in her arms. He went down and opened the door.

"IT'S MY STUFF," she said, handing Leo a leather case he vaguely remembered buying for her ages and ages ago. "Meaning, I wrote those pages."

"You still have this," he said, examining the satchel. "I don't remember it being so nice. This is *nice*."

"To be honest, I haven't used it in years. I thought it was lucky and then I thought it was unlucky and, well, here it is, here they are, and here I am. Ha."

Leo examined Bea's face, tried to make eye contact. She looked stoned. He undid the front straps and peered inside. "Lot of pages in here."

"I think it's a quick read. I don't know what it is yet, exactly, but—" Bea looked uncomfortable. "I was hoping you'd read and then pass along to Stephanie."

"You want me to read it first?" he said, surprised.

"Yes." She shoved her hands deep into her coat pockets and looked up at him with a weak smile.

"Like the old days, huh?"

Her face bloomed. She looked eighteen again, eager and bright. "That would be nice. I miss the old days."

Leo thought of the night of the hospital, Bea leaning close and saying, "I heard something else." He had an unexpected urge to bend down and hug her, tell her that whatever she was worried about was going to be okay, reassure her the way she'd done for him that night. As quickly as the odd inclination appeared, it was gone and in its place a flash of annoyance. Anger even. When was she going to grow up? He wasn't responsible for her, for reading her work anymore. "Okay. I'm looking forward to it. As soon as I can. Probably not this week."

"No hurry. When you get to it. Really." She wondered what had just happened. One minute Leo was there and the next he wasn't. Confused, she stood and kept nodding at him until she started to look like one of those bobble-head dolls of Derek Jeter or the pope.

Definitely stoned, Leo thought. "Do you want to come in?" he asked, impatient.

"No, no. I have to get to work. I just wanted to drop that off." She sighed, and he thought he saw her shudder. "I went to this party at Celia Baxter's. Lena Novak was there."

"Shit. She must be a complete nightmare by now."

Bea gave a wan smile. "She is such a fucking nightmare you wouldn't even believe."

"I believe."

They both laughed a little and things seemed lighter again, nice. Bea reached into her purse and pulled out a Ziploc bag of cookies. "I stole these from the party," she said. "The entire platter."

"I approve," he said. "Not a Celia Baxter fan either." Leo had slept with Celia once, years ago, and when he didn't return her numerous calls, she'd shown up at his office swollen faced and crying and looking as if she hadn't showered in days.

"Take them," Bea said, handing him the bag. "I have tons more at home." She gave him a quick peck on the cheek and headed off toward Flatbush Avenue, waving her hand a little behind her. He closed the door, opened the bag of cookies, and ate two. He took the leather case upstairs and put it on a shelf. He'd get to it after his meeting with Nathan. This week was all about Nathan.

CHAPTER NINETEEN

Behind the wheel of her parked car and in spite of the cold Melody had fallen deeply asleep. She was dreaming about her babies, how solid and steadying their weight was against her chest, on her lap, in her arms. *Tap, tap! Tap, tap!* Someone in her dream was tapping on a window, wanting to come in. *Tap! Tap!* Melody jerked awake and as the two figures standing outside the car lowered their grinning faces down to hers, she drew back, embarrassed and confused.

"Too early for naptime!" one of them said. Melody smothered a groan and tried to smile. It was Jane Hamilton, another mother she knew from school, laughing as if she'd just told the world's most hilarious joke. *This* she did not need today.

"Save the disco naps for the weekend!" the other woman said. Melody could never remember her name, the one with the oddly shaped curly hair she thought of as the Poodle. Jane and the Poodle were part of a clique (she'd resisted using that word at first but, incredibly, there was no other designation that fit the social stratifications of school parents) who occasionally included Melody in a monthly Mom's Night Out. The evenings were usually at someone's house (when Melody would go because the drinks were free) or sometimes at a local bar (when she would not go and hope nobody noted the distinction). Everyone would swill Chardonnay and the conversation would invariably turn into wine-lubricated screeching about sex and how the husbands wanted it too often and bargaining tips for blow jobs.

Melody didn't want to hear about *anyone*'s sex life, much less drunk suburban mothers who didn't even seem to like their spouses—or their children—all that much. Apart from the indecorousness of it all (which horrified her, she would never talk about Walt that way, she would never *think* about him that way), she thought the women were willfully shallow and tedious. Melody tended to sit through those evenings nearly silent, occasionally laughing along when everyone else laughed or nodding her head in agreement with some of the milder declarations about school: The kids had too much homework; the assistant principal was a bitch; the eleventh-grade English teacher was hot, but definitely gay.

Melody removed her keys from the ignition, grabbed her handbag, and opened the car door, bracing herself against the chill winter wind.

"We missed you at the meeting," the Poodle said.

"What meeting?" Melody asked, alarmed. She never missed school meetings.

"Oh, *she* didn't need to be there," Jane said. "Plus, it was boring."

"*So* boring," the Poodle said.

"What meeting?" Melody asked.

"The college financial aid thing," Jane said. "The forms and the requirements, blah, blah, blah."

Oh. Melody realized with a sinking feeling that when she'd dutifully copied all the parent gatherings from the college counseling calendar into her own at the end of last summer, she'd ignored the workshops about financial aid. How had things changed so quickly? And how had she not remembered that pompous bit of editing sooner.

"I'm sorry I missed it," Melody said. "I meant to go. Is the information online?"

"I thought you were all set," Jane said. "I thought you and Walt have been saving for college since your first date or something obnoxious like that."

Melody squirmed a little to remember how she'd bragged at one of the Mom Nights last spring. She hadn't explained about The Nest per se, just mentioned that she and Walt had a "college fund" and that they probably wouldn't need financial aid. She'd regretted the words as soon as they'd tumbled out of her mouth, and now she could kick herself, especially thinking about her offhanded and inaccurate phraseology—*we made saving a priority.*

"You know what investments are like these days," Melody said, inexperienced at posturing about money; she was probably the color of a beet. "We might need some help after all."

"Let me save you some time," said the Poodle. "You already make too much money and the colleges don't care about kids from Westchester, so unless you guys are going to declare bankruptcy or somebody loses a job, you're toast. The whole meeting was a colossal waste of time."

"They'll take one look at that scarf and kick you out," Jane said, gesturing at Melody's neck and the pretty lavender scarf Francie had given her.

"It was a present," Melody said.

"It's lovely," Jane said. "It suits you."

At one time, Melody had wanted nothing more than to be friends with these women, would have loved nothing else than to bump into them in town and have them admire something she was wearing. Now, she wanted to run and hide. Their conversations made her want to scream. They complained about money, while breathlessly recounting expensive house renovations (*How many blow jobs for a Sub-Zero?* she wanted to ask) or recent European vacations (*How many for a trip to Paris? Ten? One?*). And then, invariably, they'd look at each other and shrug and say, "luxury problems," cackling like some modern skinny-jean-wearing equivalent of Marie Antoinette's court.

That kale juice you're drinking is six dollars! Melody wanted to say. *Your kitchen is the size of my entire downstairs!* They made her so angry and anxious, she'd gradually learned to avoid all of them. She fingered a corner of her pretty scarf and looked at her watch. "I'd better get going," she said, gesturing to the consignment store behind them. "I have to duck in here before I go home."

"Nice," Jane nodded approvingly. "A little retail therapy."

"We just had a pleasant chat with Walt, too," the Poodle said.

"Walter?" Walt was supposed to be grocery shopping and not in the village where the only food stores were very precious and very expensive. "Where?"

"He's with Vivienne," Jane said, pointing across the street.

Melody was grateful in that moment that she'd had so much practice not visibly reacting to these galling women because she was able to keep her face calm.

"Right, of course," she said. "See you later." As she hurried, her heart was pounding so hard she thought it might cross the street ahead of her. She thought, in the moments before she charged through Vivienne's door, that this must be what it was like to catch your husband with a lover; *in flagrante delicto* was the phrase that popped into Melody's head, a *flagrant offense*. Betrayal. This is how Victoria must have felt after Leo's accident, Melody realized, experiencing a tiny flash of empathy for the woman who had never even been civil to her. And as she stepped up on the curb, careful not to slip on the slightly icy walk, she knew she'd rather catch Walter in an amorous embrace with Vivienne, would rather he have

Vivienne bent over the table in her office that was covered with local maps and magazines and restaurant coupons and be taking her from behind than *this*—calmly sitting at her desk in plain sight at Rubin & Daughters Realty. Vivienne Rubin was the Realtor who'd sold them their house.

CHAPTER TWENTY

The first time Simone kissed Nora, furtively in her family's kitchen where they were momentarily alone because Louisa was down the hall in the bathroom, she moved swiftly, before Nora understood what was happening and retreated before Nora could object—or respond or acquiesce or participate. That afternoon, when Simone heard Louisa's footsteps in the hall, she casually went back to spreading almond butter and jam on brown-rice cakes. Nora couldn't fathom how Louisa could be oblivious to the new charge in the room, not even notice how the molecules in the kitchen had briefly combusted into something intoxicating and scalding and then quickly resettled into the familiar tableau: bowl of polished apples on a butcher-block island, marble counter with a six-burner range, gleaming teakettle with a plastic whistle in its spout shaped like a little red bird. Behind Louisa's back, Simone smiled beguilingly at Nora, who was consumed for the rest of the afternoon by one thought: *Again.*

Sometimes Nora and Louisa babysat the little boy across the street, and what he loved most was for them to each take one of his hands and walk across the front lawn, swinging him by the arm, high into the air. *Again!* he would shout, gleeful, the minute they reached the perimeter of the yard. They'd turn around and go back in the other direction and before they even reached the fence on the opposite side, he'd start yelling *Again! Again!* When he'd see them in the street, he'd start bouncing in his stroller. *Again!* he'd yell, waving at them. "Tomorrow, Lucas!" they'd call. "We'll play tomorrow!" There was never enough *Again* for Lucas. No matter how many times Nora and Louisa swung him across the front lawn, until their arms were tired and their shoulders sore, no matter how they tried to refocus his attention with cookies or the swing or by playing peekaboo, when they stopped, he would cry and cry.

After Simone, Nora knew exactly how he must have felt. Thought that the sensation he must love when being lifted off the ground, propelled forward by some bigger, outside force, the swinging, the swoop of belly, the weightlessness, the sense of flying, it had to be almost sensual, a little-kid precursor to pubescent desire, lust, hunger.

Again was exactly how Nora felt after Simone kissed her. Nora couldn't stop thinking about the kiss, about the velvety feel of Simone's almond-flavored tongue in her mouth, about the almost-imperceptible brush of Simone's fingers at her waist—or about when it might happen again.

It didn't take long. The following week they went into a store to try on clothes and Simone slipped into Nora's dressing room. The minute the door was closed, Simone had Nora pressed against the wall and Nora did what she'd been thinking about doing all day and all night for a solid week—she kissed Simone back. Exploring Simone's mouth with her tongue, biting her bright and full lower lip, grabbing fistfuls of Simone's long braids and wrapping them around both hands and tugging lightly until Simone's head tilted back, exposing her long, elegant throat and Nora fastened her mouth, the tip of her tongue, to the precise spot on Simone's neck where her pulse fluttered. That day, they'd pressed against each other until a saleswoman had gently knocked on the door and said, "How's it going in there? Anything working for you?"

"Absolutely," Simone said, cupping Nora's ass and smiling, "everything in here is working great."

SOON, NORA AND SIMONE figured out that the Museum of Natural History was the easiest place to lose Louisa. Like so much of New York, the crowds lent them a privacy that Simone's two-bedroom apartment couldn't. Louisa would bring her sketch pad and set to work and Nora and Simone would say, "See you later," and then sneak away into a multitude of dimly lit corridors, empty restrooms, darkened screening areas. They became experts at exploring various body parts, triggering certain sensations, without ever fully undressing. At first they were tentative, a quick finger here, a flick of the tongue there, but they quickly learned where they could be brave, how to deftly circumvent buttons and waistbands and bra hooks while still staying clothed. Simone made Nora come for the first time in a restroom off the Hall of Invertebrates, without even moving aside the slight bit of purple thong that Nora had bought on the sly and tucked into her backpack for this exact purpose. The first time Nora took Simone's breast into her mouth, down a deserted corridor of offices that were closed on the weekend, they'd almost been discovered by a lost mother looking for a restroom with her two little kids. Simone had hurriedly pulled on her T-shirt when they heard the kids running down the hall, the mother behind them yelling, "Don't touch the walls, guys. Hands to yourselves!," which had reduced them to nearly hysterical laughter. While sitting in the deserted last row of the IMAX movie (later, neither of them would remember what the movie was about), Nora inched Simone's tights down to her knees and slipped her fingers inside Simone's underwear and then inside Simone, who was warm and wet.

"Tell me what you want me to do," Nora whispered, dizzy and momentarily brave.

Simone held herself perfectly still and spoke softly into Nora's ear, "Do me with your mouth."

When they met up later, Louisa frowned at Nora and said, "What have you guys been doing?"

"What do you mean?" Nora's hands went clammy, her ears rang a little. She had checked to make sure Louisa wasn't in the theater.

"Your knees are *filthy.*" Louisa looked genuinely perplexed, peering at Nora who seemed addled, almost feverish. "Are you guys *high*?" She lowered her voice and took a step closer to look at their eyes.

"No!" Nora said. "We just got out of the IMAX."

"I dropped an earring," Simone said. "Nora got down on the floor with me to look for it. It was dark." Simone did that thing with her voice, the tone of it, which made Louisa feel bad, like she'd said something wrong or stupid. "Oh," Louisa said. "Did you find it?"

"Yup," Simone pointed to her ear and the series of tiny silver hoops along the lobe.

Louisa didn't understand how one of those tiny hoops could have fallen. Or how they could have found it in the dark. Or why they were lying to her.

NORA HAD NEVER LIED TO LOUISA, not in their entire lives. They were a few years past telling each other everything—every stray thought that flitted through their minds, their dreams, their dislikes, the explicit details of their crushes and desires—but they'd never lied to each other. Nora wanted to talk to Louisa, but she didn't know how to start. She would stand in their shared bathroom some mornings when Louisa was already downstairs having breakfast and practice saying something, *anything,* in the mirror.

"Hi, I'm gay," she'd rehearse. She couldn't even say it with a straight face; it felt so melodramatic and dumb. "Hi," she'd say to her reflection, "I like a girl." That sounded dumb, too. *I'm sleeping with a girl?* Dumb. *I'm fucking a girl?* Wrong. *I'm in love with a girl?* Was she? She wasn't even sure. *Just be honest.* She could hear her mother's voice in her head. *Telling the truth is never wrong and always easier.*

"Hi," she'd try. "I'm totally obsessed with a girl and I don't know if I'm in love—or even if I'm gay—but I'm so horny I can't see straight." Well, that was the truth, anyway.

"Oh, lord," Simone had said when Nora tried to talk to her about it one afternoon at the museum; they were both sitting on the floor, backs against the wall, in a relatively quiet spot, legs idly touching. "Are you all topsy-turvy inside? All staring in a mirror and thinking, *What does this mean? Who am I? What is my essential self now that I've kissed a girl?*"

Nora was embarrassed. She didn't like being on the receiving end of Simone's pointed tongue (well, except in certain ways). "Are you all, *Now I have to listen to Melissa Etheridge all day and stop shaving my legs?*" Nora slapped Simone's arm lightly. "It's going to be so sad when you have to get your lesbian regulation crew cut," Simone continued, taking a healthy amount of Nora's chestnut curls in her hand. "I'm really going to miss this hair. But rules are rules."

"Forget it," Nora said. Now she felt dumb *and* angry. "Forget I said anything."

"I'm sorry I'm teasing you," Simone said, still playing with Nora's hair. "I can't help it. I like watching you blush. It's cute. You only turn pink right *there*." She touched the middle of Nora's cheeks with her fingertips. "It's like a trick."

Nora batted Simone's hand away. "It's just— I had a boyfriend last year!"

"So did I."

"You did?"

"Sure. I don't have him anymore. He was very beautiful. Supersexy but dumb as a rock. He kept talking about how he wanted to visit China because moo shu pork is the perfect food. God, he was dumb. But beautiful!" Simone flashed her brilliant smile. "Not as beautiful as you. I like you better, if that's what you're worried about."

"So what do you tell people?"

"What people?"

"I don't know. Everyone. Your friends, your parents. I mean. Are you *out*?"

"First of all, I don't tell them anything because it's none of their business. I bring home boys. I bring home girls. It's not a big deal." Nora was staring at Simone, disbelieving. It couldn't possibly be that easy. It couldn't. "Am I hurting your feelings?" Simone said. "I'm not trying to hurt your feelings. I'm just not into labels."

"I don't believe you."

"Why? I mean, if I were a boy would you have to 'come out' about it? Would you go home and say, 'Mom, there's something you need to know. I kissed a boy and I liked it.'"

"It's not the same thing. Or maybe my parents are just nothing like yours."

Simone shrugged. "I'd say that's a safe bet." She rebuttoned her lime-green cardigan and stood up. "My parents are cool. My mom's brother is gay and it wasn't easy for him. My grandparents were super religious and, well, they were really hard on him. Always. But my mom and him—he's Simon, I'm named after him—they're really close. We're his family now."

"My mother has a gay brother, too." Nora was still sitting, looking up at Simone.

"Really?" Simone said. "Does she not approve?"

"No, no," Nora said, trying to think of an easy way to explain the Plumb family and their various alliances and grievances. "They're not close, but it's complicated. They're all kind of weird."

"Everybody's kind of weird." Simone put her hand out for Nora, helping her to her feet. "Your problem is you're worried about being everyone's mirror and that's not your job."

Nora braced herself; she could tell Simone was gearing up for one of her frequent—and sometimes baffling—extemporaneous lectures. Nora knew now just to listen and nod and say, *Wow, I never thought of it that way,* and then Simone would say, *I live to elucidate,* and then they could talk about something else. "Mirror?" Nora said, because Simone seemed to be waiting.

"Everyone's always on the hunt for a mirror. It's basic psychology. You want to see yourself reflected in others. Others—your sister, your parents—they want to look at you and see themselves. They want *you* to be a flattering reflection of *them*—and vice-versa. It's normal. I suppose it's really normal if you're a twin. But being somebody else's mirror? That is not your job."

Nora slumped against the wall a little. What Simone said made sense, a lot of sense, but so did wanting to see yourself in the people you love. So did wanting to reflect the people you love. "How do you know all this stuff?" she asked Simone.

"Some people have to learn *this stuff* sooner than others."

Nora didn't have to ask what Simone meant. The previous week they'd been in the museum gift shop looking for candy when a couple had walked up to Simone and asked whether she knew where they could find a rock tumbling kit.

"No, I don't," she'd said, concentrating on the shelf of candy in front of her.

They'd persisted. "Well, can you find someone who will help us?"

Simone had turned to face them then and crossed her arms. "No, I can't," she'd said. "Because I am not employed here. Like you, I am a customer." Even by Simone standards, her tone was blistering.

The couple, flustered, apologized. "We were just confused because you weren't wearing an overcoat," the woman said.

"Oh, I know *exactly* why you were confused," Simone had said.

"Hello?" Simone tapped the top of Nora's shoe with hers, reclaiming her attention. "Do you understand what I'm saying? Being somebody's looking glass is *not your job*."

"I understand. I get it. But it's not just everyone else; it's me, too. I like definitions. I like to be sure of what's happening."

Simone put a consoling arm around Nora. "You can be sure about me."

Nora wished they were alone. She wished they could go somewhere and just be *alone*. If she told Louisa what was going on, maybe they could. Maybe they could stop these stupid afternoons at the museum, stop sneaking around.

"If somebody insists on a definition," Simone said, "tell them you're bicurious. That will shut them up, trust me."

Nora was imagining telling her parents that she was *bicurious*. God. She knew exactly what Melody would say and she said it to Simone: "That doesn't even sound like a real word."

"Maybe. But how does it feel?" Simone asked, pressing Nora against the darkened back wall in a remote corner of the Hall of Biodiversity. "How does it *feel*?"

NORA AND LOUISA TALKED ABOUT BOYS all the time and it had never occurred to Louisa that Nora might actually want to be talking about girls. There were plenty of lesbians at their school, but they all seemed so dramatically lesbian with their short haircuts and black boots and tattoos and multiple piercings; they were so in-your-face lesbian, holding hands and making out in cars in the parking lot. Or there were the girls who playacted at being lesbian, usually to flirt with boys, touching each other's hair and tentatively kissing on the lips, sometimes with tongues and then laughing and pulling away, wiping their mouths with the back of their hands. But Louisa knew that what she'd seen between Nora and Simone wasn't either of those things; it wasn't statement and it wasn't fashion. What she saw in the darkness of the museum was something else. It was lust.

If Nora was gay and they were twins, was she gay, too? She liked boys, but she had to admit that when she'd seen Simone kiss Nora, watched the rise and fall of Nora's chest and Simone's hand move over Nora, her entire consciousness had reduced to one lasting image: Simone's thumb stroking Nora's nipple. But what did she want? To be touched by another person? A boy? A girl? Either? Both? She'd always imagined herself with a boy, but seeing Nora with a girl had upended something, introduced a new possibility that was rooted in their twinness. This was the thing about having a twin, the envelop-

ing, comforting, disconcerting thing: They were equal parts and seeing the other doing something was almost like doing it yourself.

You are each other's pulse, Melody would tell them all the time,
and Louisa believed it; she didn't always like it, but she believed it.
When their father had taught them how to ride a two-wheeler, Louisa
was terrified. Every time he let go of her bike, she felt the loosening
at the back wheel and stopped pedaling in sheer terror and her bike
would slow and wobble and tip and she'd have to jump off and free
herself from the spinning spokes and whirring pedals.

"Let's let Nora have a go," Walt finally said.

Then it was Nora's turn, Nora who was always more fearless, more
agile, and when Louisa watched her father run with Nora's bike and
then release the back tire and saw Nora lean into the pedals, pump
her legs faster, give the bike the speed and ballast it needed to stay
upright, it was almost as if she'd done it herself. She could feel it
exactly. Watching Nora's body do something gave her the concurrent
muscle memory.

The next time Louisa tried the bike and her father let go, she flew.

CHAPTER TWENTY-ONE

Woman. *Runner. Literary agent. Single.* Stephanie looked over her list, the four words she'd hastily written to describe herself to a room mostly full of strangers.

"Don't think too hard," Cheryl, the cheerful woman running the team-building session, had said. "Jot down the first four words that pop into your head. No editing your first impulse and no job titles."

Stephanie crossed out *literary agent* and in its place wrote *reader,* which was more accurate anyway, describing what she was supposed to be doing all day but never actually had time to do until the evenings or weekends. She was a little stung that she'd written *single,* was surprised to see it emerge from the spongy ooze of her uncaffeinated subconscious. It had been four days since she surreptitiously switched the coffee beans to decaf (Leo hadn't even noticed), and she still felt groggy, as if her brain stayed at half-mast for most of the morning. But *single* was not how she ever thought of herself. She considered her list again, thought about erasing *single* and replacing it with something else (*New Yorker? Foodie? Gardener?),* but that would be cheating and everyone else at the table seemed to be finished.

Stephanie very much wanted this day to end, the first of three infuriating, obligatory days of employee orientation. The corporation she'd sold her agency to, a behemoth of entertainment representation—film, television, music—headquartered in Los Angeles and wanting a literary presence for their New York office, insisted on the training. She knew this was just the first of many irritations she would have to endure after running her own office with the beloved, if quirky, group of employees she'd worked with for so long. She was trying to be patient, but this was bullshit—days of icebreakers, group dynamics, and sexual harassment seminars. What did any of this have to do with her or her employees? They already knew how to work together, and they worked together well because each and every one had been handpicked by Stephanie for their specific intellectual gifts, for their discerning taste and, most important, for their ability to work with her.

Cheryl (who'd introduced herself as a human capital consultant, getting the first snicker of the morning from Stephanie and her longtime assistant, Pilar) was leading them through the second icebreaker of the morning. The first had not gone well. It was the old classic, Two Truths and a Lie. Stephanie'd endured it on several previous occasions, conferences and meetings, when everyone had to stand in front of the room and read three statements about themselves: two that were true, one a lie, and the rest of the group had to guess which was which. Stephanie always used the same three.

I was in an Academy Award–winning movie. (True. When she was seventeen, she'd worked for a caterer in Queens that provided craft services for the cast and crew of *Goodfellas.* She noticed Scorsese staring at her from beneath his Panama hat one day as she dumped an enormous bag of lettuce onto a white plastic platter. She smiled at him. He walked over, grabbed four oatmeal cookies from the table, and said, "Wanna be in a movie?" He sent her off to hair and makeup and used her as an extra for the Copacabana scene. Eight takes, all in one day. She stood for hours, tottering on high heels and wearing a tight gold lamé dress and black mink stole, her hair teased into a mile-high twist. It was her red hair that Scorsese liked; he put her front and center in the shot where Ray Liotta guides Lorraine Bracco down the stairs to their table.)

I can butcher a pig. (True. She spent one summer in high school at her uncle's farm in Vermont. She'd had a summer fling with the son of a local butcher and had spent her afternoons sitting on a metal stool watching his shoulder blades glide beneath his white coat, transfixed by how he could deftly break down a glistening side of beef or pork. He showed her how to slice along the fat line, spatchcock a chicken, separate a pork shoulder into butt and shank. They'd drive around town at night in his truck and drink Wild Turkey from tiny flowered Dixie cups, park near the pond, and touch each other until they were dizzy. She'd bring his substantial hands to her face and inhale, smells she still associated with heady New England nights: Castile soap and pennies, the coppery scent of animal blood.)

I was born in Dublin, Ireland. (Lie. She was born in Bayside, Queens, but between her hair and brownish-greenish eyes she looked like she could have been.) Nobody ever guessed Ireland was the lie; they always went for the pig.

The first participant that morning to stand in front of the room and read his truths and lie was a new hire from the Interactive Group. A gaunt twentysomething, wearing a vintage-looking cardigan and Clark Kent eyeglasses that magnified his smudged eyeliner. He had a tattoo of a squid down his left forearm. He stood, stoop shouldered, and introduced himself.

"Hey. I'm Gideon and okay, well, here goes." He shoved his hands in his pockets and read from the paper on the table in front of him in a quick, even monotone.

"I nearly died from overdosing on pills. I nearly died from bleeding out. I nearly died from autoerotic asphyxiation."

"Whoa, whoa, whoa." Cheryl jumped up, waving both hands before anyone had a chance to respond. "Thank you, Gideon, for your candor." She paused for a beat. "But I guess I should have spelled out the guidelines a little more clearly. We want you to reveal something *interesting* about yourself, but nothing quite that personal in nature and, please, everybody, nothing sexual. Think *professional*."

"Sorry," Gideon had said, shrugging idly. "Clinical depression and suicidal ideation are more common than most people realize, and they're both a really important part of who I am."

"I understand." Cheryl kept a smile affixed to the lower half of her face. "We're just going for something a little lighter here."

"The lie was autoerotic asphyxiation," he'd added. "FYI."

STEPHANIE OPENED HER MOLESKINE and tried to tune out the rest of the room as Cheryl asked for someone to read their four words. She started making a list of things she needed for dinner.

"You said not to self-edit," an amiable guy spoke from the other end of the table, "so this is what I've got: *Fat. Happy. Golfer. Husband.*"

Her cell phone, sitting on the table in front of her, started to vibrate. Without even looking at the number, she waved at Cheryl. *I have to take this,* she mouthed and left the room as quietly as she could. Relief.

She looked down at the incoming ID: Beatrice Plumb.

Standing in the hallway outside the meeting room, Stephanie was surprised to find how happy she was to hear Bea's voice. She'd begged off the phone quickly, telling Bea she wanted to talk but was in a meeting (true) and couldn't stay on the phone (true) and that, yes, Leo *had* mentioned something about new work but they'd both been incredibly busy and maybe they'd talk about it tonight (lie).

Bea sounded so anxious that Stephanie found herself feeling protective, maternal almost. She didn't know if Leo had read Bea's stuff; she doubted it, but she could ask. She briefly wondered why Bea had handed the pages to Leo and not her, but then again—they probably weren't new pages, they were probably old pages that she was passing off as new and Leo wouldn't know the difference. Stephanie would remind Leo to read them, and she would help him come up with something to say to Bea, something nice and noncommittal. She'd put it on her list.

Back in the conference room Gideon was up again, this time reading his four words (*musician, pessimist, wizard, Democrat*). A slight wave of nausea roiled her stomach; she sipped the lemon water she'd brought into the meeting. She was going to have to eat something soon.

She slid her phone out of her jacket pocket to check the time. Once it was in her hand, she couldn't resist opening the app she'd downloaded that tracked the development of the baby based on due date. *This week your baby is the size of an apple seed! This week your baby is as big as an almond. This week an olive!* She hit the button and watched the photo appear of what her embryo looked like at nine weeks—like a tiny bay shrimp, a curled crustacean with an immense head and sci-fi budding arms. As she did almost every time she looked at the eerie images, she felt herself blush. It was unseemly, really, how addled she found herself to be forty-one and single and accidentally pregnant by Leo Plumb, beyond a shadow of a doubt the most irresponsible and least paternal of all the men she'd ever loved in her entire life.

She knew it was crazy, told herself a million times a day that it was crazy, but she found she couldn't completely suppress a few fleeting moments of optimism—about the baby for sure, about Leo, maybe. She was surprised by how responsible he'd been lately, how *present*. He helped around the house. He seemed to be working every day and was enthused about meeting with Nathan. He read all the time. Nothing in his behavior made her believe he was anything other than completely clean and sober. She couldn't help but wonder if everything in her life had been pitched toward this moment—agency sold, money in the bank, some time on her hands, a seemingly renewed Leo in her bed, trying to make some kind of amends to someone or something. That she was on the receiving end of this newly burnished Leo, the very thing she'd desired and abandoned as so much wasted effort all those years ago—Leo in the living room scribbling on a legal pad, Leo in her bed in the morning running a finger down her back, Leo in her kitchen every night, closing a book and pulling her onto his lap—well, she'd decided not to question it. She'd decided to selfishly, greedily, take it. All of it. Maybe even this new wrinkle, the unexpected residue of the power outage.

Over the years, she'd considered having a baby with any number of people. Marriage was not part of her plan; she wasn't against it, she just wasn't for it. She treated her occasional yearning for a baby the same way she treated her occasional yearning for a dog. Let it linger and wait to see if it passed, which it always did, which she took as a good sign. Because other things she desired (her house, a particular author signed, a midcentury table in good condition) didn't flit through, they planted themselves until she turned desire into ownership. That her fleeting thoughts of motherhood never truly haunted her the way, say, her quest for the magenta peony bushes in her yard did was comforting as she imagined her ovaries surrendering the final vestiges of fertile eggs into the hinterlands of her reproductive system.

THEN THE STORM. The expected-unexpected arrival of Leo. The power outage. Leo. A little too much wine (hers), the familiar mouth (his). Leo had seemed the tiniest bit broken. She made him laugh. They talked. He took her wrists and circled them with his thumb and forefinger, pulling her to him (the way he had that first night their friendship became something else, the night he turned to her in a hidden booth at a small burger joint and said, "I've been wondering what you keep beneath your blouse") and then he'd two-stepped her across her kitchen, in the dark, under the moonlight, and kissed her with such acquisitive purpose, she thought she might combust. Leo. What else was there to do when the lights were out—wind howling, branches splitting and falling—but fuel the fire, let him lift the sweater over her

head, unzip her pants, and fuck her silly under the unblinking, mar-
bled gaze of Lillian.

She looked back down at the list she'd written. Her four words. She
was going to have to talk to Leo very soon. Whatever he said, whatever
his reaction, the decision was *hers*. This belonged to her. She took the
cap off her pen and crossed out *single,* wrote *mother.*

It didn't look terrible.

CHAPTER TWENTY-TWO

When Matilda was recovering in the hospital and found out how much money she was getting from the Plumb family, she'd had all kinds of fantasies about what to do with it. (Shamefully, she remembered that her first involuntary thought was a pair of suede boots she'd coveted, the ones that went over the knee and stopped midthigh; then she remembered.) She thought about trips and clothes and cars and flat-screen televisions. She thought about buying her sister her own beauty salon, which she'd always wanted. She thought about buying her mother a divorce.

The staff at the rehabilitation hospital tried to prepare her for all her future expenses, not just her prosthetic foot (which would need to be replaced every few years) and its various related medical issues and costs, but the accommodations she'd have to make to her home. "It sounds like your living situation is not ideal," one of the social workers said to her. "You might need to reassess." Matilda took the financial worksheets and nodded her head, but she didn't really listen.

Everything seemed so much sunnier at the rehab hospital where she was a little bit of a star, so young and determined and doggedly cheerful. She learned each skill quickly and was able to go home sooner than most patients. When she returned to her parents' cramped apartment in the Bronx, Matilda started to understand what she was up against.

The problems began at the building's front door, which opened to three flights of stained, uneven, peeling linoleum stairs that were discouraging in the best of circumstances but were horrific with crutches and wouldn't be much better once her prosthetic foot was ready. Inside the apartment to the left of the front door was a corridor, too narrow for a wheelchair (which she sometimes needed, especially at night), leading to the apartment's one bathroom and galley kitchen. Straight ahead, four small steps down, was the sunken living area that thirteen-year-old two-footed Matilda believed was the height of design sophistication and now made amputee Matilda want to weep in frustration.

And there was her mother's decor, what she and her sister used to call South of the Border kitsch—mismatched throw rugs from Mexico, colorful baskets full of fabric, tiny rickety tables holding religious statuary—all of it now seemed like a concerted effort to kill her. Small things she'd never noticed about the apartment loomed large: The toilet was very low, the shower required stepping over the side of a challengingly deep bathtub, there were no railings—not even a towel bar—for her to grab onto.

Beyond the physical discomfort with the apartment and the utter lack of privacy, which was psychologically draining, there was the emotional stress of being around her two parents. Even though they'd been unusually kind to each other in the wake of the accident, uniting in their worry and grief for the first time in years, they never left her alone. They watched her move around the rooms guardedly, her mother clutching a rosary, her father trying to avert his gaze.

She had to get out of there.

Matilda didn't believe in God as much as she believed in signs. (She knew she'd gotten a sign the night of the accident in the front seat of Leo Plumb's Porsche, the setting sun glinting off his wedding ring, and she'd ignored it and now look at her. God had taken her right foot.) She said a rosary every morning when she woke, praying to know what to do, where to live. So when she saw the billboard in front of a brand-new condominium complex on her favorite street, the one lined with cherry trees that bloomed exuberantly in the spring, she knew: The sign was her sign.

PRICES SLASHED it said. And in tiny print on the bottom: ACCESSIBLE UNITS AVAILABLE.

She bought two apartments. One on an upper floor for her sister who had three kids and a deadbeat husband, and a smaller one on the ground floor for herself. She paid cash, only asking her sister to cover her own maintenance costs. The leftover money had still seemed monumental. A lawyer-friend of Fernando's helped her open a money market account attached to her checking. She was being as frugal as she could, but it went so fast! And someone in her family was always asking her for a loan: a down payment for a car, plane tickets to visit family back in Mexico, a new dress for a daughter's prom. It never ended and how could she say no? She couldn't. Because when she thought about why she had the money, she was ashamed.

And now she was scared, because she had to find a way to be more mobile. She had to get a job. Once the morphine from the night of the accident wore off, she admitted what she'd always known: She'd never be a singer. "You're smart, Matilda," one of the nurses in rehab said to her. "What kind of career are you thinking about?" Nobody had ever used that word with her before: *career*. She liked the sound of it. She liked imagining herself going to an office every day. After high school, she'd wanted to go to college but there was no money, and the day she'd come home, excited after her allotted fifteen minutes with one of the school's overworked counselors, with community college applications and student loan forms her parents had been so negative, so discouraging. She knew they were afraid of their undocumented status, of being found out and losing their jobs. She heard them later that night arguing over whether to let her apply, her father becoming increasingly angry and volatile. The next day she'd asked Fernando about catering work.

Now she had some money; she could take classes if she wanted, but not if she was on crutches—or in constant pain.

Vinnie wasn't the first person during her stay at the rehabilitation hospital to mention elective amputation to Matilda, not the first person to gently suggest (or in Vinnie's case, aggressively suggest) that as far as amputations went, hers was a particularly shitty one and she should consider another operation to amputate below the knee, which would open up a world of better prosthetics. Matilda didn't understand because at first everyone had seemed excited by how much of her leg had been saved. She didn't remember much from the recovery room, but she did remember the surgeon triumphantly telling her that he'd taken "as little bone as possible." When she repeated his boast to her physical therapist, who was examining her stump and frowning, the woman said: "Sometimes more bone is a good thing and sometimes it's not."

She was right. Matilda's prosthetic foot hurt almost all the time. No matter how she paced herself or rested or how hard she worked to strengthen her body's other muscles, no matter how many (or few) barrier socks she wore or how much therapeutic massage she had, after only an hour or two with the foot, her stump would start to throb, the pain gradually working its way up her calf and then past her knee until there was a concentrated knot of tension and an almost unbearable ache at the top of her hamstring where it joined her lower gluteal muscles. (How blissfully ignorant she'd been of the infrastructure of upper thigh to ass before the accident! Only wondering if there was a cure for the tiny cellulite bumps that peeked out from her very short shorts.) Most days the pain would creep into her hip; many days her neck would start to ache by late afternoon and she'd end up in bed before dinner.

Her doorbell rang, loud and insistent, angry. Vinnie. Matilda opened the door to find him standing there with a pizza box balanced on his left arm and a full-length mirror tucked under his bionic arm. She eyed the long mirror warily when he came through the door.

"I don't want that thing in here," she said.

"Maybe you don't want it, but you need it. Your foot is bad, right?" He could tell just by looking at her how much pain she was in. She would still laugh and smile, but her eyes would be unfocused. He understood.

"It's not too bad," Matilda lied. On good days, Matilda's nonexistent foot would tingle or just feel like it was there, its ghostly presence driving her crazy. But on bad days it hurt to distraction. Today, it felt like needles were piercing her nonexistent foot. For weeks, she'd had a persistent itch on one of her missing toes. She found herself in the ludicrous position of fantasizing about amputating a foot that didn't exist.

"Sit down," Vinnie said, placing the pizza on her kitchen table. "Take a slice while it's hot. You can eat while we do this."

She reluctantly sat on one of her kitchen chairs. Took a slice and blew a little before she bit into it. "How did you manage to get it here while it's still hot?" she asked him.

"Trade secret," he said.

"What's in the sauce that makes this so good anyway?"

"Nice try. We can talk my miracle sauce later. Let's do some work."

Vinnie had been talking about mirror therapy for weeks, and Matilda thought it sounded ridiculous, like voodoo. Still, he was in front of her and he'd carted a mirror all the way to her house, so she reluctantly did what he said. She straightened her knees and let Vinnie position the mirror between them so that when she looked down, she saw her intact foot on one side and its mirrored image on the other. "Oh," she said.

"Move your left foot," Vinnie said. She did and the optical illusion was of two perfect feet, moving in concert. "Scratch your toe," he said, "the one that's been itching."

"How?"

He pointed. "Scratch the itchy spot on your left foot, but keep looking in the mirror."

She leaned over and gently scratched. "Oh my God," she said. "It helps." She scratched harder. "I can't believe it helps. I don't understand."

"Nobody understands, really. The simple way to think about it is that you're helping rewire the old signals in your brain. You're teaching your brain a new story."

She moved her foot to the left and to the right, flexed and pointed and flexed again. She wiggled her toes. She rotated her ankle and the foot in the mirror, her missing foot, seemed like it was back and was working. She scratched again, it helped again. "It already feels better," she said. "Not great but different."

"Good. Four or five times a week for fifteen minutes. And use the mirror whenever the foot hurts or itches. Got it?"

Matilda nodded and smiled. "It sounded so stupid," she said. "I didn't want to go buy a mirror just to do something that sounded so dumb. Thank you, Papi," she said. She spoke softly and put a light hand on his shoulder. "Thank you for bringing the mirror."

"It's temporary," Vinnie said, standing abruptly. The charge that shot through his arm, his chest, and other places he didn't want to dwell on when Matilda touched him was dismaying.

"I'll buy my own. You can have this back—"

"No, no," he said. "I don't mean the mirror is temporary; it's yours. I bought it for you. I mean you still need to deal with the underlying problem." He sounded angrier than he intended. Matilda was frowning. He took a breath. *Stop. Rewind.* He started again, keeping his voice even. "The mirror is just a temporary fix is what I meant."

In her heart, Matilda knew Vinnie was right. Of all the things people had said to her over the past six months, all the useless advice and meaningless platitudes (*God never gives you more than you can handle, everything happens for a reason*) and quoting of Bible verses, what Vinnie said about elective amputation and losing her ankle made the most sense. Matilda grew up knowing that you didn't get anything without giving something up. In her world, that was the prevailing logic. It was just a matter of knowing how much you were

willing to lose, how many pounds of flesh, which in her case would
be literal. ("If thy foot offend thee, cast it off"—*that* Bible verse she
understood.)

When she was in rehab, one of the nurses told her Vinnie was
someone they called a "superuser." He healed so swiftly and learned
so fast that he'd been chosen to test the cutting-edge prosthetic he
wore. And here she was, barely able to hobble around on her clunky,
ugly rubber foot. She was the opposite of Vinnie. She wasn't a superuser, she was a superloser.

But more surgery, more rehab, better prosthetics? It would all cost
money. A lot of money. "I don't have that kind of insurance. I don't
have that kind of money, and I don't know anyone who does," Matilda
said. She sounded defeated, resigned.

"Yes, you do," Vinnie said. "You do."

IT HAD TAKEN VINNIE A FEW TRIES, but before he took the mirror to Matilda, he'd managed to convince her cousin Fernando to meet
with him privately. Fernando was suspicious at first and Vinnie quickly
realized the source of all the wariness, the secrecy and protectiveness
around Matilda: fear of deportation. Vinnie slowly pulled the story
from Fernando—the wedding, the ride in the fancy car, the emergency
room, the hastily called meeting in an attorney's office only days later,
the rush to sign papers and take the check, the refusal to fight Leo
Plumb in court or insist on an insurance claim. The family wanted to
avoid a police report because a police report would mean that Matilda's
parents—and Fernando's mother who was also illegal, not to mention
most of the rest of their extended family—would come to the attention of the immigration authorities, as George Plumb had repeatedly
threatened, according to Fernando. Vinnie tried to understand exactly
what kind of agreement Matilda had signed (in the hospital, hopped
up on morphine; it was ridiculous, a travesty). He finally convinced
Fernando that a conversation with Leo Plumb was not going to incite
legal action. "I just want to have a friendly chat with him," Vinnie said.

Fernando had burst out laughing. "You understand why that doesn't sound entirely plausible to me?" Fernando had almost punched Vinnie the day he'd yelled at Matilda in the pizza parlor; he didn't trust the guy.

"I swear to you," Vinnie said. "On my mother's grave. I wouldn't do anything to hurt Matilda. You have to believe me. I would never, ever bring harm to Matilda."

Fernando *did* believe that part because Vinnie was clearly head over heels. And Fernando also felt a not-insignificant amount of guilt about the weeks following the accident. He had panicked; they all had. He'd been blinded by the sum of money the Plumbs were offering as much as anyone and was ashamed to think of how Matilda had helped him pay off some of his law school loans. He'd been so relieved, he'd barely protested.

"Okay," he finally said to Vinnie. "But you have to tell Matilda what you're planning and she has to agree. Promise me you will tread carefully."

"You have my word," Vinnie said. He wasn't scared of anyone, and the mysterious Leo Plumb sure didn't intimidate him. He respected Fernando's hesitation, but he knew without ever having to meet him what kind of a person Leo Plumb was: He was a fucking coward.

Matilda was so full of shame about the night of the accident she couldn't see clearly, but Vinnie could. What kind of person leaves his wife at a wedding and lures a young girl out to his car with a lie? What kind of person doesn't even think twice about driving given his blood alcohol and drug levels? What kind of person doesn't fucking apologize and check on the girl who, because of his spectacular hard-on, no longer has a foot? A coward, that's who. And here was another thing Vinnie knew about cowards: They were easy to break.

Vinnie had a plan. He was going to request a meeting with Leo Plumb and make it clear they weren't after money, because they weren't. Vinnie wanted access. He'd done his research and he knew Leo had traveled in the right circles. Leo could put Matilda in touch with the right people and help her with any number of programs where she would get assistance with her prosthetics, including further surgery if necessary. He wanted Leo to pull some strings, and he wasn't going to give him a choice. He was going to make it clear that he wasn't afraid to expose him for the coward he was. He'd put on his uniform, stand with Matilda at his side, and humiliate Leo Plumb until he buckled. Leo could come after him and Vinnie would welcome that fight, but he'd never have to engage. Because the other thing he knew about cowards? They were most afraid of being unmasked. This was going to be easy.

"NO," MATILDA SAID. "Absolutely not." She'd let the mirror fall to the floor, and she was furiously hopping across the kitchen. "I'm not going to talk about this."

"We're going to talk about it." Vinnie stood firm.

"Get out of here. Please. Thank you for the pizza, the mirror. I'm tired and I want—"

"This—" Vinnie said, pointing to Matilda's stump, "is bullshit."

Matilda had her back to him, holding on to the kitchen sink. "Why are you yelling?" she said, turning to him. "Why are you always fighting? Always mad at everyone and everything."

"Why aren't *you*?" In the harsh light of Matilda's kitchen, Vinnie's left hand was clenching and unclenching. "Why aren't you fucking pissed off?"

"Because it doesn't do any good."

"I disagree."

"Maybe you need to tell *your* brain a new story. Go ahead, use the mirror. Take a look at your face and see how ugly it is when you're mad."

He took a deep breath and then he slammed his palm against the refrigerator next to her. She flinched. "Why aren't you mad enough to ask for what you deserve?" he said.

She sat down heavily on one of the kitchen chairs, her face drawn and bleak. She looked like she might cry; Vinnie had never seen her cry. Matilda couldn't even look at Vinnie. She'd tried so many times to will herself back into that pantry, back into the *before,* when Leo was waltzing her to the music. If only she could do it all over again, disengage, walk away from Leo and back to Fernando in the kitchen and pick up her squeeze bottle of vinaigrette. She looked up, somber. "I can't ask for more because I did get what I deserved," she said. "I got *exactly* what I deserved."

CHAPTER TWENTY-THREE

Nathan Chowdhury had been livid when Leo wanted to sell SpeakEasyMedia.

"It's ours," he'd said. "We made the fucking thing and it's finally doing well and getting bigger and better and now you want to hand it over to a bunch of corporate drones? Why? And do what?" Nathan had argued for weeks but Leo held firm and Nathan couldn't afford to buy Leo's half of the business. "I'm done," Leo told Nathan. "I'm out."

Leo was tired. Tired of working around the clock and the crappy offices that were one step up from his living room but barely. Tired of the young, clever, petulant glorified interns they employed and had to manage in every conceivable way—Leo felt like a housemother half the time. He'd walked into the tiny conference room twice in one week to find two different couples making out. Someone was constantly letting food go to mold in the tiny refrigerator; the sink was always full of dirty coffee mugs.

He was tired of being broke. Tired of running into friends from college and hearing about expensive trips and shares in the Hamptons and admiring their nicer clothes. Tired of not wanting anyone to visit his apartment because it was still the depressingly nondescript postwar one-bedroom that he'd always illegally sublet, a second-floor apartment where every window looked out onto a neighboring roof of below-code air-conditioning compressors; the rooms actually rattled when they were all going at once.

He was tired of gossip. God, was he tired of gossip. By the time he sold it, SpeakEasyMedia had fully morphed into the very thing Leo most loathed. It had become a pathetic parody of itself, not any more admirable or honest or transparent than the many publications and people they ruthlessly ridiculed—twenty-two to thirty-four times a day to be exact, that was the number the accountants had come up with, how many daily posts they needed on each of their fourteen sites to generate enough clickthroughs to keep the advertisers happy. An absurd amount, a number that meant they had to give prominence to the mundane, shine a spotlight of mockery on the unlucky and often undeserving—publishing stories that were immediately forgotten except by the poor sods who'd been fed to the ever-hungry machine that was SpeakEasyMedia. "The cockroaches of the Internet," one national magazine had dubbed them, illustrating the article with a cartoon drawing of Leo as King Roach. He was tired of being King Roach.

The numbers the larger media company dangled seemed huge to Leo who was also, at that particular moment, besotted with his new publicist, Victoria Gross, who had come from money and was accustomed to money and looked around the room of Leo's tiny apartment the first time she visited as if she'd just stepped into a homeless shelter. ("When you said you lived near Gramercy," she said, confused, "I thought you'd have a key to the park or something.")

Heading to his meeting with Nathan, Leo remembered what it was like to be charged with adrenaline, optimistically nervous. He almost walked right past Nathan who was sitting at the bar in front of an open laptop, head bent. Leo was glad to have a minute to observe his old friend, his years-long companion in the pursuit of business and pleasure and a winning season for the Jets. The welling affection he felt at seeing Nathan's familiar profile was genuine. Nathan, who had a seemingly endless ability to stare at spreadsheets and pie charts and see a story. Nathan, who was still wearing his pants too short and his jacket a little tight and drinking his standard drink: a Shirley Temple.

And when Nathan looked up, he was visibly happy to see Leo, too. He stood and they hugged. Not the backslapping hug Leo was used to, the bro hug that was more exuberant handshake and head dip than body contact, but a true hug. Nathan drew Leo close and held him tight, and Leo was unnerved to feel himself tear up. Anyone watching might mistake their moment of reunion for something sadder. Then they straightened, did the hearty backslap, and took a few seconds to appraise each other.

Nathan grinned, nodding. "Yup, yup. I'm still the better-looking one. By many fathoms." This was a long-running joke. To say Nathan was not conventionally handsome was generous. For a big guy, his shoulders were unusually narrow and all his weight gathered around his midsection. He had the kind of pear-shaped body more common on women. The enormous gap between his two front teeth managed to be charming. His hair was completely gone, but the bald head worked with his strong features, the fleshy nose, the severely arched brows that nearly had a life of their own.

"Want a real one of those?" Leo said, pointing to Nathan's drink and ordering himself a whiskey.

"Afraid not. I have precisely twenty minutes until I have to leave for an uptown charity thing and I'm introducing someone so . . ." Leo was not encouraged to hear that he'd been apportioned such a tiny slice of Nathan's day. He'd have to talk fast. He went through the motions, asked after Nathan's family, saw a few photos, listened to a recap of his "nightmare" town house renovation.

"I heard about you and Victoria," Nathan said. "I'm sorry."

"Don't be. It's better for both of us." Leo hoped he hit the right mix of reassurance and regret. He was glad Nathan brought up the divorce, he wanted to use it. "You were right back then when you told me we brought out the worst in each other."

Nathan plucked the bright cherry out of his ginger ale and ate it, chewing on the stem. "I don't take any satisfaction in being right about that."

"I know. Just coming clean with an old friend. I should have listened to you—and not just about Victoria, about a lot of things."

"Water under the bridge," Nathan said. "You look good. And unless the grapevine is just desperately gnawing on very old intel, I think I heard something about you and Stephanie. True?"

"True. Yes. For now. We're going slowly, but it's good so far."

"I'm happy for you, mate. Don't fuck it up this time."

"I'm not planning to," Leo said, bristling a little at the sanctimonious comment. Nathan had fucked up plenty of relationships in his day. "I'm ready to get back in the game, so to speak. That's one of the reasons I wanted to see you."

"I thought as much. I've heard you've been dropping my name around town. Telling people we're working together."

"That's not true," Leo said, stunned that his movements had already been reported to Nathan.

"I've heard it from more than one person."

"Stephanie told me about your idea and I was curious. Really curious. I'm interested. I've been making calls and doing research and asking questions, but I never misrepresented myself. I never told anyone I was working with you or that we had any official affiliation. The conclusions people draw on their own when they hear my name and your name are not my doing."

Nathan stared at Leo for a few minutes, assessing. "Okay. I see how that's possible. I hope it's true."

"It is true."

"Because I can't hire you."

"Can we back up a little?" Leo couldn't believe he'd lost control of the conversation so quickly. "Can we start over? I know you're busy and I came prepared."

"I'm confused as to why you'd want to be involved with this fairly modest project I'm considering."

"It doesn't sound modest. It sounds ambitious and worthwhile."

"Believe me, it's modest."

"It also sounds like something that was once my idea." Leo stopped; he hadn't intended to bring that up at all and certainly not so quickly. He couldn't let Nathan rattle him.

Nathan looked up at the ceiling, as if seeking for patience from above. "You hardly invented the concept of an online literary magazine. Don't go Al Gore on me, Leo."

"I know. I'm sorry. That came out wrong. I—we—have the experience. We were a good team. You don't even want to hear my thoughts? You know what I can do."

Now Nathan let go his booming laugh. Leo was unnerved by how casual he seemed, how matter-of-fact. "Sadly, that is very, very true."

"Let me just give you a quick overview, how I think you could expand *Paper Fibres* in some really interesting and fruitful ways." Leo opened up his folder and took out the stack of printed pages.

"Jesus," Nathan said. "Did you make a PowerPoint deck?"

Leo ignored him, paging through the sheets in front of him and pulled out one with a mocked-up logo. "Right down to an event-based app that would also push content." Leo put the page in front of Nathan who stared at it, confused.

"An app?"

"You've got to have an app."

"This is not news to me, Leo. Every sixteen-year-old in New York City is trying to build an app."

Leo said, "That's one tiny element. I have an entire—"

Nathan interrupted. "Leo, I appreciate that you put thought into this. And I'm genuinely thrilled to find out you're with Stephanie. Really. When I heard that, I thought, Okay, whatever shit has gone down for the last few years, he's got his head back on straight. And I hope you do. I hope you find a gig that makes you happy. But even if I wanted to work with you—and I don't—I need someone young who will work for next to nothing. Someone who is already up to speed and isn't"—Nathan gestured dismissively at the page in front of him—"breaking ground with an event app."

"But what about experience? What about name recognition."

"Name recognition?" Nathan was incredulous. "That, my friend, is part of the problem. What have you done since we sold SpeakEasy? Seriously, Leo. What have you done?"

What had he done? First, he and Victoria had lived in Paris for six months and then Florence, all without improving his French or Italian one iota. Those days and weeks were long blurs of visiting friends and meals and trips to "the country" that somehow he ended up paying for. Then Victoria declared New York "boring," so they went west and leased an apartment in Santa Monica for a few years. He was supposed to be working on a screenplay, but he really went to the beach every day and tried to surf and then got stoned while Victoria spent a lot of time meditating and doing some kind of aromatherapy shit. They talked incessantly about opening up a small art gallery but never did. When her dermatologist found a precancerous mole on her otherwise unblemished décolletage, it was back to New York where she convinced him to fund a small theater group downtown so they could "nurture emerging talent," which pretty much meant Victoria "producing"—and starring in—bad plays written by people she'd grown up with in the West Village. He'd gone for long walks and taught himself all about single-barrel whiskey. He read, quietly resenting anything he deemed good. He spent months designing a custom bike that he never rode.

"I wish I'd done a lot of things differently," Leo said. "But I can't go back in time."

"I agree," Nathan said. "You and me?" He wagged a finger between the two of them. "That's trying to move back in time. We had a good run." He slapped Leo on the arm, hard. Leo winced. "A bloody good run." Leo knew the meeting was over when Nathan amped up the Briticisms. He watched Nathan gather his folders and slide his laptop into a briefcase. "I'll have my assistant call you. We'll have dinner. You, me, my wife, Stephanie. It will be fun. You can come uptown to take a look at the massive money pit and laugh at my folly."

Leo hadn't had a chance to say anything he'd planned. "Let's reschedule. I realize now I should have sent you my ideas ahead of this meeting—"

"This isn't a meeting." Nathan tossed a credit card on the bar, started pulling on his coat.

Now Leo was annoyed. He deserved better. "Come on, Nathan. Don't be like this."

"Like what? In a hurry?"

Leo tried to think of what he could say to persuade Nathan to stay. The credit card on the bar was a black Amex. Leo couldn't believe Nathan was doing that well.

"Do you need money?" Nathan asked, noticing Leo staring at the card.

"What? No."

"Because if this is about money, I can float you a loan. I can do that."

"It's not about money. Christ. Why would you think I need money?" Leo was furious remembering that he *had* thought about borrowing money from Nathan. Hell would have to freeze over.

"I talk to Victoria now and then."

"Fantastic. Fucking fantastic. Victoria, the most unreliable narrator of all time."

"To her credit, I had to drag the information out of her."

"It's not to her credit; she signed an agreement. In fact, I find it very interesting that she's trying to turn people against me—"

"Cut the bull, Leo. I asked about you as a friend. I was worried. Nobody's *against* you."

Leo took a deep breath. "So put me on your calendar. Let me give you my presentation. Just hear me out."

"You say you've done your homework?" Nathan said.

"I have."

"So you know who our CFO is?"

"I didn't memorize the organization chart, no."

"Peter Rothstein." Nathan signed the bar copy and started ripping his receipt into tiny pieces, which he carefully placed back on the edge of the plastic bill tray. Leo frantically tried to remember why the name might be significant. Nothing.

"His brother was Ari Rothstein," Nathan said.

Leo felt a vague familiar nagging, but still—nothing. "Do I know him?"

"That's one way to put it. The one who gets it done. Sound familiar?"

Leo's heart sank. Ari Rothstein had been one of the last SpeakEasy stories of his tenure. A community college kid—kind of portly, dull looking—who sent in a video résumé for a tech-support job. Leo had come to the office one morning to find everyone standing around a monitor, hooting and laughing. The tape started with Ari Rothstein in an ill-fitting suit reeling off his technical experience and then absurdly and awkwardly interrupting himself by removing his jacket, putting on a baseball cap, and singing a nonsensical rap parody about tech support. The chorus was the inelegant and forgettable "I'm the one to get it done." (I'm the ONE. I'm the ONE. I'm the ONE to get it DONE!) It was awful, and hilarious.

"We're putting it on the site," Leo had said, before he'd even watched the entire four minutes and thirty-two seconds. Everyone thought he was kidding at first, but he knew click-through gold when he saw it. It was SpeakEasyMedia's first huge viral video, and Ari Rothstein had been vilified and mocked for weeks, everywhere—online, in print, on television. His clip ended up on a *Today Show* segment called, "How NOT to Get That Job You Really Want."

"You hired that guy?"

"Noooo." Nathan drew out the word as if he were talking to someone incredibly dim. "*That guy* is dead. He overdosed a few years ago.

His brother was with the company before they acquired us, and he didn't speak to me for more than a year. It took a long time to gain his trust, convince him that I didn't have anything to do with the incident, and that I regretted it, which I do. What we did back then? It was okay. It was fun. But it wasn't exactly honorable, Leo. It's not what I want to be remembered for."

"I don't either. That's my point."

"I can't, Leo. I can't. I'm not saying the Ari thing is your fault—our fault—or anything like that. I'm saying things are different. The business world is different. I'm different. I hope you're different. And I can't hire you."

Leo sat for the first time since entering the bar. He was trying to think of the right thing to say, the sensitive and appropriate thing, but what came out instead was a joke, one the old Nathan might have found amusing. "I guess Ari Rothstein really was the one to get it done."

After a long silence, Nathan said, "I'm going to pretend you didn't say that. Good luck, Leo. Sorry to disappoint you."

"Don't be. I have other irons in the fire."

"Good."

"Not that you asked, but I'd be remiss if I didn't mention that in my opinion you should have some concerns about throwing your financial efforts behind Paul Underwood."

"Is that right?"

"I like *Paper Fibres,* too, but things are completely chaotic over there. I don't think Paul has the kind of leadership you're going to need to bring this forward. I don't think he's your guy."

Nathan stared at the floor and then slowly looked back up at Leo, pityingly. "I was hoping you wouldn't show up here and still be a prick, Leo. I was really hoping."

"Don't misunderstand. I like Paul—"

Nathan put out his hand and Leo reluctantly stood and shook it. "Best of luck, Leo. I hope you get your shit together. For Stephanie's sake."

"I'm going to have to take my ideas elsewhere."

"Be my guest. Just don't ever drop my name again."

"Fuck you, Nathan."

"Right back at you, mate."

Leo watched Nathan make his way out the bar. He sat back down and took a deep breath, trying to process what had just happened. His phone on the bar started vibrating. He looked at the incoming call display and at seeing the name, his heart nearly stopped. Matilda Rodriguez.

CHAPTER TWENTY-FOUR

Before he'd stupidly let Jack Plumb inside his house, Tommy had had only one scare concerning *The Kiss*. An FBI unit had knocked on his door one morning when he still lived out in the Rockaways, wanting to talk to him about a missing object from the World Trade site. He'd almost passed out until they explained that they were investigating reported thefts at Fresh Kills and just wanted to know if Tommy remembered seeing the Rodin and, if so, where he'd seen it last. Tommy assured the investigator that he'd delivered it to the Port Authority trailer just like he had with countless other artifacts and left it with someone there whose name he didn't remember but who had said she'd take care of it.

"That's the last time I saw it. Sorry, guys," he told them. "Wish I could be more of a help. It looked like a banged-up piece of crap, to be honest." The investigators shook his hand, told him how sorry they were for his loss, and that was the last he heard from anyone.

At first, Tommy kept the statue hidden in his bedroom closet in the house in Queens, covered with a pillowcase. He didn't want his daughters to see it when they visited, approximately a thousand times a week. "Just checking in!" they always said in chirpy voices he'd never heard them employ until he was a widower. But having his wife's gift in a closet like a shameful secret bothered him. He started to think about moving. The house he'd shared with Ronnie, where they'd raised their children, where they'd had family movie night with popcorn every Friday and had managed to make love every Sunday even when the girls were little, sometimes having to fit it in between commercial breaks on Nickelodeon—but they did, they always did— was too empty, too lonely.

His old friend Will from the fire department told him about Stephanie needing a new tenant. He'd always liked Stephanie. She was a good egg—funny and smart, a hard worker and completely down-to-earth. "What they used to call a real dame," Ronnie had said, approvingly, when Will brought her to one of their legendary holiday parties and Stephanie had charmed the entire room by singing "(Christmas) Baby Please Come Home," Darlene Love style, into the karaoke machine they'd hooked up to their TV.

The garden apartment was a little run-down, but he didn't need much. He just wanted his own place where he could keep the statue and see it every day, somewhere far enough from the Rockaways so his kids wouldn't drop by without calling first, where he wouldn't have to answer a lot of questions. The statue had been his well-kept secret. Until Jack Plumb walked into his dining room.

Having Jack Plumb inside his house, walking in circles around the statue like he was evaluating a used car, had caused an unpleasant shift in Tommy. Maybe it wasn't only Jack, maybe it was the passing of time, the nature of grief, but when he took the statue out of its hiding place now, all he could hear was Jack Plumb saying, *Where did you get this?* For years, Tommy had worried about somebody seeing the statue, his daughters mostly. And now that someone had, he started to think more clearly about what might happen if he was caught. He hadn't looked at the statue in more than a week.

Today, two of his three daughters were visiting. He almost always went to them, but a few times a year they planned a trip into "the city" and would detour to Tommy's place first, delivering bags of groceries they imagined he needed.

His family never managed to hide their dismay at his living conditions and as Maggie and Val barged through the front door, five grandchildren between them now, he braced himself for their familiar complaints and pinched mouths.

"This place could be nice, Dad," Val said for the hundredth time, "if you'd put in a little effort." She was unloading groceries onto the kitchen shelves, opening up a package of bright green sponges and using one to wipe down the cabinetry.

"You don't have to do that," Tommy said. "Sit."

"I don't mind," she said.

"Why don't you get some furniture that actually fits in here?" Maggie said. "We could go look for a new sofa today if you want. We could help you pick something out." She was right. The sofa he'd kept was meant for a much larger room, not the narrow proportions of a brownstone parlor.

"It's fine. I'm fine. I'm not expecting *Better Homes and Gardens* to drop by and take photos."

"Why is this locked?" Val was standing now in front of the built-in china cabinet in the dining room. The top half was meant for display and Tommy had put a few pieces of their wedding china on the shelves, his one attempt at "decorating." The bottom half of the cabinet was meant for storage. He'd removed the interior shelves and bottom baseboard but left the doors in place to conceal the cavernous interior, which neatly fit the statue on its dolly. He could wheel it in and out when he wanted. The doors were padlocked now.

"It's nothing. A few valuables."

"Mom's stuff?" Maggie had an edge to her voice.

"Everything that belonged to Mom is in the boxes I gave you. Like I've told you."

She was staring at the cabinet. "Is this neighborhood that bad? You need to padlock valuables?"

He didn't know how to answer (the neighborhood was fine), so he just made a dismissive sound and tried to move everyone back to the living room.

"Oh my God," Maggie said. She grabbed his arm and spoke quietly so the kids wouldn't hear. "Do you have a gun in there?"

"What?"

"You look as guilty as sin. You have a goddamn gun in this house, the house where we bring your grandchildren."

"There's no gun. Calm down. And I don't like your tone, young lady. I'm still your father." Tommy was desperate to distract her from the cabinet.

"What else do you own that you need to keep under lock and key in an empty dining room?"

Maggie's youngest son (Ron, named for the grandmother he'd never met) was clinging to his mother's leg and whimpering.

"What?" she asked, bending down and making her voice bright. "What's wrong, peanut?"

"I don't like it here."

"Don't be silly," she said. "This is Grandpa's house."

"I like his old house better."

Tommy didn't know what to say so he just watched Maggie stroking the child's head, comforting him. "Let's have some lunch and then we'll go for a nice walk," she said. "There's a park nearby with a playground. Right, Dad?"

But Ron couldn't be soothed. "This house isn't friendly," he said, crying in earnest now. He whispered something into Maggie's ear, and she shook her head and hugged him tight. "No, no, baby. That's not true. Everything here is friendly."

Val took the kids into the kitchen to make lunch, and Maggie pulled Tommy aside. "Dad, I've got to tell you. There is something *wrong* about"—she waved her arm, taking in the surroundings, the misfit furniture, the leftovers from previous tenants, the dust and disorder—"all this. After all this time."

"I'm one person," Tommy said. "It's all I need."

"I'm not talking about space." She crossed her arms and he could tell she was steeling herself to say something difficult. She looked so much like her mother he had to stop himself from staring at, touching, her face. "Do you know what Ron said when he was crying? He said this felt like a *haunted* house. Like there was a *ghost* here. I mean he's a kid, but kids pick up on things. It's dark and dreary and depressing. At least buy some lights. A couple of floor lamps. Up your wattage." She pointed to the lone living room ceiling fixture.

"Maybe he's right," Tommy said, fed up. He never asked for their help, hadn't invited them to visit. "Maybe it is haunted."

"Daddy," Maggie's eyes filled with tears. She bit her lip. He felt bad, but he felt worse not talking about Ronnie, trying to ignore the ghost they all carried with them.

"It just breaks my heart," she finally said, wiping her eyes with the back of one hand.

"You think my heart isn't broken, too?" he asked.

"I'm not talking about Mom. I know she's at peace. I know it. I'm talking about you, Dad. *You* break my heart. If there's a ghost in here . . . it's *you*."

CHAPTER TWENTY-FIVE

Melody believed in battle plans; she believed in analysis and strategy and contingencies, and that was a good thing because she and Walter were most definitely at war. He was advancing on two fronts: mortgage and college tuition. Melody was truly out of her mind at the thought of losing their house. It wasn't even like they were selling to cash out since their mortgage was still significant.

"It's not about equity," Walt said over and over. "We have to reduce our monthly nut. Especially with college coming. It's that simple. Unless you can think of a way to bring in more money every month, we have no choice."

She wouldn't let him "officially" list the house. She would not see a picture of her house in the window at Rubin Realty in the center of town for everyone to see and speculate over. Vivienne agreed to show the house "quietly," a pocket listing.

"We're just testing the waters," Walter explained. "Just seeing what *might* happen."

Walter also wanted to sit Nora and Louisa down immediately and discuss the *financial realities* of the coming years and what it meant for college—in his opinion, state schools only. Melody refused. Some families took summer vacations; Melody loaded the girls into the car and they went on college tours. They'd go out for a nice lunch afterward, check out the local town, compare notes on what they'd seen. They had their list! The reaches and the possibles and the likelys— and every last one was private and required mind-blowing amounts of money.

When Vivienne Rubin called while Walter was at work one day to tell Melody about two good offers, one all cash, Melody didn't panic. She thought for a minute and then told Vivienne to make a counteroffer. The number she named was ridiculous.

"Are you sure?" Vivienne said. "Walter is on board with this?"

"Absolutely," Melody said. She wasn't lying, she told herself, feeling calm and oddly optimistic when she hung up. This was a battlefield. Generals knew when to hold steady and when to deploy a strategic maneuver, when to retreat and when to advance. This was war and she wasn't surrendering. Not yet. Not until she saw Leo.

CHAPTER TWENTY-SIX

After leaving repeated voice mails that Tommy ignored, Jack just showed up at his door one day—as Tommy feared he might.

"You know you could get into a lot of trouble for having that thing," Jack said when Tommy reluctantly opened his door after Jack waved a computer printout of a news story about the statue in Tommy's face. Tommy had spent a few minutes denying that the statue in the article was the statue in his house, but then something within him, some resolve that had been slowly eroding over the past decade, gave way. He was tired. He slumped onto the folding chair in his front hall, despondent.

"Who did you say gave this to you?" Jack asked.

"My wife," Tommy said, staring at the floor. "My wife gave it to me—"

"Cut the bullshit," Jack said. "I seriously don't care how you *obtained* the object in question. If you or your wife or one of your many fellow *heroes* took it as a prank or to sell or—"

Tommy moved so fast and with such strength Jack didn't understand what was happening until he was pinned against the wall with Tommy's forearm jammed under his chin. He couldn't speak. It was hard to breathe.

"I didn't steal this, you motherfucking asshole," Tommy said; his face was so close that Jack could see the small spread of whiskers at the top of Tommy's cheekbone that he'd missed that morning while shaving. Tommy spoke and spit a little in Jack's face with each word: "This was a gift from my wife."

Jack was surprised to find lurking somewhere in his memory the trick they were taught back when he was with ACT UP and they were constantly being hassled and arrested by the police. To just relax, not fight. He held Tommy's gaze, maintaining a neutral face. Tommy's face fell and his whole body sagged as he stepped away from Jack.

"Jesus Christ," he said, and the words barely came out. He sat back down and looked at his hands as if they weren't his own. "What's wrong with me?" He turned to Jack. "It was a gift," he said, as he put his head in his hands and started sobbing. "It was a gift from my wife."

JACK FOUND HIMSELF in the peculiar situation of making tea for Tommy. He rummaged through the cupboards, a sad collection of items he imagined Tommy bought (Cap'n Crunch, Ramen, boxed mac and cheese) and things someone else had clearly delivered (organic canned chili, packaged quinoa, chamomile tea), and got him to sit at the kitchen table. Tommy spilled the story with little urging and Jack found himself feeling oddly sympathetic. Poor bastard. He would have to proceed delicately.

Jack made his proposal, poured more tea, opened a stale pack of vanilla wafers, and waited for Tommy to respond.

"I don't know," Tommy said. He was staring at the closed cabinet door, behind which the statue lived. "I don't know."

"You can trust me," Jack said. "I won't make a move until you tell me you're ready. You know if anyone finds out—"

"I know. Believe me, I have nightmares about dropping dead and my daughters having to deal with this."

"If you want to keep it, I get it." And Jack did get it. He understood the need for talismans from the dead. He and Walker had lost dozens of friends, had been pulled aside multiple times by a grieving mother or sister or cousin who offered a remembrance of the deceased to take home, like a party gift. *Please,* a friend's stepsister had pleaded once, *my parents will just drive it all to Goodwill; please take something that will remind you of him.* And they did. Multiple things. Michael's lime-green pocket square, Andrew's aviator sunglasses, the tiny bistro chairs David used to make from discarded champagne-cork cages, countless framed photos and out-of-order watches and the odd tie or belt. Jack kept everything neatly folded and arranged on one shelf of a bedroom bookcase. *The Museum of Death,* Walker would grimly joke, but he cherished the tokens, too. All the remembering. The shelf held nothing of value and it held everything of value. It was the past they'd both endured and escaped. It was despair and hope. It was life and death.

"I understand if you want to keep it," Jack said. "But I also understand"—and here he scooted his chair a little closer and put his hand on Tommy's and his concern was unfeigned—"I also understand if you need to get rid of it. And I can help you."

CHAPTER TWENTY-SEVEN

Leo had never been an early riser, but since he'd been living at Stephanie's the early morning hours had returned to his day, the hours he used to spend fighting consciousness, not wanting to feel the radiating burn of Victoria's fury from the other side of the bed, not ready for the muddled, self-recriminatory walk to the bathroom for water to soothe his parched, funky mouth, or the inglorious rattle of Advil tumbling into his trembling palm. Those days, there wasn't a single morning he didn't wake and swear the day ahead would be different. And not a single day where he didn't break his promise to himself, usually by midafternoon, gradually denuded by a day of boredom, by the specter of the evening in the company of his bitter, hostile wife.

But these days, he woke as the morning light slowly shifted the sky from black to the watery blue of winter. He'd quietly leave the bed and head to the bathroom, keeping his step light along the warped hardwood floors and stairs that creaked beneath the tiniest bit of pressure. He'd retrieve the *New York Times* from the front stoop and head into the kitchen to boil water for coffee. Stephanie had the same French press she'd owned when they met, when everyone else he knew thought coffee came brewed from the local deli or a street vendor. Once he'd poured the boiling water over the grounds, he'd sit at the kitchen table and slowly page through the paper, waiting to hear a thump in the pipes, hot water making its way up from the basement, signaling Stephanie was up and had turned on the shower. Around the time he was done with the world and national news, he'd hear the shower turn off with a healthy screech. He'd plunge the center filter on the French press and pour himself a cup.

And it was at that exact moment on the day after meeting with Nathan, sitting in Stephanie's kitchen, watching a fat slice of sun creep across the marble countertop and magnify every discoloration and imperfection, mulling the day ahead, that he started to feel the familiar darkness gathering inside, the glint of fear around its edges. It reminded him of that children's book Melody had loved as a little girl, the one he'd read to her over and over when his parents demanded he babysit, about a French girl with a straw hat and the towering woman—he'd never understood who she was, a teacher? A nun? A nurse?—who had a second sense for trouble. "Something is not right," she would say, abruptly waking in the middle of the night. *No shit,* Leo thought.

Leo hadn't really trusted this new world order—the pretty house in Brooklyn, the comely redhead moving around upstairs, his triumphant return at Nathan's side. He'd regarded the whole picture warily, like it was an opalescent shell found on the beach that was concealing something unsavory inside—the stink of seaweed, a putrefying mollusk, or, worse, something still alive, its pincers stirred and groping for a tender bit of flesh.

Decisions needed to be made. Deadlines were approaching. He was thinking about who he could send his proposal to; he knew it was worth something. If he wanted to stay, he was going to have to figure out what to do about the money he owed The Nest. *If* he wanted to stay.

Many days, he'd considered paying off his siblings because it could be nice, the grand gesture, the rescuing hero. But this is what he kept coming back to: What if he needed that money someday? What if he needed an escape hatch? He'd always had one. Thinking about not having one almost made him dizzy. He kept trying decisions on like jackets: *stay, go, pay everyone off.* In the past, he'd always been able to thrive in this place, the familiar sweet spot of avoidance, keeping a million plates spinning until they all gradually fell and he quickly moved along to something shinier, but this felt different.

Stephanie. He could hear her coming down the stairs now, ready for work, boots pounding the steps hard and fast, too fast; he always braced a little, expected to hear her slip and fall and tumble, but she never did. He'd downplayed the meeting with Nathan, said they'd spent "too much time catching up" and were going to meet again. He would present a milder version of what had happened once he had someone else interested. "Slow down," he said as Stephanie rounded the corner into the kitchen. "You're going to kill yourself on those stairs."

She grinned at him and grabbed a banana from a bowl on the counter. "Already moving too fast for you, Leo?" She peeled the banana, poured milk in her coffee.

He smiled, too, but what he thought, reflexively, was, *Here we go.*

"Hey," she said. "Were you supposed to read something for Bea? She called me yesterday."

Crap. Bea. Her pages. "Crap," Leo said. "I forgot. I'll take a look."

"If recent experience is any indicator, it won't be a long read. Call me at the office if they're decent."

"I guess I'll talk to you tonight," he said, brightly.

"Funny." She leaned over and kissed him. She tasted like banana and coffee, and he pulled her close. He slipped his hands inside her jacket, holding her tight, trying to right whatever was listing inside.

He smoothed back her hair and kissed her, deeply, opening himself to her, and the darkness moving through him lightened. She seemed distracted, stiff, so he ran his hand over her silk blouse until he felt her nipple harden and then moved his tongue the way she liked, lightly across her lip first and then harder, more probing, until he felt her relax against him.

"No fair," she said, softly, pulling away. "I have to go to work." Stephanie knew she had to stop procrastinating and tell Leo what was going on. Tonight, she figured, was as good as any night. "Maybe I'll leave early today."

"Sounds good," he said.

She gave him a quick kiss on the cheek. "Bea," she said, grabbing her bag. "Don't forget."

AFTER STEPHANIE LEFT, he made another pot of coffee. For the first time in weeks, he didn't have any desire to open his computer. Go to his "office." Do work. The thought of sitting and looking out the small back window to the dreary quilt of adjacent brown yards was depressing. His phone vibrated on the counter. He picked it up to see the incoming call. There it was, again. Matilda Rodriguez. He dimly remembered insisting on getting her number the night of the accident and texting her repeatedly when she was still back in the kitchen getting her things before they headed for the car. She wasn't supposed to call. He was going to have to talk to George. It wasn't only Matilda he was avoiding; Jack was sending daily e-mails about a dinner party for Melody's birthday, and Melody had left a handful of messages asking to have lunch. "Just the two of us. It's urgent."

Something here is not right.

He went upstairs and found Bea's leather bag on the bookshelf where he'd left it, back when he believed he had more important things in play. Maybe the story would be good. Maybe he'd have something useful to say about it. He tried to settle his troubled brain and concentrate on the first few paragraphs. It was about some guy named

Marcus. (Leo was surprised to feel a flicker of disappointment that it wasn't an Archie story.) Some guy named Marcus. A wedding. A caterer. A car. Leo's pulse started to race. He flipped through more quickly as words floated off the pages, *headlights, severed limb, emergency room, suture.* "Tomelo, Mami," he read. "Take it." Christ. He turned back to the first page again. The story was about his accident. The story was about him.

CHAPTER TWENTY-EIGHT

The night Stephanie was planning to tell Leo she was
pregnant—but didn't—she came home to find him wearing
the same clothes as when she'd left that morning, including the T-shirt he'd slept in. He was apoplectic about Bea's story. He
must have started reading right after she left and then spent the rest
of the day working himself into his Leo lather. It took her a good five
minutes to calm him down enough to understand what was happening, that the story was about his accident and about someone who
had been hurt during the accident in ways that Leo was not calm
enough—or willing—to explain.

"Did you kill someone?" she finally asked. In the seconds before he
answered she was sure that he had, sure that the wild terror she saw
in his eyes was because he had to tell her that he'd gotten behind the
wheel, inebriated and high, and committed involuntary manslaughter
but had somehow gotten off the hook. But he hadn't. A *severe* injury
was all he would say, something that was bad but had also been taken

care of and if Bea published this story, he insisted, the truth would be out and everyone who had it in for him would not hold back—all this came out in one invective, evasive stream; it was a lot for Stephanie to take in.

Leo stood in front of her, shaking the pages. "This is bullshit!" he said. "It's an Archie story!"

"It is?" Stephanie was surprised. An Archie story. Interesting. "Is it any good?"

"Are you kidding me? That's not the point!" He threw the pages on the table and a couple of the sheets slowly drifted to the floor. He stepped on one, tearing the paper under his heel. "She's pretending it's not an Archie story—she gave the character a different name—but it is. It's about last summer and there is no way on earth she is going to fucking publish that story."

"Have you talked to her?"

"No, not yet. I'm not sure I ever want to talk to Bea again."

"Let's take a deep breath and slow down," Stephanie said. She pulled out a chair and motioned to him. He sat and furiously rubbed his head with his hands and gave a sharp groan. His unwashed hair stuck out at odd angles, the day's beard darkened the lower half of his face, and his eyes were bloodshot and a little crazed.

"Maybe she just needs to know how upsetting this is to you. Maybe there's a way to fix the story. She's writing fiction, for God's sake. It's *one* story—"

"It's not even finished."

"Okay, so it's just a draft. Even better. Let's take one thing at a time." She managed to calm Leo a bit and eventually coax him upstairs to shower and change while she ordered takeout. She reassured him that when he came back downstairs, they'd figure out how to talk to Bea who might be many things but was not cruel or unkind.

Stephanie remembered her earlier phone conversation with Bea and wished she'd known then what she knew now. She could have set the stage for discouraging her, warned her that Leo was not happy.

Shit. Her announcement would have to wait for another day. This was not the night to talk to Leo about fatherhood, not when he was already feeling paranoid and trapped, blindsided.

Stephanie started leafing through her take-out menus, annoyed. This was the part she hated, the part of a relationship that always nudged her to bail, the part where someone else's misery or expectations or neediness crept into her carefully prescribed world. It was such a burden, other people's lives. She *did* love Leo. She'd loved him in a host of different ways at different times in their lives, and she *did* want whatever their current thing was to continue. Probably. But she always came back to this: She was so much better at being alone; being alone came more naturally to her. She led a life of deliberate solitude, and if occasional loneliness crept in, she knew how to work her way out of that particular divot. Or even better, how to sink in and absorb its particular comforts.

On the one hand, she knew that Leo was never going to really change. On the other hand, she knew that Leo had spoiled something for her. She wasn't going to enter into the type of willful ignorance that life with Leo might require, but she wasn't going to settle for less than the charge, the excitement she felt when Leo was around. She was open to love, but she was best at managing her own happiness; it was other people's happiness that sunk her.

She realized (abstractly, she knew) that parenthood was nothing more than being responsible for someone else's happiness all the time, day after day, probably for the rest of her life, but it had to be a little different. It couldn't be the same as feeling responsible for another adult who came to the party full of existing hopes and behaviors and intentions. She and her lovers had always managed to break what they built between them. She never figured out how to nurture the affection so it grew; it always ended up diminished. She knew parents and children could break each other's hearts, but it had to be harder, didn't it?

Stephanie bent to pick up a torn page from the floor and placed it on the table with the rest, which were in disarray. She gathered the pages and put them in order. She sat and started reading from the beginning.

LEO DID FEEL BETTER AFTER A SHOWER. He'd made the water as hot as he could bear, and standing in Stephanie's bathroom as he wiped steam off the mirror, he could see how pink and healthy his skin was. He had lost weight in rehab, and all the running he'd been doing showed. He hadn't let himself go, that was for sure. As he toweled off, he realized that Stephanie was probably downstairs reading. Good. That was easier than explaining to her—in his own words—the details of the accident and its aftermath. Stephanie would know how to handle this; she was an expert at telling people their work needed to be euthanized—she delivered that news all the time—and she was going to have to help him bury Bea's story.

Without even trying, Leo could come up with a list of people, starting with Nathan Chowdhury, who would be only too thrilled to write a scathing exposé about his accident, the hand job, the poor caterer from the Bronx hobbling around on one foot. (They would conveniently ignore or somehow downplay that he'd made her a millionaire.) He could see the accompanying pictures, the old drawing of him as King Roach. God. He hadn't gotten this far—endured rehab, stayed clean for fuck's sake, protected and carefully camouflaged his savings—just to attract the wrong kind of heat now. Or to end up the laughingstock of New York City, to have people pointing and whispering every time he walked into a room, to be the most e-mailed article on Gawker. He couldn't have this looming over his head as he tried to set up meetings. Stephanie needed to help him put the whole thing to rest quickly.

When he walked into the kitchen, Stephanie was slowly leafing through the pages, repeatedly returning to one toward the middle (he knew which one). She was pale. She looked up at him and, ah, yes, he remembered that look. He fought back irritation.

"You see what I'm saying. It's an Archie story," he said. She sat perfectly still. He watched her, nervously. "Just because she doesn't call the guy Archie—"

"This all happened?" she asked, as Leo walked over to the sink and got a glass of water. "She lost her foot?"

"Yes."

"Where is she now?" Stephanie said, still not looking at Leo but at the pages spread on the table in front of her.

"I don't know."

"You haven't heard from her?"

"No," Leo said. "Well, kind of."

"Kind of?"

"She's called a few times, but I haven't responded. George's taking care of it. There was a settlement—a very generous one—and part of the agreement was no contact once the papers were signed."

"I see," Stephanie said. "I guess you better get George on the amputee right away."

"I wasn't privy to the terms of the agreement, Stephanie. I was in rehab. But I have to follow the rules and so does she. It's in everyone's best interest, including hers. If she's caught violating the terms—"

"You guys get the other foot?" Stephanie said. She carefully stacked the papers in the middle of the table, smoothing a page that was wrinkled. Leo thought her hand was trembling a little. He sat down next to her.

"I'm sorry," he said. "I wanted to tell you. I really did. But I have a hard time even thinking about it."

"Aren't you a little bit curious?"

"Curious?"

"To see how she's doing. Why she's calling you? God, Leo, she lost a *foot*."

"I know she's being taken care of. I know she had the absolute best care. I'm not allowed to be curious and contact her."

Stephanie had one hand on her abdomen like she'd just been gut-punched. "But you wouldn't call her even if you were allowed to, right?" she said. "Out of sight, out of mind? Write a check and move on?"

"I'm not sure how I could help her. And, yes, I do want to move on. That's what I've been trying to do here!"

"The money? Is this why—"

"Yes. Francie funded the settlement from the trust," said Leo. "There's not a lot left, not as much as everyone was counting on, and that's why they're circling around here like fucking vultures. Everyone wants me to magically come up with what they think they're owed. You can see my predicament."

"*Your* predicament?"

"How am I supposed to make that kind of sum appear out of thin air? Those three aren't thinking clearly."

"But *you're* thinking clearly?"

"Comparatively? Very much so."

"I see." Stephanie stood and took a wineglass down from the cabinet, opened a corked bottle on the counter, and poured herself an enormous glass. She thought about the pregnancy app on her phone. The first day she opened it, she'd paged through all nine months and had been amused to see week sixteen, the one that said, *This week your baby is a plum!* A Plumb. She dumped the wine down the sink.

"What's her name?" Stephanie asked Leo.

"What difference does that make?" Leo sounded irritated.

"Do you even *know* her name, Leo?" Stephanie watched him carefully. His cheeks were pink from the shower, his hair slicked back. His eyes were guarded, flinty—ugly within his otherwise lovely face.

"Matilda." He bit the word hard, as if there were something illegal about lingering too long on each syllable. His unwillingness to hold her name in his mouth made Stephanie mad.

"What was that?" she said.

Leo straightened and spoke more clearly. "Her name is Matilda Rodriguez."

"And she was nineteen? She was a teenager?"

"Yeah, well." Leo pictured Matilda's fingers and remembered how she'd nervously licked her palm before taking him in her hand. He shook his head, trying to block the image, which had already caused a regrettable hardening in his pants. "She was old enough," he said.

That was the thing he would take back, the words that evoked the tiny but perceptible flinch from Stephanie. She walked over to the table and picked up Bea's story.

"What are you doing with those?" Leo said.

"What are *you* going to do with them?" Stephanie gripped the pages in her hands.

"You see why it can't be published. Forget about me," Leo said. The heat radiating from Stephanie alarmed him. "What if Matilda reads it?"

"Matilda's a big reader of literary fiction?" Stephanie said. "You were able to figure that out during your brief car ride?"

"Okay, forget about Matilda," Leo said. "I'm trying to re-create a life here. Rebuild some kind of business. Bea publishes a new Archie story? Come on. That's news. She publishes *this* story—it's even bigger news and everyone finds out what happened and that's it. I'm fucked. Who's going to work with me?"

Stephanie felt dizzy and nauseated. She had to eat. She was afraid she was going to vomit.

"You know I'm right," Leo said, pacing the kitchen now. "You know if this story is published, people are going to know it's really about me. She can call the guy Archie or Marcus or Barack Obama, it's about ME."

"Even if it is about you, Leo," Stephanie said, shoving a cracker in her mouth, trying to steady the room, soothe her gullet, quell her anger, and ignore her fear. "Even if it is about you, and even *if* Bea gets the thing published, and even *if* someone reads it and connects it to you—" Stephanie took a long sip of water. Exhaled. "Even if all those things happen, who is going to care?"

It was that last sentence she would call back if she could. That was the one where she saw the shift, the slightest narrowing of his gaze, the moment when she had—inadvertently and slightly, but clearly in Leo's eyes, concisely in his mind—positioned herself on the wrong side of a dividing line.

That was the thing she would take back.

CHAPTER TWENTY-NINE

Early morning on the Brooklyn waterfront. The sheer number of people out on a brilliantly sunny but bitingly cold February day surprised Leo. The chill of the wooden bench beneath his legs seeped through his wool trousers and heavy coat. The blue sky felt like a harbinger of spring, but the water was still a dire wintry gray. The leather satchel containing Bea's story was on his lap. It had only been days since he read it but it felt like weeks. He closed his eyes and tried to clear his mind, suppress his rising anxiety, but instead he found himself picturing Matilda's right foot in what would be its waning minutes. Before they got into the car and when she was slipping on her silver shoe, he'd noticed how her toenails were painted bright pink, how the pink glowed against her golden skin, how the elegant arch of her foot sat against the shoe and how, when she stood and looked at him and tugged at her shirt, she was perfectly steady on her two intact feet. Quite possibly the worst thing for him about Bea's new story was this, how it conjured Matilda and everything about Matilda from where he'd buried her deep, deep in a tiny box in some remote corner of his brain.

He reached in his coat pocket for the pack of American Spirit cigarettes he'd bought on a whim but hadn't opened yet, not wanting to further irritate Stephanie by smelling like tobacco. He opened the pack, withdrew a cigarette, and, leaving Bea's leather satchel on the bench, walked over to the railing on the water. He felt sheepish about smoking, which also irritated him. And then he was irritated to feel irritation. Irritation was pretty much his primary sentiment lately, when it wasn't anxiety.

Things were not good inside the little jewel of a brownstone that was Stephanie's. From the street, the rooms behind the new but historically accurate windows glowed with an amber-infused warmth, inviting and cheerful. From the outside, the house looked like the perfect place to take shelter from any variety of storms, but inside? Inside, he and Stephanie were barely maintaining a civil politeness. The softness that had taken root between them since the night of the snowstorm and slowly blossomed into something expansive and occasionally exuberant had collapsed—not a slow leak either, but a sudden deflation, like a sad, sunken soufflé.

They'd fallen into their old ways, accusatory and evasive, which was reassuring in a perverted way. Leo understood the nasty pull of the regrettable familiar, how the old grooves could be so much more satisfying than the looming unknown. It's why addicts stayed addicts. Why he'd walked away from buying cocaine before the family lunch at the Oyster Bar but now had a neat glassine envelope in his pocket. Why he was fingering an unlit cigarette in his hand and wondering what to do about Stephanie as he had countless times before.

Leo could see his future with her and he didn't like it: He would be one of those people who started to parcel time into "years clean." He'd build a callus of superiority around his own self-denial and would become, because of the accident and its aftermath, someone with a bifurcated past, all the accomplishments he valued would be relegated to "before," and his narrative would build around the "after"—

the accident, rehab, divorce, how he straightened up, straightened out, rebuilt from the beginning. If he stayed, he'd have to divide up his money. He'd have to get a job, like every other chump. Since his meeting with Nathan he'd e-mailed or called countless old contacts and all his inquiries added up to a big fat nothing. A few polite brush-offs at best; some never bothered to respond. He didn't know if Nathan had been pissed enough to actually blackball him around town or if he had just gravely miscalculated his own relevance. He didn't want to figure it out.

However he parsed it, his future in New York could only be a diluted reflection of his before, a whiter shade of pale. *Evenness* defined his present, the by-product, he often thought, of small minds and safe living. In his new *after,* there would be no ups and downs, no private jets or unexpected fucking in a tiny bathroom of a bar, or walking home from a riotous evening under a pinkening sky. It wasn't luxury he missed, it was surprise. The things money could buy weren't the reward; the reward was to feel lifted above everyone else, to get a look at the other side of the fence where the grass was rarely greener but always different and what he loved was the contrast—and the choice. The ability to take it in was what mattered; the ability to choose was what mattered.

He'd always leaned into the unknown. Stephanie, too. So why, he wondered, when it came to each other, did they always find themselves spinning their wheels in the same old rut, in the same exact way? He turned his broad back away from the wind coming off the water, enjoyed the familiar feeling of hunching his shoulders and cupping his hand around a lit match until the end of the cigarette glowed a steady amber. He took a deep drag and exhaled energetically. He felt better almost immediately.

Two women walking by with rolled yoga mats under their arms frowned, both furiously waving the air in front of them, as if his nearly imperceptible trickle of smoke was a swarm of stinging wasps. When had New York become so wimpy and pathetic? The city had completely lost its edge. He needed to get out, head somewhere untamed and more deserving of his talents and energy. He turned back to the water, took another satisfying drag off the cigarette, closed his eyes and thought again about his newly concocted plan, ran over the details and tested it for leaks, looked for any scraps of regret or hesitation about his decision. Nope. He felt good. He felt sad about Stephanie, that was a given, but feeling sad about Stephanie was so familiar it was becoming boring or a dangerous habit, or both. He'd casually thought about asking her to take off with him, even for a few weeks, but she never would. That kind of daring wasn't part of her fiber.

He was still annoyed with Bea. Not as angry as he'd been the day he read the story, but still irritated. (There it was again, how had his life suddenly reduced to irritation?) And although he tried not to dwell on it, he was stung by Stephanie's careless comment while knowing she might be right. He'd been out of the public eye so long he might not even be a story. Or he'd just be another in a long line of Internet millionaires who'd been at the right place at the right time doing the new thing and had made a ridiculous sum of money and then lost the money and done something dumb while wasted and maybe screwed the wrong person and wrecked his marriage and who, really, at this point would give a fuckity fuck. In some ways, that was almost harder for Leo to contemplate: the information about his implosion being made public and landing with an echoless whimper.

And then there was Stephanie's inexplicable insistence that he should at least talk to Matilda Rodriguez, find out what she wanted. He knew what she wanted, and even if he did decide to distribute some of his money, it wasn't going to be to the waitress, who'd already profited a nice tidy sum. Stephanie didn't seem to understand that he was prohibited—legally—from talking to Matilda. (Technically, he wasn't completely sure this was true but practically he knew it was the right thing to do. Nothing good could come of establishing contact with her.)

Something odd was going on with Jack, too, who was asking a lot of questions, *a lot of questions,* about trying to set something up that sounded like money laundering. He was asking what Leo knew about offshore accounts and although he didn't precisely word it this way, how to conceal ill-gotten gains. Leo couldn't imagine Jack pulling off something that would require such sophisticated financial maneuvers; he didn't have the balls or the brains. Leo suspected Jack was trying to trick or trap him.

And something else was tugging at Leo. The other day, when he and Stephanie were sitting at her bay window, trading sections of the newspaper, a wary silence between them, one of the neighbors had walked by with a baby in one of those sling contraptions. He'd watched Stephanie watch the mother with the bundle strapped to her chest. She watched them from the minute they came into view until the minute they could no longer be seen. He'd gone clammy. Surely she wouldn't—couldn't, she had to be too old—change her mind about wanting a kid now? She'd sensed Leo assessing her and had ducked behind her hair, but not before he saw something resolute in her face, something private and determined and deeply terrifying.

But maybe worst of all was how she looked at Leo these days, like he was a sad sack, like she was just waiting for him to bail. Well, why wait?

The divorce decree had finally come down; Leo was free. He could leave New York whenever he wanted. He could go straight to the airport with nothing but a small duffel and provision himself more fully when he landed. He didn't mind leaving everything behind, starting from scratch. In fact, he reassured himself, he was looking forward to it. Another thing he'd learned that the other Plumbs hadn't: the beauty of rediscovering the starting line.

He'd get a few things together and head down to the Caribbean for a bit. See old friends and sort out some financial stuff. Then maybe he'd head west, far west, to Saigon. Vietnam was hot now. He could spend the foreseeable future traveling around Southeast Asia. Keep moving until the Plumbs got the picture. He wasn't coming back for a good long time, if ever.

"Hey." A young woman walking her dog appeared at Leo's shoulder. "I don't suppose I could bum a cigarette off you?" she asked.

She was tall, fair skinned, and her cheeks and nose were tinged red from the cold and the exertion of her walk. Her black hair was pulled into a high ponytail, her light eyes striking. Her voice was radio pretty. An actress, he thought. She smiled at him apologetically.

"Sure," he said, taking the pack out of his pocket.

"I'd be happy to reimburse you," she said, winding the leash around her hand to pull the dog closer. "What are they? Twenty bucks a pack now?"

"Almost," Leo said. "I haven't bought one in years, I thought the guy charged me for a carton by mistake." He turned away from the water again and lit her cigarette from the end of his.

"I know. It's crazy. Still, if my boyfriend didn't freak every time I smoked, I'd happily pay for them. I don't care how much they cost." She took the cigarette from Leo and took a long, deep drag, groaning a little as she exhaled. "Oh, that's so good. So good. Does that sound awful?"

"Not to me," Leo said.

"Do you mind if I stand here and smoke with you for a minute?" They both stood at the railing, watching the water. "Remember when everyone used to be able to take cigarette breaks?" she said. "How you could leave the office and stand in front of the building smoking and gossiping and watching people walk by? God, I miss those days."

"I remember when you could smoke *inside* the building," Leo said.

"Oh. From the olden days."

He was pretty sure she was flirting with him. It was hard to tell what might be beneath her bright green, puffy jacket, but if her long, lean legs were a clue, it was bound to be nice. They were facing each other now and Leo noticed a tiny constellation of freckles down her left cheek that looked just like Orion's belt. The single imperfection made her face even more perfect. Her skin was smooth and tight and Leo couldn't help but think of Stephanie and how she was starting to show her age a little—deeper wrinkles around her eyes and mouth, a slight hollowing of her cheeks, a bit of droop around the jowls. The girl turned back toward the water and took another drag off the cigarette; she held her profile serenely, someone accustomed to being admired from all angles. She glanced at her watch.

"Some place you need to be?" Leo said.

"Not today. How about you? Do you work around here?"

"Sometimes," Leo said. "I move from project to project. And you?"

"I live nearby. This is my boyfriend's dog. He's out of town for a few days, so I'm dog sitting. Right, Rupert?" she said to the dog. "Just you and me until Saturday." Leo let the out-of-town boyfriend sit there and acquire a little heft. "Seriously," she said, fiddling now with the zipper on her jacket. "Can I give you money for the cigarette?"

"Absolutely not," Leo said. "My treat." He was gauging whether he should ask her to grab a cup of coffee now or just ask for her number.

"I'm Kristen." She pulled off a glove and put out her hand and Leo shook it. Her palm was warm and dry. She held his gaze and tilted her head a bit, hesitating. "Are you Leo?"

Leo sighed. "I guess that depends," he said.

Kristen laughed. "We met a few times. At that theater in Tribeca? I, uh, I know Victoria."

"Ah," Leo said. He didn't know which night she was talking about. Victoria was always dragging him to some awful performance in that tiny theater.

"I was in a play. You probably don't remember, it was kind of stupid, but I was the younger brother's girlfriend."

"I do remember!" Leo lied. "You were terrific."

"Oh, thanks, but you don't have to say that."

Leo studied her face and had a tiny flash of memory. This girl, standing on stage in a ripped sweater, sobbing and going on and on and on and on. He also thought he remembered her from a long, boozy dinner afterward. Had there been flirting? "You had the monologue at the end, right? You were wearing a brown sweater."

"Wow." She beamed. "You do remember."

"I remember *you*. Couldn't tell you anything else about the play but your performance—it stuck with me."

"Wow." A tiny line appeared on her brow, so isolated and faint that it had to be a minor failure of Botox. "That's so great to hear. I worked really hard on that monologue. For weeks I drove everyone crazy practicing."

"The effort showed," Leo said. He held her gaze. This was exactly what he needed today. "We talked afterward, right? At that French place?"

"Yeah," she said, amused. "We talked."

And then he remembered. He'd cornered her in a small hallway leading to a bathroom. Nothing had really happened, a little body contact, she was there with someone, too.

"So . . ." She trailed off, laughed a little, and looked down at the dog then back at Leo smiling.

"So," Leo said.

"I'm not friends with Victoria or anything."

"Me neither. We're divorced."

"I'm sorry," she said, not sounding the tiniest bit sorry.

"Don't be."

She looked back out at the water and he waited. "Are you off to work right now?" she asked.

"Nope," Leo said. "There's nothing going on at work today that needs my attention."

"Want to get some coffee? Breakfast? There's a good place nearby. I just have to drop the dog off at home."

"I could do that," Leo said.

"Excellent." She smiled at him and then looked down at the dog. "C'mon, Rupert," she said. "Let's show our friend where you live." As they turned to leave, she stopped and pointed to Bea's leather satchel sitting on the bench. "Is that yours?" she asked.

Leo looked at the brown leather case. He remembered buying it, how proud he'd been when he bargained the seller in London down to less than half the listed price. When he got the thing home, he decided it was a little on the twee side, a little too uptown, so he'd given it to Bea. "That is definitely not mine," he said, relieved to note his ebbing anxiety, his elevated mood. He probably shouldn't leave the case sitting there. But then he saw Paul Underwood approaching from less than a block away, right on schedule, set to arrive at the bench precisely at 8:55 A.M., as he did every weekday. Leo dropped his cigarette and ground it beneath his heel. He was doing everyone a favor by getting out of town, he thought. People abandoned one another constantly without performing the courtesy of actually disappearing. They left but they didn't, lurking about, a constant reminder of what could or should or might have been. Not him.

"You think it's okay to just leave it there?" she asked.

Leo looked at the satchel again and then back at Paul, who'd seen him and raised a hand in recognition. "Sure," Leo said. "If it's important, whoever left it will come back. Okay, Rupert," he said to the dog, clapping his hands. "Lead the way."

CHAPTER THIRTY

L et me do the talking," Vinnie said, sitting at Matilda's kitchen table and paging through her contacts, looking for Leo's name.

"It'll go straight to voice mail," she said. "I'm telling you."

If it was possible, Vinnie was even more pissed to learn that Matilda had called Leo Plumb after the night he'd brought over the mirror, after they'd argued. "I thought about what you said," she told him. "I decided maybe you were right." She had dialed Leo's number a few times, she finally confessed to Vinnie, but it always went straight to voice mail and she didn't want to leave a message.

"We'll dial all night if we have to." He touched the screen and put the phone on speaker and, as Matilda predicted, the computer-generated voice mail came on. Vinnie disconnected and hit redial. This time, after only two rings, someone answered. A woman. Vinnie and Matilda were momentarily stunned.

"Hello," they both said at once.

"Hello?" the woman said.

Vinnie held a hand up, signaling for Matilda to be quiet. She shook her head and pointed to herself. She could do this. Vinnie nodded at her. *Go,* he mouthed.

"My name is Matilda Rodriguez." Silence. She cleared her throat and leaned closer to the phone sitting on the table to make sure her voice could be heard. "And I would like to speak to Leo Plumb."

"That makes two of us," Stephanie said.

CHAPTER THIRTY-ONE

Melody's birthday was usually a grim-weather affair occurring when it did, in the waning days of February. New York in February was still weeks away from any sustained sun or morning birdsong or tender plant shoots breaking through the mottled dirt. The holidays and New Year celebrations were already a distant memory, as diminished as the lingering, soot-covered curbside snowpack that would finally melt under a gloomy March rain only to expose neat little piles of desiccated dog shit.

But every so often, like the day of her fortieth birthday, the weather gods would smile upon Melody and lift the hem of the jet stream just far enough north to create a brilliant preview of spring, embryonically warm and inviting. It was the kind of day that can fool the crocuses into blooming too soon and the twentysomething denizens of New York into baring their winter-white legs and walking down the recently salted pavement in arch-destroying flip-flops, dirtying the

bottoms of their feet still tender and pink from months of being cod-
dled by socks and boots and sheepskin slippers.

Heading south on the Taconic, a furious Walt was driving exactly
four miles above the speed limit; the mood in the car was tense. After
Melody's absurd counteroffer and her subsequent refusal to budge, the
two potential buyers for their house became impatient and moved on.
When Walter discovered her deception, he was more dumbfounded
than enraged. He was about to call Vivienne Rubin to reopen negotiations when the promising e-mail from Leo had arrived. Melody managed to convince him to wait until after her birthday dinner.

Melody knew Walt was also annoyed at how giddy she was being
about the birthday celebration. Easy for him to say, he had forty-five
years of wonderful birthdays behind him. Easy for him to be all blasé
and world-weary, but she was turning forty and this was the first real
birthday celebration she'd had, well, pretty much ever.

Melody's first and last birthday party happened the year she'd
turned twelve, a rare capitulation on Francie's part. Walking home
from school that day with her three closest friends, Melody could
barely contain her excitement—while repressing the distant drum-
beat of concern. She'd asked her mother to buy a variety of foods, to
set the table, to organize games. Francie had waved off her instruc-
tions, saying "I think I know how to keep people entertained."

But the only party Melody remembered having taken place at the
Plumb house was a birthday party for Francie the previous summer
that had become so raucous and gone on so late that the neighbors
had complained to the police. The cops, all friends of Leonard and
Francie, joined the festivities and sat in the back sipping beer. Melody
watched from the upstairs bathroom window as her mother gently
bounced on the lap of the policeman who showed up at her school
every year to talk to them about stranger danger; he called himself
"Officer Friendly." Officer Friendly's hands rested easily on either side
of Francie's waist, right above the swell of her hips. "Hands up!" he
kept saying and Francie would raise her arms high above her head
and laugh as his open palms slid up her torso, stopping when his fin-

gers grazed the underside of her breasts. Melody was certain there hadn't been any games at that party. Or gift bags. Just a cake and music and lots of cigarettes and cocktails.

Francie greeted Melody and her school friends at the door wearing a silk kimono and holding a martini. Melody's heart sank. The robe this early in the day was a very bad sign. As was the cocktail.

"Welcome, ladies, welcome." Francie waved the group through the front door. Melody could see the girls looking around the Plumb house and then eyeing each other, warily but with interest. The Tudor house was stately from the outside, but the inside was worn and neglected, chaotic. The foyer where the girls stood in their winter coats was a muddle of outerwear from all seasons. Coats were piled on a bench, hats and mittens spilled out of baskets on the floor, there were shoes everywhere—broken flip-flops, evening sandals, insulated boots, snowshoes.

"You're right on time," Francie said. "I admire punctuality in guests."

"We came straight from school," Melody's friend Kate said. "It's a quick walk."

"So you did. So you did," Francie said, focusing on Kate, looking her over. "Are you the logical one, the A student?"

"Mom," Melody said. She wanted her mother to stop talking to her friends. She especially wanted to stop this line of inquiry, one of Francie's favorite gambits, assigning people a descriptor based on her first—often uncanny—impression. Melody wanted Francie to go upstairs and put on a pair of pants and a sweater and pull her hair back with a black velvet headband like Kate's mother, or to carry cookies and hot cocoa out on a tray like Beth's mother and ask about their homework, or to burst through the door after a day spent working at an office in the city like Leah's mother and hustle straight to the kitchen saying, in her thrilling Irish timbre, "Supper soon, loves. You must be starved!"

"Logic is an underrated attribute," Francie said, continuing to address Kate. "Logic goes a long way in life, longer than lots of other things." She turned to the other two girls and squinted a little as if bringing them into clearer focus, plucking a cocktail onion from her martini. "You're the pretty one," she said, pointing a gin-dampened finger at Beth who was, in fact, the prettiest girl at school; Melody had been quietly thrilled when Beth started chatting with her after French class one day, telling Melody what products to use to get her bangs to stick up higher and sharing her glitter mascara.

"And you," Francie said, eyeing Leah, who took a step backward and clenched her fists, almost as if she knew to brace herself for Francie's reductive assessment, "must be the lesbian."

"Mom!"

"What's a lesbian?" said Kate.

"Never mind," Melody said, grabbing Leah by the arm and motioning for the other two to follow her. "She's kidding. It's a family joke. I'll explain later."

It *was* a kind of family joke, although not one Melody could explain. Leah was Melody's oldest friend, a nondescript blurry kind of girl whose most noticeable feature was a persistently runny nose from year-round hay fever. Leah tended to moon a little while following Melody around school, sniffling and sneezing.

"How's your lesbian lover?" Bea would ask Melody, referring to Leah. "You guys going steady yet?"

"Shut up," Melody would say. She didn't even know at first what lesbian meant. She sneaked into Leonard's study one day to look it up in the dictionary and then had to look up *homosexual* and although she knew right away that the word didn't describe her, she knew who it did describe: Jack. She pictured Jack and his friends sitting in the summer sun, lounging by the pool at the club, rubbing baby oil on each other's shoulders. *Homosexuals,* she thought, slamming the book closed.

Melody had led everyone to the kitchen at the back of the first floor. There were no streamers, no balloons, no festive paper plates and matching cups or shiny cardboard letters spelling out *Happy Birthday* strung above the breakfast nook, but there was a cake box.

Melody was hugely relieved to see that there would, at the very least, be cake.

"Where's the party?" Kate said, staring at the kitchen sink full of dirty dishes and the table scattered with catalogs and empty grocery bags.

"The party is wherever you make it, ladies." Francie had followed the girls to the kitchen to refill her glass, the martini shaker glistening on the butter-and-crumb-streaked counter. "Party is an attitude, not a destination."

The girls looked at her, confused. Even though it was February, Francie marched the girls outside to the lawn beyond the patio, which was devoid of snow but still frozen and bare, and led an anemic game of Pin the Tail on the Donkey. "For God's sake," Francie yelled, standing on the patio in a fur coat, smoking, as the girls walked gingerly forward, mittened hands stretched out in front of them, "how hard can it be to locate an enormous tree trunk?"

The Pin the Tail game was old, had been sitting in the storage area under the stairs for years. Melody frantically tried to remember what else was housed in that space overloaded with broken toys and old board games. How could she fake a party for two whole hours?

"I think you girls have the hang of it," Francie said after bringing them back inside and handing Leah a key chain with a tiny dangling Rubik's cube from the junk drawer as a prize for pinning her tail closest to the donkey's ass. "I'll check back with you in a little bit."

Melody started sifting through the boxes under the stairs, wondering if she could salvage enough Monopoly money to keep a game going. "I have Twister," she said to her friends. "The spinner is broken, but we can close our eyes and point to a color and play that way. It works just as well."

"Maybe I should just call my mom," Beth said. All the girls were still wearing their coats.

"I'm thirsty," said Leah.

"We could have cake?" Kate suggested. The other two girls nodded eagerly.

Melody knew that cake was the *last* thing to happen at a birthday party. After all the games and snacks, the birthday cake was cut and everyone grabbed their gift bag and went home. Melody did not want to cut the cake. As she stood there with the broken Twister spinner in her hand, trying not to surrender to the tears that had been threatening to spill forth with humiliating force since her mother had greeted them, the front door opened. Leo.

Leo had taken pity on Melody that day. He made huge bowls of buttered popcorn for the girls. He went up to his room and brought back a deck of cards and taught them how to play blackjack with pennies; he played the dealer. He brought down the vinyl records he kept under lock and key in his room and let them dance and lip-synch behind his air guitar version of "Start Me Up." Just when things were looking up, Francie reappeared, ushering the girls—sweaty and breathless and all a little in love with Leo—into the living room for cake, a cake she'd clearly forgotten to order in advance. "Congratulations, Betty!" the cake said, with a little frosting stork underneath, carrying a folded diaper in its beak.

"Who's Betty?" Beth asked.

"That's another family joke," Melody said, enjoying the versatility of this new excuse, tucking it away for future use. The cake tasted delicious, though, and the girls all took huge pieces and moved to the sofa, where Francie made them sit and listen to her play Harold Arlen songs on the piano. At first it was fun and watching her mother's fingers almost dance above the keyboard, Melody thought that if the party ended right then, right after the rousing version of "If I Only Had a Brain," everything would be fine. The party would be dubbed a success the next day at school. Her reputation saved.

But then Francie started singing "Over the Rainbow" and only a few verses in she started to weep. "Mom?" Melody said, weakly.

"It's just so, so sad," Francie said. She turned to them. "The studios killed Judy Garland. *They killed her.* That voice and what a tragedy. They made her and then they killed her." The girls were sitting quietly, nervously giggling. "Uppers to work all day. Downers to sleep at night. She was just a kid." Francie stood now, facing them, her robe gaping a little in front. "I wanted to be an actress. I could have gone to Hollywood."

"You could have been a real contender, Fran," Leo said, leaning against the doorjamb, amused.

"Why didn't you?" Beth said, brightening a little. She wanted to go to Hollywood, talked about it all the time. Her parents had taken her on a family trip to Universal Studios the previous summer and she'd loved every minute of it, talked about the studio tour like she'd flown to Los Angeles for a screen test.

"My father wouldn't let me." Francie sat on a large enormous club chair across from the girls. "He thought it was unseemly. He insisted I go to college, stay home. Then I met Leonard and got knocked up and that was that."

"Mom!"

Francie scowled at Melody and waved her hand like she was waving away tiny gnats. "Oh, relax, Emily Post." She closed her eyes and put her feet up on an ottoman and started to nod off. From across the room, Leo shrugged at Melody. The shrug was more resigned than sympathetic. *See?* the shrug said. *Remember this the next time you want to invite friends over.*

When Beth's mother arrived to take the girls home, she surveyed the scene—the baby-shower cake, Francie lightly snoring in a robe, the empty martini glass on the piano—and quietly closed the pocket doors between the living room and the front hall. As she helped the girls button their coats and locate mittens, Melody heard Beth tell her mother, "She said I was the pretty one. Why did she say Leah was a lesbian?"

Melody had been scared to show up at school the next day, worried about what her friends would say about her weepy, inebriated, odd mother. But all they talked about was the extremely cool birthday party where Leo Plumb, a high school senior, had sung and danced with them and taught them how to gamble.

"Hey, Betty!" the three girls would say—with affection, not

mockery—when they saw Melody in the hall. She'd never been happier than those weeks and months at the end of sixth grade.

So Melody had been stunned—and thrilled—when Jack and Walker offered to host a fortieth birthday dinner in her honor. Every year she told Walt that all she wanted was a quiet birthday celebration at home with her family and she was always, *always* disappointed when he believed her.

"I really think Leo is going to come through tonight," she said, flipping down the sun visor and applying lipstick in the tiny mirror. "I think he's going to surprise everyone with good news."

"That certainly would be a surprise."

"I don't know why, but something about birthdays brings out the best in Leo. Really."

"If you say so."

"I do!" Melody turned the radio up and hummed along with a song she sort of knew. Leo's e-mail had been vague, true, but it was also encouraging. She'd nearly memorized the long paragraph, something about an exciting project for Nathan that was coming together "very quickly," how he'd left town to meet with some investors and would be out of touch but back with a progress report in time for her birthday dinner. "I'm very optimistic," he'd written.

Walter raised his voice a little to be heard above the radio. "What I really think," he said, "is the sooner everyone lets go of Leo as their personal savior, the better off everyone will be. Including you. Including us."

Melody turned the radio volume higher. She didn't want him to ruin her hopeful mood. He'd never believed in The Nest and sometimes she thought he was almost enjoying being right. She believed Leo was going to come through tonight. On her birthday! She'd spent the entire day as if she were preparing for a date. Bought a new dress (on the secret card, *that's* how sure she felt), got her nails done, had dug out the pretty dangly (faux) diamond earrings Walt had bought for her after the girls were born. She checked herself in the mirror again. Maybe the earrings were too much. She shouldn't have used so much hair stuff. She started playing with her bangs. Melody always felt wrong around her siblings, just a little off. She could see them assessing her clothing, judging Walt. (How *dare* they! They wouldn't know a kind, good, capable person if—well, if their sister married one.) She shook her head. Tonight was going to be different. It was.

Walter gripped the steering wheel a little harder, biting back his words, dreading the ride home when Melody would be a basket case. He'd give her a day or two to recover from whatever went down with (*without*) Leo tonight and then the house was going back on the market. He felt sorry thinking about what were surely the difficult weeks ahead, but he was also eager to get the necessary changes under way. They would get through it. Melody would rise to the occasion. She always did. He'd always been able to count on her.

LOUISA WAITED IMPATIENTLY at the front door of the SAT offices on West Sixty-Eighth Street, eyeing the threatening clouds that were moving in swiftly ahead of a cold front bringing weather that was more typical for this time of year. It was going to rain and Louisa wanted to get to Jack's house before it started. She knew Nora was upstairs saying good-bye to Simone for the week. She stood in the foyer of the building that smelled like bleach and rancid mop and tried not to think about what her sister was doing with Simone that very minute.

THREE FLOORS DIRECTLY ABOVE LOUISA, Nora was wishing she could skip her mother's birthday dinner and spend the rest of the night in the bathroom stall with Simone who was kneeling on the closed toilet lid so none of the other girls in the bathroom knew they were both in there. Simone had a finger over Nora's lips and Nora lifted the hem of Simone's skirt and found skin where she expected to find underwear.

"Oh," Nora said, and Simone mouthed, *Shhh,* as they gripped each other and swayed to a tinny bossa nova beat that rose from someone's open window up through the back alley and into the tiny stall.

It was so simple, but ever since Simone's easy incantation—*you don't have to be anyone's mirror*—Nora had felt released, giddy. She loved her family—her father, her sister, her mother; they were so dear to her and she would never hurt them or intentionally disappoint them—but Simone was right. Nora had to stop worrying about what everyone else needed and think about herself. And what she needed was to come clean to Louisa because she hated having a secret from her sister. It made her feel like she was doing something wrong. And she wasn't.

When Nora met Louisa at the front door, she'd run so fast down three flights of stairs that she was dizzy, dry mouthed. When Louisa saw her flushed face, swollen lips, she frowned. They both swallowed hard. "We're going to be late," Louisa said, pushing through the swinging doors and stepping out into the rain. "Mom is going to freak."

WALKER HAD CANCELED his Saturday afternoon clients and left work early to cook. He was standing in his and Jack's tiny but artfully designed kitchen, ebulliently pounding chicken breasts between two slices of parchment paper. He'd planned a spring-themed dinner and even though it wasn't quite spring, the universe had cooperated; it was a beautiful evening, temperate enough to open the windows in the living room and enjoy the faint earthy scent of the softening ground.

Walker couldn't remember the last time they'd entertained Jack's family. It had been years. Melody's birthday dinner had been Walker's idea. He'd been itching to get them all together in one room and try to make a tiny inroad into facilitating some kind of agreement about the infernal sum of money they still insisted on calling The Nest, which drove Walker mad. Aside from being infantile, he couldn't fathom how a group of adults could use that term in apparent earnestness and never even casually contemplate the twisted metaphor of the thing, and how it related to their dysfunctional behavior as individuals and a group. Just one of many things about the Plumb family he'd stopped trying to understand.

But Walker did understand conflict resolution, and as an attorney who had to mediate many a divorce, many a broken business partnership, he also understood how money—and the entitlement that often accompanied just the *idea* of money—could warp relationships and memories and decisions. He'd seen it happening with Jack and his family for years, and enough was enough.

He thought Jack was probably right; Leo probably had money somewhere, but chasing Leo was a loser's game. Leo, Walker thought, was a loser. They all mythologized him like he was some kind of brilliant withholding god who just needed the right sacrifice to let loose his abundant blessings. As far as Walker could tell, Leo was just someone who'd been relatively bold at the right time and had lucked out very young. SpeakEasyMedia was a formula that made him wealthy. He wasn't even rich by New York standards and what had he done since then? Nothing. Blown his wad. Become a leech.

But since Leo's accident Walker had observed an interesting dynamic: The siblings were communicating again, and although the conversations usually began with Leo and the money, something else had started to happen. They were making casual forays into one another's lives. He'd heard Jack and Melody on the phone countless times talking about things other than Leo, other than The Nest. Bea had always been the most amiable and accessible of the bunch; he thought she would welcome some kind of coming together. If Leo could just agree to *something* tonight, anything, some kind of payment plan, installments, just throw everyone a bone so they could stop gnawing the worn and brittle cartilage of The Nest—maybe they could move on, try to forge relationships with one another that weren't about that blasted inheritance.

Walker excelled at mediation, delivering people from their own self-inflicted misery. Families were the hardest, he knew, but he also knew how to try to bring adults past their own wounds and help them find their way, if not to affection at least to accommodation. It didn't always happen, but it could. There was no reason the Plumbs couldn't start to accommodate one another and work toward some semblance of family, no matter how tentative or messy.

Walker also suspected that Jack was in some kind of financial pickle. So what else was new? He'd tell Walker in his own time and they'd figure it out. Tonight's plan: Bring them together over food. Stay focused on Melody's birthday at first. A bit of bubbly, a gorgeous chicken scaloppini, the coconut cake he remembered Melody saying she liked once. Then a gentle discussion about kindness. *Accommodation*. A different and sturdier kind of nest.

AS JACK LIT THE VOTIVES lining the windowsill, which would lend a warm glow to the whole room, softening its ordinary, postwar architecture, parquet flooring, and flimsy plasterboard, he was also surreptitiously e-mailing his contact for selling the Rodin. The initial interest in the sculpture had been impressive, but Jack had quickly narrowed the field to two buyers and one had dropped out when figures started being discussed. The remaining individual, someone he'd never met but had heard about, was a collector from Saudi Arabia who lived full time in London and part time in New York. He was a frequent buyer of black-market pieces with questionable—or infamous—provenance. What any of these guys did with art they essentially had to keep secret from the rest of the world Jack didn't know. Not his problem or concern.

When Jack first offered Tommy O'Toole his assistance getting rid of the Rodin, Tommy was under the mistaken impression that Jack could find a way to return the statue to its original owners. "That would be extremely unwise," Jack told him. "You will wind up arrested and on the front page of the paper." He explained about the person he had in mind, a foreigner of vague business pursuits. "We're going to go in high on the price, but even after negotiating, this will be a lot of money," Jack told Tommy.

"I don't care about the money," Tommy said. "I just want it to end up in a safe place, taken care of."

"Of course," Jack said soothingly. Nobody ever admitted it was about the money. Grandma's engagement ring, Aunt Gertie's emerald bracelet, the Chippendale table that had been passed down for generations—it was never about the money. Except that it was always, completely and totally, about the money.

And the money, the vast sum, was causing Jack concern. They were going to have to find a way to handle the amount without attracting the wrong kind of attention. He was going to get Leo alone tonight and ask for specific advice, which would satisfy him on two fronts: how to handle his and Tommy's windfall, and determining exactly how familiar Leo was with concealing funds.

Jack could hear Walker in the kitchen, whistling off-key along with the classical music station. Schubert something. Walker was always happiest when he was entertaining. Jack sent a little plea out to the universe. If he could sell the statue, pay off the loan, he would be a changed man. He wouldn't even care about The Nest. If he could save the summerhouse, he would forgive Leo about the accident. Tabula rasa and so on. He would be a better person, a kinder and more responsible person, a person of integrity and honesty—the type of person Walker deserved.

BEA WAS STANDING CLUELESSLY in front of the office espresso machine, a ridiculously elaborate Italian contraption that required setting pressure gauges and estimating water flow in relation to espresso grind and examining steam thermometers clipped to milk pitchers. Bea was a tea drinker but every once in a while she wanted, needed, coffee. Every time she approached the gleaming machine she wound up timidly turning a few knobs, peering at its undercarriage, and then just walking downstairs to the corner deli. But today she didn't feel like going back outside.

She was in the office on a Saturday trying to catch up, and she was exhausted from a series of insomniac nights and near constant worry about Leo who had been completely incommunicado since she delivered her new story to him. She hadn't been able to get back in touch with Stephanie either to ask about the strange e-mail from Leo about being "off the grid" that sounded like complete Leo bullshit or to find out if they were going to show up for Melody's birthday dinner as planned. She didn't even know what to hope for: Leo or no Leo; furious Leo or indifferent Leo—given his silence, enthusiastic Leo didn't seem remotely possible. If Leo didn't show, all hell was going to break loose.

"How much did this dumb machine cost, anyway?" Bea asked Paul. Technically, office expenses were her domain, but she barely paid attention.

"I paid for it," Paul said. "It was my gift to the office. Would you like me to make you something?"

"Yes, please." Bea sat on the couch opposite the coffee machine. It was low to the ground, and the cushions were stiff and covered with a nubby fabric. She was wearing one of her favorite outfits in an attempt to lift her mood. A bright red jumper with knee-high patent-leather boots. The back of her legs were exposed and the sofa was scratchy.

"Why can't we have a comfy sofa?" she said. She knew she sounded like an entitled and petulant teenager but didn't care. "Something you can sink into and maybe read and hang out."

"Because this is an office and I want people doing the opposite of getting comfy and hanging out." Paul liked to see everyone sitting upright at their desks, good posture, intently looking at computers and pecking away at their keyboards in the center of their otherwise orderly desks.

She checked the e-mail on her phone again as the espresso machine started to thump and hiss like a steam engine. If Leo was truly gone, Stephanie either had helped him and was covering it up or Leo was duping her, too. Bea moved from the sofa and sat at the office communal table. Lowered her head onto her crossed arms and felt the cool of the wood against her cheek. She felt like crying. She felt like screaming. She just wanted to be able to hear Leo's voice and try to figure out what was really going on. She wanted to know what Leo thought about the story. She wanted her lucky leather bag back.

PAUL WOULD CREDIT his nearly perfect cappuccino (the foam could have been a little *brighter* but the richness of the coffee itself was superb) for working its magic on Bea, loosening her tongue, as he'd been patiently waiting for her to do. She'd taken two long sips and smiled, feebly but genuinely, and said, "This is *exactly* what I needed."

He asked if something was wrong and it all came out in one breathless stream. She thought Leo was on a bender. Or that he'd skipped town. She told him about the accident, about the night in the hospital and how she'd become complicit in silencing the poor girl who had gone to work one night and ended up minus a foot. She told him about her story and how she'd given it to Leo and then he had, essentially, vanished. She told him about the Tuck nightmares. She finished pale and depleted. The quick pulse at the corner of her eye was beating as if there were tiny wings trapped beneath the skin.

Paul watched her as she spoke, enjoying—perhaps more than he should have—the slow realization that he had the thing she was looking for. The natty leather folder had been sitting in his office for days, ever since he'd seen Leo saunter away from the waterfront bench with some woman who wasn't Stephanie. He assumed the leather bag belonged to one of them and had put it in his office for safekeeping. He'd left a message for Leo saying he had it, but Bea's recent report explained why Leo wasn't responding to—or maybe even getting—his messages.

Paul would be lying if he said that he didn't estimate—as Bea was talking—how the depth of her relief and gratitude toward him would increase in direct proportion to her visible distress. He could have stopped her, but he let her go on. He wasn't even listening to what she said as much as watching her lips move, eyeing the pink flush that crept out the top of her white blouse and worked its way up her neck, watching her furiously fight off tears and try to steady her chin.

"What do you think?" she finally said. He realized she had stopped talking and was staring at him staring at her.

"Think?" he managed.

"Where do you think he is? What he's doing?"

"I don't know where Leo is or what he's doing," Paul said, walking over to his office and coming back with Bea's satchel. "But is this what you're talking about?" He handed it to her and she gasped.

"Oh my God," she said. "How do you have this? Did Leo leave this for you?"

Had Leo left it for him? "Maybe?" Paul said to Bea.

Bea was loosening the straps and she pulled out the stack of pages. "They're marked up," she said. "He marked them up."

"Leo?"

"Yes, this is Leo's writing." Quickly flipping through, she saw scribbling on almost every page in the blue pencil Leo favored and in his tiny crimped hand and in their shared and peculiar vernacular (*use, use with caution, do not use*).

"He read it," she said, not really believing it yet. The pages in her hands, marked with Leo's edits, had to be his way of giving her—if not approval—permission. Because she knew Leo. If he wanted the story to go away, he never would have taken the time to sit and make it better. He would have burned the pages in Stephanie's hearth. He would have deposited the entire bundle into a trash can on the street. He would have dumped the whole thing into the river. If she knew anything, she knew that. But he hadn't. She looked for a longer note on the last page that might offer some kind of explanation, a clearer benediction, but there wasn't one.

She flipped back to the beginning. "What?" Paul said, seeing the look on her face, the wonder and relief. It was right there, right on the first page where Leo had crossed out the name she'd chosen for her character, "Marcus," and in its place wrote "Archie" and in the left-hand margin, underlined twice: *use*.

CHAPTER THIRTY-TWO

Nora and Louisa were not used to being the center of attention at a family gathering and they liked it. When they arrived at Jack and Walker's place, their parents and Bea were already there. As they entered the living room, folding their rickety black street umbrellas, all motion and conversation stopped. The girls, at sixteen, were mesmerizing to the assembled crowd in a way they hadn't been when they were shy little girls who buried their faces in their father's meaty thigh at the occasional family event.

Louisa was the spitting image of Melody as a teenager, so much so that Jack was staring at her uneasily, atavistically braced for the familiar visage from the past to crumple and weep over some imagined slight. Instead, Louisa's version of Melody's face smiled at him, curious and warm and sweet. He felt like running his hand over her hair to feel the shape of her skull. Unnerved, he squeezed her upper arm a little too hard and she winced.

Bea hugged both girls tightly and then held them at arm's length, exclaiming over their hair, their height, their identical smattering of freckles on unidentical faces. "You are such beauties!" she kept saying, pulling them close to her and kissing them on both cheeks, making them both think of a word they'd never had occasion to use before: *continental.* "How have you grown so much since last summer? You're young women."

Nora and Louisa beamed with pleasure. Walker filled everyone's glasses with champagne and offered Nora and Louisa flutes of lemonade. His spirits were high and so was the color in his cheeks. Jack watched him appraising the room and the table, eyes darting, making sure everything was perfectly in its place, before bustling back to the kitchen.

Nora and Louisa were fascinated by everything: the apartment, the table, their mother's unlikely flirtatious demeanor ("Appetizers! Plural? More than one?" Melody was nearly giddy); their uncle Jack who was a more petite, elfin version of their uncle Leo; their high-spirited aunt Beatrice who they both reticently realized was a slightly prettier version of their mother. They both instinctively gravitated toward Walker, who was wearing a chef's apron over his gently protruding middle. The only unsurprising presence in the room was their father, who sat at the table, reassuring and solid, tearing into a piece of bread, sniffing one of the runny cheeses, and winking at his girls as if to say, *This is something else, isn't it?*

Walker beckoned the girls into the kitchen and they eagerly followed him. He topped off their flutes of lemonade with a generous glug of champagne. "Don't tell your mother," he said. "And I'm not keeping track of how much is in this bottle." He plunged the champagne into a sweaty copper ice bucket and headed back to the living room. Louisa and Nora drank their cocktails quickly and made new ones, adding just enough lemonade to not have the contents look suspicious.

Out in the living room, Walker announced they'd give Stephanie and Leo ten more minutes and then dinner would be served. Walker had lined the table with platters of bread and cheese, tiny ceramic bowls with olives. He'd scattered lemons and twigs of rosemary down the center. Melody's admiration was worth the extra effort.

"It looks just like Italy," she said to Walker.

"And when have you been to Italy?" Jack asked.

Walker threw Jack a look that said *don't*. Melody was too pleased to even notice. "Oh, I haven't, but I watch the Travel Channel all the time. Right, Walt? Don't I watch the Travel Channel nonstop? They just did a piece on Sorrento, all the lemons, so pretty. Limoncello."

"Don't say another word." Walker ran to the kitchen and returned seconds later waving a bright bottle of unopened limoncello in his hand. "For dessert!" Melody actually jumped up and down a little and clapped her hands. Jack reluctantly recognized that this was nice: his family admiring Walker's exquisite taste. Wait until dinner, they were all going to be blown away.

On the other side of the river, lightning was illuminating the New Jersey skyline. Everyone moved to the window to watch the storm make its way across the Hudson. Nora slipped away, unnoticed, down the hall. She couldn't have named the impulse that made her want to see Jack and Walker's bedroom, she just wanted to see it. The door was closed and she gently knocked even though she knew everyone was still in the living room. She opened the door, crossed the threshold, and quickly closed the door behind her. She felt against the wall for the light switch, flipped the light on.

She didn't know what she expected to see, but it wasn't the room she found herself standing in—an entirely ordinary bedroom housing what she assumed was an antique bed and rocker, a long dresser with lots of framed photos on top. The bed looked small to Nora, especially for Walker who was—well, he was substantial. The bed was neatly made. There were no clothes scattered around like her parents' room. It was just a tidy bedroom.

She walked over to the dresser and started looking at the pictures. The biggest one, the one in the center, was of Jack and Walker. She picked it up to take a closer look. They were both wearing tuxedos and boutonnieres and both holding their left hands up to the camera and showing off wedding bands. As she was putting the picture back, the door swung open and Louisa came in. "There you are!" she said. "What are you doing?"

"Nothing," Nora said. "Looking."

"Snooping," Louisa said.

"Look." Nora pointed to the photo. "They got married."

Louisa walked over and stared at the photo. "Wow," she said. "I wonder if Mom knows."

"It would kind of suck if she knew and didn't go."

"Maybe she doesn't even know. Maybe she wasn't invited."

"That would kind of suck, too."

"Yeah," Louisa said. She stood and took in the bedroom as Nora had been doing minutes before. "I didn't expect it to look like this," Louisa said.

"What does that mean?" Nora said. Even though she knew exactly what Louisa meant; she'd had the same reaction. She'd expected the room to be more—something.

"I just mean, it's so—" Louisa was trying not to use the word *normal,* she knew that wasn't right, but it was all she could think of. "It's so plain," she finally said.

Nora and Louisa stood quietly. They were both a little light-headed from the champagne on an empty stomach. Outside the window, a sharp crack of lightning. They jumped. A deep roll of thunder. They looked at each other, the air stormy between them, charged. Louisa sat on the bed. Her head was starting to throb. She suddenly wanted to go home.

"I have to talk to you about something," Nora said. She hadn't been planning on having this conversation now, but the champagne loosened her tongue.

"I know," Louisa said. "I saw. You and Simone. At the museum one day."

"You did?" Nora was embarrassed, trying to think of what Louisa might have seen. God, what if she had been at the IMAX.

"Are you—?" Louisa said. "Are you—?"

"I don't know," Nora said. She sat down on the bed next to Louisa. "I like Simone. That's all I know. I like her."

"She intimidates me."

"I know she does."

"She's so sure of herself."

Nora nodded. "She is. But she's also smart and funny and nice. And I really like her."

The rain was coming down harder. Jack and Walker's bedroom faced an inner courtyard. People coming home from work were running to get inside, holding briefcases and coats over their heads. "Do you think I'm gay?" Louisa said. Nora laughed, relieved they were finally talking. "Please don't laugh at me," Louisa said, covering her face with her hands, trying not to cry.

"Do you like boys or girls? You know what you like."

Louisa spoke into her hands. "Boys."

"Okay."

"I don't think I can be a lesbian."

"Okay." Nora was grateful that Louisa wasn't criticizing Simone or freaking out in some other way. Louisa lowered her hands. Her face flushed in the same exact way Nora's did, two vivid red patches right in the middle of each cheek.

"Are you mad at me?" Louisa asked.

"Why would I be mad? I thought *you'd* be mad at *me*."

"I'm mad you didn't tell me."

"I tried. I just— I didn't—"

"I know," Louisa said. They sat for a minute, both staring out the window. The thunder and lightning had passed, the clouds were moving swiftly, and the rain was tapering off. It still smelled like spring outside the bedroom window. "It's a little weird, right?"

"Me being with a girl?"

"No, not that. Well, maybe a little that. Mostly it's strange not being the same."

"I'm just me," Nora said. "I'm here. I'm the same." Now she was afraid she was going to cry.

Louisa shook her head. "I'm not saying it right. It's like we used to *want* the same things and *see* the same things and now we don't and it feels strange. Lonely almost. Almost like I'm doing something wrong because I don't want the same thing as you."

Oh, Nora thought. *This part is going to be easy.* She knelt on the floor in front of Louisa and took her hands. "It's not your job to be anyone's mirror," she began.

WHERE HAD THE GIRLS GONE? Melody looked everywhere before she thought to check the bedroom. She opened the door slowly and saw them sitting on the bed. "Did you ask Jack if it was okay to be in here?" She stepped inside and, just like Nora and Louisa had, started looking around, interested.

"We were just about to come out," Louisa said, blowing her nose and trying to collect herself. Melody saw that Louisa was crying.

"Oh, no." She rushed over and knelt in front of them. "What happened? Oh my God, did something happen on the street? Did someone hurt you?"

"No," Nora said. "Nothing's wrong."

"I want to know the truth!" Melody grabbed each of their hands and shook them a little. "If someone hurt you, you have to tell me. I don't want you keeping things from me."

Louisa started to laugh. "Mom. God. Nobody hurt us. We're completely fine."

"We were just talking about school," Nora said.

Melody looked back and forth at both of their faces. Louisa was staring at her lap. "Is she telling the truth," Melody asked Louisa. Louisa shrugged. Nora looked worried. Melody held Nora's gaze, trying to spot any tiny sign of deception. "What's going on in here? What are you not telling me?" Louisa fiddled with the tissue in her hand. Melody put a finger under Louisa's chin and lifted it until Louisa looked her in the eye.

"We're not leaving this bedroom until you two tell me what's going on."

CHAPTER THIRTY-THREE

Y ou're so beautiful," Leo had said to Stephanie the first night
they'd slept together in her dingy apartment on the ground
floor of an even dingier building. It was late August and
air-conditioning was a luxury she couldn't afford. The box fan, which
made an aggressive click with every full rotation, whirred and rattled
in the bedroom window, muffling the sounds from the street: the teens
across the way who hung out on the stoop blaring a car radio and arguing until sunrise; the bleating taxi horns three blocks over where traffic
backed up from the entrance ramp to the Manhattan Bridge. But that
night, the night Leo told her how fucked up he was, the cacophony that
usually made her grind her teeth in frustration had seemed romantic,
urban and wild, the perfect sound track for her lust.

"You're so beautiful," he'd said to her, as she slowly undressed in
front of him and he watched, still and admiring on the edge of her
unmade twin bed. His voice held such a rare note of wonderment that
her throat tightened. And then he covered his face with his hands.

"Leo?" she whispered.

"I'm so fucked up," he said into his palms.

Oh God, not now, Stephanie thought. Not a precoital unburdening, a completely unnecessary recitation of all the ways he was so fucked up. Hadn't she seen him in action for years already? Didn't she know his flaws? She looked down at the curve of his back, the thread of his spine, how his dark curls, on the long side then, rested against his almost feminine neck. His skin glowed in the moonlight, like the lustrous surface of a pearl.

He looked back up at her. "I'm really fucked up, Stephanie."

She understood with complete lucidity what he was offering her in that moment—not a confession or a plea, but a warning. He was offering her an elegant escape. In those days, one of Leo's gifts was an uncanny ability to predict how things would play out. His favorite expression was from a speech he'd heard some king of finance give once: *If you want to predict a person's behavior, identify his or her incentives.* Leo wasn't saying, *I'm so fucked up,* he was saying, *I'm going to fuck this up.* He knew something about his incentives that she didn't.

But there he was, shirtless, on her bed. Leo, whom she'd been a little in love with for always, and all she cared about in that moment was the length of his body against hers.

"Everyone's fucked up," she said, even though she didn't believe that for a second. She wasn't. Most people she knew weren't. But she also knew this: Nothing was a sure thing; every choice was just an educated guess, or a leap into a mysterious abyss. People might not change but their incentives could.

So the first time she and Leo combusted she'd practically been poised for the breakup. In some inexplicable way she'd been looking forward to it and all its attendant drama, because wasn't there something nearly lovely—when you were young enough—about guts churning and tear ducts being put to glorious overuse? She recognized the undeniable satisfaction of the first emotional fissure because an unraveling was still something grown-up and, therefore, life affirming. *See?* the broken heart signaled. *I loved enough to lose; I felt enough to weep.* Because when you were young enough, the stakes of love were so very small, nearly insignificant. How tragic could a breakup be when it was a part of the fabric of expectation from the beginning? The hackneyed fights, the late-night phone calls, the indignant recounting for friends over multiple drinks and in earshot of an appropriately flirtatious bartender—it was theater for a certain type of person, a certain well-educated New Yorker, and it was, then, for Stephanie, too.

Until it wasn't. Until she stopped being young enough. Until, like an allergic reaction, every time she exposed herself to Leo, the welts rose more rapidly, itched more intensely, and took longer to go away.

She didn't remember which time (second? third?) she'd caught Leo cheating and kicked him out and he was apologizing and begging and she was mustering her reinforcements (whose patience was almost gone, strained to the limit, incredulity replacing empathy, *what did you expect? why would this time be different?*) and her assistant, Pilar, wrote the Kübler-Ross stages of grief on a cocktail napkin to chart her breakups with Leo: denial, anger, bargaining, depression, acceptance.

"You get exactly forty-eight hours for each," Pilar said. "It's all you need, believe me." She opened her Filofax. "That puts you smack at acceptance next Thursday at six in time for cocktails. See you then."

"Don't act like I'm the most pathetic person on earth," Stephanie had said to Pilar. "Because I'm not, not by a long shot."

"I'm acting like you're the most pathetic version of you. Because you are, times a million."

And that was finally what she had to ask herself, *Did loving Leo make her a lesser version of herself?*

WHEN LEO LEFT HER HOUSE IN BROOKLYN, he left almost everything behind, including his cell phone and wallet, which was a nice touch, a convincing feint. When he didn't come home the first night, Stephanie vowed to kick him out the minute he was off his bender and reappeared contrite and exhausted.

The second night, she started poking around the house and realized certain things were missing: a small duffel of hers and a few of his nicer clothes. The shoes he'd had custom made in Italy. The shoes were the tip-off; he treated those fucking shoes like they were infants, wrapping them in burgundy-felt swaddling clothes. Also gone: a small picture she'd taken of the two of them with her iPhone one night, a picture of her laughing while he was playfully biting her left ear that she'd printed out and tucked into the corner of a mirror above her dresser. The one thing she hoped he left behind, the thing she searched the house from top to bottom looking for, wasn't there: Bea's leather bag with the new story inside. Later, she would realize it never even occurred to her to look for a note from Leo. That he might leave Bea's story seemed possible; that he would leave Stephanie an explanation, an admission of wrongdoing in and of itself, did not. And she would be more stung than she'd ever admit to discover he'd taken the time to send his siblings the decoy e-mail buying himself the space to flee.

Tonight was Melody's birthday dinner and Stephanie had told herself all day she wasn't going, but then finally felt obliged to tell his family in person that Leo was missing. *Missing* was probably too optimistic a word, she knew. *Missing* implied something accidental might have happened, that Leo had run up against some trouble, was trying to get home and was somehow being prevented. And although those things could have been true, Stephanie knew they weren't. As she headed toward Jack's place, she decided she would be brief. Say what she knew and then quickly leave. She wouldn't stick around for the likely hysteria.

Acceptance. She had to be honest with herself; she hadn't told anyone about Leo's disappearance and the pregnancy because she was holding on to a sliver of hope, and hope, when it came to Leo, was a one-way ticket to despair. She would go to the dinner, tell the truth, and unburden herself, because that's what someone would do who was not Leo, who had moved beyond anger—and hope—to acceptance.

Standing in the rain in front of Jack's apartment building on West Street, she steeled herself and rang his buzzer.

CHAPTER THIRTY-FOUR

Nora and Louisa were sitting toward the middle of the long table and Melody was standing over them, livid.

"Tell them," she said, gesturing around the table where everyone was seated. "Tell them what you just told me."

"Jack got married," Nora said.

"Not that!" Melody said. "Tell them about seeing Leo."

"You're *married*?" Bea said to Jack and Walker. Walker raised his hands in a gesture of surrender and shook his head, absolving himself. He'd wanted to invite them all.

"When did you see Leo?" Jack asked Nora, ignoring Bea.

"Last October," Nora said.

"Tell them the other part," Melody said.

"He was in Central Park. Flat on his back," Louisa said.

"In the park?" Bea turned her attention to Louisa now. "He was on his back in Central Park?"

"Drugs," Melody said, biting off the word. "He was buying drugs."

"I didn't say that!" Louisa said. "I said he *could have been* buying drugs."

"But you didn't see him with drugs?" Jack asked.

"We just saw him on his back," Nora said. "It was after that snowstorm, it was super icy. I think he just slipped."

"It was the day we all met him at the Oyster Bar," Melody said. "He supposedly came straight from Brooklyn. Remember? He said he was late because of the subway, so why was he up in Central Park?"

The three Plumbs sat, thinking. Why *had* Leo been in the park?

"Even if he was in the park to buy something," Bea said, "what does that mean?"

Melody snorted. "Seriously? He'd been out of rehab for all of three days."

"Okay," Bea said. "But what does that have to do with us?" She was already tired of this conversation, tired of talking and thinking about and waiting on Leo, and also feeling secretly relieved and pleased about the stack of pages in her bag, the ones with his notes on them.

"When did *you* see Leo last?" Jack asked Bea.

Bea cowered a little in her chair; she'd hoped not to have to answer that question tonight. "I haven't seen him in a few weeks," she said, pouring herself more champagne.

"I thought he'd been hanging around your office. That's what Jack told me," Melody said.

"He had been," Bea said. "But he hasn't been around lately."

"Jack's seen Leo quite a bit," Walker offered, amiably, placing a huge platter of chicken in the middle of the table that Melody looked at mournfully. She was losing her appetite. "Just last week, right?"

"You saw Leo last week?" Bea said.

Jack didn't know how to respond. Every time he'd met with Tommy or one of the potential buyers for Tommy's statue, he'd lied and told Walker he was meeting with Leo. "I, uh, I don't know exactly when I saw him last—"

Before he could assemble some kind of sentence, the buzzer rang. Three short beats, followed by two long, just the way Leo always rang the bell. Jack's shoulders slumped in relief. Bea stood so quickly she banged into the table and the water glasses rattled. Nora and Louisa straightened and looked at the door expectantly. Walt poured a little more olive oil on his plate for dunking bread.

"Oh, thank God," Melody said as Walker moved to the door, wiping his hands on his apron. "He's here."

CHAPTER THIRTY-FIVE

When Walker opened the door and Stephanie crossed the threshold, the disappointment on everyone's face was nearly comical. Jack began blathering immediately, wanting to know where Leo was and saying something about Melody's daughters running into Leo *buying drugs* the very first weekend he'd been out of rehab.

"Is he in the park *now*?" Jack said, hands on hips, speaking to her as if Leo were her truant child. "Is he buying cocaine *this very minute*?"

"Excuse me," she said. "Where's the bathroom?"

"Is Leo coming?" Bea asked.

Stephanie covered her mouth with her palm, shook her head and ran to a small wastebasket in the corner, bent over and started retching. The room quieted and everyone reluctantly listened until she was done. She picked up the small container and calmly walked down the hall to the bathroom. Rinsed out the basket. Washed her hands and put a small dab of toothpaste on her finger to freshen her mouth. All the while trying to process what Jack had just said. *Leo in the park, buying drugs, the weekend of the snowstorm.* She walked back into the living room where everyone was quiet and concerned looking and seated around a long table that looked like something out of a magazine. Walker must have done it.

"The table is pretty," she said to him with a shaky smile. "Sorry about that spectacle. I usually have time to get to the bathroom." She sat on the edge of a chair and unzipped her purse.

"Are you sick?" Bea said.

"Not exactly." Stephanie opened a pack of sugarless spearmint gum. "Happy birthday, Melody."

"Do you know where Leo is?" Melody asked hopefully.

"Not exactly," Stephanie said. "That little *incident* in the corner is because I'm pregnant. Leo's the father. I haven't seen him in two weeks." She placed a crumpled plastic gum wrapper on the table next to her and held the pack of gum out to the table. "Anybody want a piece?"

THE NIGHT HAD DEVOLVED FROM THERE. Melody hustled her daughters away but not before Stephanie got the play-by-play of them seeing Leo in the park. It was hard to fathom how he'd been doing anything else but buying drugs, flat out on his back, way uptown where he didn't need to be, where—she remembered—he'd always gone to meet some guy named Rico, Nico, Tico, whatever. That very first weekend! The weekend she'd conceived. The weekend she had opened her door to him and asked him not to do drugs.

Stephanie was still sitting at the abandoned table next to Bea, who poured them both champagne. "No thanks," Stephanie said, pointing to her stomach.

"Really?" Bea said. "A baby?"

"Really," Stephanie said, not even trying to hide her pleasure. From the kitchen they could hear Walker's uncharacteristically raised and furious voice, "If you weren't spending that time with Leo—*who were you with?*"

"What's going on in there?" Stephanie asked.

"I'm not exactly following," Bea said, "but it doesn't sound good. Something about Jack lying about seeing Leo. Has Jack been out to Brooklyn?"

Stephanie thought back to the morning she'd stayed home to do a pregnancy test and how when she was standing at her upstairs window, stunned, she'd spotted Jack walking down the street. She'd hidden in the back bedroom and ignored the doorbell. "No," she said. "I haven't seen Jack in years."

More raised voices from the kitchen. A slamming door.

"I guess we should probably leave," Bea said.

"Yeah." Stephanie wrapped the baguette she'd been gnawing on in a napkin and put it in her purse. "For the subway," she explained, apologetically.

THE NIGHT ALL THOSE YEARS AGO that Pilar had lectured Stephanie about the stages of grief and written them out on a napkin, she'd sat at the bar after Pilar left, moping. She'd drawn a little sad face on the napkin next to *acceptance*. The bartender, who'd heard it all and more than once from Stephanie, scratched out the sad face and in its place he drew a tiny red bird, wings spread, flying over the ocean, surrounded with glowing marks like one of Keith Haring's radiant babies.

For a long time she'd kept the napkin in her purse. Then in a kitchen drawer. Then it got put away in a box somewhere and when she'd sealed that box with packaging tape she thought she was through.

Stephanie was thinking about the bird as she disembarked the subway and walked home after the birthday dinner that wasn't. For years whenever she'd had a pang about Leo she would imagine the napkin and the little red bird packed away in a box deep in her basement. As she strolled down her street among the stately homes and warmly lighted front windows, she thought of the napkin and the meaning she'd always attached to the image: Leo flying away from her, heading straight out to the ocean, unburdened and free. She thought about how grateful she was for her life, her house—emptier now, but not for long. She thought about the small back room that she'd turn into a nursery and how it would be summer when the baby was born and her garden would be in bloom. She'd have to replace the tree that had fallen during the storm so the baby could look out and watch the seasons pass. She thought about the napkin again and realized she'd been telling herself the wrong story all these years. Leo wasn't the red bird, *she* was—ecstatically darting over the church spires of Brooklyn, heading home, expectant but unburdened. Free. Her incentives had finally changed.

PART THREE

FINDING LEO

CHAPTER THIRTY-SIX

This time there was no tea or coffee or little butter cookies or imperious Francie (who, upon hearing that Leo had gone missing, sighed and said, "Oh, he'll get sick of roaming and wander back. He's a Long Islander at heart." As if she were talking about one of her border collies). This time, it was just the three Plumb siblings and George, who wasn't even sitting down, that's how eager he was for the meeting to be over.

"Even if I knew something," George was saying, hurrying to add, "and I don't. I don't know *anything*. But even if I did, Leo is my client and I probably couldn't tell you."

"But you don't?" Melody said, surprising herself by hitting what sounded to her like the perfect caustic, disbelieving note. It was so perfect, she tried again. "You *don't*," she said, drawing out the syllables a bit too much this time. Still. Not bad.

"I don't. I swear to you, I don't. But again, Leo is my client—"

"We all understand attorney-client privilege, George," Jack said. "You don't have to keep saying it."

"Well, then—respectfully—why are you here?"

"We're here because your cousin—our brother—has essentially fallen off the face of the earth," Bea said. "He's vanished and it's worrisome, to say the least. We want to try to figure out where he is and if he's okay. What if he needs help?"

George pulled out a chair and sat. "Look," he said. "I don't think Leo needs help."

"You *do* know where he is," Jack said.

"I don't. I have my suspicions. I could make an educated guess. But I don't know anything for sure."

"Then how do you know he doesn't need help?" Melody asked.

George rubbed both sides of his face with his hands vigorously, inhaled deeply, and exhaled. "At one time, Leo had money that Victoria didn't know about. An account in Grand Cayman. To be clear, I don't know this as his attorney. He mentioned it years ago when he first opened it and, you know, I thought it was not a bad idea, given how things started to go with Victoria, to keep some money separate."

"And you hid it during the divorce?" Jack said.

"I didn't hide anything. Leo filled out the asset sheets, I asked if they were truthful, he said yes. He didn't list an offshore account and I didn't ask."

"How much money?" Jack said, evenly.

"I don't know," George said.

"Enough to have paid all of us back?" Jack asked.

"At one time, I believe there was enough in there to have paid you all back. But now? Who knows. It's Leo. He could have spent that money a long time ago."

"Or he could have doubled it," Jack said. "He had enough money to take off. It had to be a decent amount." Even though he'd told himself over and over that Leo had money hidden, he was stunned.

"I would agree with that assessment," George said. "But I'm guessing, just like you are."

"You were right," Melody said to Jack. "You were right all along."

"This is so messed up," Bea said.

The three Plumbs looked at one another, lost in their confusion, trying to process a betrayal much more significant than the one they'd been dealing with mere minutes earlier.

"I don't understand how this happened," Melody said.

"It's not hard," George said. "Anyone can open an account like that. It's perfectly legal—"

"I'm not talking about banking!" Melody snapped at George, who leaned back as if she'd slapped him. Melody's face fell. She started crying. Bea poured everyone water. For many agonizing minutes, the only sound in the room was Melody hiccuping and blowing her nose. "I'm sorry," she finally said. "I'll be okay."

"Of course you will," George said, attempting to soothe.

"I mean, I'll be broke and we're going to have to sell our house and tell the girls there is no college fund and I guess we're genetically connected to a sociopath—" The tears started flowing again and when she spoke, her voice was choked, "But I'll be fine!"

"If it makes you feel any better," Jack said, "we're probably losing our summer place."

"It doesn't make me feel better," Melody said. "Why would that make me feel better? I feel absolutely horrible for all of us."

Jack tried to console her. He wanted her to pull it together; he hated displays. "It's just an expression, Mel. I mean that I know how you feel. I do."

"I'm worried this is my fault," Bea said. She told them all about her story, how it was based on the night of the accident and how she gave it to Leo to read, wanting his approval. "Maybe if I hadn't done that, if I'd just thrown it away—"

Jack interrupted. "Don't. This isn't anybody's fault. This is who Leo is." What he didn't say out loud was that he knew who Leo was because he was that person, too. He'd always seen too much of Leo in himself. Maybe not quite as bad as Leo (*Leo Lite,* for once and for always), but close enough to know that if he had a big bank account somewhere and could get on a plane and disappear, he might do it, too. "Leo has always been this person. Self-preservation at all costs."

"What about Stephanie?" Melody turned to George. "She's pregnant."

"Shit," George said, clearly surprised. "Did he know?"

"I don't think so."

"Shit." George sat and tapped his pen on a legal pad, it sounded like tiny bullets firing. "We could hire a private detective. People do that. We could try to trace his steps and see if we can find him."

"Then what?" Melody said.

Nobody spoke.

"Let me make some calls," George said. "One step at a time. Let's just see if we can track him down."

"God. My eyes are going to be so swollen tomorrow," Melody said, pressing her lids with her fingertips. "I feel nauseated."

"Can we have a minute alone, George?" Bea asked. "The three of us?"

"Absolutely," George stood, looking like a kid who'd just been let out of detention hours early. "As much time as you want."

Bea dunked her hand in the water pitcher and grabbed a fistful of ice, wrapped it in a cloth napkin, and handed the makeshift ice pack to Melody. "Here. For your face."

"Thank you," Melody said, leaning back in her chair a little and pressing the ice to her eyes. She started humming. Jack rolled his eyes at Bea, who motioned for him to zip it.

"Relax," Melody said, sensing Jack's disapproval through shut eyes. "This is Sondheim."

"I didn't say a word," Jack said.

"You didn't need to."

"Sondheim?" Jack asked. "I approve."

"Hooray," Melody said.

They sat listening to Melody hum for a minute or two, something from *West Side Story*. "Sondheim didn't actually compose that show," Jack said. "He wrote the lyrics—"

"Jack?" Bea cut him off. "Not now." She stood and smoothed her skirt, cleared her throat. "Listen. I have an idea. A proposal. I don't need my share of The Nest. I'm okay right now. I'm not going to lose my apartment, I don't have kids with immediate financial needs. Leo has obviously forfeited his claim. So if you two split what's there, the $200,000, that should help, right?"

"No," Melody said, removing the soggy napkin from her eyes. Her mascara was smeared, her nostrils red. "I'm not taking your money. That's not fair."

"But I want you to," Bea said. "We can call it a loan if that makes you feel better. A no-interest, no-deadline loan. I know it's not enough for either of you to completely resolve the loss, but it's something."

"Are you sure?" Melody said, quickly calculating that Bea was giving them one entire year of tuition—more if it wasn't a private school, which, increasingly, did not seem to be in the cards. "You don't want to take some more time and think about it?"

"I've thought about it a lot in the last week. I don't need more time."

"Because if you're sure," Melody said, "yes, it would help."

"I'm sure," Bea said, visibly pleased. "Jack?"

"Yes," Jack said. "I consider it a loan, but yes." The extra money wasn't enough to completely extricate him from his mess, but it might—just might—be enough to buy time for the house or maybe to get Walker to start taking his phone calls again. "It won't be quick, but I'll pay you back."

"Okay," Bea said, sitting back down, pleased. "Good. Good! This is progress. And if George can find Leo, I'll go and talk to him."

"He won't find him," Jack said. "And even if he does, nothing will change."

"I can try," Bea said. "I can try to change things."

Melody blew her nose, rooted through her purse for more tissues. She had the hiccups. "When did Leo start hating us?" she said. Nobody responded. "How was it so easy for him to leave?" She wasn't crying anymore, she was spent. "Was it really just about money? Was it about *us*?"

"People leave," Jack said. "Life gets hard and people bail." Bea and Melody exchanged a worried look. Jack didn't look good, and he wouldn't talk about Walker or the fight at the birthday dinner. He'd fiddled incessantly with his wedding ring since they sat down. "Besides," he said, a little brighter now, arms spread wide, "what could possibly be wrong with any of us?"

Bea grinned. Melody, too. Jack laughed a little. And as they sat, trying to muster the momentum to make their way out of the office, they all thought about that day at the Oyster Bar, seeing Leo's agreeability then for what it really was. Jack wondered how he—of all of them, the one the least susceptible to Leo—could not have been more suspicious about how disarming and humble Leo had been. Bea remembered how it had seemed that Leo was maybe, kind of, taking responsibility and evincing a desire to make good. How he'd leaned forward and put his palms on the table and looked each of them in the eye—sincerely, affectionately—and told them he was going to find a way to pay them back, he just needed time. She remembered how he'd asked them to trust him and how she'd believed, too, because Leo had lowered his head and when he looked back up at them, damn if his eyes weren't the tiniest bit damp, damn if he didn't seduce them all into giving him the slack he probably imagined he'd have to work much harder to obtain. How grateful he must have been in that moment, Melody thought, to discover how little they were asking from him, to realize how eager they were to believe him.

CHAPTER THIRTY-SEVEN

Exactly ten days after the birthday dinner, Walker moved to a new place. He would have left the next morning, but it took him that long to find a short-term rental that wasn't too far from his office. Until the minute Walker wordlessly lugged two boxes and three suitcases loaded with clothes into a taxi, both he and Jack thought he was bluffing.

The story about the statue had unraveled with stunning celerity the night of the dinner party. After Stephanie's unfortunately timed announcement about Leo's disappearance, Walker had pulled Jack into the kitchen.

"If Leo hasn't been around for weeks, how have you been meeting with Leo?"

Jack equivocated, but that only made Walker assume he was covering up an indiscretion, an affair. Jack had no choice but to explain, and as he watched the color drain from Walker's face, he almost wished he'd made up some kind of flirtation to confess instead.

Walker had slowly removed his apron and folded it into a neat square. "What you are doing is not only against the law, it's completely unethical," Walker said, practically spitting out every syllable.

"I know how it sounds," Jack said.

"Don't," Walker said. "Please. Please do *not* try to justify what you're doing right now."

"But if you could see this guy," Jack said, "you might understand. He's a complete wreck about having that thing in his house. He needs to get rid of it. I'm doing him a favor."

"Do you even hear yourself?"

"Walker, he lost his wife when the towers fell."

"What does that even *mean*?" Walker was shouting now. "I'm sorry about his wife, but how on earth does that justify what *you're* doing? Aiding and abetting a black-market art sale." Walker was pacing now and he stopped and slammed his fist on the counter. Jack was scared. This was worse than he expected. "When the towers fell? Jesus Christ. What else, Jack, *what else*? If you don't help, the terrorists win? These colors don't run? Never forget? Am I ignoring any other pat jingoistic sentiments that you've previously reviled but might now summon to defend your abhorrent greed?"

"It's not greed. It's, it's—"

"It's what?"

The last thing Jack wanted to do at that moment was confess the home equity scheme, but he didn't see how he couldn't. If he waited, it would just be worse. "There's something else," he said.

Walker listened to Jack without saying a word. When Jack was finished, Walker walked to their bedroom and closed the door behind him. All their communication since then had been through terse e-mails. Jack learned from Arthur that Walker had put the summer property on the market. He sent Walker a series of imploring e-mails begging to talk, however briefly. They all disappeared into the great abyss of Walker's fury and silence.

WALKER HAD SURPRISED HIMSELF. It wasn't like he didn't know Jack; he did. He knew exactly what Jack was—and was not—capable of. It wasn't as if Jack hadn't done dumb things over the years and tried to hide them. (God, where to begin with the dumb shit Jack had done over the years—always failing, always, he was terrible about covering his tracks.) Walker realized that he'd tacitly agreed to subsidize Jack's failing efforts years ago. He pretended optimism every time Jack had a new trick up his sleeve, quietly paying off lines of credit that never materialized into revenue because that was what you did when you loved someone, when you were building a life together. Your strengths compensated for their weaknesses. You became the grounding leverage to their impulses, ego to their id. You *accommodated*. And if Walker got impatient, if he sometimes wished things were a little more balanced, he would just imagine his life without Jack and recalibrate, because he couldn't imagine life without Jack.

But something inside him had snapped the night of Melody's birthday. He was genuinely horrified when the story came pouring out of Jack about the illegal sale of the Rodin. It was *illegal*! Whatever stupid things Jack had done over the years, breaking the law was a first (he assumed, he hoped). If he'd gone ahead with the ridiculous scheme and gotten caught, Walker couldn't even bear to imagine what they'd be facing and not just personally—for him the repercussions would be professional. It was beyond imagining.

As he'd stood in their kitchen that night, watching Jack try to explain himself and toggle between evasive and indignant, Walker's years of resigned tolerance evaporated. In the coming weeks, he would spend a lot of time trying to unpack that moment, not understanding himself how years of commitment and love and tolerance could just vanish. But they did. As he stood and watched Jack, he realized that for more than twenty years he had parented his partner. And on the heels of that debilitating thought, a brief flash of insight that leveled him: The reason they'd never had a child, something Walker had dearly wanted but had never been able to persuade Jack to want, was because Jack was the child—and Walker had let him be the child, enabled him. His husband was his forty-four-year-old petulant, needy, responsibility-avoiding son, and now it was too late for other children, and with that realization Walker was undone.

He thought he'd come to peace with the child decision years ago; it didn't bother him that much anymore, just the occasional twinge. But seeing Melody's daughters—so lovely, so sweet—had set something off and then when Stephanie said she was pregnant, he was overwhelmed by such a sudden and unexpected melancholy that he had to leave the room to breathe. Then the confessions, forcing Walker to stop ignoring Jack's careless, greedy heart. It was as if on the night of Melody's birthday a yawning crevasse had opened beneath him and he couldn't clamber up the side to safety. Every day, all day, he felt a kind of vertigo, as if there were nothing holding him up, just a dangerous looming beneath, a valley of regret and waste.

The night before he moved out, he panicked. What if he was ascribing grief from his own decisions to Jack's behavior? What if he was being unfair? What if he owed both of them another chance? He walked into the apartment after work if not entirely willing to reconsider a separation, at least willing to have a conversation. Jack was in the bedroom with the door partially closed, talking on the phone. He was arguing with someone. He was insisting he could find another "buyer," encouraging the person on the other end to reconsider. He hadn't, as he'd e-mailed Walker repeatedly, called off the sale of the statue. He was still trying to make it happen.

That was that.

Walker would take whatever proceeds he could get from the house on Long Island and buy his own place. He'd help negotiate Jack's line of credit. He supposed they'd have to get divorced, but he was in no hurry to start legal proceedings. He'd probably end up paying for all of that, too.

CHAPTER THIRTY-EIGHT

The night of her nonbirthday dinner when she'd found Nora and Louisa in Jack's bedroom and asked them what was wrong and why Louisa was crying, the night she wouldn't let up until Nora finally blurted that they'd seen Leo in the park in a compromising position and then they both (in an effort, Melody now realized, to deflect from what would come out days later, the missing SAT classes; Simone) pointed to the wedding photo of Jack and Walker, Melody still believed the evening could be salvaged. Absurdly, she continued to believe it the whole time Jack and Bea were interrogating Nora and Louisa about the day they'd seen Leo in the park, and she'd even held out hope while Stephanie was disgorging the contents of her stomach in the corner of the living room and then the news of Leo's disappearance. It wasn't until Jack and Walker started fighting in the kitchen, hushed voices quickly giving way to shouting, that Melody finally realized dinner was never going to be eaten, the cake never cut, the pretty limoncello never poured.

She'd drained her champagne glass, removed her dressy sandals because her feet were killing her, and wondered if it would be rude to sneak into the kitchen and grab the remaining champagne from the ice bucket. "Come on, birthday girl," Walt had said to Melody. "Put on your coat and let's get pizza."

In the following weeks, Melody stewed and nursed her disappointment like it was a tiny ember that couldn't die because she was carrying fire for the whole tribe. Then the phone rang one Saturday, the SAT place asking if she was willing to fill out an online survey explaining why Nora and Louisa had dropped the program. Had there been a problem with the tutor? Because they'd received other complaints.

It was Walt who finally stepped in and calmed everyone down. It was Walt who negotiated a refund for the tutoring. It was Walt who Nora found in his office one late night when she went to apologize for lying about the SAT classes and admitted, eyes apprehensive, smile blinding, that she liked a girl. It was Walt who Louisa and Nora approached together to tell him they didn't care about the college list; they *wanted* to look at the state schools.

"I'll take a year off," Louisa told him. "I would love to take art classes and live here with you guys."

"I can take a year off, too," Nora said. "We can work and save money."

It was Walt who treated each of them with equanimity and grace and pure unadulterated love. Who enveloped them with his comforting arms and said about everything, "Please stop worrying. This is not your problem. We love you so much. Everything will be fine." It was Walt, finally, who put the house back on the market and found them a clean and spacious short-term rental. It was Walt who became the General.

The day they accepted an offer on the house, he hustled everyone out for Chinese food.

"To *celebrate*," Melody said, bitterly.

"No," Walt said, "to eat."

Sitting in a roomy corner booth, Melody was trying to be calm, civil. She was on her second beer and the alcohol was going to her head. The food arrived and it looked wrong. All wrong. The relentless glistening brown of the platter of chicken and cashews offended her. The pink-tinged pork (why was it *fluorescent pink*?) scattered in the greasy fried rice nauseated her. The steamed dumplings that looked like wrinkled water-soaked fingers made her want to scream. Walt's idle chatter about their new bedrooms and shorter commute infuriated her. (He didn't seem to realize that the apartment being closer to the school was *not* something to brag about.)

"Aren't you hungry?" Walt asked, pointing to an untouched egg roll on her plate. She looked down at the egg roll. It looked fine, plump and crispy. She remembered how much she'd loved egg rolls as a little girl until the night she'd grabbed one and dunked it in the neon-orange duck sauce and took an enormous bite and just as she started to chew Leo had leaned over and said, *Do you know what they put in those to make them so good? Dead dog.*

It took years for her to believe that he'd been kidding and try an egg roll again. Leo always ruined everything.

"I'm not hungry," Melody said, pushing her plate away. "You can have this."

"Do you want to order something else? Is something wrong?" Walt asked.

"Is something wrong?" Melody said. She was holding a fortune cookie in her fist and gripped it so hard it shattered and pieces flew across the table. "Yes. Something's wrong. A million things are wrong. In case you haven't noticed, Walter, our *entire world has recently turned to shit.*"

Something hard flashed across his face, an almost subliminal message like the words you were supposed to see spelled out in the ice cubes of liquor ads, something that in this case might say, *You've gone too far.*

"Excuse us," Walt said to Nora and Louisa. Melody sat and watched Walt stand. "Can I speak with you, please?" he said. Melody looked at Nora and Louisa, sitting wide-eyed, and finally Walt took Melody by her upper arm and half guided, half pulled her to the back of the restaurant, near the restrooms.

"Enough," Walt said.

"What are you doing? Why are you manhandling me!"

"I'm tired of you insisting on being miserable. Nothing here is 'going to shit' to use your charming phrase, including our children who might take your outlook a tiny bit personally. *Enough*. Get back to the table and apologize to Nora and be the person you've always been for them."

"I wasn't talking about Nora," Melody said. Walt walked away in disgust. She was stunned. He'd never spoken to her in that tone or touched her in any way that wasn't purely affectionate. She stepped into the restroom to compose herself. How dare he! She hadn't been talking about Nora! (Okay, maybe she had been talking about Nora. A little. God forgive her.) She bent over and washed her face and looked at herself in the mirror. She looked horrible because she *was* horrible. How had she been so wrong about everything and everyone? Not realizing Nora was gay and not knowing how to talk to her about it and, by extension, about anything; not noticing the girls' deception; not understanding Leo was a liar and a thief. Not being the type of mother who would sacrifice a house for her daughters' college tuition—not willingly, anyway, not lovingly.

She didn't know who she was anymore. She didn't know how to be the person she'd always been. Besides, that person had been a bit of a chump, hadn't she? She walked back to the table where everyone was silently chewing, watching her approach with, she ruefully noted, dread. She sat and picked up her egg roll. She tried to say, *I'm sorry,* but she couldn't speak. She took a bite and thought, *dead dog,* and spit out the food in her napkin.

Without a word, she grabbed her purse and went and sat alone in the car. Through the large restaurant window, she could see Walt and Nora and Louisa. They were eating, but not talking. All of them silently passing platters and chewing while looking down at their plates. She tried to imagine she'd gone somewhere, just disappeared without a trace, and this was their life now. A husband without a wife, daughters without a mother. The tableau was so unbalanced and incomplete and *sad*.

Walt said something and the girls shook their heads. They each took a little more food from the big platter in the center. They kept looking over at the other side of the room, away from the window, all of them. She wondered if someone they knew was sitting over there or if they needed the waitress for drink refills or take-out cartons. The staff at this place had a habit of disappearing when you needed something. Nora probably wanted more fortune cookies. Walt leaned across the table and took one hand of each daughter. He said something to them. She squinted and leaned forward, as if she might be able to read his lips. She wondered what he was saying. The girls were looking at him and nodding. Then smiling. Then they all turned and looked across the room again and she realized what they were doing; they were looking toward the door. They were looking for her.

CHAPTER THIRTY-NINE

It was a Tuesday, which meant Jack opened the shop a little early after having been closed on Sundays and Mondays. Tuesdays were the days that most of the decorators made their rounds because the stores weren't full of weekend amateurs or tourists, but the morning had been slow. So what else was new? Jack was sitting at a small desk in the back of the shop. He'd been making a few calls, writing e-mails. The front door opened and the little bell rang announcing someone's arrival. Jack stood and couldn't quite make out the person in the door; the sun was shining through the transom and hitting him square in the eyes.

"Jack?"

"Yes." He squinted and moved out of the light and let his eyes adjust. "Melody?"

"Hi," she said, a little meekly. "I brought you some lunch."

"SO LET ME GET THIS STRAIGHT," Jack said. "You've brought me these delightful sandwiches and cookies and even an overpriced bottle of sparkling water because you want my advice on having a lesbian daughter?"

Melody sighed and picked some kind of dark wilted lettuce off her sandwich. Why was it so hard to find just a plain turkey sandwich? "What is this stuff?" she said, sniffing it. "Arugula. Ugh. Whatever happened to good old iceberg lettuce?" She put the sandwich down and looked at Jack. "I don't want advice exactly . . . I just . . . I don't know what I want, to be honest. I guess I'm a little scared."

"Of having a gay child?"

"No! Of being a crappy parent."

"Because she's a lesbian?"

"I'm not trying to be an asshole, Jack. I've never cared that you were gay. You know that. None of us did. You were the one who didn't invite anyone to your wedding, which is a shame because we all would have liked being there. It might have been nice for your nieces, too, to see their two gay uncles marry."

"Well, now they have a front seat for the groundbreaking divorce."

Melody put her sandwich down. "Seriously?"

"I'm afraid so."

"But why? There's no chance of putting things back together? What happened?"

"I did a very dumb thing. Can we talk about something else?"

"Sure." They were sitting at the counter at the front of the shop, next to the jewelry display. "This is nice," Melody said, picking up a red leather box with a vintage watch inside.

"Yes, it is nice. It's the watch I gave Walker as a wedding gift."

"He gave it back?"

"Actually, he sold it back to the person I bought it from who alerted me and I reacquired it."

"I'm sorry. That sounds upsetting."

"It was. Very. Especially since he sold the watch to buy combs for my long hair and without knowing what he had done I sold my hair to buy a leather case for this watch."

Melody smiled at him and put the watch back on the counter. "We're selling our house." She pinched the bridge of her nose between her thumb and forefinger. She really didn't want to cry again in front of Jack.

"Our house is on the market, too."

"They say it's picking up, the market," Melody said, mouthing Walt's words.

"Fuck the market," Jack said.

"Yeah." They both sat chewing their turkey sandwiches for a few minutes, avoiding looking at each other. Then Melody said, "Remember those friends you had in high school?"

"God, is this going to be a lunch of *examination* and *remembrances*? Because I'm not in the mood."

"No. I have a point."

"Which friends?"

"All those boys."

"Again, I'll need you to be more specific."

"All those boys that summer. The ones from the pool club. Remember? You'd bring them home and hang out in back under the trees."

Jack's eyes lit up. He did remember. The summer before he left for college, he'd brazenly brought home a series of beautiful boys from the family beach club, all of whom worked at the restaurant, clearing tables and refilling water glasses. (The coveted waitstaff jobs in the dining room were doled out to the collegiate sons and daughters of the membership who pocketed the tip money they didn't really need to fuel their alcohol or drug habits—or both.) Even then, Melody knew there was something different about how Jack and his friends would pull their chaise longues to the far end of the yard and slather each other's backs with Hawaiian Tropic, misting themselves occasionally with her mother's little plant atomizer, the pretty brass one meant for the African violets on the sill of the summer porch. Melody would try to find an excuse to wander over whenever she could, offering glasses of lemonade or Fudgsicles from the freezer. The boys would stop laughing and talking as she made her way across the lawn, squinting to see what she had in her hands.

"Want one?" she'd ask. She always brought an extra for herself, hoping to be invited to join them. But Jack always grabbed whatever she had and shooed her away.

"I remember very well," Jack said to Melody. "The good old days under the pine trees. When life was so much simpler and merry and *gay*."

"They *were* gay, right."

"Not all of them. Some of them. Enough."

"Why didn't they like me?"

"What?"

"They never liked me, those gay boys." Melody was trying to keep her voice light, casual. "I was always trying to hang around and you all were always trying to get me to go away."

"You were a little girl."

"So? I brought you guys stuff. I brought you drinks and ice cream and all I wanted was to maybe play cards or listen to you talk or *anything*. But you and your friends never liked me. So I was wondering why. If it was something specific."

Jack sat back and crossed his arms, grinning at Melody like she was telling a particularly excellent joke. He started to laugh, but her expression became so raw, so Melody-walking-wounded that he stopped. "Mel," he said, putting a hand over hers. "They didn't hate you. You were adorable, stumbling over the grass in your saggy two-piece bathing suit, carrying a pitcher of warm lemonade or melting Popsicles that tasted like freezer burn. You were adorable."

Melody stared down at her half-eaten sandwich. She couldn't look at Jack. She was mortified now that she'd brought the whole thing up and mortified to hear his take on her pilgrimages across the grass and particularly mortified that hearing him say "you were adorable" made her so happy.

He continued and his voice lost its usual sardonic edge. "Whatever happened—under the pines—it wasn't about you or liking you or not liking you. That's just crazy. I was seventeen. I didn't want to have you around because I had a twenty-four-hour erection. I didn't want my little sister there."

"Gross."

"Exactly. Think of it as a different form of brotherly love. Is that what you've been obsessing about because of Nora? Whether you have some kind of built-in gay repellent?"

"No. I'm just thinking. I want to do the right thing. I want to understand and be supportive, but I'm scared. I don't know what she needs anymore, how she feels."

"Yes, you do."

"I don't, Jack, I *don't*. I never wanted a girl—"

"You *do* know," he insisted. He stood and gathered the garbage from lunch and shoved it into an empty grocery bag. "You wish she weren't gay," he said, calmly.

"Yes. I'm sorry. I'm not saying that to be hurtful. I don't want her life to be any harder than life already is. I don't know how to smooth the way for this, make it easier. I don't know what to say or what to think or how to behave and I don't know who to talk to. Except you."

Jack was staring out the window of the shop, tapping his fingers impatiently against a display case. "Walker wanted children," he finally said.

"Really?"

"I was nervous about the whole thing. You know me. He wanted to adopt and all I could think about was how do we know what we're getting? It seems like such a crapshoot. How does the kid know? Nobody signs up for two gay fathers. It seemed like such an easy thing to fuck up. Walker would always say I was overthinking. He would always say, 'There's a reason they call it *giving custody*. Parents are temporary custodians, keeping watch and offering love and trying to leave the child better than they found him. *Do no harm*.' That's what Walker would say anyway. I don't know if it helps."

"It helps a little," she said.

"Just another example of my selfishness, according to Walker as he walked out the door."

"Not wanting to adopt?"

"Yes."

Melody thought for a minute. Why was it so easy to wound the people you loved the most? She pointed to an art deco bar cart a few feet away with crystal bottles filled with a dark liquid. "Is that real alcohol?" she said.

"It most certainly is," Jack said. "Are you suggesting a drink? Because if you are, you are my favorite person in New York right now."

"Yes," she said.

Jack filled half their plastic cups with scotch and they sat and sipped in a companionable silence for a few minutes.

"I don't think you were being selfish," Melody said.

"About adopting?"

"Yes," she said. "I think you were being thoughtful and cautious and honestly airing your concerns. Having kids isn't easy."

"I know!"

"Don't get me wrong; it's great and I think you and Walker would have been great parents—if you both wanted it. But it's not for everyone." She finished her scotch and poured a little more. She was building some alcohol-fueled momentum. "*Do no harm.*" She laughed. "It sounds so, so easy, but do you know what else is easy? Doing harm! Accidentally *doing harm* is distressingly easy. I don't think you were being selfish. I think you were being realistic."

Jack watched Melody, amused. He wasn't surprised she was a cheap date in the booze department, but what she said also resonated with him—and made him feel better. "Tell that to Walker," Jack said, joking.

"I'll tell him." Melody straightened. "Where is he? He thinks being a parent is so easy, such a cakewalk? Get him on the phone. I'll tell Mr. Attorney just how easy it is. Where is he?"

"I don't know, let's see." Jack took out his phone and she was abashed to see him open the Stalkerville app, the one she'd talked him into using. "Let's take a peek," he said, waiting for it to load. "Here we go. He's at work and, look!" He pressed the "call" button on his phone and held it up for Melody to see as the screen said "Walker" and the phone rang and rang. He banged the phone onto the counter. Melody picked it up. "What are you doing?" Jack said.

"I'm deleting this. If you want to tell Walker something, you should go find him. This thing?" She raised the phone and shook it a little. "It's not telling you what you need to know. It's one tiny part of the story; it's bullshit." She typed in a few commands, and the app was gone. Jack was looking past her lowered head and out the window, watching the pedestrians walking down the street on a heart-wrenchingly perfect spring day. He'd never felt so alone in his entire life. Handing him back his phone, Melody realized that Jack's scattered, slightly unfocused gaze, his too-long hair, and his wrinkled shirt—it all added up to heartbreak. He wasn't mad or blithe; he was empty. She sat with him for a while, wishing she could erase the look on his face, a world of comeuppance and regret.

"Mel?" he finally said. "Nora just needs to know you love her as much and exactly as you did before. She needs to know she's not alone."

"I know," Melody said.

CHAPTER FORTY

I t was the day before Mother's Day and Stephanie was still wearing her down vest. May in New York City was fickle. On Friday she
hadn't needed any kind of overcoat, but Saturday dawned cloudy
and cold, more autumnal than springlike. Still, there were bunches
of pink and purple and blue sweet peas at the farmers' market and
she splurged and bought four bouquets for herself. She'd scatter them
around the house and their heady scent would permeate every room.

Vinnie and Matilda were coming over to her house for lunch. The
day when she'd answered Leo's phone, she'd quickly ended the call
with Matilda, saying Leo was *out*. She didn't forget about the call—or
the poor girl who'd been in the car with Leo—but there was so much
else for her to contend with; weeks later, she'd called back, out of duty
more than anything else.

Stephanie knew she wasn't responsible for Leo's mess, but as
Matilda nervously and somewhat disjointedly explained why she was
calling, Stephanie realized she might be able to help. One of her favor-

ite clients, Olivia Russell, was a hugely successful journalist who had written extensively about artificial limbs, especially the challenges facing Gulf War veterans. Olivia had lost a leg herself when she was young. She knew everyone and how to work every program and now ran a nonprofit that helped amputees navigate the expensive and complicated world of artificial limbs. Stephanie offered to broker an introduction. Matilda asked if she could bring her friend Vinnie. So they were all coming for lunch: Vinnie, Matilda, and Olivia, who'd already agreed to help Matilda as a favor to Stephanie. Then Stephanie's job would be done.

"Happy Mother's Day," the farmer who took her money said. She assumed he was a farmer anyway; he was scruffy and already sun weathered. His fingers were thick and blunt and dirt stained, and he was wearing a bright blue baseball cap that said SHEPHERD FARMS ORGANIC in orange script on the front. It took Stephanie a minute to realize he was addressing her.

"Oh, thanks," she said. With her height, she was carrying the pregnancy well but at six months her bulge was prominent, unmistakable.

"You have other kids at home?"

"Nope. First and last," she said, employing the emotionally neutered tone that she'd learned usually shut down baby conversation, shifting her bags of spring potatoes and asparagus and strawberries into the crook of one elbow so she could carry the vibrant flowers in one hand, like a spring bride.

"Yeah, that's what they all say," the farmer said, grinning. "Then the kid starts walking and talking. Soon he won't sit in your lap anymore and before you know it"—he gestured toward her middle—"you're cooking number two."

"Hmmmm," she said noncommittally, holding a palm out for her change.

She'd listened to her pregnant friends complain for years about the invasiveness a protruding belly engendered, how even in New York where you could stand inches away from someone's face on the subway secure in the tacit but universal agreement that nobody (sane) would engage with you, ever, all bets were off when you were pregnant.

Boy or girl? First one? When are you due? (Stephanie always heard *When are you due?* as *What do you do?* Always.) So she had been prepared for the annoying questions, but the thing she found most infuriating was how everyone needed to talk not only about the baby she was gestating, but also about her unplanned, unwanted *future* children. It was so odd. As if only wanting one child was already undercutting the motherhood that hadn't even officially begun. As if these strangers had something at stake in the process. As if having one baby, alone, was some kind of halfhearted gesture, a part-time commitment. (*Oh, they're just jealous,* Pilar, mother of one astonishingly charming and erudite nine-year-old son, told her. *They want to make sure you're going to be knocked back on your ass as soon as you're sleeping all night. Misery loves company, my friend.*)

"So do you know what it is?" the farmer said, counting out her ones.

"It's a girl."

"Got your name."

"Yes," she said, smiling thinly. "But that's my secret." She'd learned to keep her counsel on baby names the hard way. When she started mentioning names she was considering, before the obvious one occurred to her, everyone had an opinion based on logic so subjective and personal that it was utterly bizarre: "My first wife was named Hannah and she was a cold bitch." "My daughter has *four* Charlottes in her class." "Natasha is kind of cold war, no?"

It also seemed to Stephanie that like so much else surrounding parenting, naming had become a competitive sport. Some dude in her childbirth class couldn't stop talking about his Lotus spreadsheet for baby names. "We have three priorities," he explained to a bored Stephanie and a bemused childbirth instructor (*she'd* seen it all). "The name needs to be unique, it needs to reflect the ethnic background of both my wife and me—a little bit Brit, a little bit Jew—and"—he paused for effect—"it needs to be mellifluous. Pleasing to the ear."

"I know what mellifluous means," Stephanie said.

"Sophia is the type of name we're going for," his wife added in her clipped BBC accent, "but it's much too popular these days."

"It's popular because it's pretty," Stephanie said. "A classic old-fashioned name."

"*Too* popular, I'm afraid, and the classic tips to trendy," the wife said, putting a sympathetic palm on Stephanie's arm, who she clearly thought was hapless and uninformed.

"In addition to the top three priorities," the husband continued, "we have subset qualifications." He ticked off the items on his fingers. "What happens when you Google the name? How many syllables? Is it easy to understand over the phone? Is it easy to type on a keyboard?"

The last one was too much; Stephanie burst out laughing. The couple hadn't really spoken with her again.

"Good luck," the farmer said, waving his hand as she walked away. "This will be the only quiet Mother's Day you have for a long time. You let your husband pamper you."

This was another thing that surprised Stephanie, although she supposed it shouldn't. How everyone assumed because she was pregnant that she was also married. She lived in New York City, for Pete's sake. Not just New York, *Brooklyn*! She wasn't the first fortysomething woman to have a baby alone, but even if she was having the baby *with* someone, who said she was married? Who said her someone wasn't another woman? She wasn't only offended by the near unanimous conventionality of everyone's automatic assumptions, she was unsettled because she knew her daughter would eventually face the same kind of cavalier reasoning about a father who—well, who knew what the story with her father was, what it might be when the baby was old enough to ask.

Stephanie redistributed the shopping bags so her shoulders and arms were evenly weighted and started to walk home. It was downhill from the park to her house, thank goodness. Her legs felt strong, but her center of gravity was shifting and her back hurt if she walked too far while carrying packages. She should get one of those shopping carts on wheels, but she'd be pushing a stroller soon enough.

Stephanie was still annoyed about the farmer's *husband* comment. There wasn't much about having a baby alone that stymied her except what to tell people about Leo—*whether* to tell them about Leo. Her closest friends and coworkers knew the story, sort of. They all knew about Leo and their past, how he had briefly resurfaced and that she'd been surprised but happy to find herself pregnant and now he was no longer in the picture.

It was harder with the casual acquaintance or the out-and-out bold and nosy stranger. Many people were stopped with a curt, "I'm a single mom." But many weren't. She was going to have to come up with something specific enough to shut everyone up but not intriguing enough to encourage questions.

She also hated the looks of pity and concern that accompanied her deliberately upbeat clarification that she was having the baby alone. Pity was such an absurd sentiment to be on the receiving end of because all she felt was lucky. Lucky to be having a baby, lucky to be forming slow but encouraging bonds with Leo's siblings and their families, which she was doing specifically for her daughter so that she would have a sense of her extended family.

Stephanie was the only child of a widowed mother who had died years ago. She'd loved her childhood and her doting, accessible, smart, and funny mom. The only regret she had about not having a baby sooner was that her mother was gone and her mother would have been an amazing grandmother. But Stephanie had been lonely sometimes as a girl, too, so she hoped the Plumbs would embrace her and Leo's baby and so far, they had.

If Stephanie was perfectly honest with herself, she knew that the particular family configuration hers was about to take was her preferred configuration because it was what she knew. If she was being scrupulously honest, one of the reasons she'd never had a kid was because having a father in the picture was something she didn't know what to do with. It wasn't really something she'd missed. Her mother and her cousins and summers in Vermont with her beloved uncle satisfied her craving for family. In the middle of the night, in the dark, where nobody could see the satisfied smile on her face, her hand on her rising belly, she recognized that although this baby hadn't been premeditated (it *hadn't*, Leo had shown up at *her* door), the night of the snowstorm she didn't insist on a condom, something she had, quite literally, never done before—not during the most inebriated hookup, not during the most spontaneous erotic moment.

She hadn't planned the pregnancy (*hadn't),* but she hadn't prevented it and if she was being *brutally* honest, deep in the night in the privacy of her room, *her* room, hand on her belly gently rising and falling with the undulating motion of her rolling, kicking, hiccuping baby, listening to the quiet of her creaky house under the duvet arranged exactly as she liked, she could admit the truth about the night of the snowstorm: that she'd let a tiny aperture of possibility open to something that was *of* Leo but wasn't Leo. And that she liked it that way.

"You're more like a guy than a girl," Will Peck had said to her once when they were together and she suggested he might want to sleep at his place a little more often. He didn't appreciate her love of solitude. She supposed that was true in a way. Although she didn't buy the stereotype of women being the needy ones. It seemed wrong. Sure there were women hell-bent on getting married, but men were just as bad once they decided they were ready to pair off. Wasn't it the divorced or widowed men who always remarried right away, who had to be taken care of? Wasn't it the elderly women who reinvented their lives alone? Of all her friends whose marriages had split up—and by now there were quite a few—it was usually the woman who had the courage to step away from something broken. The men held on for dear life.

You'll be beating the divorced Brooklyn dads off with a stick, Pilar warned her. That was the last thing she needed! A guy with his own kids. She'd dated and dismissed a number of divorced men she suspected were mainly on the prowl to have someone around every other weekend to help with their kids. They didn't particularly charm her, the men she thought of, collectively, as "the dads." She had to admit, though, that there was something captivating and even a little sexy about a man fumbling to pin back his daughter's curls with a barrette or braid a ponytail.

As she turned onto her block, she could see Tommy O'Toole sitting out on their stoop. Oh, good. He'd insist on carrying her bags up the stairs and into the kitchen and she'd be happy to let him. She waved; she wouldn't mind some help carrying the bags the rest of the way. But he wasn't facing her; he was looking at a couple walking from the other direction. The woman was on crutches and—shit—it had to be Matilda. And the person walking next to her must be Vinnie. They were early. Oh, well, she'd put them to work chopping vegetables. Maybe Vinnie could carry some bags, too.

CHAPTER FORTY-ONE

Even though it was a little chilly to be outside, Tommy and Frank Sinatra were sitting on the stoop, which they both loved to do. Sinatra took up his usual position, on the third step from the bottom, snout high, bulging eyes alert, tail happily thumping the cement riser behind him.

Next to him, Tommy put his head in his hands and prayed. It had been a while since he prayed to God or anyone. When he was younger, he used to believe he could pray to his missing friends and relatives. He felt envious of his old self, the one who thought someone was listening. At first he'd stopped believing out of laziness and then out of anger and now it was more an apathetic meander. He wouldn't have called himself an atheist; being an atheist required more belief than he had, a kind of determined certainty about mystery that he didn't think was feasible or possible, admirable or even desirable. Who could deny a guiding hand of some kind, a design to the world? Calling it science didn't explain it all to him either. He wasn't a believer and he wasn't a nonbeliever. He wasn't something and he wasn't nothing. He was a survivor.

For a long time after Ronnie's death, he'd prayed to her. Not just those endless months on the pile when he was desperate and lost, but for years afterward. He was embarrassed to think about this, but he'd prayed to the statue, too. It had become a shrine in his house until one day he saw himself, caught his reflection in a window, sitting on a folding chair, talking to the statue and he got scared that he was losing his mind. That's when he put the thing behind doors in a china cabinet.

At first he'd been terrified by Jack Plumb's offer to sell the statue, but once he got used to the idea, Tommy was filled with relief. He'd had some sleepless nights imagining what would happen if he died suddenly—hit by a car, massive heart attack—and his daughters found the statue in the closet. Eventually, they would figure out what it was and what he'd done. Reshaping the story of their hero father would be bad enough, but if they knew he'd stolen from the pile and hidden the contraband, it would change their relationship to the story of their mother, too. He knew, God how he knew, that if your memories of someone couldn't carry you from grief to recovery, the loss would be that much more incontrovertible. He'd seen firsthand how his children started writing the mythology of Ronnie mere hours after she was dead. If they knew about the statue, her death would become tainted by his actions, and he wouldn't put his kids through another loss surrounding their mother. He couldn't leave them with a stolen statue that would become the thing in the closet they had to hide. He'd dump it in the river first.

He knew there would be complications to the sale. How to move it, where to put the money, but Jack Plumb reassured him he would help with, as he put it, all the particulars. He was full service. But before they'd even gotten into the particulars, Jack had let slip that the London buyer was from Saudi Arabia.

"An Arab?" Tommy said to Jack, clenching his fists, not believing what he was hearing.

"A Londoner," Jack said, clearing his throat. "Everyone in the Middle East isn't a terrorist, for heaven's sake. He's a finance guy. Very successful businessman and a very successful collector. Highly respected."

Tommy was enraged. "But he came from oil money, right? And don't tell me he didn't because you'll be lying."

"I have no idea," Jack said. "That's irrelevant. You want to sell on the black market you don't get to run a credit check and an employment history. He's rich and he wants the statue and he's discreet. Bingo."

Tommy had practically carried Jack out the front door. Not even giving him the courtesy of a lecture about why he—someone who'd lost a wife and countless friends and fellow firefighters on 9/11—couldn't possibly take Middle Eastern oil money in exchange for a ground zero artifact from anyone, anytime, *ever*.

He was relieved by the turn of events because it snapped him out of his funk. He'd been crazy to think selling the statue was possible, or ethical. He'd meant it when he'd told Jack that it wasn't about money. All he cared about was where the statue ended up because he needed to honor Ronnie's memory. But if he exposed himself—accidentally or on purpose—he'd *harm* her memory for his kids. And that was the never-ending loop he'd been caught in for weeks. He yawned. He hadn't been sleeping. How to get the statue somewhere safe? For days Jack had called him hourly wanting to reopen negotiations until Tommy finally threatened to call his friends in the police department and turn them both in. "I'll do it, asshole," he told Jack. "Don't think I won't." At least there'd be some honor in being honest.

Sinatra lifted his head and whined a little. "What do you say, Mr. S.?" He rubbed a few knuckles across Sinatra's head, the place where his skin was a little slack and the fur soft. The dog panted with pleasure. From down the street he could see Stephanie waving at him. She probably wanted help with her bags. Sinatra started barking at something in the opposite direction.

"Shush, boy," Tommy said, looking to see what was agitating the dog. It was a couple. The woman was on crutches and there was something uneven about her companion's profile. They were walking slowly and looking at house numbers. As they got closer, Tommy couldn't believe what he was seeing. A tall muscular man with one arm and a long-haired woman with a missing foot walking together down his street. It was his statue come to life. He stood and Sinatra's barks turned to a menacing growl.

"Shhhh." He picked the dog up and tucked him under one arm to keep him calm. He really needed to get some sleep. He blinked and shook his head a little, looked again but his vision hadn't cleared. The statue was still there and it was coming toward him. He felt lightheaded and looked up at the sky. He didn't know why, what he expected to see up there. He thought for a minute he might faint. What was happening couldn't be happening. He could feel his breaths becoming shallow and then a constriction around his chest, like someone was tightening a belt. The dog scrambled out of his arms and down the stoop and turned to face Tommy, barking in earnest now, scared.

Oh, please, Tommy thought, *not now.* Not the heart attack he'd feared, not while that statue was still in the house. He put a hand on the iron railing to try to steady himself. If the statue was in his house, how was it also walking down the street? Stephanie was yelling his name from one direction. From the other direction, the statue-come-to-life was getting closer. Sweat streamed down his back, and his palms were clammy. Sinatra was barking even harder. Holy Jesus, he was dying. He was having a stroke or a heart attack or both. He tried to take a deep breath, but couldn't.

"Quiet," he said to Sinatra, but he wasn't sure anything came out. His throat was tight and dry.

"Excuse me." Now the statue was in front of him, talking, wanting to climb the stoop.

Tommy tried to speak but his lips wouldn't work. *They were coming for him,* that's what he was thinking even though he didn't really understand what he meant. Coming for him? Who?

"Hey." The man stepped closer and reached out with his one arm. "You okay, buddy? You don't look so good."

"What's wrong, baby, why are you so upset?" Tommy thought the woman was talking to him, but she'd leaned her crutches against the stoop and was trying to soothe Sinatra who was barking at her outstretched hand. Tommy stared at her missing foot and then back at the man with one arm. He couldn't tell in that moment if he was hallucinating or if he was dying, but whichever it was he knew it wasn't good. *Ronnie,* he thought. *Help.*

"Call 911," Tommy heard the man say. "Do you need a hand there, mister? What's your name?" Vinnie's voice sounded like it was coming through a long tunnel or across a static-filled connection. He couldn't make out the words, but he heard the man say something about 9/11. Fuck. And right before Tommy pitched forward, he looked at them both beseechingly, his hand at his heart, his mouth a tight slash of pain.

"What?" Matilda said, her voice thick with concern and fear. "What is it, Papi?"

"Forgive me," Tommy said. And then he fell, landing at Matilda's missing foot.

CHAPTER FORTY-TWO

Tomorrow was Mother's Day and Melody would wake up and spend the last day in her beloved house. Monday morning, the moving truck would come and load all the boxes and wrap their furniture in quilted moving blankets and they would get in their car and follow the van to their temporary condo on the other side of the tracks.

And then the bulldozers would arrive.

Walt had kept that piece of information from her until he couldn't any longer: The person who bought their house was a developer who planned to raze the entire thing and build a spanking new monstrosity. She moved through the rooms now with a fresh sorrow; soon they wouldn't even exist.

Today, they were waiting for a salvage firm to show up. The developer was not only going to demolish her house, but he was going to strip it first—the wood, molding, the oak banister, her painstakingly cared for heart pine living room floor—and sell it all to an architectural salvage firm. Walt tried to get Melody to leave, but she wouldn't. She wanted to look the asshole in the eye who was dismantling beauty and reselling it at a profit. She and Nora and Louisa were in the living room packing up the last of the books when the doorbell rang. When Walt opened the door, she thought she was seeing things. It was Jack.

She wanted to pummel him at first. She was outraged. *He* was the salvager? *He* was going to rip out the soul of her home and sell it? It took a few minutes for Jack and Walter to calm her down and help her understand: Jack was salvaging what he could for *her*.

"I don't get it," she said.

"I know people," Jack said, gesturing to the crew with him. "These guys will take what you want and store it."

"For what?"

"To use again, Mom," Nora said. She and Louisa were expectant, excited. They'd known about the plan for weeks as Jack and Walt conspired to figure out the details. "If you build your own house someday. Or to put in one that's already built. You can keep the best things and reuse them."

"Keep them where?"

"I have a storage unit," Jack said. "A place for backup inventory. If it turns out you don't want the stuff, we can always sell it."

"You guys did this for me?" Melody was dazed and grateful.

"We can only keep what you really want," Jack said. He started organizing everyone. They needed to make a list, figure out what was worth storing. Choose the most important things.

"Why don't you guys start upstairs," Melody said. "I'll make us some tea. The kettle isn't packed yet."

Nora and Louisa ran up the stairs with Walt. "How about the stained-glass window in the hall?" she could hear Louisa say. "Mom loves that window." Jack followed her into the kitchen. He looked around the room.

"I don't think there's much in here to keep," he said. "These cabinets are from the '70s."

"Jack." Melody stood at the sink, filling a kettle with water. "I don't know how to thank you," she said. "This is—"

"It's what I do. It's easy. But we're paying this crew by the hour so we should move quickly."

"It won't take long," she said. She put the kettle on the stove, lit the gas. "What's going on with Walker?"

Jack shrugged. "Things are getting settled. I handed over my share of The Nest and he made up the difference to pay off my debt. We're selling the house. He's being generous. I won't get half, but I'll get enough to keep the store afloat for a bit while I figure out whether to sell it or not. He's letting me keep the apartment."

"But what's going on *between* you? Other than business."

Jack sat down at the kitchen table. Melody thought he looked thinner than usual but he seemed better than the last time she'd seen him. "How old were you when you got married?" he asked.

"Barely twenty-two. A baby."

"I was twenty-four when I met Walker. Do you know I've never lived alone? I'm forty-four years old and I've never lived alone. The first few weeks Walker was gone, I didn't know what to do with myself. I'd stay in the store until late, pick up some takeout, and just watch television until I fell asleep."

Melody looked around the kitchen. She'd spent every night for weeks dismantling their lives and wrapping it in newspaper for packing. Her nails were ragged and black with newsprint; her arms and shoulders were sore from heaving boxes around. "Sounds kind of great right now."

Jack looked at her and nodded. "It *is* kind of great. That's my point. I miss Walker. I miss him terribly and I don't know what's going to happen. But for the first time ever, I'm only accountable to myself and I like it. I'm not proud of why I'm at this point, but I'm doing my best to figure it out, and I'm kind of enjoying it, parts of it anyway."

Melody wondered what it would be like to live alone—to come home every night and turn on the lights of a darkened house and have nobody waiting to hear about your day or eat dinner with you or argue about which show to watch or help clear the table. She wouldn't tell Jack how sad it sounded to her. Upstairs, she could hear an electric saw.

"I'll be sorry if you and Walker don't get back together," she finally said.

"Oh, I'm sure I'll go running and crying back to his capable meaty arms soon enough. But I doubt he'll have me."

Just then, Walt and the girls came into the kitchen. "Look!" Nora said. She had a piece of woodwork in her hand. Melody recognized it immediately. It was from the upstairs hall closet, the piece of wood where she'd recorded the girls' heights at least once a year: red for Nora; blue for Louisa. "This is the first thing I asked for," Nora said.

"You did?" Melody was pleased that Nora thought to take it because Louisa had always been the more sentimental of the two. "What a perfect idea."

"We started a list," Walt said. "Look it over and see if you agree." Someone above them was hammering; the kitchen light fixture swayed a little.

Melody looked at the list. It was extensive. She couldn't imagine all those things—floorboards, windows, banisters, molding—sitting in Jack's storage space gathering dust. A house but not quite; bits of a building that didn't add up to a home.

"I don't want to keep anything," Melody said.

The room went quiet. "Funny," Walt said, laughing and then stopping when he saw that Melody was serious.

"I want *that*." Melody pointed to the piece of wood in Nora's hand, marking the years they'd lived there and how much the girls had grown; it was covered with fingerprints and gray with grime because she'd never cleaned that bit, afraid of accidentally smearing or erasing the carefully drawn lines with dates next to them. "That's the only thing I want."

Jack was watching Melody carefully. "I don't mind storing things for you," he said.

"I know," Melody said. "Let's get anything out of here you think is worth money and sell it."

"Melody," Walt said, frustrated, "I'm confused."

"I'm so grateful to you both for thinking of this. Please don't think I'm not grateful. But— Let's sell it. Use the money to fix up our new place."

"You're sure?" Walt said.

"I'm positive." She turned to Jack. "You can sell all this and make a commission, right?"

"If that's what you want, yes." He was surprised, but pleased. He didn't really have the room to keep everything he'd imagined she'd want to keep.

"And you two are okay with this?" she asked Nora and Louisa. She felt good, lighter, in charge.

They both nodded. "We just wanted to do something to make you feel better," Louisa said. "We wanted to make you happy."

"I have what makes me happy," she said. Melody wasn't even sure she understood the impulse making her want to let go, but she decided not to overthink it for once. Having things from the house wasn't the same as having the house. Given all that had happened over the past year, nothing was the same, and it was time to stop holding on for dear life. And just like that, she felt like the General again. Their family might look like they were in retreat, but she knew better. She was the General and if anything was an advance, this was it.

CHAPTER FORTY-THREE

*I*t was the craziest thing. When Matilda would tell the story later, and she and Vinnie would tell the story a lot in the coming years, the story of *The Kiss* would be their story and after the tenth, the hundredth, the thousandth time would still be told in almost exactly the same way, always starting with the same sentence, *It was the craziest thing.* How they went to Brooklyn the day before Mother's Day, and because some adjustments were being done to Vinnie's prosthetic arm, he wasn't wearing it, a rare occurrence. How Matilda had fought him about taking the subway because her stump was particularly painful and she wanted her crutches and was worried about being late, how they'd taken a car service and because there was no traffic had arrived absurdly early. How they'd walked around for a while, admiring the neat blocks of brownstones, the daffodils and pansies in the window boxes, the number of families out on the street pushing strollers, jogging lightly behind kids on bikes with training wheels, planting the tiny garden beds around the tree trunks. How they finally decided to go over to Stephanie's a little early and see if she was home. How the man on the stoop had stood there and stared at them like he was seeing a ghost. How even with one arm Vinnie had caught Tommy O'Toole as he fainted, preventing him from hitting the sidewalk facedown and *God only knows!* Matilda would tell their wide-eyed children then, *God only knows what would have happened if he'd hit his head. If your daddy hadn't caught him? He could have been dead. Worse! His brain could have been damaged and he'd never be the same. But no! Your father reached out—with one arm—and caught him around the waist and set him down like he was no heavier than a big bag of rice. A full grown man!*

Matilda would tell how Stephanie had dropped her bags and flowers and started running down the street when she saw Tommy fall, how she'd sat and cradled his head in her lap and held his hand and made him stay still until the paramedics came and told them he was going to be fine. How they'd finally gotten him to his feet and helped him inside and then they knew why Tommy had fainted, why seeing Vinnie and Matilda on the street had made him dizzy and confused.

It was a statue of Mommy and Daddy! As soon as Vinnie Jr. was old enough to know the story, he'd always interrupt and say that part. *It was a statue of you guys!*

That's right. Matilda would run her hand over his head, his glossy hair dark like his mother's, curly like his father's. *It was a famous statue from France. The lady was missing a foot and the man was missing an arm, just like your mommy and daddy. I took one look at that statue and I* knew.

Here, if Matilda and Vinnie were in the same room, she would always pause, always give him the look, a look like she'd given him that day brimming with awe and revelation, a look that fixed his world and made him whole and filled him with such unbearable desire and hope that he was always the first to turn away because the look was almost too much, a virtual sun flooding his world with light.

I saw that statue, Matilda would say, smiling at her boys (first Vinnie Jr., then little Fernando, then Arturo for Vinnie's grandfather), *and I knew. That statue? It was my sign.*

CHAPTER FORTY-FOUR

Nearly ten months after the unexpected nor'easter blew through Manhattan in late October, freezing branches, killing 185 stately trees in Central Park, destroying nearly all the autumnal foliage of the five boroughs, including the colorful mums that lined Park Avenue and the decorative pots of kale the denizens of Brooklyn favored for their front stoops while trying to effect a kind of incongruent country gentility, the birthing centers of New York City were hit with a miniature baby boom. As spring turned to summer and the days grew longer and the humidity crept northward and eastward, slowly making its way up the Jersey shore until it settled over the city like a clammy, uninvited embrace, the citywide birth rate for July nearly doubled, forcing doctors and nurses and midwifes and anesthesiologists to work double shifts, cancel vacations, operate on zero sleep.

"Snowtober babies" they started calling them, the Ethans and Liams and Isabellas and Chloes that appeared in late July in place of the corn, which had failed to thrive because after that early snowstorm the rest of the winter was dry as a bone and the winter's drought extended into spring and summer. But the babies came—their hair as abundant and soft as corn silk, their new bodies unfurling to expose tiny grasping fingers and clenched toes that looked as sweet as newly bared kernels of corn.

Stephanie had been having prelabor contractions for weeks, but she was five days past her due date and still didn't have a baby. She'd stopped going into her office, preferring to spend a few desultory hours at the computer before taking a long afternoon nap. She was bored. She was ready. She was beyond ready. Downstairs, Tommy was hammering. She still couldn't believe the change that had come over him once he got that ridiculous artifact out of his apartment. The day Tommy collapsed on the stoop, EMS declared him fine. Exhausted and dehydrated, but fine. When they finally got him inside and she saw the statue, she'd nearly fainted herself. She knew all about the theft at ground zero because one of her clients had written an entire book about the recovery efforts downtown and was currently covering the rebuilding of the new Freedom Tower.

Logistics of statue moving aside, the transfer was absurdly simple. Stephanie asked her old friend Will to help, knowing she could trust him to protect Tommy. A rented truck, a late-night drop-off at a collection spot that had been set up for anyone wanting to donate 9/11 artifacts. Ever since the statue had been returned to its rightful place, Tommy had taken to his living quarters with a new zeal, renovating the entire garden level himself. It was going to be beautiful.

Five days late. Stephanie had taken her nap, refolded the baby blankets in the spanking new crib in the pretty new nursery. The July heat was blistering and the afternoons were too miserable to do anything but sit in her air-conditioned living room, watch reality TV, and saunter down the block for an overpriced gelato before dinner. Standing in front of a neighboring stoop, listlessly rummaging through a pile of books left out for the taking, she felt a little pop, like a balloon bursting quietly and deep inside. And then the telltale gush between her legs, followed by a long, throbbing ache, longer and heavier than the small precontractions she'd been having. She leaned against a neighbor's stone balustrade with one hand and took a deep breath. She felt the sweat trickle down the back of her neck, between her tender breasts. She closed her eyes and the sun beat down on her face and shoulder and arms, the peach gelato in her other hand dripping down her palm and wrist. She wanted to remember this moment. She looked at the wet spot on the pavement and thought: *This is before.* The trickle down her inner thighs, the swelling ache at her back, they were ushering her to a completely different place, to *after.* She was ready.

As she stood, mesmerized by her amniotic fluid meandering down the slope of the bluestone sidewalk (the first and last moment, as it would happen, that she had the luxury of observing the process with any aplomb), the first contraction hit and was so sustained it took her breath away, doubled her over, and she was stunned to hear herself audibly groan.

Okay, she thought, *I guess this is going to be fucking intense.*

As the pain receded and she tried to catch her breath and move toward her house, another contraction, right on the heels of the first and this one—she didn't even know how it was possible that she registered it but she did—a little stronger and longer than the first.

As the second contraction subsided, she stood and waited. Nothing. She took the phone out of her pocket and hit the stopwatch function so she could time the intervals between contractions. Everything was happening too fast. Gingerly, she started to walk and when she was directly in front of Tommy's living room windows, the third contraction. She grabbed onto the wrought-iron railing with both hands and the sound that came out of her was so primal and involuntary that she scared herself; she felt as if she were being torn in two.

Tommy loved telling this part of the story, how he heard her before he saw her. "Three kids," he'd say. "I knew that sound. Oh, boy, did I know *that* sound." He ran out the front door and managed to get Stephanie up the stairs and through the front door (contractions four and five). He tried to settle her on the floor (contraction six).

"Not on the rug!" she'd screamed at him. He'd run upstairs to grab some sheets out of the linen closet and a blanket to wrap the baby because it was evident that there would be no time to get to the hospital. A pair of scissors from the bathroom. Peroxide? Why not. He started toward her bedroom thinking he could use a few pillows when he heard her bellowing.

Downstairs, Stephanie was just trying to control her breathing. Shit! Why hadn't she paid more attention to the breathing? Practiced? She couldn't manage her breathing, couldn't get ahead of the pain. She sat on the living room floor, pulled out her phone, and after a brief, unsettling conversation with her doctor during which she had two contractions and the doctor said, "I'm hanging up and sending an ambulance," and before she could even check the time again—and she knew this was *very* wrong, way too soon—she had to push.

"Tommy?" she wailed up to him. Where was he? "I have to push."

"No, no, no," he yelled down to her. "No pushing. Absolutely no pushing."

But telling her not to push was like telling her not to breathe. Her body was pushing, her body wouldn't *not* push. She reached up from the floor and pulled a cashmere blanket off the back of the sofa. She could hear sirens, but it was too soon for her ambulance and she knew she wasn't going anywhere. She tried to remember if she'd learned anything about what to do once the baby was out. Would she have to cut the cord? Oh, God. The afterbirth? What the fuck was she going to do! The contractions were seamless; a constant tsunami of pressure, there was no break, no moment when she didn't feel like every internal organ was trying to exit her body in one concerted rush. She pulled up her maternity skirt, managed to work her underpants off, and place the cashmere blanket next to her on the floor.

Nothing but the best for baby, she thought, hoping she would remember later that she'd had the presence of mind to make a tiny joke.

She was trying to fight the urge to push, but she knew she'd already lost. Her body was doing what it needed to do and it was completely clear that her job was to surrender. Tommy had come down the stairs and dumped a pile of things near her head and was in the kitchen washing his hands. At least she thought that's what he was doing. She'd lost count of the contractions. She'd lost track of time. She thought she could feel something emerging, but how could that be true? It couldn't be true. She remembered she was supposed to be trying short little breaths—*ha, ha, ha, ha*. No use. She reached down between her legs and felt it: her daughter's head, slick and wet and grainy with hair. Her daughter was in a hurry.

"Tommy," she yelled into the kitchen. "She's coming."

Her daughter was here.

CHAPTER FORTY-FIVE

There were three things Paul Underwood assiduously avoided: the beach, watercraft, and so-called street food. He genuinely disliked the beach, enjoyed neither the sand nor the beating sun nor the occasional whiff of putrefying sea creatures, nor the practically prehensile barnacles cleaving to a twist of brown otherworldly, goose-fleshed kelp. He made certain exceptions. On a cool, cloudy day, preferably in winter, preferably with an offshore breeze, he could be persuaded to walk along the waterfront for atmosphere if, say, a bowl of chowder or a bucket of steamers were offered as recompense at the end. But otherwise? Thank you very much, but no thank you. He'd never learned to swim, and marine vessels of any kind from kayaks to cruise ships petrified him. (He'd never even learned to drive a car, so the prospect of a stalled boat was also disturbing.) And the entire concept of street food was befuddling and abhorrent: the greasy cart with its questionable sanitation, the paper plates that lost all tensile strength before you were finished, eating while standing, having things drip down your hand or onto your pants, and how to accommodate a beverage along with flatware and napkins? He didn't even approve of dining al fresco—what was the point when there was a perfectly wonderful, bug-free, climate-controlled room nearby? Street food was dining al fresco minus the petty luxuries of a table and a chair. In other words, minus civilization.

So Paul's discomfort, while standing on a slightly swaying dock, under the relentless afternoon Caribbean sun, waiting to board a ferry while eating a plate of jerk chicken and fried plantains served from a truck in confounding proximity to the diesel fumes from the nearby idling ferry, was immense. Immense and vaguely nauseating.

His consolation? Bea. She was across the dock, sitting on a bench, her face bent to her plate of food and momentarily hidden by the wide-brimmed straw hat he'd bought her the minute they arrived at the ferry terminal from the airport, ten days ago. Although their trip hadn't been successful by Bea's measure (she hadn't found Leo), the trip for Paul had gone exceedingly well. Bea's spirits had oddly—or maybe predictably—risen a bit each day. Partly it was their surroundings, being away from New York, being away from the Plumbs. But partly it was because Bea seemed to let go a little bit more each day of the need to find Leo. It wasn't anything she said—she wouldn't talk about not finding Leo—but her dissipating urgency was obvious to Paul. Her brow seemed to smooth a little each day. Her shoulders unwound. She'd stopped chewing the side of her mouth.

Everyone else seemed convinced that Bea was on a fool's errand. Well, if that made him the fool's accomplice, so be it. He'd eagerly volunteered to accompany Bea when she confided how anxious she was about going alone, and not just for the opportunity of her company or to offer support for her fraught mission, but to be there to help her confront Leo if he actually appeared. Paul would be quite happy to confront Leo.

He enjoyed parts of their trip, especially the tiny side-by-side but separate wooden cottages they rented near the water, both with green tile roofs and cherry-colored bougainvillea surrounding the front doors. He appreciated the expansive view of the shimmering blue water that he could admire safely from his shaded deck. And the trip had begun with promise. An airport worker recognized Leo's photo as someone who'd landed on a small charter from Miami some weeks ago and who hadn't left, at least not by plane.

But after that initial hopeful sign, nothing. Nobody recognized his photo or—as Paul strongly suspected was the case—they did and didn't say so. As Bea became increasingly frustrated, he started going out on his own some afternoons, looking in the more remote bars on the island, the places not frequented by tourists and, Paul believed, not appropriate for Bea. But those efforts ran dry, too. Two nights ago he'd coaxed her out for dinner at a small inn on the island. He took her hand in his and made his case for returning to New York. That's as far as his physical intrusion went. She was preoccupied with Leo, occasionally despondent, and he didn't want her to turn to him out of sadness or desperation. He'd waited this long, he could wait until they got back to New York. Or he could wait for her to make the first move. They'd been so simpatico lately that he thought he wasn't crazy in believing she might just make the first move.

And she'd been writing nearly every day. *Clickety-clack, clickety-clack.* He could hear her from his deck when the door to her room was open, typing on the keyboard. She demurred when he asked what she was working on, but he could tell she was pleased. And he was patient. If Paul Underwood was anything, he was extremely patient.

Then this morning, she'd excitedly knocked on his door before breakfast. She was talking so fast, he didn't understand her at first. She'd sent fifty pages of something new to Stephanie, she told him.

"More Archie—"

"No, no," she said, shaking her head vigorously. "No Archie. No more freaking Archie. Something else. I don't even know what it is yet, but listen." Bea read from Stephanie's e-mail, lavish with praise for the pages and ending with "Keep going. I love this. I can sell it." And just like that, Bea was ready to go home.

They'd slipped some cash to a local police officer, asking him to "keep his eyes open" for Leo. They packed their things and booked their flights. They were waiting for the ferry to take them to the larger island's airport. Paul walked over to Bea as she stood and tossed her empty plate of mediocre food in a nearby trash can. He had a headache.

"I'm going to go across the street to look for aspirin," he said. "I'll be right back." He walked over to the small gas station and accompanying rickety wooden building that sold mechanical parts and a smattering of groceries and other sundries. Flanking the doors were two small stands with boxes of mangoes in various states of ripening, swarms of fruit flies hovering over each crate. Inside, Paul went to grab the guava soda Bea liked. He could hear a lively crowd in a side room, a bunch of men laughing. He smelled weed.

Paul heard Leo before he saw him, recognized the barking laugh that was distinctly Leo's. He told himself he was just imagining things, that they'd spent so many hours of so many days looking for Leo that he was constituting him out of thin air in the very last minutes before boarding the ferry. But then he heard the laugh again, closer, and the man with the laugh was heading to a rear restroom. Paul ducked behind a cardboard display for Kodak film that had to be at least twenty years old, two life-size all-American teens holding tennis rackets and laughing; the sun had faded all the pigment on the display to various shades of blue so the models looked ghostly in spite of their jauntily cocked elbows and toothy smiles. From his spot behind the display, he saw the back of the laugher's head, took in his height, his hair, the particular profile that was, absolutely and beyond any doubt, Leo Plumb.

He'd found Leo.

LATER PAUL WOULD TELL HIMSELF he hesitated that afternoon in the bodega because he'd had too much sun. Or that it was the jerk chicken that was already roiling his stomach with ill portent given that they were about to get on a ferry and then a small plane to Miami and then a bigger plane to New York. Or shock, sheer shock. He'd never really expected to find Leo. He hurriedly paid for the soda and a tiny bottle of baby aspirin, which was all they had. As he made his way across the street, he thought about what to tell Bea. Back at the ferry terminal, he found a bit of shade at the side of the building and stopped to think for a minute. Seeing Leo again made Paul realize how much he loathed him. Nathan had told Paul about Leo's undermining tactics, how he'd questioned Paul's leadership and competence. Paul had been furious but he also recognized that Leo's misstep had angered Nathan enough to tip the scale in Paul's favor. The first influx of Nathan's funding had already arrived and Paul was working night and day to prove to Nathan that he'd made the right choice.

From afar he could see Bea, still sitting where he'd left her. The straw hat was on the bench beside her; she was getting too much sun. She was wearing the old yellow dress he remembered from her first *SpeakEasy* photo, the picture he'd chosen for the cover, a decision that somehow ended up being credited to Leo. Like then, her face was in profile, her expression undimmed, hopeful. He walked over and handed her the drink.

"Nice and cold," she said, holding the bottle with two hands and putting it to her cheek. "What?" she said, looking up at his face. "What's wrong?"

"Nothing," he said, attempting to clear whatever was clouding his expression. "I was just thinking that you look really happy right now." His heart galloped, knowing what he knew and what he wanted to do with what he knew.

"I *am* kind of happy," she said, sounding surprised. Their ferry had arrived and its disembarking passengers streamed out onto the dock.

"Are you ready?" Paul offered his hand to Bea and in that moment he did a quick calculation: Who was Bea with Leo and who might she be without him? Who might *he* be without Leo in the picture? Who might they be together? Bea placed her palm in Paul's hand and stood to face him and his answer was as clear as the easy, radiant expres-

sion on her face, which was—even given the beating sun and the smell
of street food and the stink of the ocean nearby—positively transport-
ing. Beatific. Exhilarating and emollient.

WHEN BEA PLACED her hand in Paul's, she felt an unexpected
rush. It was nice. He'd been so patient, so good, so helpful and loyal
and true. His ordinarily pale skin had an almost pretty glow from the
sun, in spite of his incessant application of sunscreen with an SPF
factor at or above 70. She'd badgered him into wearing a T-shirt and,
true, it was solid navy and topped with a seersucker jacket but he still
looked different to her somehow. Taller. More confident. As she stood
and faced him, she saw something determined move across his face,
something—she could tell—having to do with her and that made her
feel safe, calm. He was, she realized, nearly handsome.

He had been deeply disappointed when she decided to put the last
Archie story into a desk drawer. For good. "It's not mine," she'd told
him. "It belongs to Leo and Matilda and someone who hasn't even
been born yet. It's not the story I need to tell." And still, he'd been so
stalwart about helping her look for Leo, she knew he'd even gone off
on his own a few times.

"I liked this place," she said to him. "In spite of everything."

"I liked it, too," he said. They stood there, her hand in his, both of
them looking a little giddy and a little tentative and a little sun-kissed
and a little sweaty, and though she didn't understand the heady optimism moving through her (she hoped it was her new work, but maybe
it was just the sway of the dock? the swell of the water? Paul?), she
decided to embrace it. To bear her own joy.

"Do you know what else I like?" she said, putting a hand on each of
Paul Underwood's shoulders.

FROM HIS USUAL CHAIR at the regular Friday morning bodega
card game, the one facing the door, Leo had seen Paul the minute he
crossed over to the drink cooler. He'd moved off to the side of the room
and tried to stay calm while wondering what to do. The guys he was

playing with would cover for him. He wouldn't have to explain, just tell
them that Underwood was trouble and they'd clam right up. He made
his way to the restroom out back and locked the door behind him,
wanting to think for a minute where Paul couldn't ambush him. There
were advantages to running, of course, but he was also curious, wondered who was with Paul. Bea, that seemed obvious. Paul and Bea had
to be waiting for the 5:15 P.M. ferry, which was always at least fifteen
minutes late. He wondered if anyone else had come looking for him.
He had time to sneak over to the terminal and see who else was there.
Melody maybe? Stephanie?

Or he could just walk up to Paul and ask. Man to man. Man to half
man. Man to Underdog. Whatever. His siblings could find him but
they couldn't force him to do anything. He'd kind of been expecting
this moment. Truthfully, he was surprised it took so long. Technically, he should have been in South Vietnam right now but—he'd gotten a little lazy.

He splashed his face with some questionable water from the sink
marked NONPOTABLE and stepped back into the bodega. Paul Underwood was nowhere in sight. Had he not seen Leo? Leo was sure he
had. Paul never did have a poker face. Leo decided to investigate.

Across the street, from a spot inside the tiny terminal building, he
saw Bea sitting on the outside pier right away. Even in a crowd of American tourists, her clothes were ridiculously colorful. She was sitting on
a bench, her legs out in front of her. Her gold sandals caught the sun. A
tall woman stood next to Bea; her back was to Leo but he would know
that long red hair anywhere. Stephanie.

He quickly moved toward the open doorway and right before he
crossed the threshold, the redhead turned toward Leo and he stopped.
It wasn't Stephanie, not even close. This woman was too heavy and
her face was sunburned and pudgy, almost piglike. He felt a surge of
fury for this stranger who dared to look from behind like someone he
now realized he'd been expecting to see. She hadn't come.

As the ferry docked and started unloading its passengers, a few
local teens began to play the steel drums, hoping to be the first recipi-

ents of the newly arrived tourists' dollars. Leo watched Bea stand and say something to Paul that made him smile as she lazily dropped her arms over his shoulders. Even from a distance, Leo swore he could see Paul blush.

"Come on, Underdog," Leo found himself silently coaxing. "Grow a pair."

Paul slid one hand along Bea's waist and pulled her closer, ran a finger along the line of her jaw and then cupped her face with his hand; right there, right in that moment, Leo watched Bea surrender. Exhale. He watched her knees collapse a bit and her elbows bend as she leaned into Paul and then they were kissing—as if they were alone, as if they were in love, as if for all time.

AFTER THE LONG AND HEADY KISS (Bea hadn't ever expected to be kissed like that again in her entire life, not after Tucker died), she and Paul stood quietly for a minute in a close embrace. Everyone was boarding the ferry now. Her eyes were still closed and she could feel how neatly her body aligned with Paul's—how her tidy breasts matched up with his narrow chest, how his slight potbelly fit perfectly into her slender middle, and how her chin fit just so into the crook of his shoulder. She drew back, wanting to see his face, but as she lifted her gaze, a familiar profile caught her eye. A stream of people temporarily blocked her line of sight, but when they passed, she could see the figure walking toward her. The lowering, late-afternoon sun shone straight into her eyes and the glare made everything hazy, including the man, who was nearly a shadow. She froze. It couldn't be.

WHEN LEO STARTED TOWARD BEA, he had no plan, no idea what he was going to say, he'd just impulsively moved in her direction. When she raised her head and saw him, he stopped. As he hesitated, he watched everything about her change. She stiffened. Her face went dark with worry and confusion. She closed her eyes and lowered her chin.

BREATHE, BEA TOLD HERSELF, *JUST BREATHE.* She remained perfectly still, afraid to move or look up, waiting to hear his voice calling her name. Afraid to hear his voice calling her name. Paul held her a little tighter. He smelled like shampoo and sunscreen and faintly of jerk chicken. A nearby seagull squawked, sounding as if it were laughing. The ferry horn blared three times. Final boarding.

"Ready?" Paul said. She lifted her head and blinked a little. The figure was gone. She looked again, shielding her eyes. No one.

She thought she'd seen Leo a thousand times on this trip, a million times, every day, sometimes every hour. She thought she'd seen him dancing to a calypso band at their hotel, serving fish to a nearby table at a restaurant, and buying mangoes at the side of the road. She thought she'd seen him walking down the beach flip-flops in hand, in the backseat of a taxi weaving through traffic, playing pool through an open door, on countless barstools and down countless sun-drenched alleys under the swaying palms. But it had never been him. It had never been Leo.

"I'm ready," she said, retrieving her hat from the bench, placing her straw bag on her shoulder. "Let's go home."

EPILOGUE

One Year Later

The day of the baby's first birthday was every bit as muggy and miserable as the day of her birth. That's what everyone said to Stephanie when they arrived at the celebratory lunch. *Remember? It was a day exactly like this!* As if it had happened decades or centuries ago, not fifty-two measly weeks and their meteorological recall was something magical and marvelous.

"Oh, I remember," Stephanie said. How could she forget? The heat, the ice cream melting down her arm, the onset of a labor so sudden and fierce that it had a name: *precipitate labor.*

Lillian Plumb Palmer, called "Lila" for short (her first name was a sweet secret to Stephanie, just between her and her mantel), was born in her mother's living room exactly forty-two minutes after Stephanie's water broke. She slid into Tommy's hands as the paramedics were ringing the front doorbell. "It's a girl! It's a girl!" Tommy said over and over, forgetting that Stephanie knew she was having a girl but remembering all three times the doctor had delivered the same joyful news to him as he clutched Ronnie's hand after the final agonizing push.

And today Lila was one!

In spite of the heat, Stephanie was setting up in the yard. It wouldn't be too bad. She'd expressly asked everyone not to bring a gift. Lila'd never had a birthday before and she wouldn't know the difference and Stephanie didn't want more junk in her house, but she knew the request was pointless and, sure enough, as the Plumbs arrived most of them not only brought a gift, they were *laden* with gifts.

Melody and Walt arrived first. Louisa had recently moved into Stephanie's second bedroom and was preparing for the upcoming school year when she'd be studying art at Pratt, just one neighborhood over. She'd gotten a generous scholarship but not enough to cover room and board. When Stephanie heard she was thinking of commuting into Brooklyn every day, she offered Louisa a free room in exchange for the occasional weeknight or weekend babysitting. They'd only been living together for a week, but Stephanie was surprised by how much she enjoyed Louisa's company. And Lila was crazy about her big-girl cousins. Louisa—and Nora when she visited—were so good with her, happy to swing her back and forth between them as they walked the length of the yard again and again, willing to sit and amuse her with silly voices or by building towers with colorful foam blocks. Nora had brought her friend Simone today and as Stephanie and Melody stood at the kitchen window watching the girls with Lila out beneath the newly planted maple, they saw Simone lean in and give Nora a quick kiss.

"I won't lie. It's a little weird," Melody said. Her tone was affectionate, if a little melancholy.

"Do you like her?" Stephanie asked.

"Simone?" Melody said. "I guess. She's intense. I don't know what's going to happen when she's at Brown and Nora moves to Buffalo." *It would be state college for Nora after all.* "I kind of hope they do stay in touch. Simone pressured Nora all year to work harder, it's the reason she got into the honors college."

"Love can be an excellent motivator," Stephanie said.

When it doesn't wreck your heart, Melody wanted to say, but that would have been cruel, so she didn't. And Melody had to admit Stephanie's post-Leo life seemed far from wrecked; she seemed happy.

The doorbell rang, Jack, Bea, and Paul all arriving. More presents and ribbons and passing around of Lila, who pulled so insistently at the collar of her party dress that Stephanie took it off and soon Lila was toddling around the backyard in a soggy diaper, red-faced and sweaty. She was wild-eyed and overstimulated and they hadn't even given her any sugar yet. Stephanie knew she'd never go down for a nap later. Oh, well.

Out back, Jack was hoping to find a bit of shade. The new tree Stephanie planted to replace the one felled during the storm was small. Jack thought she should have splurged a little to buy one that was more mature. He pulled a chair close to the trunk where it was marginally cooler. (Years later, when the tree had grown and formed the perfect canopy over the rear of the yard, Lila would marry beneath the massive leafy boughs turning red and orange on a blindingly beautiful October afternoon. She would ask Jack to escort her down the leaf-strewn path to her partner. Jack would be good to Lila all her life, showing up whenever she was missing a father. On the day of her wedding when Lila appeared on Jack's almost-seventy-year-old arm, Stephanie would see Leo at her side and for a debilitating moment would be crushed by the enormity of everything he'd missed.) Now, sitting under the tree, keeping an eye on Lila in case she moved too fast and fell—she was still a little unsteady on her feet—Jack was also wishing for Walker, albeit with more melancholy than grief these days. Walker was the only person he could think of who would actually look forward to a baby's birthday party. He'd heard from his old friend Arthur that Walker was already living with someone new and in a way it was nice to learn that, ultimately, Walker had been the one who wasn't good at being alone. Jack was more relieved than surprised to find how very good he was at living alone. He'd fall in love many more times in his life, but he would never want another man to share his home.

Bea was corralling the group, insisting that Lila open gifts. She was crazy about Lila but she really wanted the party to be over so she could get home and back to work. She was more than halfway through her novel about an artist who has stopped painting and then, through a series of losses and loves (as she pitched to Stephanie), finds her way back to herself and her art. It wasn't quite autobiographical, but whatever Bea had loosened by turning her lens away from Leo and onto herself made it all work. Every time Stephanie got new chapters, they were better than the ones that came before. Bea didn't know the ending of the book yet, but she knew if she kept working, she'd find it; she knew it was in front of her.

"I always knew you had this in you," Stephanie told her, thrilled and relieved not to be reading about a thinly disguised Leo; she couldn't have done it. After much urging on Paul's part, Bea had finally sold her apartment, put the money in the bank, and moved in with Paul. She was writing full time. She'd brought at least five gifts for Lila.

Stephanie put Lila on her lap and let her tear pieces of wrapping paper into tiny bits while Bea tried to interest her in the parade of presents: the little red fire engine with wheels that Lila could sit on and ride down the sidewalk, propelling herself forward with her meaty legs, a teddy bear twice her size that briefly made her cry, three Marimekko dresses bought at a fancy baby boutique that would make Lila look like a mini-Bea, a multicolored plastic monstrosity called Baby's First Smart Phone from Melody (Stephanie would take the phone—and most of the other needless toys—to Goodwill the following Monday), an exquisite tiny antique bracelet from Jack, pink gold with inlaid chips of ruby, Lila's birthstone. "What a remarkably beautiful choking hazard," Melody joked as Stephanie tried to get Lila to sit still long enough to clip it around her chubby wrist; no dice.

After the presents were opened and the wrappings collected and lunch was served, they all gathered around the table in the yard and sat Lila at the head in her high chair. Lila tugged at the elastic from the sparkly party hat Melody had put on her head. She finally pulled the hat loose and flung it to the ground, legs swinging, feet banging against the rungs of the chair. She started squirming to be let down, but when a cupcake with an unlit candle was placed in front of her and everyone started singing "Happy Birthday," she quieted and stared at the joyful looming faces above her.

Stephanie knew what everyone was doing while Lila offered a rare still moment to search her resplendent face: They were looking for Leo. It was impossible *not* to see Leo in Lila, the way her bright eyes would narrow when she was angry, her pointed chin was his, as was her broad forehead, the elegant tapered eyebrows and overbearing mouth, all sitting below bright red curls just like Stephanie's. Leo was gone but he was right there in front of them. And as they concluded their off-key warbling and started to cheer, Lila looked up and shyly smiled and applauded herself.

"Throw a kiss, Lila," Louisa said, wanting to show off the trick she'd taught her cousin that week.

Lila brought her fleshy, sticky palm to her mouth and then flung an imaginary kiss to the crowd; she squealed as everyone pretended to catch it and threw one again, and again, flinging kisses to the left and to the right, until suddenly it was too much! Spent, she rubbed her eyes, her face crumpled. Then she raised both arms high. "Up," she said, looking desperately from one eager face to another. "Up!" She opened and closed both hands as if she were grabbing fistfuls of air. "Up!" she said again, as her family rushed toward her all at once, each of them hoping to get to her first.